CW00505899

THE
MERMAID

ALSO BY ANKI EDVINSSON

Detectives von Klint and Berg

The Snow Angel

THE MERMAID

ANKI EDVINSSON

Translated by
Paul Norlen

AMAZON **CROSSING**

Text copyright © 2021 by Anki Edvinsson by agreement with Grand Agency
Translation copyright (English edition) © 2024 by Paul Norlen
All rights reserved.

Previously published as *Sjöjungfrun* by Norstedts in Sweden in 2021. Translated from Swedish by Paul Norlen. First published in English by Thomas & Mercer in collaboration with Amazon Crossing in 2024.

www.apub.com

Amazon, the Amazon logo, and Thomas & Mercer are trademarks of Amazon. com, Inc., or its affiliates.

ISBN-13: 9781662516009
eISBN: 9781662515996

Cover design by kid-ethic
Cover image: © Andreas Gradin © Willyam Bradberry / Shutterstock

Printed in the United States of America

'Often the fear of one evil leads us into a worse.'

Nicolas Boileau

PROLOGUE

Rådhus Square, Umeå

Erik stuck his hand in his jeans pocket to make sure that the mobile was there as he walked past the ice cream stand on Rådhus Square. The line was somewhat shorter than it had been earlier in the summer but long enough to keep the woman in the serving window very busy. He thought back to when he and Helen often stood in that line with the children. That was only a few months ago, but it felt like another life.

The sun warmed his face and the late summer day had enticed the residents of Umeå into town. Erik took out the phone and saw that it was already twelve thirty. He had to go home. Helen would be back after collecting the children from their weekend activities.

The red hue of the bricks in City Hall was deepened by the sun. He looked past the building toward the hot-dog vendor who'd stood in the same place, every Saturday, as long as Erik had lived in Umeå. He raised his hand to greet him and got a smile in return. A little girl was standing with her mother in line to buy a hot dog. She had pink ribbons in her hair and matching shoes.

'Hey there, how's it going?'

Erik turned around and stood eye to eye with his neighbour. He noticed immediately that the neck brace was gone. The neighbour had been in a car accident a while ago and for a long time used a neck support. This neighbour also liked to have a beer or a hot toddy, preferably in Erik's company. Unfortunately. Presumably it was because Erik didn't usually talk that much, which let the neighbour talk even more.

'Hey there. Yes, we've been quite busy now school has started up again after the summer holidays,' Erik replied, searching for a way out. He wasn't in the mood and the neighbour could be long-winded.

'So how are things with Helen now? Have you got her straightened out?' the neighbour said, laughing.

'Oh yes, she's doing fine,' Erik said, slightly stressed.

What else could he say?

Conveniently the neighbour got a call on his mobile and Erik quickly aimed his steps toward a vacant bench by the bronze sculpture. The bronze fellow was considerably taller than him and that day someone had wrapped around his neck a scarf with the logo for Björklöven's hockey team. Erik sat down on the bench and called Helen again. No answer.

A teacher from the school waved in the distance and Erik waved back. *Is everyone in town today?* he thought.

Just then a scream was heard across the square. It was followed by more. Erik stood and saw how a father picked his child up in his arms and ran. His eyes were wide. The little girl with pink ribbons and her mother seemed paralyzed at first. Ketchup from the hot dog ran down the girl's hand. Eventually the mother dragged her away, so fast that she dropped the hot dog.

The same people who had just been enjoying an ordinary Saturday were now fleeing in every direction, like ants in an anthill under attack. A man that Erik had never seen before took hold of Erik's jacket and tried to drag him away.

'Run, damn it!' the man screamed.

But Erik stood there. He forgot to breathe, and it was only when his lungs demanded oxygen that he took in air.

He heard the sound of police cars approaching, turned his head and followed everyone else's gazes – all aimed in the same direction. A young man was standing by the entrance to the Utopia shopping centre. Erik knew who he was – an immigrant youth who had come to Umeå a year or so ago. He would sometimes hang around outside the school where Erik was a counsellor. There were rumours that he robbed people and sold drugs for a criminal gang. He was someone the young people were afraid of. Now the guy was wearing a green vest loaded with plastic explosives and metal pipes. People who had taken cover could not keep from filming – Erik saw several mobiles sticking out from behind corners of buildings. His mouth was dry, his lips were tight and his heart was pounding in his chest. He was in a bad position – too close. Uniformed police screamed at everyone to leave the area – a few were taken away by force.

Erik took a few steps back but was stopped by the bench he had just been sitting on. He started to run, veered off to the right past a large advertising board behind which he took cover. The young guy with the vest screamed something that Erik didn't understand.

EIGHT DAYS EARLIER

1

Friday, 26 August

Charlotte's cheeks flushed as she stepped into the offices of Major Crimes. The scent of Ola still lingered in her memory. They'd been sleeping together for several weeks and it was starting to feel serious. No one except Per knew about the relationship with her colleague. Every day felt like a 'walk of shame' as she entered the police station.

Charlotte took off her jacket and hung it on the already overflowing coat rack, ran both hands over her dark hair – feeling the bun at the back was tight and firm – checked that her blouse was buttoned correctly and finished by putting on red lipstick.

Her colleagues were already in place; Anna was taking off her cycling shoes, her helmet on the desk and her hair damp with sweat. Clearly the team's most physically fit member, she biked six kilometres every day to and from work. She had been with Major Crimes for several years but had no desire to rise in her profession. Anna was content where she was because it left time for other things – like exercise.

Charlotte looked into her boss's office, but Per wasn't there. His jacket on the office chair testified that he was in the building, and she jumped when he showed up behind her.

'Good morning. Ready for a Friday?' he asked, retrieving a folder from the desk.

Charlotte nodded and followed him to the briefing room.

'We can only hope it stays calm. We've got a bit spoiled by that recently,' said Charlotte, slipping in before Per, who shook his head.

'We have one, or actually several, youth robberies to deal with,' he said, following her in.

Charlotte nodded seriously. 'It's unbelievable that so many robberies are happening here in Umeå.'

'Why shouldn't that happen in Umeå?' Kicki interjected.

The team's data analyst was already sitting there, ready as always to assert herself against Charlotte. From the first day she stepped into the police station, Kicki had tried to make life difficult for Charlotte. Small, subtle digs as well as quite open ostracism. Like when she invited everyone in the group with their significant others to her home, except Charlotte. Adult bullying.

Charlotte's mobile phone vibrated. A text from Ola, whom she had just kissed in the car outside.

Miss you already.

Charlotte replied, and the next moment the very same Ola was standing in front of her in the conference room, talking with Per, as he flashed a blinding-white smile. Sometimes she thought he looked like a Ken doll. Everything about his appearance was just so perfect. Per called him the Dressman, because he resembled Dressmann's advertising models. Ola was part of the division that handled witness protection, so he and Charlotte worked under the same roof but not in the same department. That was probably fortunate.

Charlotte looked at him. Under that well-ironed shirt hid something that she couldn't tear herself away from. And she perceived his scent again, with a hint of lavender. It came from Charlotte's shower gel that Ola borrowed when he slept over. The only negative thing about him so far was that he was too keen. Always ready, like a scout. On holiday he'd wanted to take her on a mountain hike. Among mosquitoes and snakes. They were different in that way, because she preferred five-star hotels on her time off.

'Hello, Charlotte?'

She tore her eyes away from Ola and turned her head to Kicki.

'Are you awake or what?' her colleague said. 'I'm talking to you.'

'Are you? Unbelievable, I wasn't prepared for that,' Charlotte replied, smiling broadly at her.

Kicki's gaze turned black. 'The papers sitting in front of you – can you pass them out to everyone? I've produced a chart on the robberies,' she said, pointing at Charlotte's desk.

'Of course,' she replied, wondering whether Kicki truly had done it herself. The intelligence service usually did this type of analysis. Maybe she wanted to present herself in a better light.

Ola went toward the door, but before he left the room their eyes met and Charlotte dropped her musings about Kicki. *It's going to be a fine day*, she thought, directing her attention to Per who had started the briefing.

'Yesterday evening we got a call from Roger Ren, a man I know through my son's hockey practice,' said Per. 'His kid, Adrian, plays on the same team as my eldest son and yesterday he was robbed by three guys in a park. It was violent, aggravated assault, and it's left the kid traumatized. I want us to go after these robberies that have spread across the city. What Adrian was subjected to was more serious than the previous incidents and we need to start working preventively.' Per looked out over his group.

'But hasn't that already been done?' asked Anna, who was still wearing her sweaty exercise clothes.

'As you can see in the chart that Kicki compiled, there have been four robberies in as many weeks. Four reports have come in quickly, but two of the victims don't want to cooperate with the investigation out of fear. Rumours are flourishing about a group of guys with a foreign background, but we have nothing concrete to go on, no clear facial descriptions or anything else that means we can bring them in for questioning. But a lot indicates that they are prime suspects in the robberies. Kicki will soon tell us more about that, and report on what we've done so far.'

'But this Adrian? Did he report that he was robbed?' Charlotte asked.

'Yes, although clearly he was very frightened and didn't dare participate as a witness in the investigation, but—'

Per was interrupted by his phone. He held it up to show the team.

'Roger, the dad, is calling me constantly. He's going crazy over the fact that we can't just bring in the ones that everyone believes – or, according to him, *knows* – are guilty. It's hard to explain that, in principle, we need to catch them in the act.'

Per let the call from Roger go to voicemail, but Charlotte sympathized with the father. Being the victim of a crime often restricted your freedom more than being a perpetrator.

'But can't we bring these guys in for questioning, talk with them a little?' said Charlotte.

'As long as we don't have anything that supports the suspicions against them we won't get any further. We can't bring them in only based on rumours.'

'Witnesses? Surveillance cameras? Isn't there anything that can even link them to the place?' Anna asked.

'No, nothing, and the victims' unwillingness to testify makes the investigation more difficult. On the other hand, there are indications that point toward these guys, and it's our intention to go further with those.'

'So what should we do?' asked Charlotte.

'What we can do with this kind of gang is what we usually do. Check them when we encounter them in the city. Frisk them to see if they're armed or have drugs on them. Simply disturb them. Make them feel they're being watched,' said Per.

'Okay, then we have to coordinate that internally with the patrol officers so that more of them actively disturb these people,' said Charlotte.

Per nodded.

'So these guys can go around robbing youths just as they please?' Anna said, without meaning it as a question.

Per sighed. Charlotte could see that Roger was calling him again, but he let it be.

'I want Anna and Kicki to focus on trawling social media – Roger thinks that young people are posting about this gang. They give tips to each other about places to avoid and write where the group in question has been seen. See if there's anything in that material we can use. And look at surveillance cameras in the area. Maybe we can connect the gang or some others to the park at the time the robbery took place.'

'But can't it be youths from one of the criminal gangs in the city? Like the ones from Stockholm and Karlstad who have established themselves more and more up here. They deal in drugs and have robbed stores before,' Charlotte suggested.

'The juvenile unit is keeping an eye on them and apparently the new guys have taken over the robberies in particular.'

Per paused and pointed at Kicki, who took over.

'As you see in my chart, all the robberies have roughly the same approach,' she said. 'And in addition, there are always three perpetrators. Two who rob, one who stands guard. Black clothing, ski masks or scarves as face cover, which means that we don't have any effective facial descriptions. A sharp object like a knife is used to threaten.'

It was silent in the room; everyone was reading.

'Adrian's debit card was stolen, along with his jacket and mobile. Watch that card – if there's a withdrawal, we can act,' said Per. 'Kicki has looked more closely at our three prime suspects.'

'They are recent arrivals,' she said. 'Two of them, Samir Al Tajir and Omar Athar, live at a campground in Nydala. According to the Migration Agency, they claimed they were sixteen years old when they arrived in Sweden a year ago. They came to Europe without papers, and to Sweden with one of the freighters that arrived via Spain or perhaps Germany. Those two are under review. The third is the same age, Ibrahim Hatim, and he's been given a residency permit.'

Per set up photographs of the three guys on the whiteboard and wrote their names above them. Major Crimes alternated between using a physical whiteboard and making presentations digitally on a TV screen, depending on who was the investigation leader. The digital way was becoming more common, but Charlotte still wasn't used to smartphones and tablets. Clearly Per, who did a little of both, wasn't either.

The only one of the prime suspects who appeared to be his stated age was Ibrahim, in Charlotte's opinion. His face was like a seventeen-year-old's, where mouth and nose were not done growing.

'Personally, I think that Samir and Omar seem older, based on the pictures we have of them, but that's not anything we can prove,' said Per, as if he'd heard Charlotte's thoughts. 'We have to proceed from the Migration Agency's database. Although it's rather common that new arrivals state a younger age because it helps them in the process of getting to stay.'

'Yes, who wouldn't have done that in the same situation?' said Charlotte, and Kicki nodded before she continued.

'Ibrahim is from Syria and the one in the group who seems misplaced here. Thanks to the residence permit, he's been placed in a foster home in Umeå. He is studying Swedish and according to previous interviews with the Migration Agency he wants to go to high school. The family he lives with has reported that he is well-behaved, diligent and wants to take advantage of the chance he's been given in Sweden. He lost his whole family when they made their way across the Mediterranean and has been alone since he was eleven.'

Charlotte looked more closely at the pictures. Ibrahim's black hair was shiny, natural curls that framed a narrow face. His dark eyes were surrounded by long eyelashes. His gaze was intense. The smile ended up crooked and gave a rowdy impression.

'Did his family drown, or what happened?' Per asked.

'Yes, the mother, father and two younger siblings. Horrible,' said Kicki.

'How did he manage to get all the way to Sweden by himself?' asked Charlotte.

'Reportedly this is where Omar and Samir come into the picture,' said Kicki. 'They took the young boy under their wings on their journey through Europe.'

'And how did Ibrahim get his residency permit so quickly?'

Kicki shrugged her shoulders. 'Presumably because his identity could be confirmed from the start. He's also the only one of the three guys who seems to want to create a functioning life here. Ibrahim showed up at the Swedish for Immigrants course, while Omar and Samir haven't taken that opportunity. According to the

Migration Agency, Ibrahim wanted to go to Sweden because his family was on their way here.'

'Does he have any relatives here, do we know that? Because the family was supposed to come here,' said Charlotte.

'Not that I'm aware of.'

Per pointed at Samir to show Kicki that she should continue.

'Samir also reports coming from Syria,' she said, 'but we don't really know that for sure. Many gave Syria as their homeland during the refugee wave in 2015. He showed up in Sweden in the company of Omar and Ibrahim, and has reported threats against him as reason for his application for asylum. That hasn't been possible to confirm because his identity hasn't been established. He is said to have been recruited as a child soldier when ISIS made their way into Syria. His family was murdered because his father was an English-speaking interpreter, but Samir's life was spared so that he could fight. Two years later he had an opportunity to flee to Iraq, according to him.'

'So the kid was forced to fight for the same gang that murdered his family?' said Charlotte.

Kicki nodded.

'My God, what a fate. Imagine all the refugees who bear such cruel, unprocessed trauma,' said Anna.

'Omar then?' asked Per.

'Afghanistan is his country of origin, according to the Migration Agency database. He hasn't reported any family, so we know nothing more. All three made their way to Sweden with the help of human traffickers. None of the boys is in our police database.'

Charlotte sighed. She thought about the many people who lived like that. What did it do to a person to be stateless, without rights and responsibilities?

Per cleared his throat. 'Okay, let's move ahead. You all know what you have to do. To put a stop to these youth robberies we have to be able to arrest. Be precise. This could escalate quickly if we don't make progress.'

He paused for a moment.

'Charlotte, you and I will go to see Roger Ren and his son Adrian and talk with them,' said Per, turning to her.

She nodded, thought about her daughter Anja. Charlotte would have been hysterical if she'd been brutally robbed.

Per's phone rang again. He held it up in front of her. Roger.

'If we don't get hold of these guys, he's probably going to do it,' said Per, shaking his head.

2

Erik looked down at his feet. His grey socks blended in with the light blue bathmat. The fringes pressed against the balls of his feet. He waited for his young daughter to finish brushing her teeth, checked to make sure she hadn't been careless. The sweet scent of the toothpaste reminded him of strawberries. Erik moved his gaze to his own reflection. Thin shoulders, which in his youth he had tried to build up without success. His body didn't respond to exercise; no matter how much he toiled, he stayed thin. Erik had been told that his muscles were long, which was the reason for the absent muscle mass. At the age of forty-four, he'd learned to accept this fact, and these days he was content with a run now and then to keep the pot belly away.

'I'm done now, Daddy,' said Elsa, spitting into the sink.

Erik patted his daughter on the head but didn't say anything. She went ahead of him to her room to change, and as he observed her, Erik thought that her nightgown was starting to get too small.

'Hurry up,' he said, stopping by the door to her bedroom. She would turn six in a few weeks and could certainly dress herself.

Then he went out to the kitchen where his wife Helen was putting the plates from breakfast into the dishwasher. She did it efficiently, as if she had a degree in it. Erik sat down at his usual place at the table and watched as she cleaned the kitchen counter. At their home it was always sparkling clean.

'Are you angry?' he asked, taking a sip of the coffee that was still on the table. Today he would start work at noon and was in no hurry.

Helen closed the door to the machine, dampened the dishrag in the water running from the tap, squeezed it out and wiped down. She interrupted herself and brought her hand to her face, wiping something away from her forehead. The whole time she was standing with her back to him.

'Listen, it can't be that bad. Turn around.'

She did as he said. With the dishrag in her hand, she looked straight at him.

'I just have to know,' he said. 'You've been strange lately. You disappear for long periods without being in touch. You're short with me. Don't even want to touch me.'

Helen stood leaning against the counter and set both hands on the surface.

'I'm not seeing anyone else. When would I have time for that?'

Her tone was gentle but her gaze hard. All of her behaviour screamed infidelity, he thought. The previous evening he had asked flat out and Helen looked as if she'd been caught with her fingers in the cookie jar.

Erik got up and went over to her, raised his hand and guided a light curl behind her ear. He liked the blonde curly hair that stuck out in all directions. The first time they met, twelve years ago, it was those very curls that had caught his attention. He'd been in the district court as support for a child from his school at the time. Helen, who was twenty-seven then, was there because her father was accused of aggravated assault, after starting an argument with a man at a bar about climate politics. So silly, in Erik's opinion. It almost cost the man his life and her father was sentenced to three

17

years in prison. Erik had started talking with Helen at the coffee vending machine and eventually she'd given him her number.

Then things moved fast. After dating for six months Helen got pregnant with their son and they moved in together. To start with, when they first started seeing each other, she was a confused woman. Indoctrinated by her father's radical opinions and belief that everything that was wrong with Sweden was due to immigrants. A steady stream of racist comments came out of her mouth. But Erik managed to convince her not to see her father. At first Helen protested, but after being away from her dad for a while she realized that his way of thinking was wrong. Erik had taken her out of a destructive environment. Rescued her. Just as he'd done with many young people he met at his job – those who didn't have a chance from the start, who every day were fed with their parents' twisted reality.

Erik had helped Helen. It was the two of them against the world. When Liam was born he proposed to Helen in the obstetrics ward. She cried with happiness and he was proud to have a family. One year later they got married in Malmö.

Helen looked at Erik from her place in the kitchen. 'I've signed up as a volunteer to be class parent in Liam's class, and we're planning a school trip,' said Helen. 'The rest of the time I'm at work, when I'm not here.'

'Okay,' said Erik. 'I just feel that you're very absent. That's all.'

He cocked his head and with his hand on her chin he brought Helen's mouth toward his.

'I love you,' said Erik, kissing her, trying to put her in a better mood.

They were interrupted when Liam came into the kitchen.

'Mum, where's my new hoodie?' the eleven-year-old asked, throwing out his arms as if he'd lost the most precious thing he owned.

Helen slipped past her son. 'I have to go to work. Dad will help you.' She took her jacket, grabbed her handbag and left the house.

Liam went berserk in the hunt for his new top. 'I have to wear it today!' he said, raising his voice.

Erik pointed in warning at him.

'Sorry,' said Liam.

'I'll help you look,' said Erik, joining his son in the search. 'I'll check the bathroom and the laundry basket.'

He didn't really think it was there, because Helen would never wash something unnecessarily and the top was brand new. But he took everything out of the basket and set it on the floor. No hoodie. At the very bottom were Helen's jeans and Erik picked them up too, to make sure that the top wasn't under it. There was a red spot on one leg that looked like blood. As he was about to set it back in the basket something fell out of the pocket: a Nokia mobile that looked quite old, not an Android. He hadn't seen it before. Erik picked it up and pressed the buttons. Turned it off. He sat down on the toilet seat and looked at the phone. Whose was it?

'Found the hoodie!' he heard Liam call. 'It was on the couch!'

Erik didn't reply. He tried to get into the phone but it required a code. What should he do? Confront Helen? She had just sworn that she wasn't seeing anyone else, but here was evidence that she was hiding something from him. He was still sitting on the toilet seat when Liam came in.

'What are you doing?' his son asked.

Erik looked up. 'Is this yours?' he said, holding up the phone.

'What? No. Why would I have two phones? And that one's old. I'm riding my bike to school now,' Liam said and left Erik, who remained sitting in the bathroom.

It felt as if he'd been socked in the jaw. He'd sensed it, and maybe he could rely on his gut feeling. He wanted to scream out loud, but instead he leaned over the sink, cupped his hands under the tap, captured the water and wet his face. She was doing something behind his back.

3

Per and Charlotte turned into the driveway to Roger and Adrian's home. A rake was lying outside the closed gate.

'Do you think it's possible to convince them to cooperate with the investigation?' Charlotte asked.

Per turned off the car engine.

'We'll have to see. Adrian is home from school and isn't doing so well. We'll have to be compelling.'

Per had been here before to pick up Adrian before hockey practice. Sometimes the parents weren't able to make the schedule work out with all the practices and matches, and then they helped each other. But he'd never been inside the house – Adrian always came out punctually. The boy was one year older than his son Simon, but it appeared they worked well together.

Charlotte got out of the car. Per followed.

'Very nice residence, I must say,' she said, pulling her jacket closer to her body.

Residence, Per noted, and did the same. The wind never seemed to let up and made his jacket flutter. He'd never thought about the house itself. It was probably an ordinary villa, he thought, albeit fairly large. Per could see it suited Charlotte's taste, with the two white pillars by the front door and a veranda reminiscent of the American South. Architecture that stuck out in the Teg area of Umeå.

'Grandiose,' she said, ringing a doorbell that played a jaunty melody. 'Less grandiose,' she added with a smile.

Roger opened the door before the doorbell fell silent. His short hair was perfectly in place, and the shine revealed that it involved some form of wax. A bit of summer tan was still on his face and emphasized his blue eyes.

'Step in,' said Roger with a serious expression. 'You can keep your shoes on.'

Per took his off. Charlotte on the other hand wiped her shoes off on the doormat and went in.

The house offered open space – a combined living room and kitchen. Adrian was sitting at the dining table right in front of them with his mother. His arm was in a cast, his face was patched up with bandages and stitches. His back was bent. He was dressed in a hoodie and tracksuit bottoms like the ones Simon and Hannes spent their days in – Björklöven's kit. His team jersey number, fifteen, was on one trouser leg.

'Would you like coffee?' his mother asked.

'Yes, please. With milk,' said Per at the same time as Charlotte. They laughed about that.

Per sat down next to the boy and Charlotte at the end of the table. The coffeemaker made a loud sound as it ground the beans, and the aroma spread in the room. Per was a bit of a coffee nerd at home, preferring Italian beans with strong flavour. Evidently this family also appreciated good coffee, considering the advanced apparatus.

'How are you feeling?' Per asked, taking a cup. He looked at Adrian, at the marks that the perpetrators had left, and wanted to hug him. It could just as easily have been Simon or Hannes who'd been robbed.

Adrian met Per's gaze. 'Have you arrested them yet?' he asked.

'No. We're here to check if you, or both of you, have changed your mind about taking part in the investigation.'

Adrian looked tiredly at Per. 'Are you completely nuts? Not on your life. They'll come back then.'

Per nodded. The boy was right, of course, but he couldn't say that. Charlotte intervened.

'Unfortunately we need your testimony to be able to arrest them, and in particular to go for a conviction. Otherwise there's a great risk that they'll go free.'

'How the hell can it be that way?' Roger roared. 'Everyone knows who these guys are. Goddamned immigrants who come here and rob our young people.'

Per looked at him. 'Now we can't say with certainty that they're the ones you're talking about. That's why we need your help, Adrian. It would provide us with more tools in the investigation and the chance to pick up the guys and question them.'

'Bullshit,' said Roger. 'We know, the young people know, you know. Just bring them in, pressure them a little. Goddamned namby-pamby country, Sweden.'

'Dad, knock it off,' said Adrian, looking down at the table.

'I just get so damned angry. My son refuses to go out the door because of them, and now apparently you have to catch them in the act in order to arrest them,' said Roger, pacing back and forth in the room. 'I'm a doctor and I've bandaged other youths who've been assaulted by this gang. What kind of world are we living in? Huh? Why aren't they sent home, or at least punished?'

'Because we have to prove that it's them. We can't just bring someone in on hearsay and rumours, that's not how our legal system works,' said Charlotte.

Adrian squeezed his arm with the cast, and sighed.

'What kind of injury did you get to your arm?' Per asked.

'A break. I'll be away from hockey until it's healed,' he said, pressing his lips together.

'You can do physical therapy – exercise your legs, balance, mobility,' said Per, knowing that it hurt to miss the first part of the season that had just started. Half the thing with hockey was hanging out with your teammates in the changing room, the bus trips to away matches. It gave them a sense of being a team.

Adrian didn't reply. Looked vacantly down at the table. Per leaned toward him.

'When our colleagues talked with you right after the robbery yesterday, you said that the group threatened you. Can you tell us more about that?' said Per, taking a sip of the perfect coffee.

Adrian shrugged his shoulders. 'They filmed me and said that the pictures would be posted, and that I could count on more beatings if I snitched to you all. And they . . .'

His gaze moved quickly to his mother.

'And they did what, Adrian? Tell us,' his mother said, placing herself behind him and putting both her hands on his shoulders. 'You must tell us everything that happened, dear.'

Adrian leaned forward to remove his mother's hands. His free elbow hit the tabletop.

'They're going to do things to me . . . Do you understand? They . . .' He drew air into his lungs, grimaced in pain when his ribcage expanded. 'I don't want to talk about it. They're sick in the head. I just want this to be over.' Adrian stared straight ahead.

'I understand that, but—'

His mother got no further, because Adrian stood up, clenching his jaw so hard that it was visible, and looked right at Per.

'Don't you get it?' Adrian raised his voice. 'If I talk, they'll come after me again! They're capable of just about anything. A girl at school was forced to sleep with him – that idiot, Samir. That's rape, damn it. He just takes what he wants and no one stops him.

No one is talking with you because he's dangerous and you can't do a thing. He gets away with everything!'

Adrian's face was red and screamed out his anxiety. Tears dampened his cheeks. He took a few steps away and disappeared into another room.

His mother followed him. Roger threw out his arms.

'A few days ago my son was happy, looking forward to the hockey season, school . . . Now he's . . . a wreck. And for what? Because Samir or whatever his name is wanted to have a little fun? No, if that guy comes near my family again I intend to personally kill him.'

He said that so calmly that Per believed him.

'That's not something I recommend,' said Charlotte, who must have understood it in a similar way.

Roger looked at her. 'Do you have kids?' he asked.

'Yes, an eighteen-year-old daughter.'

'Then she's just a few years older than Adrian. How would you have acted if Samir had done anything with her?'

Per held his breath, hoped that she wouldn't give an honest answer. He knew that she would have gone after Samir.

Charlotte stood up. Placed herself face to face with Roger.

'To be honest I don't know what I would have done. Although I know that I would have felt just like you do. The powerlessness. The frustration. The anger. I would have probably instinctively wanted to shoot him. But—'

'Exactly,' said Roger. 'So what is—'

'If you'll let me finish speaking,' Charlotte interrupted. 'But then I would go to prison and the criminals win anyway.'

Per breathed out.

Charlotte continued to speak while she looked toward the room where Adrian had gone. 'Per and I understand that this is

24

not a simple matter. But think about it at least. That's all we can ask,' she said, going to the front door. Per gulped the last of the coffee and followed her.

'In the meantime we'll just have to hope these guys don't rob anyone else,' she concluded and opened the door.

4

Klara pulled the blanket over her naked body. Ibrahim was asleep beside her. With a light movement she ran her index finger across his thick eyebrows. His face was relaxed. Smoothed out. Sometimes he dreamed things that made him roll from side to side and mumble anxiously. That frightened her. But she knew what caused it. Memories from his time in flight.

She leaned forward, let her lips meet his and then lay down with her cheek against his chest. Her index finger continued to explore. Two scars on the right side of his stomach revealed some of what he'd gone through. Cut with a knife when he was little. Another scar on his shoulder. A dispute with Samir that Ibrahim refused to talk about. He hadn't told her everything about his background – certain things were too hard to hear, he thought. She knew that he came from Syria. That his family was Christian and for that reason had to leave the country. Ibrahim had lived in flight since he was little. He had no clear memories of his homeland. But in his dreams he saw the city of Raqqa, he said. Quite clearly, like in a movie. And he remembered his family.

Klara had thought a lot about that. How it might feel to be without a family, without a homeland. When you were born in Sweden it was so usual to have a passport, an identity, a sense of belonging. Ibrahim lacked all that. He slept in a room with a family who had chosen to give him security and a context. The rest was up to him to arrange.

Ibrahim was studying Swedish as a second language and with every week he got better and better. When she first got to know him, the words came haltingly, hesitantly. Today they flowed, even if the word order was often incorrect and past tense sometimes became present and vice versa. It was sweet, she thought.

It was Friday and Klara had bunked off school to be able to stay in bed until late in the day. When Ibrahim was off, she wanted to be too. He was lying here beside her. Relaxed and near. She listened for sounds outside the room. No one from the family he lived with seemed to be at home. It was calm and lovely at his place.

Klara's phone vibrated on the nightstand. She raised her head from his chest. A friend had sent a message.

Where r u?

She replied.

I—

Klara looked at the blinking icon with three dots. Her friend wrote back.

Watch out in case you're forced to wear a burka soon. LOL

Klara turned away from Ibrahim.

Knock it off. He's not like that.

Joking. See you tomorrow night? Party with A. Hugs

27

Ibrahim started to wake up. She wrote a quick reply.

Nah, gonna hang out here with I. Hugs

Klara felt his arm around her body and crept closer so he could embrace her. Ibrahim was the nicest guy she'd met. None of the rumours she'd heard about immigrant guys were true of him. He was gentle, let her be who she was. Never judged her. The first time they were going to have sex he asked if Klara was sure she wanted to three times before he dared touch her. Sometimes she felt the differences, like when he went with her to parties. He always stood close to her. Like a shield. Never drank alcohol. Could be unpleasantly rude to other guys.

'Good morning,' said Ibrahim, pressing his arms tighter around her.

'Sleepyhead,' she said with a laugh. Klara turned and looked at him. At his perfect face. Ibrahim was beautiful, if a guy could be that. Her friends always talked about it. He would have been a drop-dead gorgeous girl too. 'Tell me something that your mum used to say to you, if you remember.' She stroked his cheek.

He said something in his language and Klara's facial expression showed clearly that she understood zip.

'So what does that mean?'

'When the stomach sleeps, the man sleeps too.'

Klara burst into laughter. 'Tell me about your mum,' she said.

Ibrahim lay on his back. 'I remember her dark hair smelled like oranges. Her hands were thin, with slender fingers. She was . . . what's it called . . . when you don't take help from anyone, when you manage by yourself?'

'Strong?' Klara asked.

'No, not dependent on anyone?' he said.

'Independent?'

28

'Yes, she was independent. She came and went as she wished. I remember that, because it was a big deal among my friends' mothers.'

Ibrahim laughed at the memory.

'But we were Christians who lived in a Muslim culture, so outside the home she wore a hijab,' he said. 'When we lived in refugee camps she often cried. Flight made her sad, hollow. I don't know.'

Ibrahim lay down on his side, facing Klara. It almost took her breath away when she looked into his eyes. He was so gorgeous.

'Dad said to me once that women are wiser than men. "Marry a wise woman and listen to her",' said Ibrahim, brushing her fringe away from her face.

Klara was about to ask more questions when Ibrahim's phone rang. There was no name on the display. Just a number. He sighed audibly but bounced up out of bed.

'Leave it,' she said.

'Not possible.'

Naked, he wrapped his bathrobe around his thin body and answered as he left the room and closed the door behind him.

Klara hated it when he left her to talk on the phone. As if he wanted to hide something. The cosy feeling was replaced by suspicion, though for no reason. The suspicion was simply something that showed up sometimes, like an irritating fly that landed on your arm. She waved it away but maddeningly it came back.

Ibrahim was speaking softly in the other room, but it still sounded like he was angry at the person who called.

She put on pants and a T-shirt, sat up in bed with her back against the wall, and checked her phone while waiting for him to be done talking. Klara answered a few messages in Snapchat while she tried to hear what he was saying.

Ibrahim suddenly opened the door with such force that her hair fluttered from the draught.

'What happened?' she asked, pulling up her legs.

'We can't hang out tomorrow night,' he said. 'I have to help some people with something. Sorry.'

'What do you mean? Who are you going to help?' Klara didn't believe him.

He sat down on the edge of the bed without answering.

'What are you going to do?' she asked.

'Pick up some things outside the city. I have to go along to interpret and carry.'

'Can't they learn Swedish themselves and stop exploiting you?' said Klara, sounding just as irritated as she was. It felt like he was just obeying orders and didn't have anything to say about it.

'It's not that simple. Samir can't sit at a school desk, his body is too restless. He's been through too much shit.'

'You don't always have to do what they say, do you?' she said defiantly.

Ibrahim's eyebrows raised, his mouth opened, his arms moved out to the sides.

She regretted it the moment she said it. It sounded as if she was accusing him of being a weakling. Klara just wanted him to stand up for himself. Swat the fly away for her.

Ibrahim shook his head, running his hands through his thick hair. 'We've talked about this. You know I can't do anything about it. Can't you just let it go?'

He seemed sincerely sad and Klara regretted it. *Damn*, she thought, forcing away the tears that were welling up.

'Sorry. I just think they're playing with you.'

'It's not something you can understand,' said Ibrahim.

Klara wiped a tear that had managed to come out anyway.

'It's just tomorrow night, then we can meet again. I promise,' he said with a sigh, noticeably irritated. He brought his hand over her leg.

'Okay,' she replied.

Klara's phone vibrated with a text. It came from a number she recognized but hadn't put in her contact list.

Can you babysit tomorrow night between 6 p.m. and midnight?

She showed the message to Ibrahim.

'Timely. So I can work tomorrow instead of hanging out with you,' she said in an attempt to smooth over her accusation. She smiled cautiously. Tried to see in his face if he loved her less because she'd accused him of being weak.

'Come here,' he said and pulled her to him, serious now. Klara closed her eyes. She loved his warm body. Loved how he smelled.

'If anything happens to me you should know that you're the best thing that has ever happened to me.'

Klara looked at him. Her heart dropped down into her stomach.

'What do you mean? What could happen to you?'

5

Per held his wife Mia's hand. Her doctor was sitting in front of them, writing on her computer. The wooden armrest pressed on his forearm, but Per didn't want to change position and let go of her.

'Well, we've done what we can and all that remains now is to analyze the test results and the X-ray images,' the doctor said.

Mia leaned forward. 'How long does that usually take?'

'We're not going to drag it out. We'll know within a few days whether the cancer has spread or not. But don't worry. From what we saw today it seems positive.'

Per tried to appear calm on the outside, but inside he was shaking like an aspen leaf in a storm. The stress of having a life partner sick with cancer was like living your life hanging over a precipice. At any moment you could fall down into the abyss.

'So when exactly are we going to find out?' asked Mia.

The doctor looked at her from behind her reading glasses. 'I understand that this is a tough time right now. But I promise you, Mia, as soon as I know I'll call you. Try to live like normal during these next few days. Think about all the things that you and Per have gone through. You're strong and you've managed this before.'

Per turned to his wife. She was wearing a black sweatshirt and jeans. All her clothes hung off her. Slowly but surely she'd had to buy smaller sizes. Her cheekbones stuck out. The headscarf sat tightly and accentuated her emaciated face. The disease had not been kind to her. The treatments nauseated her. A sore on her upper lip was several weeks old.

'Okay, thanks.'

Mia got up, and Per followed her as they left the room. They stopped outside. Unable to go further.

'Listen to what she said – the doctor thinks it looks hopeful. We should hold on to that now. If something else comes up we'll deal with it at that time.'

Mia leaned her forehead against his chest. Nodded. 'I'm just so tired of waiting, tired of news that only takes us further down the hole. So far we've only had bad news. I don't dare hope . . .'

Per put his arms around her, felt her ribs clearly through her clothes. 'You'll be healthy. And we'll solve this together. Go home and rest now.'

Mia looked up at him. 'My eternal optimist,' she said with a faint smile.

'What's the alternative?'

'Pessimism with hope for a surprise.'

Per laughed. 'Yes, you can look at life that way too.'

She believed the worst about everything. Always prepared for a battle. Every bit of news they'd received during the past year had given Mia grist for the mill. He kept his fingers crossed that soon they would get that surprise she mentioned.

They were just leaving the clinic where they'd seen the doctor when Per's phone vibrated. It was the district chief of police, Kennet Eriksson.

'Answer, it may be important,' said Mia.

Per stopped and let her go ahead without him. 'Hi, Kennet. Can I call you back in a bit? I'm with Mia at the hospital.'

'Yes, but there's something I need to talk over with you. Can you come to my office when you're done?'

'Now?' asked Per. 'I have to meet up with Charlotte after lunch and keep working. Can we do it this afternoon?'

'No, come here as soon as possible.'

They ended the call and he caught up with Mia.

'What did he want?' she asked.

Per shrugged his shoulders. 'Don't know. Kennet wants me to come in. But he sounded strange, to be honest. Curt.'

'Maybe it's time for yet another reorg?' said Mia, laughing.

Per didn't know if he could cope with more of that sort of thing. The whole police force had been reorganized in a major shift, and for the worse, in his opinion. Per thought it needed to be clearer what responsibility and mandate the bosses had now. Lack of clarity created uncertainty which paralyzed them and affected the efficiency of the whole of the police. The main idea was to get closer to the public, but Per sensed that it had turned out exactly the opposite.

He had a bad feeling in his gut. Kennet had basically ordered him in, which suggested that something major was going on within management.

'Maybe you'll get fired, or someone else on the team?' said Mia, winking at him in an attempt at a joke.

The same thought had occurred to Per.

6

Charlotte was sitting across from Ola, ready to order lunch. Friday was half over and they'd got a lot done at work, she thought. The waiter took their order and left the table. Ola insisted on treating her. It was important to him. To start with, Charlotte insisted on paying for herself when they went out to eat, but after a while she understood that he wanted to be a gentleman and let him pick up the bill. It was a bit sweet and irritating at the same time.

Today he picked the restaurant and it was Orangeriet Boule & Bistro. The last time she was there she had played a game of boule against Per. It was one of the few times they'd gone out after work. Charlotte had lost and wasn't at all eager for a rematch.

She looked up at the waiter, who had brought their food. He placed the salad on her side of the table. The hamburger ended up in front of Ola.

'Typical,' she said, exchanging plates.

Charlotte took a big bite of burger while Ola started poking at his salad. He had lost his father early to a heart attack. She knew that was why he was a bit obsessed by his health. Exercise and healthy food were a way for him to get control, to try to avoid his dad's fate.

'I've signed up for Vasaloppet this year,' he said.

'Oh, that's impressive.'

Ola chewed on his salad. 'Mum started crying when I told her. She's done the race twenty years in a row.'

'Will you ski with her?'

He looked at Charlotte. 'Maybe?' he said, raising his eyebrows.

'Oh no,' she answered. 'You won't get me on a ski run. Not even to exercise.'

Ola offered a broad smile. 'My ex and I did a lot of cross-country skiing. It's sexy,' he said, winking.

'What?' She shook her head. 'All the more reason for me not to ski. You and I will create our own memories, not share yours and your ex's.'

'How shall we do that? Give me some suggestions for an activity that you want to do with me.'

'Rock climbing?'

They both burst into laughter at the unlikely thought and started joking wildly about the image of Charlotte in a sling against a stone wall. She loved Ola because he made her laugh reach all the way to her toes. True, sometimes he was more boring than watching paint dry, but the next moment he could be the funniest man she'd met.

Charlotte looked at him. His shirt bulged from his muscles. She remembered the first time she saw Ola at the police station in Umeå. He came walking toward her in the Major Crimes offices and it took her breath away. Straight-backed, self-confident and masculine. And then that well-toned body. Ola was known for his appearance and was generally called 'Hot Ola' among the police. Really, he and Anna should be a couple. Although they would exercise themselves to death, thought Charlotte, dipping her fries in a bowl of ketchup.

Ola looked at her for a moment, before he took up the question again of a joint activity.

'I'm going to drive to Riksgränsen and hike in the mountains for a month – would you go with me? Please?'

She took the napkin from her lap and wiped her mouth. 'Never. I don't consider that a pleasure.'

'Why? You haven't tried it, as far as I know?'

'I did, many years ago. All I got out of hiking was chafed skin, mosquito bites, muscle cramps and ticks. So . . . No, thanks. You can hike where you want, but without me.'

Ola took her hand, which was on its way to pick up more fries. 'You need to get away from Umeå, see something else.'

'Then I'll go down to Italy, check in at Villa Cordevigo and wander among the grapevines in Valpolicella,' she said, squeezing his hand.

Ola turned his attention to his salad again. 'You're so terribly snobbish. Be a little daring,' he said.

'Ditto.'

When Per called it felt like being rescued. Without apologizing to Ola, she answered.

'Hi, Ola and I are having lunch. Can I call you back in a bit?'

'Well, I've just had a meeting with Kennet. Can you come over to me? I'm sitting at boules court number one.'

'What? Are you at Orangeriet too?'

'Yep.'

'How did you know that Ola and I were here at the restaurant? Are you spying on me, Per?'

He laughed in her ear, at the same time as she watched Ola wave his hand at someone behind her. He was happy that someone else knew about their relationship.

'Come over, Charlotte. I need ten minutes.'

She looked around and there sat Per, waving like an idiot.

'Leave Ola at the table, he'll get you back soon.'

Charlotte stood up, excused herself to Ola and explained that Per had something important to say. Then she turned on her heels and walked to the exit, where she sat down in one of the chairs closest to boules court number one with her knees angled toward her boss and colleague.

'What in the world is going on? Has Mia got worse?'

He shook his head. 'We haven't got an answer yet. This concerns us – you and me.'

'Have you been fired?' she said, intending it as a joke, but Per didn't pick up on that.

'Kennet is going to be on sick leave for six months,' he said instead. 'He's going to undergo a couple of operations. They've discovered a heart defect . . .'

'Oh, is he okay?'

'Well, he's in good spirits. But I'm going to take over as acting district chief of police during that time.'

Charlotte was both happy and disappointed.

'How nice! Although boring for me. I don't want any other partner,' she said, looking at a man who had just made an extremely bad throw on the boules court.

'Nicely put, but—'

Charlotte interrupted Per before he could say more. 'Who will take over your position? Don't say Kicki. Don't say Kicki!' she said repeatedly.

Per burst into laughter. 'That's why I came here to talk with you. You're not going to get a different boss.'

'What do you mean?'

'I couldn't wait to tell you. You . . . You'll become acting chief inspector at Major Crimes during that time.'

Charlotte straightened up and looked at Per. Her mouth opened to say something but she didn't know what. She hadn't seen that promotion coming.

'I'm going to be acting chief inspector?'

'Just say yes,' said Per, laughing again.

'Admittedly I'm already detective inspector, but I've been at Major Crimes the shortest time. You're going to get your balls cut off by the others, pardon my language.'

'It was Kennet's suggestion and decision. You're the best suited of everyone in the department.'

She leaned back. 'Are you serious?'

'Yes.'

There was a tingle in her stomach – she wanted to stand up and jump, she was so happy. Charlotte smiled at the man on the boules court who was drinking what appeared to be beer. At the same time another thought popped up.

'We'll be understaffed. Who's going to come in and cover my position?'

'That's already been solved externally. Kennet is going to introduce that person in the next few days.'

'Externally?' Charlotte repeated. 'How did Kennet manage that? We aren't allowed to recruit from other parts of the country. Besides, the recruitment process is terribly slow in our organization. He must have known for a while.'

'Yes, he's fought for it. From what I understand Kennet put his foot down with HR in Stockholm, and with the development of events up here they had a hard time saying no.'

'Who will the reinforcement be?'

'His name is Alex Alvarez and he comes from Major Crimes in Gothenburg,' said Per.

Charlotte felt all the blood drain from her head.

She knew Alex Alvarez well. She even knew what brand of underwear he favoured.

39

7

Ibrahim looked out of the window and observed the buildings passing by. The bus was half full, so he could take two seats. In front of him a young man was sitting with a designer jacket and Ibrahim was glad that Samir wasn't with him – otherwise he would have taken that guy's jacket.

Samir and Omar had started hanging out with a gang in Umeå that was involved in a lot of shady things. Samir was firmly resolved to rise in the hierarchy and did what was required. He'd tried to get into other criminal gangs in Europe but always started fights and was forced to flee. Samir was constantly running from something. Ibrahim was tired of that.

He thought about Klara. She was suspicious of Samir and Omar, and Ibrahim couldn't blame her. There were things he hid from her and she knew it.

The landscape outside the window changed along the bus's route toward Nydala; buildings were replaced by trees. He got a Snap from Klara.

Sorry I'm difficult. Promise you'll call tonight. Kisses.

She often did that. Quarrelled with him to then regret it and say she was sorry. Worry was something he often associated with her. It was a little sweet, because in Ibrahim's world that wasn't a fight. But it was hard for him to be called a coward.

Ibrahim looked at his leg, which was moving up and down in a rapid tempo. His jaw was tightly clenched and it felt as if his nerves were outside his body. He knew what Samir wanted. If Klara found out the truth she would hate him. The guy she loved was an illusion.

He replied to her Snap.

It's fine. Call later. Kisses.

He stretched to press on the red 'Stop' button, and just as the bus turned into the stop, Samir called.

'Hey, bro, where are you? We're going to eat.'

'There in five. I'm not hungry, man,' Ibrahim replied and switched to Arabic, which they always used when they were talking with each other – even Omar, although it wasn't really his native language.

'Come here now, we're going to hang out tonight. It'll be great. Big plans.' Samir hung up.

Ibrahim sighed. The first time he saw Samir had been on an overcrowded boat in the Mediterranean. When it capsized, everyone fell into the water. Ibrahim's whole family disappeared into the dark depths. He remembered his mother's screams, how she came up to the surface only to disappear again – several times. His father held his little sister, his arms flailing so that they wouldn't be dragged down. Suddenly both were gone. His mother's red shawl floated beside Ibrahim. He never saw his brother again.

He had clung tightly to a plank. He'd screamed but couldn't let go of the piece of wood that held his head right above death. Total anarchy prevailed there on the sea. Everyone clambered on everyone else to keep themselves alive. Ibrahim struck at a man who tried to take his plank. It was the difference between life and death. No one in his family knew how to swim. Ibrahim wanted to learn now, in Sweden, but summer had quickly passed and he hadn't dared. He stayed out of the water.

A vessel had picked up the survivors out there on the sea, and Samir and Omar had been among them. They sat together across from him. After that Ibrahim's memory was blurry. He came on land in Turkey; all he remembered was the blanket around his wet body and other people crying who had lost next of kin. There and then a man came up to him, took hold of his arm and led him away from the group. Ibrahim let himself be taken, in shock and afraid, paralyzed by sorrow. Samir saw the man and ran after them. He beat him black and blue until the man was lying motionless on the ground. That was Ibrahim's clearest memory from life in flight after that of his mother's shawl on the water: the man on the ground. Samir's foot struck his head so many times that brain matter ran out. His fury had rescued Ibrahim from being the victim of the worst sort of human trafficking. That was his second contact with death. And far from the last.

Ibrahim got off the bus and walked toward the campground where his buddies were staying at the moment. Samir and Omar moved around quite a bit. Sometimes they stayed with some fellow immigrants in their apartment, sometimes here or at another campground. They didn't seem to be too particular. They liked Sweden, and Ibrahim was the one who had brought them here. He had nagged at them to learn Swedish, tried to get them to spend time on something other than the shit they were involved in. But Samir laughed and said that he was already lost, that he wasn't going to live that long. So what would he do with Swedish? He could barely read or write in his own language.

Ibrahim thought that was sad. There was no faith in the future whatsoever, nothing that gave Samir and Omar any meaning in existence. They got their kicks from violence and drugs. It was as if their own lives were slowly choking them to death, that's what

42

Klara said. It sounded right somehow, Ibrahim thought, as he entered the campground.

Inside, he was met by a gang who were sitting on a bench outside the main cabin. They nodded at him, pointed at the camper where Samir and Omar were, followed him with their eyes. They knew that he associated with Samir and for that reason Ibrahim was not someone they attacked or questioned. In a very short time Samir had gained respect among the others at the campground, because he supplied them with mobiles and drugs. The criminal gang that Samir had started hanging with pulled him to them like a magnet. He also knew that his predilection for violence came in handy with such groups. It was always like that, and Ibrahim suspected that the violence made Samir feel good too. It was something Samir recognized from when he was little; nothing that gang did was worse than what he was forced to do as a child soldier. He could take care of himself. Ibrahim no longer asked him for details about his life.

When he came up to the camper, the door flew open. A boy jumped out and ran past him. One of Samir's young couriers. Ibrahim watched him before he stepped in.

'Hey,' said Omar, who was sitting right by the door, putting pills into a little plastic bag.

Ibrahim stayed by the door. His heart knotted up when he looked around. Mouldy plates in the sink and remnants of white powder on the counter. Smoke haze from the constantly puffing Omar. Pizza boxes with half-consumed contents. A hole right through the bathroom door that testified to strong emotions. A couple of years ago that would have been normal for Ibrahim too. In flight you often ended up in misery. A camper meant a roof over your head, a refuge – whatever the standard. It was only now, when he was living in a clean home, that Ibrahim saw what he hadn't even noticed before.

He sat down on the edge of the couch and looked at Omar's actions. At the drugs that would go out into the city.

'Is that kid your new courier?' Ibrahim asked.

Omar laughed but avoided eye contact. 'Yes – or not ours, but the gang's. If the cops catch him there won't even be an interrogation or anything because he's so young. They'll just release him. He has guns at home where he lives that he's hiding for Samir.'

'Hey, man!' Samir came in through the camper door. 'We're going to arrange some things today.'

'Don't we usually do that anyway?' said Ibrahim.

Samir placed himself in front of him. 'Are you questioning me, or what?'

He took a pill from Omar's pile and stuffed it in his mouth. The whites of his eyes had red streaks and he looked generally indifferent.

'Huh?' said Samir, when Ibrahim didn't reply.

'Sorry, I just meant that we're good at arranging things.'

It didn't pay to talk back.

'Listen, by the way, your girlfriend,' Samir said suddenly. 'Can she help us bring in a little cash? That body . . . We would get rich. Is she beautiful?'

Ibrahim looked up at Samir, wanted to drive his fist right through that sneer. But he knew better than to show what he felt. If he did that Samir would never let it go.

'She's mine, no one else's,' he said instead. 'Do you get it?'

It was a language that Samir understood. Honour.

Omar and Samir said they were Muslims, but put no great store in religion, except for quoting phrases from Islamic teachings when it suited them. Ibrahim believed that somewhere on the way they had lost their faith – in everything. He had thought a lot about his own religion, that he was born Christian in a culture where the majority were Muslims. But the life he'd lived as an orphan had erased the faith; it was all about survival.

Samir's laugh filled the camper. Omar shook his head.

'Yes, damn it, I get it. No one else gets to screw her. Respect, man.'

Ibrahim didn't reply. The only thing he could think of was that Klara should never meet Samir. Sometimes he forgot how sick in the head he was. Samir had been his protector for so many years that he'd become like a brother to him, but that didn't come free. Ibrahim paid through his obedience. What Samir wanted, you did. It was in Ibrahim's marrow.

'Do you have another girl we can use? A friend of your girl-friend, or something?'

'I'll think about it,' said Ibrahim, but there wasn't a chance. 'What are we doing tonight?'

Samir sat down at the table. 'It's the weekend – the unbelievers will go out and booze and I need more stuff.'

Omar guffawed. 'Fucking infidels, they ought to be shot,' he said.

Ibrahim knew that was just something he said to impress Samir. He thought about Klara; she was also an unbeliever in their eyes.

On the floor was a box full of mobiles that really should be sent on. Samir was careless about that. Certain phones he opened to get personal information in the form of pictures that could be used for extortion. He knew a guy who could unlock smartphones and usually sent Ibrahim to arrange that. It became a pattern: the gang gave Samir assignments which he then passed on to Omar and Ibrahim to perform.

'Let's go and eat, then we'll arrange the other things later,' said Samir, pulling the hood over his head and taking a jacket from a pile of other jackets that he hadn't bought himself.

Sometimes he sold things they'd taken. Certain objects he kept. Everyone knew that Samir hadn't paid for those things and that gave him respect. When he dealt out the clothes, it was to people at the campground, although also to Swedes. They paid a few hundred kronor for a jacket that cost ten times more in the store. The watches were actually the easiest to get rid of and gave them easy money, but he passed those on to the gang. In return he got pats on the back and protection.

Samir took a couple of credit cards from his trouser pocket.

'What are we going to do tonight? What is it that's so important?' Ibrahim asked.

'You'll find out when it's time.'

The answer meant more robberies.

Who would be the next victims?

8

Per grasped the handle of the glass door and opened it, slipped past Simon and Hannes who went ahead into the 'barn' – which was really called Winpos Arena and the home of Björklöven's hockey team. It changed names so often that Per could barely keep up. Sundays these days were devoted to hockey – or really the whole weekend was. It was seven o'clock in the morning and Per remembered a time when Sundays meant sleeping in. But he could at least be grateful for the day before – a Saturday with no work or practices. Just rest.

The younger players rarely practised at this arena, but today was an exception because Simon would be trying out for the U16 team. The boys quickly disappeared along the cramped corridor and the rubber mat in the middle of the floor made their steps soundless. Per set down the holdall with all the gear and followed his oldest son with his gaze, saw his blond head of hair at the far end of the corridor.

'Simon! Come here and get your gear. You have to learn to take care of your equipment. You change in room three,' he said, pointing to the door.

His son retrieved his bag, which was the same size as his upper body. Per felt a little ashamed when he saw how heavy it was for the kid, although he carried it without complaining. Getting to practise with players two years older was a big deal. Per was mostly worried about injuries, but the team seemed convinced about trying out Simon and hoped in time to gain both brothers, who clearly demonstrated talent. Per didn't understand a thing about it. Where did that talent come from? No one in the family had any background in hockey.

He took out his phone to call Mia and wake her, while he looked in the changing room to see if Simon was doing okay. His son was sitting and talking with another player.

'Hi,' said Per when Mia answered after two rings. 'I made coffee for you at home. How are you feeling this morning?'

'Okay, actually. I think I could have come to the practice.'

Soon they would find out if the cancer was gone from Mia's body. Until then they were trying to live as normally as possible.

The price that he personally had to pay was to take care of all the chores at home, plus his job. Sometimes it felt like he would fall apart from stress. But soon Mia would be able to take part more actively in the family again and he could stop living like a single parent.

'How are the boys doing?' she asked.

'Good, I think. Hannes is hanging out with the younger players and Simon is getting ready. He said he could manage on his own.'

Mia laughed. 'That's understandable – who wants their dad with them in the changing room?'

Per leaned his back against the orange-painted brick wall. A stationary bike stood alongside it. The stench was tangible – like crotch sweat mixed with an old man who never showered. It was worse here, where the adult players changed and exercised.

'If anything happens at work, do you have the energy to come and take over from me here?' he asked.

There was a scraping sound in the receiver.

'Yes, of course. Someone has to be there to watch. And take care of Hannes, who I hear will tear down the whole training facility otherwise.'

Per smiled to himself, relieved at her sarcasm being on its way back. It had disappeared when things were toughest, when they found out that her body hadn't responded to the initial treatment. Mia was planning for her own death and Per had to go to a psychologist in order to not break down. Later when the news came that the second cancer treatment was actually starting to work, her mood became as light as her hair. The hair she'd had and would get back. Until then she wore a headscarf. A wig had never been an option for her.

'Call if anything happens,' Mia said and hung up.

Just then Simon came out in his hockey gear. With skates on he was even taller than his usual five foot eight. *My little man*, thought Per, and wanted to go up and hug his son, wish him good luck. But he refrained, and did like the parents of the older youths: stood and watched calmly as his son went past on his way out to the ice, looking serious and energized. Per knew that this was important to him. Hockey had become his life. As a dad he was both happy and nervous. Happy that his son devoted all his waking time to practising and dreaming hockey instead of sitting glued in front of a video game. Nervous because he knew that it was a tough environment to be in. Hard competition.

One of the other boys' mothers came up and stood beside him in the corridor. 'Come on, Per. Let's go and sit in the bleachers.'

He looked at her. Did they know each other? He couldn't place whose mother she was.

'We see each other every day – I work in the lunchroom at the police station,' she said in response to his questioning gaze, and Per wanted to sink through the floor. She always had her hair in a braid on the side; now it was hidden by her jacket.

'Yes! But . . . Hi! Does your son play here? I didn't know that,' said Per, sounding a bit forced. He heard it himself.

'Goalie,' the woman said, pointing at one of the two guys with heavier equipment.

He didn't dare ask her name, that would reveal that he didn't know it which would be even more awkward, he thought. Hopefully one of the other parents would address her.

Per followed 'the Braid' to the bleachers. He was used to cold skating rinks, but in here it felt like a warm spring day. They sat down a couple of seats from each other and he saw how Simon started skating round and round.

'Cool about Simon. I hope he makes the team. We need good wings,' she said.

Per replied with his gaze directed out at the ice. 'We'll have to see how it goes. It's just good to test the opposition.'

Hannes was sitting beside him. His team would practise in an hour in another rink. As usual it was double practice for Per. Weekdays and weekends.

'Listen, it was awful to hear about Adrian,' said the Braid, leaning toward Per. 'Have you arrested Samir and the gang?'

Per looked at her, wondering how she could know who the suspects were.

'I can't talk about an ongoing case and who the persons of interest are for the investigation,' said Per, observing Simon, who was taking faster and faster turns on the ice.

'What do you mean? Everyone knows who they are, anyway,' said Hannes.

Per raised his eyebrows and looked at his youngest son. 'What do you know about it?' he said, and saw how the Braid got up and left her seat.

Hannes shrugged his shoulders. His light-brown hair was a little longer at the back and his eyes were blue as a summer sky. *Stylish*, Per thought.

'You know, Dad. Aren't you a policeman? Everyone knows who they are,' his son said, taking out his phone and going into his social media. 'Here you can see them putting on their ski masks. It's so wrong. And look here, this old man is getting robbed.'

Per took Hannes' phone and watched a clip of an older man with a walking frame being relieved of his watch and wallet. Without any resistance whatsoever. He let the robbers take everything. Per could not recall a report coming in about this robbery.

He played the video again. It was hard to make out the figures completely, but Omar's face could be clearly seen. The shoes that the robbers were wearing in the clip appeared to be the same ones Adrian had described to the police when he was robbed.

'Where did this video come from, Hannes? Or do you know who posted it on the internet?'

Hannes directed his attention to his big brother on the ice. 'What do you mean? It circulates on social media, haven't any of you seen it? That video is a few weeks old. Aren't they the ones who robbed Adrian? They always hang around down by the campground in Nydala.'

'Send it to me,' said Per, returning his gaze to the rink. There was another witness to one of the robberies, that was good. They simply had to find out who had filmed it. How could they have missed that video online?

Just then he saw Simon was tackled hard by player number twelve and crashed so violently into the board that it was heard all over the arena.

Per looked for signs of injury, but his son seemed to have coped. *Little bastard*, he thought, glaring at number twelve just as his phone started ringing. It was Kennet.

'Hi there – and on a Sunday no less. What can I do for you?'

'Hi, Per, I'm calling to ruin your day off.'

9

Charlotte pulled on her bathrobe and guided the watering can to the green plants on the veranda. The leaves were hanging listlessly, tired from the lack of water.

'Shall we have coffee inside or outside?' Ola called.

'Come out, it's really nice.'

She watered the rest of the plants, which were reaching up toward the morning sun. Then she looked at Ola through the big picture windows; he was assembling breakfast in the kitchen. For some reason they were already up by eight o'clock. *Ungodly early on a Sunday*, she thought. They'd stayed in bed and talked about her new position as acting head of Major Crimes – how it would affect the team, the dynamics with Kicki and the others. She expected strong resistance, but she was also respected for her work.

Charlotte sat down in the pleasing outdoor space she had created during the spring. She and Ola had spent the summer down by the pier on the river. After the house in Falsterbo, the home on The Island was the best investment she'd made. For four weeks they'd been here together with her daughter Anja, who had just turned eighteen. Charlotte hoped that she would start studying at Umeå University in the autumn, but she hadn't got into the right course and stayed in Stockholm – in the claws of Charlotte's ex, Carl, who was quite content with how that had worked out. In any event, they had agreed to buy an apartment for Anja. It would do her good to live on her own and become independent, taking the rubbish out herself and doing without any weekly cleaning help . . . Nowadays Sundays were devoted to apartment showings for Anja. But it wasn't that easy for her because apparently there were only a couple of streets in the Östermalm neighbourhood that were suitable, where all of her social circle lived. Not a good idea, Charlotte felt. Although the alternative was that Anja would keep living with Carl, and then the risk was that she would become even more unbearable and spoiled.

While they ate breakfast outside, Ola scrolled on his phone, apparently searching for something. Charlotte set her own phone in the shadow of the flowerpot on the table. She drank coffee with her legs up on a chair and looked at her toes, which needed a pedicure. Ola sat across from her, eating an open sandwich. He tanned easily, his dark hair wet after his morning shower. He had put on shorts and a sweatshirt, and would probably go for a run. *But why did he shower then?* she thought, although she immediately let that go.

'Listen, Charlotte. There's something we have to talk about,' he said.

'What's that?' She immediately got a bad feeling. The calm in her body was replaced by apprehension.

'I've got reports about Tony Israelsson from Interpol,' he said, draining his glass of water.

Her gut feeling had been right. This was not good. Tony Israelsson was a hardened criminal who had been after Charlotte since she crossed him as a police officer in Stockholm.

'Yes?' she said cautiously.

'He's been brought in for narcotics offences by the Spanish police. It appears that he'll be convicted and most likely sentenced to a long prison term down there.'

Charlotte's muscles relaxed. She'd thought that Tony was back in Sweden. There was still a risk that he would return, but if he was locked up in Spain that risk was reduced considerably.

'We ought to celebrate tonight. Champagne!' she said, leaning toward Ola. Their lips met.

'Didn't we drink enough yesterday when we toasted to your new position?' he asked, taking the edge off the joy.

'We shared a bottle of Sassicaia. That was nothing, just pure enjoyment. Tonight we'll celebrate.'

'Okay, let's do that,' he said happily.

Ola stood up and she followed him with her gaze. He was charming, she thought. And she was extremely attracted to him, felt like a teenage girl pining for her first love. Insatiable. But she was bothered by his lack of joie de vivre. It was something she'd noticed the more time they spent together. Charlotte would gladly open a nice bottle of wine in the middle of the week because it was pleasant. Ola wanted to wait until the weekend and made her feel like a semi-alcoholic.

'Maybe we drink a maximum of three bottles a week together. That's not much, darling,' she said.

Ola kissed her on the cheek and left her. She watched his back disappear as he took the first steps of his run. At the same moment Per called.

'Did you miss me?' Charlotte asked when she answered.

'Not exactly,' he said. 'We've just got an alarm. A woman has been found murdered down by the pier, under the Teg Bridge. See you there in fifteen minutes. Bye.' Per hung up on her.

So the summer slowdown is over, she thought, finishing the rest of the coffee in her mug.

10

Erik turned to the car and pressed the key fob an extra time, saw that it blinked. He had parked not far from Rådhusparken.

'It's free to park here on Sundays, isn't it?' he said to Helen, who was walking a few steps in front.

'Yes, I think so,' she said.

The children ran ahead of them on the pavement as they passed Stora Hotellet, turning to the right by the water and the Strand promenade. In the park the flowers offered beautiful colours. Erik brought his hand to his jacket pocket and took out sunglasses, which dampened the strong sunlight to a pleasant glow. The family had cleaned all morning, a well-practised weekend routine. The kids had been promised a treat afterwards and the happiness of the approaching food made them jittery. They skipped along the pavement toward the Väven community centre, which stuck out like a lump of sugar and extended down to the Ume River. It was fairly new and very different from the other buildings in the city, looking like a spaceship with its glistening white facade and black window sections.

'Kids, you need to calm down a little,' said Helen, and the children stopped as if they'd got an order. She placed her hand on her son's shoulder in an attempt to quiet him.

'I'll go and order with the children, if you find a table?' Erik said, pointing at the Fika bakery.

Helen nodded and he went up to the register. As Erik ordered, he saw her choose an outdoor table, where she sat down and remained seated with her gaze straight ahead. She sat on the edge of the chair with her handbag in her lap, as if she were ready to leave. Her eyes were aimed at her phone – the one she didn't hide from him. Erik hadn't mentioned the mobile he'd found in the laundry basket. He was still uncertain about what he should do. The thought that she shared secrets with someone else was hard to take. His *wife*.

On the counter before him the tray was filled with coffee, soft drinks, two chocolate balls for the kids, a vanilla pastry for him and a biscotti for Helen – her favourite treat.

Erik took the tray and had to concentrate not to spill the coffee on his way out to the table. Helen was sitting by herself and he looked for Liam and Elsa. They were playing with a classmate of Liam's a short distance away.

He sat down and leaned back against the wicker, which creaked in a familiar way. The heat made him sweat. Erik followed the example of the other guests and took off his jacket.

'It's a hot day for the end of summer,' he said, setting the family's treats out on the table. A drop of coffee ended up on the saucer under the cup from the hasty movement. Helen was there immediately and wiped it up.

'Yes, it is,' she answered, but kept her jacket on. Her long, curly, blonde hair stuck out in all directions as usual. She still had a summer tan and her blue eyes were hidden by sunglasses.

'Take off your jacket, you're going to sweat to death,' he said.

She leaned back without answering, set her handbag down on the ground and raised the coffee cup, ready to drink, when the sound of sirens drowned out everything else at the outdoor cafe.

They saw an ambulance coming at high speed toward the pier, closely followed by two police cars with blinking blue lights. Erik craned his neck to see what was happening.

A short distance away, under the Teg Bridge, the police were putting up plastic tape.

Everyone at the outdoor cafe turned their heads in that direction. Some stood up. Inquisitive glances were exchanged. The only one who didn't look was Helen. She simply drank her coffee.

'What has happened?' an older woman asked, who was sitting at the table beside them.

Erik shrugged his shoulders. 'No idea.'

Gazes wandered from the other cafe visitors.

'Terrible things happen all the time, even here in Umeå,' Helen said with sarcasm in her voice, looking around her.

'Yes, but this seems serious. I'll go and check,' said Erik, getting up.

'Why?' asked Helen.

'Just out of curiosity.'

When Erik left the serving area he crossed his arms; the air was colder when you weren't sitting out of the wind. The gravel on the path crunched under his shoes. The river was to his left, concrete to the right. An old wooden shed stood under the Teg Bridge, by the edge of the pier. *Oddly placed*, he thought. His gaze instead was drawn to the bridge above, where cars were crossing in a steady stream. A group of people had gathered and were looking down on what was happening by the barricade. Among them he recognized someone, even though he'd never talked with him. The guy was in a relationship with one of his students at the school, Klara, who also babysat for them sometimes. She often talked about him and said that he wanted to go back to school next year. Apparently the kid was studying Swedish as a second language now. Erik tried to remember his name, but his thoughts were interrupted when he came up to the barricade.

A police officer asked him to back up.

'What happened?' asked Erik, but at the same moment he saw what the man and the others on the bridge were looking at.

Two policemen were leaning over the edge of the pier and pulling something out. Erik stretched to get a glimpse of the object in the water.

A body was in the river, just below the shed at the edge of the pier, right under the bridge. Erik could only see hair floating on the surface, the person was facing down. He stared. Then he turned around, saw people gathering. Death attracted attention.

'There's nothing to see here, let them work in peace,' said a policewoman, pushing back the curious observers by the pier. Erik felt embarrassed, like a peeping Tom. He backed up but looked around and up to the offices of Umeå Energi. The vegetation-covered facade was full of windows toward the river. Maybe someone there saw something, he thought. Below it was the skate park, which was usually full of activity and young people. He went back to the cafe with his arms pressed against his chest, passing the Hamnmagasinet building, and was glad that the children hadn't seen the corpse.

When Erik came to the outdoor serving area, Liam and Elsa were eating their chocolate balls, unaware of the dead body not far away. He cast a final glance at the cordoned-off area before he sat down. Helen didn't ask about anything, but the elderly woman was curious.

'What happened?'

'Don't know. Looked like someone was in the water under the bridge.'

'Oh, dear me,' she said, shaking her head.

Helen smiled cautiously. 'Maybe it's someone who was drunk and fell in,' she said abruptly. She still had her jacket on, buttoned all the way up.

'Are you cold?' Erik asked. 'Or are you sick?'

'No, but I want to keep it on,' she said, sounding like a testy teenager.

Erik laughed in an attempt to lighten the mood. 'You're a grown woman and you can do as you wish.'

She looked at him with a smile, but Erik couldn't decide whether it was a sweet or scornful smile. Did she no longer love him? He searched for signs that it wasn't true.

His thoughts went to the mobile in the laundry basket again. His stomach was in knots. Worry sat like concrete in his whole body, weighing him down. He had taken out the Nokia phone one more time after finding it, sat with it in his hand, trying to understand that his wife had someone else. The questions whirled in his head about where and how they must meet. At a hotel? At the man's home? And when? He was about to go crazy. One moment he wanted to scream at her, tell her that he knew, and in the next moment forge plans about how he would catch them in the act.

Erik leaned toward his wife, inspected her as she sat there on the edge of her chair. On the sleeve of her jacket was a red spot, like the one he'd found on her trousers in the laundry basket.

'What's this?' he asked, trying to scrape it away with his fingernail.

'Nose blood,' she answered, irritated, pulling back her arm.

Erik looked at her. She was so angry all the time.

11

Per had to put on a white overall and face mask, and was just about to pull on the rubber gloves when Charlotte turned into the area in her brand-new Porsche Cayenne. It was electric, which allowed her to arrive without a sound. Per was grateful for that, as it meant fewer glances at the car and less talk behind her back. Carola, the responsible CSI at the scene, waved at her. Per stuck his hand in the tight-fitting glove. The rubber crackled. Charlotte looked relaxed in jeans and simple sweater under her jacket. No watch and no jewellery that needed to be locked in her desk at the police station.

They were standing in the car park by Hamnmagasinet. Nearby was a cafe, which today was full of people at the outdoor tables. Per had been there many times with the boys.

'Hi, what do we have here?' Charlotte asked, getting gloves from Carola. The forensic technician was like a copy of Crown Princess Victoria with her lively eyes and broad smile.

'A woman in her fifties, suspected homicide. We fished her out of the water,' said Carola, pointing at a body bag on the edge of the pier. 'The woman has injuries that resemble torture.'

'Can you describe them?' asked Per.

'I'll get to that,' said Carola, starting to walk toward the bridge. The water glistened in the sun.

Charlotte put on gloves.

'A forensic investigation is still going on here,' said Carola, sweeping her arm over the cordoned-off area, which the police were in the process of expanding to be able to work undisturbed. 'You know what applies, and you may only stand where I point.'

She raised the plastic tape and let Per and Charlotte in.

'Signs of rape?' asked Charlotte.

'No idea yet, but she has clothes on,' said Carola. 'When we found her she looked like a mermaid.'

'Mermaid?'

'Yes, it had to do with the design of her trousers and how her legs were together in the water. She was found with her face down and the currents in the river made her bob. It looked like she was swimming, like a mermaid. Her hair was floating on the surface.'

Per pictured the Disney character Ariel. 'Was there any identification on her?'

'No, we haven't found anything that can confirm her identity. We suspect that she was tortured somewhere else and dumped here. But that's only speculation so far. Come with me and you'll see.'

Per and Charlotte followed Carola, who walked to the wooden shed under the bridge. Outside it was the body, already placed in a body bag. Carola pulled down the zipper and a female face appeared. The eyes were closed, the skin white, the lips blue. She was swollen after some time in the water.

'How long has she been in the river?' asked Charlotte.

'Making a rough guess, I would say six to eight hours. She didn't sink to the bottom, but the tissue has had time to swell.'

Per was grateful that the body hadn't started to smell strongly yet. The woman had on a dirty sweater that had risen up a bit and exposed her stomach. There were leaves in the dark, shoulder-length hair. That was all he could see.

'Does she have clothes on her lower body?' asked Per.

'Yes, jeans. They are blue down to the thighs, where it changes to violet and a sequin-like fabric, I think it was. It was colourful anyway,' said Carola, pointing at the woman's legs, which were hidden by the bag.

'Why didn't she sink below the surface?'

'Somehow her jeans got stuck on a hook on the edge of the pier,' said Carola, pointing to the water.

Per took two steps forward and looked down.

'Did the victim drown or was she dead before she ended up here?' he asked.

'I'll have to examine her before I can give an answer. But she has none of what you normally see with drowning, such as white foam around nose and mouth. Although an autopsy is needed to decide for sure.'

'Have you been able to establish the time of death?' asked Charlotte.

'No, not yet. The decomposition process goes considerably faster in the water. As I said, we'll have to see what the autopsy shows.'

Per watched as Carola zipped up the bag again.

'Then there's another thing,' she said, getting up and stretching her back. 'Something that is going to make things difficult for you.'

'What?' Charlotte asked impatiently.

'The medical examiner will have to examine the woman more closely, but we've already seen that all of her teeth have been extracted. Every single one. That requires both technique and force. It would be extremely painful, assuming she was still conscious,' said Carola, pulling her face mask down to her chin. Per followed her example and breathed air into his lungs.

'What the hell are you saying?' he said, exhaling. 'That sounds like something personal, not just a robbery or an assault that went wrong.'

'Yes, and it makes the identification process more difficult if her fingerprints aren't in your database. In any case, so far we haven't found any teeth.'

'You think the assault didn't happen here?' said Per.

Carola inspected the body bag with the woman. 'I'm fairly certain that she was moved. As perhaps you saw, she has marks on her wrists, which indicates that she's been bound,' said Carola, looking up at them.

'And someone ought to have heard her otherwise, I think,' said Per, looking around. 'Or maybe not, if it happened at night. Then this is a deserted place.'

He saw how Charlotte took off the gloves and seemed to be feeling whether her hair sat as it should on her neck.

'We'll need to bring divers here,' she said. 'If she had a handbag or something like that it may also have been thrown into the water. The teeth may be there too.'

Per looked out over the water. It was calm. The sun created a shadow of the bridge on the surface, like an exact copy of what was above.

'Do we have time before the sun goes down this evening?' asked Charlotte.

Per looked at his watch, which showed 10.47 a.m. 'Yes, that should work.'

He and Charlotte left the scene and discarded gloves and face masks. Their cars were parked next to each other. Per leaned toward his black Volvo XC40, let his rear end meet the bonnet. Charlotte joined him with her arms crossed.

'What are we dealing with here?' asked Per.

'An unusually brutal murder,' said Charlotte, looking out over the river. 'Who is the victim? We need an identity to be able to find a motive. The first thing we have to do is to see if anyone with her description has been reported missing in our region, but also in other counties. And we have to find out if her DNA is in our database. We'll put Kicki on that.'

'Yes, and then we should review any surveillance cameras in the vicinity,' said Per as Charlotte went over to her own car. 'Maybe it will be possible to map the woman's activity before the crime occurred. Where did she meet the perpetrator?'

'That building there should have functioning cameras, anyway,' said Charlotte, pointing at the local energy company as she opened the car door.

Per knew that she would be a damn good leader for the team when she took over his position. Better than himself.

12

Klara sat up in bed. What time was it? She reached for her phone and saw that she'd slept through half of Sunday. She'd woken up because her parents were arguing. It wasn't possible to make out what it was about. They didn't quarrel that often but sometimes things got heated.

Klara listened guardedly. Closed her eyes. Waited until one of them left the house and slammed the door. She took a few deep breaths to prevent a stomach-ache. The whole house was a Chernobyl of radioactivity.

'Damn,' she said out loud, pulling up her feet.

The sun was shining right into the room. She'd been babysitting the night before, got a ride home afterward and went straight to bed. That was twelve hours ago. Now she opened Snapchat. Ibrahim had sent her three messages. She was just about to take a picture and reply when he called.

'Hi, darling, where are you?' he asked when Klara answered.

'At home,' she said. 'When will I see you?'

'Maybe later,' he said quickly. 'There's something I have to do.'

Klara bit her lip and crossed her legs on the bed. Sometimes she wondered if there was something wrong with her. She wanted to see Ibrahim all the time. He was cooler, didn't have the same need.

Jealousy was a problem she struggled with. She knew that she had a fear of being abandoned but couldn't explain why.

'Okay, I'd really like to see you anyway,' she said.

Ibrahim was silent for a moment before he answered.

'Me too, a little later. Okay? I mostly wanted to check that you're feeling okay.'

'Why wouldn't I be?'

He laughed, but didn't reply.

Klara couldn't bear to ask more questions, it just made things awkward. She must stop being suspicious. But at the same time the things Ibrahim was involved in worried her.

She stretched her legs and leaned back against the headboard. She had a round mirror on the wall right in front of her. In it she saw herself. Her blonde hair was straight and hung down toward her breasts, framing her face. Her forehead was high and her nose straight. The long fringe was lighter at the ends. Overall she'd got even blonder, as always during the summer. Klara avoided the sun but her white skin had got some shades of golden brown anyway. Her freckles were about to disappear. That was the only thing she liked about getting sun on her face.

She held her gaze in the mirror. Her lips weren't thick enough; she wanted bigger ones. As soon as she'd saved enough money she would have them enlarged.

Ibrahim breathed into the phone.

'Come to my place later. I'll be home at five o'clock, I think. Does that work?' he asked, and Klara turned her eyes away from her own reflection, wrapping a strand of hair around her index finger.

'Yes, that will work,' she said.

Whatever he was up to she loved him. It was like a poisonous dependency. He was her drug.

'See you there then,' Ibrahim said. 'I have to go. Kisses.'

After she'd said goodbye and clicked away the call, she heard her little sister Svea calling, asking if Klara had taken her sweater. It was only then that she realized that the shouting between Mum and Dad had ceased.

'No! Why would I do that?' Klara replied, getting up from the bed. She opened the wardrobe and checked that she hadn't borrowed it, just to be on the safe side. She rummaged among the clothes with both hands. There was the sweater. *Shit*, she thought. Svea would be livid.

There were two years between them and her little sister was extremely difficult. But they stuck together when Mum and Dad screamed at each other. That made them tight somehow.

The sweater was wrinkled. She picked it up and folded it nicely. But then changed her mind and wadded it up again. She opened the door and slipped into the bathroom, throwing the sweater in the laundry basket.

Her sister was swearing in her room. Klara went in there and watched as Svea rooted among her things, which were lying everywhere. She was bad at keeping things tidy.

'Have you checked the laundry?' Klara asked, leaning against the doorframe. 'Mum does have a habit of gathering up everything she sees and tossing it in there.'

'Damn, good idea,' said Svea, rushing past her with a scent of violet hanging around her.

Klara was amused by her own cleverness, but was immediately forced to run away from her sister's room when her ringtone sounded from her room.

It was Helen, whom she'd helped the night before.

'Hi, sorry it got so late last night,' Helen said curtly.

Klara sat down on the bed. 'That's cool.'

'It struck me that you didn't get paid,' Helen continued. Her voice sounded strained. Like Klara's own voice had just been, during the call with Ibrahim.

'Yes, I was so tired that I forgot about it,' Klara replied. 'It's no problem.'

'I'll Swish you. How much was it?'

'Five hundred.'

'Coming now,' said Helen. 'I'm planning to go away next weekend, but Erik will be at home. Thanks, because you've always shown up. The kids have loved you. You should know that.'

Shown up, have loved. What did she mean?

'Thanks, they're nice kids,' Klara answered, confused. 'Are you going to be gone long?'

There was silence on the other end.

'Hello . . . ?' said Klara.

'I've sent the money.'

'Okay, see you soon then?' Klara asked.

'Bye now,' said Helen and hung up.

Klara stayed sitting on the bed and looked straight at her open wardrobe. *Strange conversation*, she thought.

Recently she'd been babysitting more and more often with the Stenlunds and felt at home in their house. She liked the children best, of course, but did also click with Erik. Helen was usually serious and cold and harder to make small talk with. The feeling that something was wrong with her lingered in Klara even though she'd hung up.

Would she and Erik get a divorce?

13

When Charlotte pressed the lift button in the police station it lit up. Per was standing alongside her, dragging his phone along his forearm. It beeped and he looked at the screen.

'How's the blood sugar today?' she asked.

He let her look at the display, which showed a line like a downhill slope. Straight down.

'Three point three and diving. I sensed something was wrong,' said Per, taking a packet of dextrose from his pocket. He took three tablets.

'Don't you hate dextrose?'

'Yes, I always took it at the start of my diabetes, gorged myself. But it's handy to have with you out in the field.'

'Why do you insist on injections? Why don't you just get a pump that gives you insulin automatically?' asked Charlotte, even though she knew the answer.

'I don't want to have yet another device implanted in my body. The meter in my arm is enough.'

The lift pinged, the doors opened and they entered.

'We have to call in the standby personnel, now we have the murdered woman. That demands more resources today,' said Charlotte.

'Already arranged. Did it in the car on the way here,' said Per. 'I've also turned over what we have about the robberies to the youth outreach group – they'll have to get involved with it now we have a brutal murder to investigate.'

The lift stopped abruptly, like it always did. Major Crimes was on Level 2.

As they stepped out, Per's phone rang. The sound of an upbeat accordion made Charlotte laugh out loud.

'Hannes loves changing my ringtone. There's a new one every day,' said Per before he answered.

Charlotte turned off to the kitchen where she met Kicki, who was filling the coffeemaker.

'Oh, thanks, we had the same idea,' said Charlotte.

Kicki smiled at her, strangely enough, but did not respond to her comment and instead pressed the 'On' button and left the room. *Hello to you too*, thought Charlotte, taking a cup from the cabinet. She removed the carafe and set her cup under the opening instead, filled it with steaming fresh coffee that Kicki had fixed and then went to the briefing room. Her thoughts went to Ola, whom she'd simply left at home after breakfast, and hadn't said anything else to since.

She took out her phone and texted him that she'd gone into the station. He answered immediately.

Figured that out – heard about the woman. Kisses, O

In the briefing room she watched as Per pulled out a TV screen. A new case – an empty screen that would be filled with investigation material and leads. Charlotte wondered how long it would take before it could all be removed. An alarmingly long process seemed to lie ahead of them. Right now they didn't even know who the dead woman was.

'Okay, listen up, everyone,' said Per, placing himself in front of the screen with an iPad in his hand. 'Some of you have been called in because a murdered woman was found in the water under the Teg Bridge this morning. Some of you are already informed, but I'm going to tell you what we have and what needs to be done right away.'

Anna came in, her hair damp and her exercise clothes even damper.

'Sorry I'm late, it does take a little time to cycle here,' she said and sat down, still with her cycling shoes on. She set the helmet on the table in front of her. Charlotte knew that she took a detour when she cycled to work to get her exercise, but avoided commenting on that. She was impressed by her colleague. Anna was single but had a son she'd acquired on her own in Denmark – something that Charlotte also admired. That was brave.

Per wrote on the iPad and then turned toward the screen, where black text showed up.

Unidentified woman – who is she?

Pictures of the dead woman appeared. One after another. Some of them were from the water, where she was floating by the edge of the pier, with hair that glistened in the sun. *She really did look like a mermaid*, thought Charlotte.

'The victim is estimated to be between forty-five and fifty-five years old and appears to have been assaulted. Forensics suspects that the woman didn't die at the scene, thus she wasn't alive when she was dumped in the water. Right now the body is at autopsy so we'll find out more when that's done.'

'The assault, did that take place in the same area?' asked Anna.

'We don't think so at the present time. All of the woman's teeth have been extracted but we haven't found any traces of blood, or any signs of a struggle or scuffle either. It also must have been a lengthy process to pull out so many teeth.'

72

'All the teeth? Every single one?' asked one of the police officers who'd been called in on their free Sunday.

'Every one of them. We don't know if this was done to make identification more difficult, or if it's a personal action against the woman.'

'DNA? Fingerprints?' asked Anna.

'No matches in our databases. So presumably she doesn't have a record.'

Once again Charlotte was struck by the thought that the woman should have been reported missing if she had disappeared in their region.

'Do we have any nationality – anything on the body that can show where she comes from?' she asked.

'No, nothing.'

'So what's the next step?' asked Anna.

'Right now we're canvassing the area and talking with possible witnesses. There are surveillance videos from several places in the area and they're being collected.'

'How is the search in the river going?' asked Kicki.

'The diving team is in place, but nothing has been found yet. And as you all know there's a major risk that the currents have carried away any objects that may have been thrown in.'

'That all her teeth were extracted seems sadistic. That's torture. Who would do such a thing?' said Anna, setting her water bottle on the table.

'Maybe she had enemies who wanted her to keep quiet? The extracted teeth could be a signal. But we're fumbling in the dark here before we know who she is.'

Kennet, the district chief of police in Umeå, knocked on the door and stepped in. He was uncommonly engaged in field work for someone in such a high position. Charlotte knew that Kennet divided opinion among the colleagues. Some in the building appreciated his interest, others thought he ought to stick to his own job description instead and not get involved. No one on the team knew yet that Per would be taking over Kennet's position for six months. They would be informed of that during the week ahead, at the same time as the new co-worker Alex was introduced. She shuddered at meeting him. It had been a long time since they'd seen each other. Back then, she'd been married and they'd run into each other in passing at the police station in Stockholm. Charlotte had been disconcerted by the sudden encounter and acted rather rudely, she thought. Only said hello and moved on. She'd felt his gaze on her back.

'Sorry to disturb you, but new information has come in concerning the murdered woman,' said Kennet, placing himself beside Per. His shirt fitted tightly across his stomach and he unbuttoned his jacket. Charlotte worried about the surgeries he would undergo.

'It appears that she was homeless,' Kennet continued. 'While canvassing, a woman who is the director of the City Mission's emergency shelter reported that she'd been worried about a homeless woman who'd been at the hostel a few days earlier. A completely new face who talked about being pursued or threatened by someone. The woman was described as scared, almost manic. Considering that the victim wasn't reported missing, it's worth investigating. Go there and check up on it.'

Kennet held his arm out to Per to show that he could continue the briefing.

'Okay, fine. Then we have something to go on. Charlotte and I will go to the City Mission down on Kungsgatan and talk with them.'

'A homeless person is an easy victim, but why was she threatened?' said Charlotte.

14

Ibrahim heaved the duffel bag on to his back. It wasn't particularly heavy, just bulky. He'd got off at the usual bus stop and took the road toward the campground. The gravel scraped under his feet. The bag said 'Umeå IK' but there was no sports equipment in it. It contained the takings from robberies. Samir had told him to hide it in his room, but Ibrahim no longer wanted it there. Every time he looked at the bag it gave him a stomach-ache. He knew there would be one hell of a row when he dumped the bag with Samir and Omar.

Ibrahim took out his phone, called Samir, but it went straight to voicemail. Since last night it had been impossible to reach him, though not surprising after what happened. He was up to something bad, Ibrahim was sure of that. The question was simply what.

When he came into the campground area the bag slipped down from his back. The hand holding the handle was damp, his knuckles white from the grip. He knew where to go and passed the same men as last time. They nodded at him. The door to the camper was ajar, and he peeked in, called to Omar.

'In here, man,' he answered, and Ibrahim stepped inside.

Omar was sitting at the table as usual. The mess in the sink was still there, flies were buzzing. A young girl was sleeping at the far end of the camper, wrapped up in blankets. Her dark skin was met by the rays of the sun that fell in through the window beside the bed. Ibrahim pointed at her and cast a questioning glance at Omar.

'I'm helping her. She can sleep here to get away from her sick dad who's crazy.'

Ibrahim shook his head. Tossed the duffel bag down on the table. Omar's eyes opened wide and he stood up quickly.

'What the hell is this!'

Ibrahim defended himself. 'I refuse to have these things at my place any more. I could get arrested. You have to take this!'

Omar slammed the front door shut, and then pushed Ibrahim up against the wall with such force that the camper rocked. The girl wakened and sat up.

'You have a whole fucking house to hide the bag in. What the hell is the problem? Are you a coward?' Omar's face came so close that Ibrahim felt his breath. His pupils were as big as saucers.

'Understand this: I'm not having this at home. I can throw the things away if you want.'

Omar stared at him. His hand was still on Ibrahim's chest. 'Is everything in the bag?' he hissed.

'Yes, what do you think?'

Once again Omar pressed Ibrahim against the wall, as a warning. Then he released him. The girl started to get dressed. Ibrahim straightened the hood that had ended up crooked.

'How the hell do you dare come here with it? When Samir finds out you're through.' Omar hissed out the threat and threw the bag at him.

Ibrahim's heart was racing, he felt pounding in his temples. Every muscle was tense. He was ready for a fight.

'I'm not going to take this home again. You can burn it. Do whatever the hell you want, but leave me out of it!'

'Out? You're already involved, man. As soon as Samir is back we're going to divvy up the goods.'

The stuffy odour in the camper was intrusive. Ibrahim threw the bag back to Omar, who let it drop to the floor. His nostrils flared when he breathed. His eyes were open wide. He sat down, staring at the bag with the things. It was Samir who divided up or sold the goods, and he couldn't be reached.

'What the hell should we do with it then?' said Omar, who had calmed down a little. 'Samir won't have it here.'

Ibrahim shrugged his shoulders. 'No fucking idea. Bury it.'

'Good suggestion,' said Omar.

Ibrahim looked at him and thought he was giving in pretty easily.

'How many have you taken?' Ibrahim asked, pointing at the pills.

'Go to hell.' Omar leaned back on the couch. High as a kite.

Ibrahim opened the door. He'd done what he came to do. Sometimes he wanted to help his buddy, but today wasn't that kind of day. Instead he started walking back to the bus stop.

Then he saw a police car pull into the car park of the campground. Everyone who'd been sitting around disappeared into various campers, and he himself took cover behind one of the cabins. Two cops in uniform marched straight to the camper where Omar was lying almost knocked out by drugs. Should he buy time for Omar, create a disturbance to give him an opportunity to escape?

'Fuck it,' he said at last and ran out of the area, grateful that he'd managed to leave the camper in time.

15

Charlotte pressed her index finger against the doorbell, which made no sound. Per was standing behind her in the stairway. The wooden building that housed the City Mission was well maintained. She listened for sounds from inside, looked at the two mailboxes that were by the door and then turned toward Per.

'They do know we're coming, don't they?' she asked, thinking that it was a Sunday after all.

Per nodded with a grim expression. 'I talked with the director before we left. Maybe she hasn't got here yet.'

Charlotte kicked away some scattered leaves that had blown up on to the stairs, knocked on the door.

There was a click in the lock and Charlotte pressed down the handle and stepped in. No one met them on the other side, so Charlotte suspected that someone had unlocked the door remotely.

'Hello, we're here from the police,' she said and was met by the flowery scent of fabric softener.

The door closed behind them and clicked when it locked automatically. On the wall by the entrance was a bulletin board with information about rules of conduct and other things. Straight ahead was a stairway that led up to the top floor. To the left was a corridor with closed doors.

Per pointed to one of the rooms to the right of the stairs.

'I think we can go in there, it's a common room.'

'You're familiar with this place,' said Charlotte, walking toward the room.

'All uniformed police in Umeå are,' Per replied.

'Fucking cops,' a hissing voice said.

Charlotte turned around and caught sight of a thin man with a bushy beard coming down the stairs. His grey hair was combed back and he looked like he'd just showered. His hand held on to the railing.

'Hey, Janne,' said Per. 'That wasn't a nice thing to say.'

The man laughed and pounded him amiably on the back.

'How are you doing?' asked Per.

'Like a satisfied prince,' said Janne, showing his smile with greyish front teeth, of which there weren't many.

'Have you seen Lollo? We're here to talk with her.'

'Yes, damn it, she's making coffee in the kitchen.' Janne extended his arm to show the police into the common room. 'Wait here, I'll fetch the old lady.'

Per went before Charlotte, who watched the man her colleague seemed to be pals with.

'He's been around a long time,' she said.

'Yes, he has. It's a wonder that he's still alive. Homeless and alcoholic for over twenty years. He has a good heart but can't stop drinking. He was principal at my school once upon a time, clearly was drinking even then.'

Janne came back, and this time he stood next to Charlotte.

'Lollo's coming right away,' he said with his hoarse voice and looked at her. 'So what's the name of this fine lady?'

'Charlotte. Lovely to meet you,' she said, sitting down on one of the couches.

The man sat down beside her with one thigh pressed against hers. Per smiled and shook his head.

'Nice too, thank you. What brings such a beautiful police officer here?'

Janne straightened his back and Charlotte inspected his face. Kind brown eyes, rough lines, reddened skin.

She placed a hand on his arm and was about to answer when she was interrupted by a woman who came bustling into the common room with a pot of coffee and cookies. Lively eyes, quick movements, big smile. Charlotte moved her focus to the person she assumed was the director, Lollo. The man remained seated beside her. His body jerked in a way that made Charlotte suspect Parkinson's.

The woman sat down on the couch opposite Charlotte and poured coffee for her without asking if she wanted any.

'All police officers drink coffee,' she said, extending the cup.

Charlotte received it with a smile.

Per on the other hand got a glass of juice and Charlotte couldn't keep from laughing.

'Why does he get juice instead of coffee?' she asked.

Lollo pointed to Per who had just sat down. 'When he was here one time, God knows how many years ago, and dropped off a homeless person, he had low blood sugar and had to take a ride in an ambulance. Now he always gets sugar when he comes here,' she said with a laugh.

'I was young and working a lot,' said Per.

'I remember when you were young, Per – the girls were drawn to you like winos to the state liquor store,' said Janne and chuckled. 'You were a real charmer.'

'I'm curious about that. You must tell me more about it later,' said Charlotte.

Janne nodded and stood up. 'Are you going to ask about the woman under the bridge?' he asked. One arm jerked and he placed the other over it to stop the muscles from twitching again.

80

Charlotte looked up at him. Took out her little notepad from her jacket pocket.

'You've heard the news, I suspect,' she said.

The director cleared her throat. 'Yes, Janne was here during the week and probably has the most to say,' she said, leaning comfortably back on the couch. The worn brown leather creaked when she moved.

When Per showed a picture of the dead woman she nodded.

'That's her,' said Lollo. 'I remember her trousers well – they were unusual with sequins and different colours.'

'Are you certain?' said Per, eyeing the director.

'Yes, I took note of her because we hadn't seen her here before.'

'Who was she?' he asked.

'Everyone here calls . . . called her Lady Lena,' said Janne, reaching for a cookie.

Charlotte interrupted herself in mid-motion to write down the name on her pad. 'Lady Lena?' she repeated.

'Her first name was Lena?' Per asked, after gulping down his juice. A scent of orange spread around the table.

'She registered as Lena. I didn't question that.'

Janne broke off a piece of cookie and stuffed it in his mouth. The lack of front teeth seemed to make chewing difficult.

'Did she have any other name besides Lena?' Charlotte asked, looking at him.

'No idea. She introduced herself as Lena and here you don't ask any follow-up questions, you know. But the rest of us talked about her when she wasn't in the room because she was so . . . so well-preserved . . .'

'What do you mean?' said Charlotte, trying not to stare at his arm which jerked now and then. Small twitches.

'She drank, reeked of alcohol when she was here. But she probably hadn't been homeless very long, because all of her teeth were white as snow. After a couple of years on the street they aren't exactly fresh.'

Janne showed his discoloured teeth.

'So you don't know what her last name was?' asked Per, turning to Lollo.

'No, sorry,' she said. 'But I know that she came here last Monday and stayed two nights. She left the shelter last Wednesday.'

'What time did she leave here, do you know?' asked Per.

Lollo looked out of the window, thinking about it. But it was Janne who answered.

'Lena left at eleven. I remember that because she asked me what time it was.'

'How did she seem then? Her manner, that is?' Charlotte asked.

'Calm – she smiled at me,' said Janne. 'I thought at the time that it was nice that she was happy. Before she'd just been . . . grim. As if afraid of something.'

He suddenly snapped his fingers.

'Yes, yes, she was,' he exclaimed. 'Said that she was threatened by someone.'

'We don't know that,' said Lollo. 'But she seemed to be an anxious soul, like a scared but nice dog. I wonder how she managed on the street. It's tough, especially for women. They're extremely vulnerable.'

'She didn't say anything more specific, for example who she thought was threatening her?' Charlotte took a sip of coffee. It didn't taste good, but the caffeine was welcome.

'She said nothing about that to me,' said Lollo, looking at Janne, who shook his head.

'Hell no, she was like a clam, that Lady Lena. And I didn't think she'd go and get murdered. If I'd thought that I would've asked more, of course, you know. I just thought it was that sort of anxiety you get sometimes.'

'Did she quarrel with anyone at the shelter?' Charlotte asked.

Lollo shook her head. 'No. Sure, conflicts arise, spats. But during the two days that Lena stayed here nothing in particular happened.'

'We'll need to question everyone who was here at the same time as Lena and may have talked more with her.'

Lollo smiled, handing over a piece of paper. 'I know how you work. Here's a list of those who were registered at the time in question. Including staff.'

Charlotte loved Lollo. 'Did Lena talk with any dialect or accent?' she asked the director.

'Fluent Swedish with no accent. The little she did say didn't make me think of any dialect.'

'Do you remember if she had a handbag or other personal possessions with her?'

Lollo seemed to think before she answered. 'Now you say it, I didn't see that she had anything other than a mobile. Often people come here with plastic bags and clothes that need washing. But Lena . . . she only had the clothes she was wearing.'

'Check the Red Scare,' said Janne, stroking his beard.

'What?' said Per and Lollo at the same time.

'Yes, she was sleeping in a car the nights she wasn't here. A red one that she called the Red Scare.'

'Where is it parked?' asked Per.

'She didn't say and I never asked.'

The ringtone of Per's mobile interrupted the conversation. As he left the room to answer, Charlotte looked at her own phone and discovered that it was already past nine o'clock. She stood up.

'Thanks for the coffee and the information,' she said, placing her hand on Janne's shoulder.

'If I think of anything else I'll be in touch, you know,' he said. 'Always happy to help out.'

She left them and went out to Per, who was standing on the steps outside the front door. It had started raining and drops landed on his glasses. The little roof above the entrance didn't provide enough shelter. He ended the call and took them off, rubbed his eyes.

'That was Anna who called. They've checked through the surveillance video from the Teg Bridge and surroundings, and there you can see Lena walking across the bridge four days before she was found under it. On the way to Teg, away from the city. That matches the time when she left the shelter.'

Per pulled his jacket more tightly around him.

'Then we must find out where she was between Wednesday at eleven o'clock and Saturday night. Someone must have met or seen her,' said Charlotte.

'I've asked the team to send out information to everyone in the field to keep an eye out for a red car that's been parked in the same spot for a long time. They should start looking in the immediate area. If we find it, we'll probably figure out who she is,' said Per.

'Yes, we'll have to see what we can produce. Until then we'll have to work with what we have. Simply a little honest police work,' said Charlotte.

16

Monday, 29 August

Per had got a good night's sleep and the investigation continued. All morning he'd wondered about the woman in the Ume River. Who was Lena?

He closed the lid on his lunchbox; yesterday's leftovers was today's lunch. Several members of the team needed to warm up their food. Anna was first in line at the microwave and what she had on her plate did not look appetizing.

'Listen, diabetes guy, you need to eat more of this kind of nutritious stuff,' she said, showing him her plate. Per saw lots of broccoli.

'Rabbit food . . . great . . .' he said.

'Brolin salad.'

'What?'

'Brolin salad.'

Per tried to understand what that meant. Anna saw his confusion.

'Yes, I call it that because I stole the recipe from Tomas Brolin,' she said, laughing.

'What do you mean, is he a chef now?'

'Nah,' she said. 'I know a couple here in Umeå who socialize a bit with Tomas and his wife. They treated me to this salad and called it Brolin salad because it was their recipe.'

Per craned his neck to look more closely at what was on her plate.

'Taste it,' said Anna. 'Raw broccoli, raisins, peanuts, red onion and Hellman's mayonnaise. That's all.'

Per took his own fork out of the lunchbox, thinking back to the 1994 Olympics when Brolin was king of the soccer pitch as he speared a big piece of broccoli and along with it some of the rest. It crunched pleasingly when he chewed.

'What do you know? This is really good,' he said spontaneously and was about to take more when Anna moved her plate away.

'Take it easy now – make your own!'

'How can it be so good with only five ingredients, and that's basically just broccoli?'

He was sincerely surprised, almost excited. But before Per could get an answer from his colleague, his phone rang. Anna went and sat down while he answered. It was his son Simon.

'Hi, Dad, I didn't make it on to the U16 team.'

Per could hear the disappointment in his voice and his shoulders collapsed. It felt like everything negative that happened to his kids was ten times worse for him.

'I'm sorry, Simon, but you'll have to practise and try again later on. They liked what they saw, the coach told me that, anyway. You're only fourteen and you have time. There will be other chances.'

Then Simon suddenly started to laugh.

'Just joking. I made it! Starting tomorrow. Get that!'

Little bastard, thought Per.

His shoulders felt lighter at once. This would mean more practices, but Per and Mia would work it out somehow. The sixteen-year-olds practised early in the morning, before school, and then at seven o'clock in the evening. Quite a lot, actually, but his son's joy was all he needed to manage all the driving. Hannes' team practised around eight o'clock in the evening. In other words, Per and Mia wouldn't get to see a single TV series until next summer.

'Have you told Mum?' he asked.

'Going to do that now. See you later, Dad,' said Simon and hung up.

Per was about to go over to Anna to talk more about Tomas Brolin's salad when Kicki stepped up. The first thing he saw was her heavy red leather boots.

'You don't answer when I call,' she said curtly.

'I was talking with my son.'

'You have to come with me.'

Per held out his lunchbox, which he had just warmed up. 'Don't I have time to eat?'

Kicki turned around and left. 'No, you have to see this now.'

Per followed Kicki to the offices of Major Crimes. Most people were at lunch, but a few were still there working. Kicki sat down at her desk and pulled up a file on the computer. The bracelet on her wrist rattled as she moved her fingers across the keyboard.

'What's so important that a poor devil with diabetes isn't allowed to eat?' asked Per.

'Here,' she said, turning the large screen so that he could see better. 'This is a surveillance video from one of Umeå Energi's cameras which faces toward Västra Strandgatan. The river where Lena was found isn't visible, but wait and you'll see . . .'

She started the video. The time stamp showed that it was the early hours of Sunday. A clock established the time and counted ahead at a furious speed. At 03:45:34 Kicki pressed pause.

'Do you see who that is?' she asked, pointing at a guy who came running into the picture from the left. Per leaned closer to the screen.

'What the hell . . . ? Samir.'

'Exactly,' said Kicki, leaning back.

'So he's not far from the place where Lena was found, only a stone's throw away, at exactly the time we think is right. It can't possibly be a coincidence,' said Per, and they played the video clip again. Samir ran along Västra Strandgatan, past the 'Sparken' skate park and then continued, away from the Teg Bridge.

'Is he capable of committing a brutal murder?' asked Kicki.

'I don't know. He seems to be one of the robbers and has a history of violence, but Lena was tortured. What's the motive? She didn't own anything of value, as far as we know. What would make him do something like that to a defenceless person? Is he completely unhinged?'

'There we have something to bite into,' said Kicki.

'I'll call the juvenile unit. Samir must be brought in for questioning,' said Per.

'He'll be hiding out somewhere,' said Kicki.

'Bring in his friends too, find out what they know.'

'His buddy Omar was already arrested for drug possession. He was picked up at the campground yesterday, so you can question him now,' said Kicki.

'Perfect! Put out an APB on Samir and bring in anyone associated with him,' said Per, going to his office. 'We have to find out what they know.'

17

Ibrahim sent a brief text to Samir.

Where are you, man? Omar's with the cops.

He'd sent a dozen similar messages earlier and realized that Samir probably wouldn't answer, but Ibrahim hoped that the information about Omar would lure him out.

He was sitting with his legs dangling over the edge of the pier, waiting for Klara who had a lunch break from school. The warmth from the ground worked its way up toward his butt. Winter was still a way off and that didn't worry him. For the first time in many years he would spend the cold season in a warm home.

The sound of a child made him turn around – a family approached with a pushchair. Ibrahim looked at the kid who was wrapped up in a blanket. He thought about the different circumstances you could have in life. It was almost comical. Which part of the world you were born in was the difference between heat and cold, hunger and fullness, security and flight. Unaware of how fortunate it was there in the pushchair, the baby looked at Ibrahim. Laughed.

'Here you sit, by the water, people watching,' said Klara, sitting down beside him. She had on a new blue jacket, and her cap pressed down the hair that framed her face. 'Aren't you afraid of the water?' She put her arm around his shoulders. Draped herself over him.

'Yes, my whole family disappeared under it,' he said, pointing at the river that ran calm and serene.

'You never talk about what happened.'

He turned his head away. Let the sun meet his skin. She was direct, asked as if it was obvious. Ibrahim wanted to, but didn't know how to talk about such things. For Klara it was simple.

'Listen,' she said, looking at Ibrahim with a warm gaze. 'It's just me. You can talk to me.'

He sighed. Every time his thoughts went to his family and the escape across the Mediterranean, it was like shaking up a bottle of emotions. There was a lot of noise in his head and he had to force away the memories in order not to go crazy. At the same time he felt compelled to try. They had never talked about this properly and he wanted to give something to Klara.

'Sorry, it's just so hard to talk about,' said Ibrahim, looking out over the river. 'Mama had a red shawl that she always wrapped loosely around her head after we fled. She stopped wearing the hijab when we left Syria, I remember. The red shawl framed her face – she almost looked like a fairy-tale character. It floated on the surface of the sea and was the last I saw of my mother.'

Klara sat with her face close to him. He picked up her scent.

'Did you take it with you? The shawl?'

Ibrahim shook his head. 'Everything is gone.'

'I can't imagine what you've gone through.'

He looked at Klara. 'Samir and Omar became my new, extremely dys-something. What's it called? A funny word. I was supposed to explain it in school one time. Dysfunk? A family that doesn't work, what's it called?'

90

Klara smiled. 'Dysfunctional?'

'Exactly, they became my dysfunctional family.'

'How did the three of you live before you came here?' she asked.

White birds circled above the surface of the water. They seemed to be searching for fish. Screeched.

Ibrahim looked at them. 'Day to day,' he said. 'We slept in different places, in apartments full of people or in rundown houses.'

'How did you get money? You did have to eat?'

He lowered his gaze. That wasn't something he wanted to share with Klara. Robbery, theft, shoplifting. Samir was good at selling drugs to local gangsters. But at last they got tired of his cockiness, became insecure, and started threatening violence. Then the three of them moved on. Never stayed longer than a few months in the same city. After a while they ended up in Spain and with the help of human traffickers came to Malmö on a freighter.

'We got by,' he said instead. 'Say what you will about Samir, he's one hell of a survivor. Did you know that he was a child soldier for ISIS before he managed to escape?'

'Shit,' she said. 'Not strange that he's the way he is.'

'He's disappeared. I can't get hold of him. Don't know what he's up to.'

'When did you talk with him last?'

'Saturday,' said Ibrahim, getting the noise back in his head, like when he thought about his family.

'Can't you see where he is on Snap Map, like you and I can find each other?'

Ibrahim laughed out loud. She was sweet.

'Samir doesn't have Snapchat. He uses different apps.'

'So where do you think he is?' she asked, kicking her feet against the edge of the pier.

He met Klara's gaze. Those innocent blue eyes. Could he trust her? That is, properly, one hundred per cent?

He thought about the woman who was found in the water not far from where they were sitting. The Mermaid, as the newspapers called her. Should he tell Klara?

18

Erik parked by the Rådhus Esplanade, across from Helen's work-place. He looked at her window on the third floor. The lights didn't appear to be on but the daylight made that hard to determine. He wanted to go up and say hi to her, maybe take her lunch, but hesitated. Helen didn't like surprises. So now he was sitting there, watching his wife's workplace. Like a real loser.

Erik tried calling Helen. No answer. He needed to make time to talk with her, wanted to know if she was unfaithful or if the hidden phone in the laundry basket was about something else alto-gether. But if that was the case, then what?

He turned off the engine but stayed in the car. Paid for parking through his app. Parking enforcement came by often and wrote tickets because there was a lot of traffic in the area. Then he lowered the sun visor and looked at himself in the little mirror. The dark beard stubble needed to be either trimmed or shaved off. It scraped when he brought his hand over it. Erik often heard that he looked nice, not handsome. The narrow chin had a thick scar from child-hood, and his hair was thinning. But he still had some, even if the hairline was receding. Helen had commented on that.

He raised the visor with a thud. Fixed his gaze on the instru-ment panel. His shoulders felt heavy, his breathing even heavier. Erik thought about how Helen had been acting recently. A little curt in tone, and she answered more and more rarely when he called. If this wasn't about infidelity, who did she have contact with through the secret Nokia phone? Her father? Erik knew that he moved in extreme right-wing circles and was active in the Nordic Resistance movement. Helen had grown up with his opinions and views of people, but she had broken free from that, thanks to Erik. What if her father was back in her head, in her life?

He shook away the thoughts. Didn't want to have them.

His stomach growled; he still hadn't had any lunch. Erik opened the compartment between the seats and took out a chocolate bar. Emergency provisions. As he broke off the first piece he saw Helen. She came out of the building and turned left toward Rådhus Square. Her coat fluttered in the wind. She tied the belt around her waist and put on the red hat she liked. He'd bought it for her as a present long ago.

Erik followed her at first with his gaze. Where was she going? Then he got out of the car and followed her on foot. Helen turned left on Kungsgatan. She walked quickly, got a headwind between the buildings and crossed her arms across her chest. She didn't have her handbag with her. Was she going out for lunch?

Erik felt like a detective on surveillance. Kept a good distance. The red hat made it easy to see where she was. She stopped outside the Apoteket pharmacy; she'd run into someone she knew who wanted to talk. But then she took two steps forward, wanted to keep going. With a strained smile she waved to the person before she trotted ahead. Erik had a hard time keeping up without running himself.

He called her mobile and saw how she took it out of her pocket, looked at it and put it back again.

No clearer sign was needed.

When Helen got to Vasagatan she stopped outside the Stadium store. She appeared to be waiting for something. She pressed herself against the wall behind a pillar and looked at the ground, pulled the hat down a little. The hat barely contained her thick head of hair. In another situation he would have thought it was almost sweet.

Erik didn't want to stand there spying on his wife. Sure, they argued sometimes, but when things were good between them it was just amazing. The arguments were about little things, as in all marriages. Who should do the shopping. Why the house was messy. The children's activities that required planning. That sort of thing. Otherwise the relationship did well and Erik was certain that Helen was happy. She and the children were the nuclear family he'd always wanted and he didn't want to lose them.

His stomach was restless and his head hurt. It felt even worse when a grey Volvo stopped and Helen jumped into it without hesitating, after which the car quickly drove on. It happened so fast that Erik wasn't able to see the driver or make a note of the number plate.

He took out his phone, brought his finger over the display and entered her number again. When she answered, his pulse rose.

'Hi, Erik,' she said curtly.

'Hi, do you want to have lunch with me?' Erik tried to keep his voice calm. 'I didn't have time to eat on break today.'

'I have lots to do. Another day?'

'Okay, are you at work now? Can I stop by and say hi?'

'Yes, I'm here, but there's no point in you coming up. I have way too much to do right now.'

Helen ended the call and Erik looked down at the phone in his hand, paralyzed. It felt like he'd been run over by a tractor.

19

Charlotte inspected her reflection in the police station's staff toilets. The wrinkles had become more prominent. They suited her, she thought. For the first time since the divorce from Carl, she felt satisfied with her existence. Ola was one reason, but it was more about a feeling of strength. She was not dependent on anyone or anything. The only thing that was missing in her life was Anja. It was Monday and perhaps her daughter would come up to Umeå for the weekend. Charlotte longed for her so much it hurt. Now the summer was largely over and Anja had started her studies at the university in Stockholm, she had no time left for her mother. She was consumed by her new life. *But it's fine that way*, thought Charlotte, taking out her lipstick, colouring her lips with the faintly pink shade that she loved. As usual she brought her hands over her hair. The bun sat firmly but a few strands had left their place, so she took out one of the pins that held it and fixed the bun again. Then pulled back her shoulders and left the narrow space. The first person she met outside the toilets was Kicki.

'You know you can't park your car where it is now. I've sent out an email about it,' her colleague said.

'What do you mean?' asked Charlotte.

Kicki turned around. 'Your car, it's parked in one of the spaces that are used by the night staff. You can't park there.'

'Everyone parks there, until the night staff start their shift. Even you do sometimes.'

'Read the email,' said Kicki, disappearing into the break room.

Charlotte raised her eyebrows and took out her phone. Sure enough, there was an email from Kicki about Charlotte's car, sent to everyone in the police station. Including the bosses.

She took three deep breaths, clenched her jaw so as not to say anything she would regret later. Sure, her colleague was factually correct, but she could have brought it up with Charlotte privately.

Kicki came back from the break room with an apple in her hand. She walked past Charlotte with a straight back. Took a big bite of the fruit.

Charlotte remained standing in the same spot for a few minutes so as not to feel irritated when she stepped into the interview with Omar. The juvenile unit had brought him in on suspicion of robbery and narcotics crimes. Now was an excellent opportunity for Major Crimes to ask a few questions about Samir, whom they were searching for after he'd shown up on that surveillance video. They had no information about their buddy Ibrahim from the robberies, but they needed to talk with him too.

Charlotte took hold of the door handle to the interview room, but realized that she'd forgotten to take off her watch. The Patek Philippe watch quickly went down into her trouser pocket before she went in.

As soon as she stepped into the room she let go of Kicki's email.

'Sorry I'm late.'

Per looked up from where he was sitting with his back to the wall, entering something on the computer.

'No problem, Omar just arrived with his attorney.'

Per pointed to a man in a suit. Charlotte had never seen him before and she nodded at him. There was also an interpreter in the room, although they weren't sure they needed one. Omar

97

sat alongside them with his legs parted wide, his arms crossed over his chest. The bomber jacket was too big but an expensive brand. Black cap. Gucci. One leg twitched constantly and he was glassy-eyed.

He was under arrest with no access to drugs, thought Charlotte. Young suspects often had problems being deprived of liberty; after a couple of days they usually cracked. It remained to be seen what timber Omar was made of.

Per started the interview with the usual introductory words and when that was done Charlotte got right to the point.

'Omar, you've been arrested on suspicion of second-degree drug possession and robbery.'

He stared at her while the interpreter translated. When he was done Omar smiled.

'I'm innocent. Those weren't my drugs and I haven't robbed anyone.'

Charlotte sighed. 'That's not why we're here. We want to talk with you about your friend Samir.'

Omar leaned forward to Charlotte. She responded with the same movement.

'No comment,' he said.

Charlotte looked at the guy who was sitting before her. He didn't know much other than how to live from day to day. The little information they'd managed to produce during the investigation showed that Omar's parents were alive, but he'd spent his childhood on the streets around Europe. Since he came to Sweden and Umeå, he'd been seen with a notorious criminal gang, which he and Samir seemed to be working their way into. There was nothing that she or Per could do to frighten him into talking. For him they were as dangerous as house pets. A piece of gravel that chafed a little in your shoe. A source of irritation, nothing more.

Omar laughed as if he'd heard her thoughts. He raised his voice and showed total contempt for her when he said something in his own language.

The interpreter did not convey the message word for word, but instead translated it as, 'I know nothing about Samir.'

Charlotte sat there with her gaze firmly nailed on Omar. They needed to resort to a different tactic in order to reach him.

'Okay, so you want to play that game,' she said.

Charlotte looked at Per, who took over.

'On Thursday the twenty-fifth of August a young boy is robbed and brutally assaulted. He is relieved of his mobile, jacket and debit card. Two days later you and Samir withdraw money from an ATM in Ersboda where you use the boy's card. How do you explain that?'

'You're lying, I never robbed anyone,' Omar exclaimed in English. 'It's Samir . . .'

Omar fell silent. Thought about what he'd said. He'd just sold out Samir.

Good, thought Charlotte. *Now we're starting to get somewhere.*

'Where is Samir now? We know that you know.'

'I have no idea where he is.'

Charlotte looked at Per, who remained expressionless.

'May I go now?' said Omar.

'You can go right back to custody, because we're not finished with you. We have the right to hold you another twenty-four hours,' said Per.

Charlotte saw that Omar was starting to breathe faster now he realized that he would have to spend more time in a cell.

'If you want to go home you should tell us where your friend Samir is.'

'Fuck you,' said Omar.

Per stood up and Charlotte took over the questioning.

'What were you and Samir doing the night between Saturday and Sunday, after midnight?' she asked.

Omar's rapid breathing was interrupted, his mouth opened and the smile he'd had during the whole interview disappeared. He pulled his arms closer to his body.

'We have reason to suspect that Samir may know something about a serious crime,' she continued. 'He is a potential witness that we must get in touch with.'

The attorney protested about loose evidence that had nothing to do with Omar. He was right, but Charlotte ignored that.

'Tell us what you were doing that night, Omar.'

He looked at her. His leg was shaking under the table. 'Don't remember.'

'You don't remember? What don't you remember?'

Omar's gaze wandered. 'I didn't kill anyone,' he said quietly in English.

'I haven't accused you of having murdered anyone. Why do you say that?'

'You sit here and ask lots of things about a serious crime. Don't you think I get that this is about the woman that everyone's talking about? I don't know anything about any murder.'

Something had happened with Omar when the subject of Saturday night came up. Either he was scared of being dragged into the investigation or else he knew something about Lena. Charlotte was convinced of the latter: that Omar knew more about the murder than he was saying.

'Tell us the truth now. What were you doing the night in question?'

'Watched a movie at home.'

'Can anyone confirm that?'

Omar stared down at the table. Bit his lip. 'Ibrahim,' he said.

'Ibrahim can confirm that,' Charlotte repeated, understanding that they would presumably give each other an alibi.

Omar brought his hand over his nose. His mouth was still open and he moistened his lips with his tongue. The water glass that stood in front of him was untouched.

'We need to get in touch with Samir. If you help us, we'll help you,' said Per.

Omar looked up. His bloodshot eyes reinforced the dark irises. He said something barely audible in his own language.

'I haven't talked with him since that night. He can't be reached. I don't know anything about any crime,' the interpreter translated.

'You know more than you're saying, but . . . We're done with you, for now. You can go back to the cell,' said Charlotte, standing up.

'Are you slow? SAMIR IS GONE!' Omar screamed in English.

Charlotte was surprised by the reaction.

'What do you mean "gone"? When did he disappear?' asked Per.

'I don't know! He doesn't answer his phone and I haven't seen him since Saturday.'

The attorney wanted to break off.

Charlotte ignored him. 'What were you doing that night, Omar?' she asked again.

But before Omar could answer there was a knock at the door and his attention was drawn to Kicki, who looked in. Per halted the interview and Charlotte thought that the young man seemed relieved now to be able to return to his cell.

When they met up with Kicki outside the interview room she handed a folder to Per, who started browsing through the papers. They had found the witness who filmed one of the robberies, so now they had additional evidence against Omar. However, they hadn't been able to find anything that contradicted what he'd said about Samir, even though his phone had been emptied of information.

He'd tried calling Samir fifty-five times since last Saturday, sent lots of texts and asked where he was staying. The tone in the messages was stressed and angry.

'Bring in Ibrahim. It's time to talk with him too,' said Per.

'Omar is afraid of something,' said Charlotte.

20

Erik sat in the school car park with both his hands on the steering wheel. The work day was over but the last thing he wanted to do right now was drive home. He leaned his head back on the neck support and watched how the windscreen filled with raindrops. He thought about Helen and about the car she jumped into outside Stadium. That she'd lied to him.

When he started the car the radio came on, louder than he was prepared for. But it soon fell silent for an incoming call.

Helen.

'Hi, sorry I was short with you earlier, but so much is happening at work today. How are you doing?'

She showed consideration, but her voice was cold. Erik didn't reply, couldn't bear to pretend.

'Where are you?' she asked.

'In the car outside the school,' he said tiredly.

'Is everything okay? You sound strange.'

Erik closed his eyes, listened to the raindrops falling on the roof of the car.

'Where are you?' he asked instead of answering.

'On my way home from work.'

Damn you and your lies, he thought.

'I'll get home at six – will you be there then?' he asked.

Silence.

'Hello? Helen?'

'Yes. I'll fix dinner.'

'Good, we need to talk,' he said.

'I have to leave after dinner,' said Helen. 'Elsa has gymnastics.'

He pressed his lips together. 'Where is the practice?'

'The Haga School, as always on Mondays.' Helen's reply was curt.

'How long will you be gone? It would be good if we had a little time to talk.'

'About two hours. And tomorrow I'm taking Liam to practice.'

Erik's hands gripped harder on the steering wheel. She found excuses to avoid talking.

'Okay, it'll have to be that way then,' he said, and she seemed content with that reply.

The call ended and Erik was left with the music on the radio. Dr Alban with an old hit. He wondered whether their babysitter Klara could watch the kids some evening during the week so that he could follow Helen. See what she was doing. He could easily lie and say he was going to a conference or something.

Klara was the kids' favourite; in record time she had sailed up to first place. Erik liked her. She was always present when she was with the kids, but she didn't draw attention to herself. Never showy, and always cheerful and nice. The principal had advised him against using a student as babysitter. Erik had ignored him. Klara herself had suggested it during one of their talks at the school. She needed money and they needed help with the kids. What was the problem?

Erik drove home as if in a fog. Suddenly he was there.

As he turned into the driveway, lights were on in all the windows even though it was still rather light outside. Erik sighed. He thought it was wasteful, and would go around and turn off lights when no one was in the room. But when he wasn't at home the house was lit up like a Christmas tree. The electric bills got higher and higher.

After turning off the engine Erik stayed in the car and scrolled on his phone. He put off going in. Every time he looked at Helen there was a knot in his chest. One moment he wanted to confront her with the betrayal she subjected her family to, and the next moment he wanted to put his head in the sand and hope that everything would simply be as usual.

Erik jumped when there was a knock on the window. The neighbour had come out in the rain with his dog.

'Hi there,' he said when Erik opened the car door.

'Hi, you scared me,' he answered and got out.

The neighbour patted the dog. Erik was no animal lover, but luckily it stayed where it was.

'So, Elsa has gymnastics this evening?' said the neighbour.

Erik laughed. 'And how do you know that?'

'I've probably seen how Helen leaves every Monday at the same time, with Elsa in her nice pink ballerina outfit. I can still put two and two together,' said the neighbour, laughing loudly at himself. 'But there is something I'd like to bring up with you. Concerning Helen.'

Erik raised his eyebrows and took his briefcase out of the car. 'What would that be?'

'Well, she stands outside and talks on the phone at night,' the neighbour said, sounding worried.

Erik's whole body froze. The rain worked its way into his scalp and ran down his cheeks. 'What do you mean?'

'Well, I've seen her a couple of times now. She stands outside on the patio and talks on the phone in the middle of the night. It's not my thing to snoop but . . . Is everything all right between you? Is she okay?'

Erik forced himself to meet the neighbour's gaze. 'Why are you checking on our house at night? Isn't that the more strange thing here?'

The neighbour laughed again. 'Well, you might think that, but just one of those nights was so warm that the wife and I couldn't sleep. We sat out on the porch and listened to the silence. Helen broke it, you might say.'

Erik saw that the neighbour seemed embarrassed, and the explanation sounded believable.

'She's okay,' he answered shortly.

'I understand, and excuse me for getting involved, but I happened to hear a little of what she was saying. It wasn't that I was eavesdropping, she simply sounded so angry there in the middle of the night.'

'What do you mean? What did she say?' asked Erik, ignoring the fact that his clothes no longer protected him from the rain.

'I only heard a little, but there was something about "solve it". "Solve it, just do it, otherwise I'll kill him," she said. Although then I stopped listening because it scared me and the wife a little. We thought that maybe she'd got into a dispute with someone.'

The neighbour kept talking but Erik didn't hear him. All he heard was the rain.

21

Klara had been waiting for Ibrahim and looked up at him when he finally stepped into his room. White T-shirt, black jeans and a hooded sweatshirt. He always looked so fresh, never pale and gloomy. Klara herself had put on make-up, taking time to make it perfect. She was a big fan of Bianca Ingrosso and tried to look like her, even though Klara wasn't nearly as good-looking.

As usual she was sitting on Ibrahim's bed and she'd got a pastry from his foster mother Apollonia. It was half-eaten on the nightstand.

'Hi, how long have you been waiting?' asked Ibrahim.

'Fifteen minutes maybe.'

He flopped down on the bed and her light body juddered from the force. She reached for his hand. Laced her fingers together with his.

'What should we do?' asked Klara.

Ibrahim pulled her to him, moved his body next to hers, hugged her from behind.

'Sleep?' he asked, and she shook her head.

'Nah, can't we hit the town or something?'

'"Hit the town"? What does that mean? You can't hit a town, can you?'

Klara was about to explain when the front doorbell rang. He sat up quickly and their bodies glided apart. They heard how the family received a visitor, but Ibrahim didn't seem terribly curious about that, and instead bent over his phone.

'Omar is with the police,' he said without looking up from the screen.

'Why?'

Ibrahim shook his head. 'Don't know, maybe it has to do with the drugs he sells.'

'What about Samir? Is he there too?'

Ibrahim shrugged and was about to answer when there was a knock on the door.

'It's the police,' said Apollonia from the other side. 'They want to talk with you.'

Ibrahim looked at Klara. He looked puzzled. 'Huh?'

The door opened and two men in uniform came into the room. Klara sat up.

'Hi, Ibrahim. We need to talk with you concerning . . . a few things. Can you come with us to the station?'

'Talk about what?' said Ibrahim, getting up from the bed.

'You're not suspected of any crime. But we need to ask a few questions about Samir.'

Klara looked at the police. 'Samir?' she said, also getting up.

'Yes, he's a person of interest in an investigation that concerns a serious crime.'

'What kind of crime?' said Apollonia, who had stepped into the room and placed herself beside Ibrahim.

'You'll find out more at the station,' the policeman said to her.

'Okay, I'll come with you,' said Ibrahim, and Klara stared at him as he started to move toward the front door.

She was preparing to follow when one of the policemen stopped her.

'Ibrahim's guardians, Apollonia and Martin, need to be there, but you'll have to wait here.'

Klara watched as Ibrahim disappeared with the policemen after him. When the front door closed she stood there alone in an intrusive silence. But in her head it was anything but silent. The questions piled up. What was Ibrahim involved in? She knew that Samir and Omar did a lot of bad things, but her boyfriend was a good person.

'Damn it!' she screamed, but there was no one left in the house to hear her.

Fucking Samir, she thought and stomped back into Ibrahim's room with her heels pounding the floor.

Suddenly she heard a buzzing sound from somewhere. Like the vibration from a phone on silent. At first she stood quite still, then she turned in an attempt to locate the sound. It couldn't be Ibrahim's phone as Klara knew that he took it with him, and her own was in her back pocket. Was he hiding a phone in the room?

Klara bit off a piece of fingernail and then started looking around in Ibrahim's things. She bent down and carefully lifted the mattress. Then went to the desk and slowly pulled out one of the drawers, picked through the things in there before she closed it again. What was she up to? Snooping like a crazy person. She ran her hands through her hair. Her jaw was clenched. Every muscle in her body was tense, and she couldn't stay still. Her heart questioned what she was doing but her brain wanted to keep searching.

She opened the next drawer, and the cautious searching turned into rooting. Like an addict on the hunt for drugs she turned the whole thing inside out, but all that was there were books, pads, chargers and other ordinary things. Instead she directed her attention to the wardrobe, opened it and looked in. Everything in there was in perfect order, as if he cared about his clothes. She was about to start digging between the garments when she heard the buzzing again. The same sound as before but louder this time. Klara tore out the clothes. A Samsung mobile phone landed by her feet with the screen facing up. It said *Darling* on the display and the picture showed a drop-dead gorgeous girl who appeared to be a few years older than Klara. She froze. Stared at the phone blinking from the incoming call. Did Ibrahim have someone else? Why did he have two mobiles?

She bent down and picked it up, and was about to answer when *Darling* hung up. Klara threw the phone on to the bed as if it were a big spider. She let her back meet the wall behind her and slid down to the floor. She remained sitting there without being able to take her eyes off the phone. Thoughts were rushing around in her head. She brought her index finger to her mouth, tore off another piece of nail. Was he unfaithful? In that case her grinding gut feeling had been right.

Tears started to well up and Klara threw herself on the bed. She landed on her stomach and used the pillow so that her crying wouldn't be heard, even though the house was empty. *No,* she thought. *It can't be true.*

She grasped the phone she'd found again and pressed on it, but it was locked. The photo of the girl was gone and had been replaced by a nature image. The phone had a protective case with a brown crocodile-hide pattern. The battery icon shone red. She would need a six-digit code to be able to open it. She tried Ibrahim's birthdate – nada. Her own – nada. Pressed and pressed and at last the phone died completely.

Klara wiped the dampness from her cheeks, took the phone and her jacket, and rushed out of the house. She had to find out who *Darling* was.

22

Charlotte laughed when she saw Per step into the interview room. His glasses were crooked and a bit of hair was sticking up like on Stig-Helmer.

'Worn out?'

'Like hell.'

Charlotte felt the same, but a detective doesn't work normal office hours. Other families were having dinner while she would have to work overtime. And before the weekend Kennet would tell the department that she would be acting chief inspector while Per took over the role of boss. The hierarchy between the various departments and the struggle over the highest positions was tiresome. A constant fight about results. Even so the Umeå police force was considerably more harmonious than Stockholm's.

Per sat down beside her at the table. 'We have to get Ibrahim to tell us where Samir might possibly be.'

Charlotte had a sense that Ibrahim would be hard to scare, but he associated with their prime suspect and the serious crime that Samir was suspected of could perhaps get Ibrahim to distance himself from his buddy. For that reason they had to focus on the murder of Lena during the interview.

The door opened. Ibrahim came in with his attorney, the couple he was living with, and a man from social services. The room was crowded. Charlotte hung her jacket on the back of the chair. Exposed her service revolver which sat in the holster across her chest.

She looked at the young man. His brown eyes were lively, in contrast to Omar whose eyes had been completely glassy. He greeted them politely – in Swedish. No interpreter was necessary, they'd been told.

Per started the interview and the young man listened attentively. He sat quietly, leaning forward. His breathing was calm.

'We've brought you in because we know that you spend a lot of time with a person we're interested in making contact with.'

'Samir Al Tajir, you've already told me that, but what has he done?' said Ibrahim, sounding more stressed than he appeared to be.

'We need to speak with him concerning a serious crime. He may be an important witness,' said Charlotte. She couldn't say that they suspected Samir of murder because they hadn't questioned him yet.

Ibrahim reacted by sitting up straight, looking up at the surveillance camera and sighing.

'What?' he said after a while. A bit too late, Charlotte felt. He didn't seem surprised by what she'd just said.

'As you know, we need to bring Samir in for questioning. You're one of his closest acquaintances. Where is he?'

Ibrahim laughed. 'I'm wondering that too.'

'When did you last see Samir?'

Ibrahim met Charlotte's gaze. 'Last Saturday, in the evening. We were just hanging out in town.'

Charlotte smiled at him. Omar had said they'd watched a movie and she was more inclined to believe Ibrahim. 'Where did you see him last?'

Ibrahim's gaze wandered. The attorney whispered something in his ear. 'At Rådhus Square,' said Ibrahim. 'It was after midnight. Omar and I went home, but I don't know where Samir went.'

'You maintain that you hung out, but what did you *actually* do in town? Tell the truth now.'

The attorney interrupted her. 'Because my client is not suspected of any crime and is cooperating with you, there is no reason to conduct yourself as if he'd committed one.'

'He's not a suspect, at least not yet. But we have sufficient evidence to arrest him for robbery.'

Charlotte stretched the truth to scare him a little.

'We have a witness who points out you, Omar and Samir at the robbery of an elderly man which happened two weeks ago. According to the witness you took the man's watch and wallet and threatened to kill him. That has also been caught on video.'

Apollonia brought her hand to her mouth, while Martin looked down at the floor. Ibrahim was silent.

'What were you doing last Thursday, the twenty-fifth of August, at 6.45 p.m.?' Charlotte continued.

'I don't remember,' Ibrahim replied. 'I think I was with Klara, my girlfriend.'

'What were you doing?'

He raised his eyebrows, took a breath. 'Uh, we were at home, watching TV.'

Every criminal who lies in an interview says that they were at home watching TV, thought Charlotte. She was always surprised at their lack of imagination.

'At home with whom?'

'Her,' he answered.

'What did you watch?'

Ibrahim sat silently.

'Ibrahim?'

'That Swedish series . . . the . . . *The Bridge*, it's called.'

Appropriate, thought Charlotte, picturing the Teg Bridge where Lena was found.

Per asked for Klara's contact information, and when he'd got that from Ibrahim he said, 'We'll check on this information, you understand that, right?'

Ibrahim pressed his lips together. Nodded. He leaned back, crossing his arms.

'The reason we're asking is that we have more evidence linking you to the robbery of a young man last Thursday,' Charlotte continued to lie. It was primarily Omar and Samir they had something on, thanks to the stolen debit card they'd used to withdraw cash.

Ibrahim's shoulders went up.

'If you know anything about these robberies you have to tell them,' said Martin to him.

Ibrahim looked at Charlotte as if he was thinking about what he should say.

'I don't know anything about this,' he said.

'I'm sure you do,' said Charlotte. 'If you help us find Samir, we're going to help you. That's how it works. We know that you're not active at the robberies, that you watch but never hit. We also know that you're working on your Swedish to be able to get an education. You have a goal, Ibrahim, a future. Don't let the crimes done by Samir and Omar ruin that.'

He cleared his throat and once more his gaze wandered. He leaned forward again, his elbows against the hard surface of the table.

'Where is Samir?' Charlotte asked yet again.

'I don't know.'

'We know that he was at Teg Bridge in the early hours of Sunday. Do you know what he was doing there?' said Per.

Ibrahim stared at him. 'Do you think he murdered that woman who was found in the water?' He sounded almost angry.

'Samir is part of our investigation. He may have seen something that is of importance for us and we need to get hold of him.'

'I get it, but I don't know where he is. He's been completely missing since . . .' But Ibrahim did not complete the sentence, simply shook his head.

'Since . . . What do you mean?' said Per.

'Nothing.'

'Since early Sunday?' Charlotte added. Omar had said the same thing. Neither of them seemed to know where Samir was staying.

Ibrahim brought his finger to his mouth, bit on the nail a little.

His attorney spoke up again. 'Now that's enough speculation. My client is not being held for anything and can't be held responsible for another person's actions.'

The attorney was right. They got no further with Ibrahim, even though Charlotte wanted to pressure him a little more. He looked irresolute, as if he wanted to tell the truth but couldn't.

Nonetheless Per ended the interview. When the door was opened and the group met the fresh air outside the interview room, it felt like a cooling breeze.

'Can you wait in reception before you leave?' Charlotte said before Martin managed to close the door behind him. The foster father nodded and went after the others.

Per looked perplexed and Charlotte took him aside.

'I'm going to try to get Ibrahim to think differently, give him one last chance,' she explained.

Per's phone pinged. He took it out and looked at the text message.

'Wait,' he said. 'The preliminary autopsy report is on its way, but Carola has sent a message. Our murdered and unidentified Lena had large quantities of Rohypnol in her blood.'

'Rohypnol?' she said. 'It's been a long time since you heard about that.'

115

'Yes, the illegal market is bigger nowadays. But perhaps this explains how she was held captive, because the drug paralyzes the body if you ingest too much of it.'

'So she may have been conscious when the murderer pulled out all her teeth, without being able to move?' said Charlotte. 'What kind of sadist are we dealing with here?'

23

When Klara arrived at the police station it was already seven o'clock in the evening. She had asked about Ibrahim, said he was here and that she wanted to speak with him, but was told to wait in reception. The woman at the desk was an uncomprehending old bag who had probably never been in love herself. She simply told Klara to wait, that you couldn't barge into the police station just like that.

Klara compulsively held on to the dead phone that she'd found in Ibrahim's room. The tears had receded – instead adrenaline pumped through her body and her thoughts were spinning in every direction. Every time the lift door opened she got up, ready to bombard Ibrahim with questions. Now it was the fourth time she had to sit down again.

When the woman at the desk had a free moment Klara went up to her. She pushed her shoulders back, straightened her hair and tried to calm herself by taking deep breaths.

'Excuse me, but how long are you going to keep him here?'

The woman looked at her over her red eyeglasses, which were attached to a chain around her neck. 'Honey, it can take several hours and it's only been one. Go home and wait. I'm sure he'll call, you'll see.'

Several hours, thought Klara. But at the same moment the lift pinged and she turned toward it. The doors glided apart. Ibrahim came out first. The couple he lived with followed close behind, along with a man she didn't recognize.

Klara's pulse rose again. She ran up to Ibrahim, while at the same time holding up the Samsung phone with the brown crocodile-hide case.

'Who is *Darling*? I found this in your room!'

Ibrahim saw the phone and stopped. He tried to tear it out of her hand, but she evaded him and held it up again. Ibrahim looked around.

'Calm down,' he said.

Apollonia and Martin stood off to the side, talking with a woman. She was not in uniform but the gun in her shoulder holster revealed that she was a police officer.

'Why do you have two phones?' Klara exclaimed. 'Answer me.' The tears welled up again and her temples were pounding.

'It's not my phone,' Ibrahim said curtly.

'Whose is it then?' the female police officer asked suddenly. Her posture was erect and her hair in a tight bun.

Ibrahim's shoulders sank. He looked at Klara, who could see irritation in his eyes.

'I got the phone from Samir. I don't know anything about it.'

'You're lying,' said Klara, shoving Ibrahim, but she had no strength left. The waiting and the anxiety she felt had turned into a stomach-ache.

'Is it Samir's phone?' the female police officer asked, looking at Ibrahim.

'Yes . . . or, well, I don't know. He just said that I should keep it with me.'

'When did he do that?'

Klara looked on while Ibrahim was questioned about the phone. Her find in his wardrobe was clearly important. Had she messed something up now?

118

'I don't really remember,' he answered. 'Last weekend. He just gave it to me.'

'Why would he want you to take care of it?'

Ibrahim shrugged his shoulders, his gaze wandered. Klara saw how he was searching for words. 'He never said. You just do what Samir says.'

The woman started to walk to a door by reception. 'Come in here,' she said.

They all had to step into a room that looked like an ordinary office, though without the decor. All that was in there was the furniture.

The female police officer didn't bother to sit down, she simply leaned against the back of a chair and crossed her legs. Ibrahim, on the other hand, sat down. His back was bent and his chin rested against his chest.

'Is that why you're not telling the truth? Because you're afraid of Samir?' said the policewoman.

Ibrahim looked up at her. 'When Samir is angry, he can do just about anything. But he protected me when I was alone, travelling here. He's rescued me so many times that I've lost count. I owe him loyalty, do you understand? I can't betray him, he . . .'

The policewoman crouched down in front of Ibrahim. 'He . . . what?' she said.

Klara was leaning against the wall and bit her lip, listening. She thought the woman was being very hard on him.

'He'll kill me,' Ibrahim replied.

Klara stared at her boyfriend.

'We can help you, Ibrahim. If you help us find him,' said the woman.

'Can we go now?' Apollonia interrupted, who seemed to see the same fear in Ibrahim's eyes that Klara saw.

'The young man who was robbed last Thursday – Adrian – he had a phone like that,' said the policewoman, pointing at the mobile phone that Klara was holding. The woman reached out her hand to take it. Klara hesitated.

Ibrahim shook his head. 'I don't know anything about that robbery or anything else that Samir has done.'

Klara heard that he was lying and clearly the policewoman did too, because she took the phone from Klara.

'We'll take care of it, thanks,' the policewoman said, looking at her. 'Are you Klara, Ibrahim's girlfriend?'

Klara nodded, surprised that the policewoman knew her name.

'Can you come with me in here?'

The policewoman opened the door to an adjacent room and Klara followed her inside. When the door was closed she was asked to sit but chose to stand.

'What were you doing on the night between Saturday and Sunday?' the policewoman asked, crossing her arms.

'What?' said Klara. 'Why do you want to know that?'

'Answer the question.'

'I was babysitting until midnight, then I went home and slept.' Klara didn't understand why that would be of interest.

'Listen now,' said the policewoman. 'If Ibrahim has got in trouble or knows where Samir is, you have the chance to help him. Get him to risk talking to us.'

'He's the world's nicest guy, he would never do anything bad,' said Klara. 'I promise, I don't know anything and he doesn't either.'

But it was as if the policewoman wasn't listening.

'We'll be in touch if we have more questions,' she said. 'But try to get Ibrahim to understand that we only want to help him.'

Klara nodded and had to leave the room through a different door. It led directly to reception and her legs were shaking while she waited for Ibrahim there. The questions from the police made her afraid. The feeling of being part of an investigation was unpleasant.

When at last the family came out from the other room she sought Ibrahim's gaze, in search of acknowledgement that she hadn't messed things up for him. She got none; he didn't even look in her direction.

The female police officer also stepped out of the room. 'If you decide to talk with us, Ibrahim, you can call me directly,' she said, handing him a business card. Apollonia and Martin also got one. Klara craned her neck to see what it said.

Charlotte von Klint.

'One more question before you go,' said Charlotte the policewoman.

Ibrahim stopped on his way out.

'Does Samir use Rohypnol? Have you seen him take, sell or buy it?'

Klara saw how her boyfriend clenched his jaw before he answered.

'In Germany he sold a lot of that shit. But I haven't seen him deal it here in Umeå.'

24

Per took off his gloves. His winter coat had made its first appearance, extremely early in the season, but the ice rink was sometimes raw, like now. It was six thirty in the morning and that surely contributed. He grabbed his homemade sandwich from a coat pocket and took out the little coffee thermos from the other. He placed it on the floor in front of him and looked out over the bleachers while he yawned. The ice looked lovely – even and hard. So far he was alone in Nolia Ice Rink. Simon was changing and no other parents were here. Per wanted to see his son's first practice with the U16 team. He opened the foil around the sandwich and sank his teeth into it. The smell of liverwurst made him hungry and he took another bite. Then it occurred to him that he hadn't taken his injection. Per hurried to take it out, pulled down the zipper on the coat and pulled up his shirt beneath, exposing his stomach. Bruises from previous injections were visible there. He preferred injecting in his thigh, but it was awkward to pull down your trousers on the bleachers. As the insulin entered his body there was a snap and a chemical odour spread in the air. He put away the syringe and reached down for the thermos, wanting to enjoy the aroma of coffee instead. He loved that.

As the first players glided out on to the ice he heard a familiar voice.

'Hi, Inspector, how's the investigation going?'

Roger Ren.

Per took another mouthful of the sandwich, waved his hand while he finished chewing. Roger sat down beside him. There were plenty of seats but he chose to sit down right next to Per. He had a black hat on which was pulled far down over his forehead. His blue eyes were clear and his cheeks slightly red, as if he'd been out in the cold too long. His snow boots were similar to Per's – grey and ugly – but ever so comfortable in cold environments. Roger made a pleasant impression, when he didn't open his mouth.

'Yes, it's moving ahead,' Per replied. 'I can't talk about the investigation process here and now, but you know that Adrian's case has been handed over to the juvenile unit.'

He saw Simon come out on to the ice and look in his direction. His son waved and Per raised his arm in response. Roger did the same, but Simon had already skated past.

'Did you read in *Västerbottens-Kuriren* that the local council wants to reduce the risk of crime by placing more streetlights in dark places?' said Roger.

Per shook his head without replying, simply kept his eyes on the ice. Roger leaned toward him.

'As if that would make any difference. These immigrants don't really care if it's light or dark.'

At first Per wanted to ignore him and continue eating his sandwich, but he couldn't stop himself. 'I think, quite honestly, that your way of talking is unpleasant.'

Roger looked surprised. 'My goodness, have I hit a sore spot?'

'No, but I'm here to watch my son play hockey and you're disturbing me in my time off. A piece of advice: try to tone down your xenophobia, don't tar everyone with the same brush.'

Roger sat silently beside him. Per wondered whether he should move a few seats away.

'All the youth robberies that happen, not just here, but in the whole country – it's the immigrants who are behind them, right?' Roger asked.

Damn it, thought Per. *I don't want to listen to you and your opinions, I want to watch my son's practice.*

'It's a big and complex issue,' Per answered. 'Can we watch the practice? Is Adrian on this team too?'

Roger placed one leg over the other, his foot almost knocking over Per's coffee.

'Sorry, it wasn't my intent to disturb you. I'm just very upset. I can't let them get away with what they've done to my family. Just so you know, Inspector.'

'It sounds like you're thinking of doing something illegal,' said Per when the hockey team's coach gathered the boys on the ice for a talk.

'Yes, it may sound that way.'

Per looked for Roger's son, but didn't see him anywhere in the arena.

'What are you doing here? It's six thirty in the morning.'

'I'm leaving. Enjoy it as long as your boys are undisturbed. Just keep in mind what I said.'

Per looked at Roger, wanted to see irony in his face. But no. Instead Roger got up and left the bleachers.

Per got stuck in work-related thoughts. What had Roger been trying to say? Why come to the ice rink just for that? Was Roger someone they needed to be worried about? Per was slightly acquainted with him through his son's hockey, but he'd never expressed himself like that before. It felt as if Roger had been radicalized somehow. That the robbery of his son had triggered a landslide of hate toward people with foreign backgrounds.

'Good, Simon!' the coach shouted, and Per brought his attention back to the practice.

He stretched his arms and yawned again before he finished the last of the sandwich. After that he leaned back and drank his morning coffee. More parents arrived, sitting scattered but making small talk with each other. A few waved at Per, who was new to the group. He sat a little further away from them but didn't move closer. He wanted to be alone and watch. Although his thoughts kept going back to Roger's statements and anger. Could he have done something with Samir?

But Per rejected that thought immediately. This was about an ordinary dad. Roger was not a dangerous person, simply upset. Although Samir was still missing.

His musings were interrupted when someone placed a hand on his shoulder. Per looked up. Charlotte.

'I suspected you might be here,' she said, wrapping her shawl tighter around her neck.

Per laughed. It didn't seem possible to get a quiet moment.

'What are you doing here?' he asked. 'In a cold skating rink at this hour?'

'What do you mean? It's almost next door to the police station. I saw your car outside. Instead of calling I wanted to meet up with you,' said Charlotte, shaking her head when she realized that he'd eaten his breakfast here.

'I left my phone in the car anyway,' said Per.

'Where's Simon?' she asked, looking out over the ice.

Per pointed to his son. 'There, green number eighteen.'

Charlotte sat down beside him and leaned back.

'Are you already so tired of Ola that you'd rather be here than having breakfast with him?' Per asked.

'Listen, Ola satisfies me on all levels, except possibly culturally. He refuses to watch a ballet performance, or go to the theatre. He just wants to watch sports,' she said, spitting out the last bit. 'Maybe the two of you should be together.'

Per sighed audibly. Simon had just missed a shot at goal.

'That Ola doesn't want to suffer through a ballet performance is probably fair enough. Who wants to do that?' he said.

'Many people. Ballet is the most graceful thing you can watch.'

'You can probably get Mia to agree to that, but not me.' Per had his eyes on what to him was the most graceful thing there was: his son.

'What do you want?' he asked.

'Omar was just released. His attorney succeeded with the age card. That and our weak evidence meant that we couldn't keep holding him.'

'What the hell?' said Per, looking up at the ceiling of the arena. 'So the interview with Ibrahim yesterday produced nothing other than that he's afraid of Samir too. Omar is free, and we still have a woman we haven't been able to identify who was murdered and tortured?'

'That's more or less it, yes. No bite at the hotels either. No one seems to have booked a room without showing up. Anything new on the phone we took from Ibrahim?' asked Charlotte.

'Not yet.'

'Did you ask Roger if it was his son's phone? I saw him driving away just now,' she said and smiled.

'Even if Samir and Omar likely robbed Adrian, we of course don't know if it's his phone. We have to go through it first. Damn that Omar was released,' he said.

126

Charlotte looked at him. She had some kind of green sludge applied in a line around her green eyes. She showed her white teeth in a self-confident smile.

'We've put surveillance on Omar, of course. Maybe it's better to have him out so we see where he goes and who he meets,' she said, startled when the puck ran into the board with a loud thud. 'Anything new on Lena's red car?'

'No, personnel in the field are keeping their eyes open, but it's like searching for a needle in a haystack. How many red cars are there?'

'It should be an older model,' Charlotte speculated. 'And parked a little out of the way. A homeless person doesn't have the means for a new car unless it's stolen. And no red cars have been reported stolen during the past few weeks.'

Per's eyes were on the ice. The practice was going extremely well for Simon. His son appeared to enjoy the pressure from the older players. Charlotte applauded eagerly so that it was heard all over the ice hall when he got the puck in goal.

Per showed with his hand that she should calm down.

'What do you mean?' she said. 'He scored a goal, didn't he? Shouldn't you appreciate that?'

'Not at practice as a parent.' He winked at her.

'But I'm not his parent, I'm just a fan.'

They sat silently for a moment and observed Simon. Then Charlotte turned to Per.

'I've been thinking about the drug that Lena had in her. Rohypnol is out there, but it's not as common as, for example, cocaine.'

'Yes, and it's been quite a few years since the tablet was redesigned to prevent pulverization,' said Per, happy that the other parents were sitting at a reasonable distance and didn't hear their conversation.

'Because we found out from Lena's autopsy that she had needle marks in her arm, that must be the way she got the drug in her,' mused Charlotte. 'So it was probably the old variety, which is still possible to grind up and mix with fluid.'

'Samir dealt Rohypnol in Germany,' said Per.

'We should ask him more about that when we get hold of him,' she said.

Charlotte's phone rang. Loudly. More sound from their side of the bleachers.

Per tried not to eavesdrop on the call and focused on the practice. But he heard her soft tone. When she was done he turned to face her.

'Anja? Ola?'

'It was the family that Ibrahim lives with. He's decided to tell us something. It was obvious that he was lying about his alibi when we last saw him. But he's not coming in until this afternoon. First he has a test at school that he refuses to miss.'

'Either he knows where Samir is or else he knows something more about the murder,' said Per.

25

Klara had spent the night at home and was forced to go to school by her mother. She didn't want to be there. Besides, it was Tuesday, and she hated Tuesdays for some reason. Her heart was down in her stomach. Everything was completely ruined. Ibrahim's family wanted to have yesterday evening to themselves, to talk about what had happened, and she was left out. It made her feel unfairly treated. She was the one who had found the hidden phone and now she couldn't find out who it belonged to. And she hadn't slept a wink. Instead she'd sent texts, Snapchat messages and tried to call. Ibrahim hadn't answered. But on Snap Map she saw that he was home anyway.

She was sitting on a bench, looking in turn at her phone and at the students passing in the corridor. Ibrahim's silence produced heavy emotions. He was her soulmate. He saw her in a way that no other boy had before, caught sight of details that not even her friends noticed. Like her birthmark behind one ear, the fact that she always brought her hand to her chest when she laughed, or that she talked baby talk with animals and bit her lip when she lied. All that he'd noticed and told her. But now she was worried that she'd ruined their relationship by her actions with the police and because of the phone she'd found. She was worried that Ibrahim was so angry that he would never want to see her again. That thought made her feel ill.

Klara stood up and walked past her locker, toward the social worker's office. Should she knock on Erik's door and talk with him? Was he there? If she couldn't talk with someone she wouldn't survive, that's how it felt. And none of her friends understood her relationship with Ibrahim. They tolerated it but were not enthused. Which was completely wrong because he made her happy. Even her own little sister was worried, although they saw each other all the time. Not to mention the general fear that Ibrahim provoked in others. Klara noticed it when they were shopping, riding the bus or having coffee. His presence made people watch them.

Klara stopped in front of the mirror outside the toilets and adjusted her backpack over one shoulder. She checked herself. The black jeans, the T-shirt that fitted tightly. Klara was *skinny*, as her friends always put it. Mum called her scrawny and Ibrahim said that she was beautiful. She never thought about her weight. She ate what she wanted, it just didn't stick.

A classmate came up and hugged her as she was standing by the mirror.

'My God, I'm so envious of your body,' she said.

'Hello to you too,' said Klara.

'Do you even eat?' the girl asked.

Klara was used to the pressure of body image in class – everyone talked about what they ate and didn't. Her friend was a normal weight, Klara thought, but anything other than *skinny* was fat, according to an unwritten law.

Klara shrugged her shoulders and looked at her own reflection. She cocked her head and ran her hand across her long fringe. The fatigue after the sleepless night was visible under her eyes. Klara hadn't had time to put make-up on.

'Yes, I eat tons. It's probably just good genes or something.'

'Fuck you,' the girl said, nudging her.

Klara didn't laugh; the lump in her stomach made everything dark. Not even a compliment helped.

'How's it going otherwise?' her classmate asked.

'Fine,' Klara lied. 'But I've got to go.'

'See you in the cafeteria later?'

'Sure,' was her brief reply.

Klara took a few stairs up to the teachers' area. Erik's office was there too. She'd been to the school counsellor previously, quite a few times. He was easy to talk with and cared about the students. And about her. It was like Erik understood and always tried to find solutions when she didn't have any herself. Besides, she liked babysitting for him and his wife. Erik was always nice when she was there.

Klara knocked on the brown wooden door and heard a 'Come in'.

'Hi, Klara!' said Erik as she stepped into the room.

The furniture in the office was of the same light wood that was a pervasive feature at the school. The fixture in the ceiling gave off a sharp light and created a sterile feeling. Klara refused to ever work in an office.

She sat down in one of the chairs in front of the desk. As soon as her butt met the seat cushion the tears came. She could no longer hold them back.

'What's happened?' he asked worriedly, leaning forward across the desk. It was clean and tidy, like his and Helen's home.

Klara looked down at her hands; the nail polish had flaked off on several fingers. She pulled one hand across her cheek. Wiped away the tears. The fog in her head produced a burning sensation behind her eyes. She was so tired.

'Talk to me,' he said calmly.

Klara breathed in and collected herself. She met Erik's gaze. 'If you found a phone at home that you didn't know whose it was and thought that Helen was unfaithful and told her that too, and she got angry and then it turned out that it wasn't her phone and maybe you'd ruined the relationship . . . What would you do then?'

Erik sat silently. Looked at her. 'What?'

He sounded nonplussed.

'Yes, well . . . I found a phone in my boyfriend's room, Ibrahim's. It rang, and the call came from a girl that was in the phone as *Darling*. He says that the phone isn't his, but instead his buddy Samir gave it to him, and now Ibrahim refuses to answer my calls. I think he's angry because I accused him of something he didn't do.'

Klara clenched her jaw to prevent more tears from welling out. She sniffed the mucus back into her nose and breathed with her mouth.

'If he says it's Samir's phone, maybe you should believe him,' said Erik. 'It may be that he's angry that you distrust him.'

'But he doesn't answer when I call. He's dissing me.'

'Give him a little time,' said Erik.

Klara nodded and pressed her lips together. 'The police say that the phone came from a robbery,' she said.

Erik stood up, went around the desk and sat down on the empty chair alongside her.

'Did Ibrahim rob someone?'

Klara breathed heavily; her nose was almost stopped up. 'I don't know,' she said, starting to cry again. 'He would never do something like that if he wasn't forced into it.'

The counsellor breathed in, holding his breath a long time before exhaling. 'So who do you think the phone belongs to?' he asked.

'No idea. What if it's Ibrahim's after all? Who's this girl, *Darling*? I'm so damn angry at myself. If I'd just had a little self-control and kept it, I could have had someone unlock it and check, and I could have found out whose it actually was.'

'How would you have been able to open it?'

Erik crossed his legs and put his hand on one knee. She looked at his gold ring, the slender fingers, like a girl's. All of him was slender. *But for a guy that's probably not so cool*, she thought.

'Ibrahim knows someone who's really good at opening locked mobiles. But now the police have the phone, so . . .' she said, hearing for herself how dumb it all sounded.

'Why does Ibrahim need to unlock phones?' Erik interrupted. 'Do they come from robberies?'

Klara shrugged her shoulders. 'I don't know, but can't people forget their passwords or enter the wrong code too many times so the phone locks itself? The phones don't have to be stolen.'

'It sounds shady, I think. Who is it who unlocks them?'

'I don't know his name, it's Ibrahim who knows him.'

'It sounds illegal,' he said.

Klara became worried. Had she said too much now? Would Erik go to the police and create even more drama around Ibrahim? She regretted talking and wanted to put the words back in her mouth.

'Ibrahim doesn't do anything wrong,' she said. 'It's only happened one time, I think.'

Erik laughed. 'It sounds like Ibrahim is involved in serious things, and that makes me worried for you, Klara. Why do you want to be involved with him if he's a criminal?'

'Ibrahim is the nicest guy in the world. He's not like everyone thinks.'

'Although the ones he hangs around with don't seem to be soft serve exactly.'

The comparison made her burst into laughter. Erik handed her a tissue and she blew her nose so that she could breathe. Behind

133

Erik's desk she saw a bookshelf with binders and books. On the top shelf was a photo of Helen and the children. The picture was old, because the daughter was in nappies. She thought about the phone call she'd had from Helen the other day, when it seemed as if she and Erik were about to separate, as if she was saying goodbye to Klara. She wanted to ask Erik flat out if they were going to get a divorce, but refrained.

'Let me give you a piece of advice,' Erik said after a moment. 'Stay away from Ibrahim for a while. Let him miss you.'

'How can I do that? I want to know if he's angry or not.' She felt her cheeks getting warm.

'Ibrahim will be in touch. He hasn't broken up with you. Focus on your studies today, and tonight you'll be babysitting for us. We can talk more then. Can you come over at five o'clock? I have to leave earlier than planned and Helen has practice with Liam.'

Klara offered a weak smile and nodded. Maybe Erik was right.

26

Charlotte's heels echoed as she walked across the glass bridge that led to the bosses' offices. The sun was peeking out through the clouds and warmed the air. She unbuttoned her jacket. On the bosses' side everything was newer and whiter and had more square footage. The offices were bigger and further apart. The coffee machine was expensive, the dry cookies replaced by juicy pastries. Soon Per would be sitting here too. She had been told that Kennet would inform the unit about the new acting positions by the weekend. But the regional chief of police was keeping it all very hush-hush. All they knew right now was that Alex was on his way in, Per had said that.

He and Charlotte had decided to talk with Ibrahim in one of the special rooms that looked less like you were in a police station. All forms of monitoring were in place, but it was furnished more like someone's living room. Couch, table, fluffy rug, TV, pictures, candle holders and flowers. And toys, which they'd removed for this occasion. The room was used for conversations with children who'd been abused. They hoped that Ibrahim would feel more secure in this environment and be easier to talk with.

Per was already sitting on the couch conversing with Kennet, who was standing with his back to the door. When Charlotte appeared in the doorway, Per peeked out from behind him.

'Come in. Ibrahim and the others are on their way up in the lift.'

Kennet turned around. 'What do you think the kid wants to tell us?' he asked.

'To be honest, I have no idea,' said Per.

Kennet left the room and Ibrahim came in with his attorney and the rest of his group. Everyone greeted each other politely. His foster mother Apollonia's hair was hanging loose down to her shoulders; the brown waves looked soft. She was slim and seemed physically fit under the knitted sweater. Martin, the dad, was wearing a suit and had his hair slicked back. He looked like he'd been plucked from a bank commercial, like someone from Charlotte's old neighbourhood. The family had a good heart to take Ibrahim into their home, she thought. They were involved and gave him tools to manage in Sweden. To think if only all unaccompanied kids got that chance.

'So, Ibrahim, there was something you wanted to tell us,' said Charlotte when everyone sat down. 'But before you do that, I simply want to ask, what made you want to talk with us? Yesterday you didn't say much. Has something happened that we need to know about?'

Ibrahim looked at Martin, who nodded to encourage him to talk.

The words came out slowly.

'We talked at home after we were here yesterday, and . . . They say that you can trust the Swedish police, that I'm going to be treated fairly.'

'That's true. Our goal is not to put you away, we want to help you,' said Per.

Ibrahim nodded. 'I would like to confess to a crime—' he said but was interrupted by Apollonia.

'We've understood that he can get a reduced sentence if he cooperates with you. Is that true?' she asked.

'Yes, that's correct, and we're going to do all we can to help you in the event of a trial,' said Per, turning toward Ibrahim.

The guy had a hard time sitting still and cast yet another glance at Martin, who looked at him kindly and nodded.

'I have . . .' Ibrahim looked down. 'I've robbed two people and I regret that very much. An elderly man and a young guy. I didn't mean to harm anyone . . .'

He shook his head and met Apollonia's gaze before he continued.

'I'm responsible for what I've done, but I want to apologize to the victims.'

Charlotte understood that the attorney had given him the words he used, but his regret sounded sincere. Ibrahim sat leaning forward, with his legs wide apart and his elbows against his knees. He massaged his fingers as if they'd fallen asleep and he needed to get the blood circulation going.

'Is that why you're here? To talk about the robberies?' Charlotte asked, her disappointment clear in her voice. She wanted to solve a murder, for heaven's sake.

'Yes, what did you think?'

'You know more than you're saying about the murder by the bridge,' she said. 'And about Samir.'

He looked at his foster mother, then at the attorney.

'Ibrahim is here to talk about what he knows and admit to his crimes. Isn't that enough for you?' said the attorney. 'He is cooperating after all.'

Charlotte sighed. *Jesus Christ,* she thought.

'Who else was at the robberies?' Per asked.

'Samir and Omar. You don't say no to Samir.'

'You mentioned the last time we talked that Samir would kill you if you weren't loyal to him. What did you mean by that?'

'He's dangerous. I've seen him kill before – he goes crazy if you aren't honest or don't do what he says. One time he killed a woman with a knife who pointed him out after he assaulted her son in a refugee camp.'

'Why do you continue to associate with Samir and Omar if you're afraid of them?' Charlotte asked.

He shrugged his shoulders. 'Like I said before: I owe him my life too. It's impossible to back away from that.'

'Although it sounds like you didn't want to participate in robbery, but did so anyway. Is that from fear or loyalty?' she asked.

'A little of both.'

Ibrahim paused for a moment before he continued admitting to the robberies of the elderly man and Adrian. Charlotte listened, but at the same time she felt irritation taking over. They were getting everything served on a silver platter, but it concerned the wrong crime.

'Ibrahim, if you know anything about what Samir has done you should tell us that now,' said Apollonia.

'I came here to talk about the robberies, not anything else,' he said indignantly. 'If Samir finds out I'm sitting here talking with you, I'm dead.'

'We're good at keeping secrets,' said Per.

'Where is Samir now?' Charlotte asked.

'That's what's so strange. He's missing. For real.'

'When did you last see him?'

Ibrahim sighed deeply. 'I've already told you that. Last Saturday. I was with Samir and Omar, we were going to . . . Samir wanted to rob someone again and we were a little here and there.'

'Where?' Charlotte asked.

'All over the place. We were looking for good victims. It's easier when people are drunk.'

'Were you down by the Strand Promenade any time after midnight?'

'No. Mostly around Rådhus Square.'

Ibrahim bit on a fingernail. He seemed honest, but at the same time not. As if there was a filter over the truth.

'Listen now,' said Charlotte. 'We know that Samir was somewhere near a place that is interesting to us in an investigation. He was leaving the Teg Bridge – he appeared to be running away from something. So if you were with him after midnight, the early hours of Sunday, you also must have been there. Right?'

'No.'

Straight answer, thought Charlotte.

'Did you find anyone to rob?' Per asked.

'No,' said Ibrahim.

'So what did you all do?'

'We went home.'

'We?'

'Omar and I. Samir . . . I don't know.' Ibrahim sighed again.

'So that was what time?'

'I dunno, I don't remember. Around midnight, I think. We were watching movies.'

Same story as Omar, thought Charlotte. But she felt that Ibrahim was lying about the times for the evening.

'Do you know if Samir went back to the campground or stayed in town after you separated?' asked Charlotte.

'I don't know. Like I said, the last I saw of him was at about midnight maybe.'

He wasn't telling the whole truth. Something felt wrong and Charlotte couldn't figure out what it was.

There was a knock at the door. Anna looked in.

Per remained seated with Ibrahim and the others while Charlotte met her outside.

'We've got into the phone that Ibrahim's girlfriend found and which Ibrahim claims he got from Samir.'

'And what was in it?' Charlotte asked. 'Whose is it?'

'I think you have to interrupt the conversation with Ibrahim and come and see for yourselves.'

27

Klara pressed her index finger on the doorbell at the Stenlund family's home. It was after five, so she was a little late. The idea had been to take her moped here, but as usual she chose the bicycle. Their son Liam opened the door and let her in. She saw immediately that he'd been crying. She hung up her jacket, took off her shoes and went into the house. The only sound that was heard came from the TV in the living room, which was showing a children's movie. Elsa sat on the couch drying tears from her cheeks. Liam sat down beside her and hugged his little sister. Whispered something that made her nod.

'Hi there, why are you sad?'

She sat down close to the children and placed her hand on Liam's knee. Both of them looked at her but didn't say anything.

'What happened?'

'Nothing,' Liam said quietly.

Klara looked around. The house had an open-floor plan and from here she could also see the kitchen. A casserole was on the stove. It smelled good. Everything appeared as usual at home with the Stenlunds. Tidy and clean. The children were really good at picking up after themselves. Every toy they played with they put away afterwards. It was normal for them to help out at home, and they even seemed to like it.

Helen came out of the bathroom and stopped when she saw the group on the couch. Her blonde, curly hair was set up in a twist.

'Liam, are you ready to go?' she asked without saying hi to Klara. She seemed to want to avoid her.

The boy remained sitting with his little sister and looked at his mother.

'Has Erik already left for the lecture?' asked Klara.

Helen put on her jacket. 'He's in the bedroom.'

Was Klara imagining it or was her tone curt?

Helen moved quickly and seemed stressed. She went from the front door to the kitchen and back. Appeared to be looking for something. Her cheeks were red, and when she put on lipstick Klara saw that her hand was shaking.

'We'll be back in a few hours. I made dinner,' she said, pointing to the kitchen. 'Come on now, Liam, your practice will start soon.'

She was also brusque toward her son. Liam got up from the couch. Slowly. He sighed, didn't seem to want to leave his little sister. Klara sat down in his place and put her arm around Elsa, whose eyes were glassy and cheeks were wet. Helen went to the hall with Liam without kissing her daughter goodbye, as she otherwise always did. When the door closed behind them Erik came out to the living room.

'Hi, I'm sorry about the sad children. Helen and I had a little difference of opinion. I think that Elsa is going to appreciate you being here this evening,' he said, then pointed to the set table. 'Liam already ate, so the two of you can take what you want.'

Erik went over to the kitchen while Klara stayed with Elsa on the couch.

'Has Ibrahim been in touch?' he asked.

'Yes, he called. He wasn't angry.'

Erik smiled at her. 'What was it I said? What have we learned from this?'

Klara shook her head in confusion. 'What do you mean?'

'Well, simply because Ibrahim didn't call you right away doesn't necessarily mean that he's angry. He may have been occupied with something that doesn't have anything at all to do with you.'

She mumbled in response.

Erik went out in the hall and started to put on his jacket. 'I need to go,' he said, looking out at the driveway through the hall window.

Elsa jumped down from the couch and moved toward the kitchen. She had a stuffed animal in her arms – a white rabbit that she set in a basket of toys before she sat down at the table. Erik went over and patted her on the shoulder. After that he leaned down and picked up the rabbit.

'You can have it at the table, Mum isn't home,' he said, starting to search for something in the kitchen drawers. Elsa hugged her stuffed animal and looked for a long time at her dad, who was rooting around in the kitchen.

'Listen, Klara . . . The last time we talked you mentioned someone who can unlock phones, do you remember that?'

Klara had also sat down at the table and was now eating the meat casserole with rice.

'Yes . . .'

'I need help from that guy to unlock a mobile,' said Erik.

Klara looked up. 'Did you rob someone too?' she said, laughing.

Erik didn't react to the joke. Instead he stopped his searching in the drawers when he found his car keys. Then he took a phone out of his jacket pocket and set it on the table. Klara looked at it, while Elsa sat quietly beside her and ate. It was a Nokia, and looked old.

'No, this is mine,' said Erik. 'I bought it a while ago and I've forgotten the code.'

She knew he was lying. Why would he forget his code? But before Klara could look more closely at it, Erik picked up the phone again and disappeared into the bathroom with it in his hand. When he came back out the Nokia was nowhere to be seen.

'See if you can make contact with the guy. I'll pay you for the trouble. Ibrahim too.'

'Okay, I'll check it out.'

'Thanks, that's all I'm asking. It's a shame to not be able to use it,' he said, going back out in the hall. 'Now I have to leave – can you clear up?'

Erik slammed the door and his daughter started from the sound.

Klara brought a pitcher of water and poured a glass for Elsa, gave her a kiss on the forehead and took out her phone. She took a selfie and sent it to Ibrahim. She wrote:

Babysitting at Stenlunds tonight, see you after?

He answered immediately.

Hell yes!

Her heart turned quite warm, as did her cheeks. She took another picture for Ibrahim and continued writing.

BTW can you see if that guy you know can unlock a mobile? The father in the family forgot his code.

Ibrahim wrote a single word in response.

Checking.

28

Charlotte crossed the glass bridge together with Per, but this time away from the bosses and toward the foot soldiers' departments. It had taken longer than expected to finish the interview with Ibrahim, and now they hurried to see what Anna wanted to show them – the phone that had been hidden in Ibrahim's room and which their colleagues had now managed to get into. Per was walking so fast that she had a hard time keeping up. She was about to ask him to slow down a little when her daughter called.

'Hi, Anja. Is this urgent or can I call you back in an hour or so?'

Charlotte fell further behind Per.

'Mum, it's important. I want to leave the pre-law course.'

She stopped and watched as Per disappeared through the security door.

'What do you mean? You've always dreamed of studying law. You even turned down moving up here with me because you wanted to study that course. What happened, honey?'

Charlotte kept walking. She came up to the door and entered the code. It clicked and she opened it.

'Mum, I've wanted to say this for a while . . . but . . .'

Anja made a dramatic pause.

'But?' Charlotte prompted her. 'I don't have time for mysteries. Say it.' She started walking faster.

'I want to drop out and become a police officer,' said her daughter.

That made Charlotte stop again.

'What?'

'Yes.'

'Police? But why?'

'Because it seems to be an exciting and fun job,' said Anja. 'I've been able to follow it up close, and I also want to have a job that I love and consumes me completely. Not a boring lawyer job.'

Charlotte laughed and shook her head, pulled her hand over her hair.

'We have to talk about this in peace and quiet, Anja. I'm the last person to want to influence you, but we have to figure out what's what here. Okay? I'll call you later tonight.'

'Sure. By the way, Dad doesn't know anything about this yet.'

'No, wait until we've spoken to tell him about this,' said Charlotte, ending the call.

There is a police training program in Umeå, was her first thought, which was quickly interrupted when an irritated Per called to her from the briefing room.

Charlotte was last to arrive and had to take a chair at the very back.

'The Samsung phone that Ibrahim's girlfriend found in his room isn't Adrian's, but our murder victim Lena's,' said Kicki, holding up the phone with the crocodile-hide case. 'We just got it open and will go through it more, but there's something you must see first.' She turned on the big TV screen and clicked up a picture of Lena dressed in a pussy-bow blouse. 'We now know that Lady Lena was not a homeless person.'

Charlotte started at the photo, which showed a heavily made-up woman with blow-dried hair and a glass of white wine in her hand. She even knew where Lena was – at Sturehof in Stockholm. A well-known restaurant if you lived there.

'And this isn't a picture from a former life, before addiction?' asked Per.

Kicki shook her head and showed more pictures. 'These were taken two weeks ago.'

Charlotte raised her eyebrows. Their homeless woman seemed to have lived a completely normal life in Stockholm. The pictures showed Lena in the company of a young woman, smiling, content. Lena in exercise clothes. Lena in a boat with friends. Lena standing by a stove, cooking.

'So the question is how she ended up in a shelter in Umeå,' said Charlotte.

'Does this mean that Ibrahim is our perpetrator?' said Anna. 'How did he get hold of the phone otherwise?'

'He claimed that he got it from Samir and I believed him,' said Per, taking out his own phone. 'But God only knows. Now we'll have to question him again. Damn it, we just let him leave. Storing the murder victim's phone at his place clearly makes him a suspect. We'll have to see what he has to say about this. I'll call right away,' he said, leaving the room.

Charlotte looked at the phone with the brown case. She never would have believed that very phone, with its well-preserved lovely crocodile-hide case, could belong to their murder victim. But Lena was no longer a homeless person, but instead a denizen of Stureplan like herself.

'Who is the person listed as *Darling* – who called when Ibrahim's girlfriend had the phone?' asked Charlotte.

'It's her daughter Emelie,' said Kicki, showing a picture of Lena and a young woman. 'Emelie is twenty-three and currently lives in New York. She's on her way to Umeå. Kennet talked very briefly with her and told her what happened. She was going to get on the first available flight here.'

So Kennet had talked with the victim's daughter. *Not common for bosses to make such a call*, thought Charlotte.

'Is Lena her real name?' asked Per, who was back after the phone call.

'Yes, her full name is Lena Bengtsson, fifty-four years old and far from homeless,' said Kicki, but was suddenly interrupted when the Samsung phone on the bench started ringing.

Lena's phone. The number started with 08, the Stockholm area code.

Kicki gave the ringing phone to Per, who set it back on the table, pressed the 'Answer' button and put it on speaker. No one in the room said anything. Charlotte held her breath.

'Hello?' said a man's voice.

'Yes, this is Per Berg with the Umeå police. Who am I speaking with?'

Someone was breathing on the other end. 'Oh, excuse me. I must have called the wrong number.'

'Are you looking for Lena Bengtsson?' asked Per.

Silence.

'Yes . . . Why does the police have her phone?'

'Who am I speaking with?' asked Per.

'I'm Lena's boss. What has happened?' The man's voice sounded strained.

'What company do you work for?' asked Per.

'Uh, Ratata Marketing, we . . . What's happened? Is she okay?'

'Unfortunately I can't go into that. We have an ongoing police investigation. Can we reach you at this number?'

'Of course . . . But what's going on?'

'Do you know what kind of car Lena drove?'

148

'Yes, she drives a red Passat that she uses as a company car. She, uh . . . She's our representative out in the field. Travels around and meets customers.'

'Do you know the number plate?' asked Per.

'No, but I can easily find out. If you'll give me a few minutes.'

'Thanks, I would appreciate that. I'll call you at this number in a bit.'

Per hung up and everyone in the room looked at the pictures being displayed on the screen. Charlotte said what each and every one of them was probably thinking.

'How did Lena Bengtsson end up homeless under a bridge in Umeå?'

'Two weeks ago at most she was living an apparently normal life,' Per added.

'Her daughter will be able to tell us about that,' said Kicki. 'For understandable reasons she was shocked when Kennet talked with her on the phone. But she said something that caught his attention. Something along the lines that this had happened before. But Kennet never got out of her what she meant by that.'

'We'll have to talk with her when she arrives,' said Charlotte.

'Now we really must grill Ibrahim again,' said Per. 'The phone still belonged to our murder victim.'

29

Erik picked up his phone from the passenger seat beside him and opened an app that could track Helen's phone via her number. A tip he'd found on the internet. Erik had thought a lot about what the neighbour told him, about Helen talking on the phone at night and saying she wanted to kill someone. Was she being serious? Who was she talking with? Erik didn't know if he felt like a detective or a paranoid lunatic, but he was firmly resolved to find out what this was about.

On his phone screen so far Helen appeared to be on the way to the IKSU sports centre, where Liam's practice would take place. Erik drove in the same direction at the same time as he searched on various car sites. He had decided to buy a new car, a bigger one. At every red light he checked where Helen was and then clicked on new cars. The latter action was a way to scatter his thoughts. Behaving like a jealous loser was not his favourite pastime. It made him shrink as a person. *Unworthy*, he thought, turning on to Ålidbacken.

It was almost eight in the evening and daylight was swiftly disappearing. When he turned on to Gösta Skoglunds väg his progress was slower due to the traffic.

The large building was for the benefit of the sports-minded in the city. Here were areas for strength training, a swimming pool, indoor bandy, basketball and everything else imaginable. Erik had been a member of IKSU for a few years for Liam's sake, but didn't exercise there himself. He preferred smaller places like the IKSU spa.

Erik signalled left and drove into the car park, cruising past all the vehicles in his search for Helen's car. When he saw it he felt an ounce of hope. Should he go in and check if she was there? He looked for where Helen's phone was located. She appeared to be inside the building. But he couldn't risk being discovered and exposed. Then he would totally lose face.

Liam's practice would go on for an hour, and Erik was about to park the car to wait until it was over when he saw Helen come out from the entrance. He observed her while she jogged to the other car park, which was farther away. She was doing it again. Sneaking off. How often did this happen when she was at the kids' practices?

While Erik watched, his wife jumped into the same car as last time – the grey Volvo that picked her up outside Stadium. It was too far away for him to see who was driving. But this time he wouldn't lose her.

Erik stayed two cars behind the Volvo to keep from being discovered and picked up the phone to look at the app in case he lost the car. The icon was still at the IKSU sports centre. She had left her phone at Liam's practice.

After driving a while Erik saw from a distance that the Volvo turned into the Innertavle School and stopped beside the only vehicle in the car park. He couldn't follow all the way there but instead had to stop on a side street. From there he had a good view of the vehicle she was sitting in. Darkness had now settled. The street lighting was weak and the cars were parked as far from the streetlights as you could get. The doors remained closed on the Volvo but someone got out of the car that was parked beside it. The person had a hood pulled up with a cap beneath it which concealed most of the face. Medium height, slim-shouldered under the hoodie. Erik's jaw was clenched. Who was it? Woman or man? He didn't dare blink, afraid to miss any detail. It was too far away for him to determine who it was, but from what he could see the person was holding something in their hand. Then the person in question disappeared into the back seat of the car Helen was sitting in, and didn't get out until a few minutes later, after which the Volvo backed out of the car park.

Erik got the number plate on both cars as they drove past.

What was this? Why was Helen meeting shady people at a school car park?

30

Thursday, 1 September

Charlotte was the first to get into the car, even though it was Per who unlocked it. It was almost four o'clock and the city was drenched in rain.

'How long can it really keep raining? This has been going on for twenty-four hours now,' she said, pulling down the sun visor, checking herself in the little mirror and smacking her lips. There was a snapping sound when she pushed the visor back into place.

'Okay, so what do you think about Ibrahim's interview yesterday?' said Per. 'Did you believe him when he stubbornly claimed that he didn't know how Samir got Lena's mobile? That Samir gave it to him on Saturday night so that he would hide it?'

'To be honest I don't know what to believe,' said Charlotte. 'We have nothing that contradicts his defence. My theory is that Ibrahim and Omar know something that they don't dare tell us out of fear of Samir. They tell the same story and give each other alibis for that time.'

Per nodded. 'At present, we can't hold Ibrahim, but at least we've put him under surveillance. We'll have to see what that leads to.'

'It's Samir who's hiding out,' Charlotte continued. 'That suggests he's guilty. There's a risk that he's already left Umeå. He's used to moving around between different cities and places.'

Charlotte was working her final days with Per at her side. She knew that. He was her security, the one who'd brought her into the team at Major Crimes, who believed in Charlotte and helped her grow in her profession. Although she also felt ready to take on greater responsibility, even if she would have to cope with the detail that Alex was new on the team. Right now he was only involved in their homicide case outside the police station, but he would start soon. On Saturday, of all days, he would apparently be introduced. Charlotte would try to avoid him as much as possible. It was idiotic, but the mere sight of Alex always made her warm and she hated that.

Per turned on the ignition. The windscreen wipers started immediately and he drove out of the police parking garage, on to Ridvägen. They were going to Hotel Uman to meet up with Lena's daughter Emelie who had come to Umeå from New York and arrived the day before.

'Lena's daughter seemed rather collected when I called her yesterday to set the meeting,' said Charlotte.

Per slowed down because of pools of water on the road. The dampness outside penetrated into the car. It smelled sour, like wet clothes.

'Maybe it was shock,' he said. 'You never know how next of kin will react. Emelie was on the other side of the Atlantic and in another time zone. She's probably struggling with a number of question marks today.'

Per stopped at a red light outside MAX Burgers, and looked at Charlotte.

'What is it? It feels like you're somewhere else,' he said.

Charlotte ran both hands through her loose dark hair. 'Anja wants to be a police officer. What do I do about that?'

Per laughed loudly as the light turned green and the traffic was unleashed.

'Ironic, because you went against your parents' wishes and became a police officer,' said Per.

'I'm well aware of that. And as a mother then I'm clearly a bad example, because she's dropping out of the pre-law course just like I did with pre-med.'

Charlotte looked out of the window. She did not envy the people outside the car, cowed by the weather.

'She wants to follow in her mother's footsteps – that's not so strange, is it?' said Per, driving along Västra Esplanaden and turning left on to Storgatan.

'But is she suited to being a police officer? She was born with a silver spoon in her mouth and knows nothing about life. The world she lives in is extremely privileged.'

'But it was in your case too, wasn't it, before you got the courage to go against your mum and dad? Don't forget that, because it resulted in the best cop I've worked with.'

Charlotte looked at Per. 'Thanks, that's very kind of you. But I'm made of tougher stuff than Anja. She is . . . how shall I put it . . . good at being spoiled.'

'Tell me so I understand.'

They cruised past the MVG shopping centre and Stora Hotellet.

'I've talked with her on the phone and tried to explain what it's like to be a police officer, that you don't become a detective immediately but instead have to put up with hard years as a patrol officer first. Wipe up vomit after driving a junkie to the hospital. Stay calm when people scream swear words at you on the street. Anja gets upset when her friends call her "the Maid" because her name is something as *trivial* as Anja. That was the name of my nanny when I was growing up.'

'What nasty friends she has then. Maybe they're the ones she should stay away from.'

Charlotte agreed; it was part of why she wanted to bring Anja up to Umeå last year, to get her away from the destructive associations.

'That was a few years ago now, her friends have grown up. But you understand the fragility in my daughter's soul.'

Per laughed. 'Well, I know Anja – she's not really that weak. She's cool as hell. I think you're basing this on her weakest moments when in reality she has many strengths.'

'Oh boy, have you gone to therapy to get so analytical?' Charlotte said, smiling.

'How serious is she?' asked Per. 'It's not something she's doing just to get your attention, is it?'

Charlotte hadn't thought of that.

'We talked for an hour and a half, and she has read up and knows what's waiting, but wants to drop out anyway. Her friends are horrified. Carl, her father, is going to jump from a bridge . . . Although on second thoughts that would be something useful.'

Per laughed and slowed down the car. They parked right outside the entrance to the hotel on Storgatan. Charlotte could barely see because of the rain, but Per pointed to the left.

'Look there, do you see? That's Omar, isn't it?' he said, putting the windscreen wipers on the fastest setting.

'Correct, that's him,' said Charlotte. Omar was walking fast, determined. Alone.

'The reports from Surveillance show that he's lying low. He hasn't made contact with Samir.'

Per followed him with his gaze. He was wet, or rather drenched, from the rain.

156

'If Samir killed Lena Bengtsson, his friends probably won't want to draw attention to themselves,' said Charlotte. 'If they even know anything about it, which I'm starting to doubt.'

'In due time maybe Omar can lead us to him,' said Per. 'How would Samir have got hold of the phone otherwise if he wasn't involved in the murder?'

Rain pattered on the roof of the car. People outside took cover as best they could. Charlotte didn't look forward to leaving the car.

'Are you ready to run?'

'Yes, boss,' Charlotte replied.

Both of them ran to the hotel entrance. It was a matter of metres but they got drenched anyway in that short distance.

Right inside the door Per stopped and took a call while Charlotte took the stairs up to reception. She dried her face with her hands. Her trousers were soaked through at the thighs.

'Quite the weather we're having,' said the guy behind the desk.

'Yes, truly,' she said, taking off her jacket.

Per caught up and showed Charlotte to one of the corners where there were two armchairs.

'That was Kicki,' he said.

'Any new information?'

'Yes, this was interesting. Right now she's analysing Samir, Omar and Ibrahim. Checking their social media or if there are other digital traces of them. She's searching for things that stick out – for example, pictures that may reveal where Samir is. And what she's found is that rather serious hate has been directed at all three, primarily on Flashback.'

'Islamophobic, or what?'

Per nodded. 'Extremely hateful comments and threats are aimed at Samir there. A separate thread sticks out that concerns violent crimes and robberies here in Umeå. One user in particular stands out, because the threats are perceived as genuine. Kicki checked the account, but it wasn't possible to identify the user.'

'Not that unusual on Flashback,' Charlotte observed laconically.

'Although it was possible to find information about the user behind one of the accounts that spreads the most threatening comments. An acquaintance of ours.'

'What? Who?'

'Roger Ren.'

'What? Has Adrian's dad threatened Samir on Flashback?' she said.

'Yes.'

'What does he say?'

'Roger posted the address of the campground where Samir and Omar live. He has also linked to videos from the robberies – the same ones that the juvenile unit is using in their investigation and that are spread all over the internet. But he has also written that Samir, Omar and Ibrahim should leave the country, because otherwise he's going to administer justice for all their victims.'

'Yikes. Could Roger Ren or another one of those nut jobs have anything to do with Samir's disappearance?'

31

It was just past four o'clock in the afternoon and Erik needed to get away from school. He was already late when there was a knock on the door to his office. He swore silently to himself before he spoke.

'Yes, come in.'

'Hi,' said Klara, standing in the doorway.

'Close the door,' he said without looking up, while he browsed through some papers that were on his desk. The only thing he could think about was Helen and what she was up to in that car in Innertavle. He'd followed the Volvo back to IKSU Sport, where she went back into Liam's practice. Erik checked the licence plate numbers afterwards. The Volvo belonged to the home nursing service and was used by several different employees, but who they were was impossible to find out. The other car he'd seen in the car park was registered to a cleaning company in the city. When he googled the company there were no pictures or any other information that might reveal who the person was that Helen met.

'Sit down,' said Erik, pointing at the same chair that Klara used last time.

'I don't have time, I have to go. I just wanted to tell you that the guy who unlocks mobiles can help you. For a price, of course.'

Erik nodded. Now he was even more convinced that he had to get into that Nokia phone that Helen kept secret from him.

He'd started to let go of the thoughts that she was unfaithful. This seemed to be about bigger things and that worried him down to the bone. In the worst case it had something to do with her past and her father. When he first met her in Malmö she had dangerously unhealthy opinions that originated from him.

'Hello? Erik?' Klara said impatiently from the doorway.

'Good,' he hastened to say. 'What's the price?'

'Five thousand, but a thousand of that is for me and Ibrahim.'

'That's not cheap,' said Erik, thinking about what he was doing. He was asking a student to commit a crime for him. 'Listen, Klara, if you don't want to I'll understand. It's not my intention to subject you to this sort of thing.'

She didn't reply.

'What's the address of the phone guy?' he asked.

Klara set one hand on her waist, in the other she was holding a bundle of photocopied papers. Maths assignments, it looked like. She was chewing gum as if it were her last day on earth.

'Don't know. I'm your contact person. No one goes to his place. He wants to be anonymous.'

Erik sighed. This wasn't what he'd hoped for, because it meant that he had no control over when he would get the phone back.

'It will go faster if I go there with it.'

'Hmm, but that's not possible. Ibrahim says the guy doesn't trust anyone. He helps a lot of dangerous people too. There are only a few people who know who he is and where he lives.'

'But I'm not dangerous, I'm a nice counsellor,' Erik attempted, but knew that the answer was no. The young lady had received clear instructions.

'Bring the phone to school tomorrow, then I'll pick it up,' she said.

'How long does he need?' he asked.

Erik's thoughts were whirling around the problem it would involve to remove the phone from the house for a longer time. If Helen discovered that it was gone, what would she do then?

'Just a few days, I think,' said Klara.

'Can't you double check with Ibrahim?'

'He's already said that he doesn't know.'

'Okay, it doesn't matter,' said Erik. 'Come here tomorrow and pick it up.'

Klara waved goodbye and left the office. Erik fixed his gaze on the closed door for a moment, until the phone rang.

'This is Erik Stenlund,' he answered.

It was his wife's boss on the other end.

'Do you know where Helen is?' she asked. 'She didn't show up at work today and I can't get hold of her. We're a little . . . worried that something has happened.'

Erik stood up. 'What?'

He sounded angry – he heard that himself and immediately apologized to Helen's boss.

'So you don't know where your wife is?' she said.

'No, but has this happened previously?'

She didn't reply.

'Hello? Are you still there? Has Helen missed work much before?' he asked.

'I just wanted to call and check if she was doing okay,' said the boss, her voice immediately sounding gentler.

'Let me investigate it. I'll ask her to get in touch with you,' said Erik, hanging up and starting to move toward the door.

Every muscle in his body was as tense as a guitar string.

'Damn it,' he said out loud to himself and pounded his fist on the door before he opened it and went out.

32

Together with Charlotte, Per moved in silence from the lobby at Hotel Uman to Lena's daughter's hotel room. The lift stopped on the third floor. As they came out, Per wondered how Emelie would be feeling. Angry? Sad? Next of kin could react in different ways when someone beloved was murdered.

'Was the room number thirty-two?' Charlotte asked, walking ahead of Per in the corridor. Her determined steps pounded the floor. Mostly it was Charlotte's boots that made a dull sound on the wall-to-wall carpeting. A cleaning woman nodded amiably to them as they passed.

Once at the right room they stopped. Per fixed his hair which was wet and Charlotte took off her jacket, draping it over her arm. She knocked on the door and Emelie opened immediately.

'Hi, come in,' said Lena's daughter.

Her face was puffy below her bloodshot eyes, but otherwise she was a copy of her mother. It felt like meeting a younger version of the murdered woman.

Emelie asked them to sit down. She was holding a coffee mug, but there appeared to be hot water in it.

'Sorry that I couldn't come sooner,' she said.

'No problem, you were in New York,' said Per. 'Please sit down too, then we'll tell you what we know.'

Lena's daughter sat down in the armchair. The light in the room was subdued and came from a floor lamp. Her suitcase was open on the floor. Everything in it was disorganized. It was obvious that she'd packed in a hurry.

'When can I see my mother?' she asked.

'As soon as the autopsy is done,' said Charlotte.

'What have you been told about what happened to your mother?' asked Per.

'That she'd been held captive, drugged and tortured,' said Emelie, wiping away a tear with a tissue. 'Who does such things to an innocent person – pulls out all their teeth?'

'That's what we're going to find out,' said Per.

'Tell us about your mother,' said Charlotte. 'We know that she worked meeting customers for Ratata Marketing, and we understand that she was in Umeå for work. But we also know that she stayed two nights at a shelter here in the city, and we don't really understand the reason for that because she should have had a hotel room.'

Lena's daughter crossed her legs and pulled her cardigan closer around her. 'My mother is amazing, but she's not like other mothers. She never has been.'

Charlotte took out her little notepad. 'What do you mean?'

Emelie looked at her, then at Per. 'Uh, well, where shall I start . . .'

'Where you feel you're able and want to,' he said. 'Keep in mind that we need to know everything, details that you perhaps don't think are important can be decisive for us in our investigation.'

'My mother has, or rather had, a number of problems. This isn't the first time she's stayed at a shelter.'

Charlotte leaned forward. 'We talked with the director and a homeless man at the shelter. Your mother said there that she felt pursued, or hunted,' she said.

Emelie nodded. 'It's true and not true at the same time, or . . . It can be both.'

Per cleared his throat before he asked, 'What do you mean?'

'My mother has a disease – she's bipolar.'

Per held his breath. He knew a little about the diagnosis from his time as a patrol officer. It meant that you had to take medication.

'This is the third time Mum has lost herself and lived as a homeless person. Sometimes she stops taking her medication and then things go quickly downhill.'

Per took off his glasses and massaged the skin between his eyes. He felt that Charlotte was looking at him.

'Do you know why your mother would stop taking her medication?' he asked.

Emelie sighed deeply. Per recognized the feeling she was giving expression to: that you're hanging over an abyss. He had experienced it himself when things were at their worst with Mia and her cancer.

'Every time she stops taking her medication it's because of stress of some sort. Then after a couple of days the manic period starts,' said Lena's daughter.

'How does that usually appear?' Per asked.

'One night I found her on the kitchen floor at home. She'd taken a toothbrush and was frantically scrubbing with it. Another time she sat in front of the mirror and brushed her hair for hours. If you don't stop it in time, Mum quickly gets worse. Then she gets confused, paranoid and hyperactive. She starts drinking, stops taking care of her hygiene and wanders around town. The only way to put an end to it is to commit her and make her take the medicine. After a couple of days she feels normal again. Or used to . . . in any case.'

Per wondered what Emelie's childhood had been like, but he didn't say anything about that.

'Do you know when your mother came to Umeå?'

'Yes, she drove up in a car a week and a half ago, around the twenty-second of August. I talked with her a few days before. She seemed to be feeling as usual then, even if it can be hard to tell on the phone, especially in the start, when she's just stopped taking the medicine.'

'Did you talk with her at any time once she'd come to Umeå?' asked Charlotte.

Lena's daughter shook her head.

'We know that she didn't check into a hotel, so we can probably assume that she was in poor shape already on her way up to Umeå,' said Per.

Emelie sighed. 'It's been a long time since she last went into a state, so I'd probably been lulled into a false sense of security that she was doing fine. Although Mum normally stayed at different hotels and never booked in advance.'

'Your father, where is he?'

Emelie shook her head again. 'My father, yes. He's a pig that neither of us have contact with any more.'

'Why not?'

'He hit my mother during their marriage. They were married for twelve years.'

'Did she report him?' asked Per, thinking that they must question the ex-husband as soon as possible. However, violence in close relationships didn't usually result in the type of sadistic torture that Lena had been subjected to. But nothing surprised him any longer.

'Once, I think,' said Emelie. 'When I was younger. Although it made everything ten times worse, so she chose to leave him and move around with me. But . . . Since a couple of years ago he has a new woman and has left Mum alone. Nice for us, in any case.'

'What's your father's name and where does he live?' asked Charlotte. Per knew that they would get that information from Kicki later, but they might just as well ask.

'Lars Bengtsson. He lives in Solna now, in Stockholm that is,' said Emelie, as if they didn't know where Solna was.

'What happened when she left him and filed for divorce?' asked Per, who knew that it was absolutely the most dangerous period for a woman who'd been married to a violent man.

'He pursued her. Sometimes Mum imagined things, but sometimes her instinct was right too. A year or two after she left him she saw my father standing in the woods outside our apartment, spying on us with binoculars. We lived on the ground floor with pine forest behind the building and he just stood there by a tree, smoking. Didn't even try to hide that he was there. He did things like that. But because he didn't directly attack her, she got no help from the authorities.'

'I understand,' said Per.

'Could it be my father who's done this?' asked Emelie, starting to cry, with the tissue pressed against her mouth.

Per thought hard. Could the ex-husband have killed Lena? He had a violent past . . . Men like him were handled with kid gloves in the Swedish legal system. A vulnerable woman had few options for protection. Most often the husband's right to privacy won, or else joint custody of the children forced the woman to stay in his power. Her life was ruined while the perpetrator lived as normal, free to continue threatening and hitting.

'Could it be him?' Emelie asked again.

'We don't know yet. We're going to investigate everything and everyone.'

'Do you know if your mother had met someone new?' asked Charlotte.

Emelie once again shook her head. 'Mum didn't want to be in a relationship, she said she was through with men. She felt freer than in a long time, but still went around looking over her shoulder.'

'Apart from your father, do you know if she'd been threatened by anyone else?'

Lena's daughter got up from the chair, tossed the tissue in a waste basket and took a new one from the holder on the desk.

'Not from what she told me. Mum is the world's nicest person, or was . . . I . . . Sorry,' she said, crying openly.

Per wanted to get up and hug her.

'Mum didn't have any enemies,' Emelie continued. 'She never created chaos or drama. She was nice . . . One thing about my dad, by the way, which perhaps you already know – he just got out of prison.'

Per and Charlotte looked at each other.

'We're still in the process of mapping everyone who was in your mother's vicinity. What was he in for?' asked Per.

'A year for aggravated assault.'

He nodded. 'Of whom?'

'His new woman, whom I've never met. You can get her name if you want.'

'Thanks,' he said.

'I need to sleep for a while,' said Emelie. 'Can you come back later?'

Per and Charlotte stood up at the same time, as if on command. They'd got a name, an ex to check on, and an explanation for Lena's homelessness. They didn't need to ask more right now.

167

'We'll be in touch when you can see your mother and if we have any more questions,' said Per, following Charlotte out of the hotel room.

They started to walk to the lift, but stopped before they got there.

'Samir is still our hottest lead,' said Per. 'But we have to talk with the violent ex-husband. Did he know that Lena was in Umeå? Where is he now?'

33

Klara sat uncomfortably on the bike rack outside the Migration Agency's offices on Kungsgatan. She yawned. It was nine o'clock, and for her that was early. Usually she slept in when her classes started later in the day. But today she'd already been at school a short time to get the Nokia phone from Erik. Now she was waiting for Ibrahim, who had a meeting with someone at the Migration Agency. He was still suspected of involvement in the robberies. It was just incredible that he'd even been part of that, thought Klara, kicking away some small stones. It had stopped raining but the ground was still wet. She leaned against the yellow facade and scrolled through her phone. There was rustling in the trees when the wind took hold of the branches, and a few scattered leaves let go and flew away. She took a picture and posted it on Instagram.

'Hi, that sure as hell took a lot of time,' said Ibrahim as he came out of the building.

Klara jumped up from the bike rack, right into his arms.

'How did it go? What were you talking about in there?' she asked, wrapping her legs around his waist and her arms around his neck.

'Just a little chat. A few questions, you know. Forget about it,' he said, holding hard on to Klara so that she wouldn't fall out of his embrace.

He started to move away but seemed reluctant to put her down.

'Man, good thing you're so light,' said Ibrahim.

'Wait, I have to bring my bike,' said Klara, getting down.

She pulled it out of the rack and started to walk it.

'Do you want to try it?' she asked, pointing at the bike.

'No,' he said.

Klara had nagged him to try it out, but he'd never learned to ride a bike. Yet another thing she wondered about. For her and many other Swedes it was second nature to be able to cycle, likewise to know how to swim. He couldn't do that either. On the other hand he was good at soccer. Sometimes she watched when he played with his buddies from SFI and he seemed to have talent. Or else it was just that his opponents were really bad. She didn't know.

Klara took out the Nokia phone that Erik had given her, the one they were going to take to the phone guy. Ibrahim took it and put it in his jacket.

'Should you really do this now, considering those robberies you're suspected of?' she said.

'Don't worry. You promised him, right?' said Ibrahim. 'Why does he want to unlock it again?'

Klara shrugged her shoulders. 'No idea, he says he can't remember the code.'

'Maybe he stole it?' said Ibrahim.

The question wasn't meant seriously, and Klara threw her head back and laughed out loud. 'Are you kidding? He's the school counsellor. He probably folds his undies before he has sex with the wife.'

'What do you mean, "folds his undies before sex"? I don't understand.'

They were walking along Kungsgatan, toward the Öbacka district where the phone guy apparently lived.

Klara took Ibrahim's hand and guided the bicycle with the other. 'You say that if someone is, like, super-boring. The kind of person who never relaxes or does anything impulsive. He's so dull that he folds his clothes before he goes to bed. No spur-of-the-moment sex, that is. Do you understand?'

Ibrahim had been looking down at the ground while they walked, but now he looked up and gave her a big smile that made her heart explode.

'I understand,' he said, pointing at the luggage rack on her bike. 'Come on, let's cycle.'

Klara straddled the bike frame, got on the seat and started pedalling. Ibrahim jumped up on the rack and the bike wobbled before she picked up speed. He wrapped his arms around her waist and extended his legs. Klara had to exert herself because of the weight behind her, but at the same time enjoyed his closeness. She wanted to take his hands in hers but didn't dare let go of the handlebars, holding hard on to them instead. The air caressed her cheeks, her hair was forced back by the breeze. An elderly woman glared at them as they rode by on the pavement.

'Here, turn right,' said Ibrahim, pointing to the left.

'Huh? Left or right?' she said, slowing down.

'There,' he said, pointing again. 'Stop by the restaurant.'

He meant Svingen Pizzeria a little further ahead.

'It's on the left side,' said Klara with a laugh while she cycled up to the building.

Ibrahim jumped off the rack while the bike was still moving. The brakes squealed when Klara stopped. She leaned the bike against the building's facade.

'I'll do the talking, okay?' he said, putting his arm around her shoulders, bringing her head to him and kissing her forehead.

'Okay. But what if he asks me something?'

Ibrahim laughed. 'Then you'll answer.'

They went up two flights and rang the doorbell. Loud music was heard from inside the apartment. Metallica.

'The eighties called and wants its music back,' said Klara.

The door opened a crack, a chain keeping it from opening completely.

'Hi, I've booked an appointment,' said Ibrahim. 'Friend of Samir – we talked on the phone yesterday?'

The apartment door closed, a clanking sound was heard from the chain, and when it opened again they stepped inside.

The man who met them on the other side of the door inspected Klara slowly up and down. His gaze made her pull up the camisole by her cleavage, but he didn't seem embarrassed. When he was done staring he went ahead of them to another room.

The first thing they saw in there were computer screens that lit up the space. She counted four of them. All the curtains in the room were drawn; it smelled like pizza mixed with farts. Instinctively Klara brought her hand to her nose. Naked ladies were on the walls. *This is so gross*, she thought.

'I can take the phone,' the guy said, extending his hand.

Ibrahim gave it to him.

'Money?'

Klara took it out of her jacket pocket. The cash she got from Erik at school earlier, less a thousand for her and Ibrahim.

'Thanks,' he said, sitting down in front of the screens with his back to them.

He was wearing baggy shorts that hung so far down that she saw more than she cared to. His T-shirt was worn and didn't hide his beer belly. His hair was long, thin and tied in a bun at his neck. *He must be the kind of man who lives in involuntary celibacy*, thought

Klara. An incel. She'd read about them on the internet – that they hated women because they couldn't get sex.

The guy twirled on the office chair so that he could see them.

'You can go now. I'll call you when I've got into the phone.'

He said that to Ibrahim, but he was looking at Klara's breasts.

She wanted nothing more than to leave the shabby apartment, so she walked ahead into the hall and was quickly out in the stairwell. Klara's skin was crawling; she never wanted to return there again. She shook her upper body to show Ibrahim her emotion.

'Is he dangerous?' she asked.

'No, I don't think so. But his customers are.'

34

Per looked at Mia, who was sitting beside him in the car. She'd been at the parents' meeting at Hannes' school during the morning. It was the first time she'd seen the other parents in a long time, but today she could manage it. Mia adjusted the scarf that was wrapped around her head. A Hermès, which apparently was a fine brand. Charlotte had bought it for her and Mia loved it.

'I wonder how long it will take before my hair starts coming back,' she said, placing her hand on his leg.

'A few months maybe, but don't feel stressed about it. You're beautiful the way you are,' he said, squeezing her thin hand.

Mia had lost lots of weight; she was only skin and bone.

'Can we invite Charlotte and Ola to dinner some weekend? It would be nice to see friends again,' she said.

Per blinked away tears of joy, prevented the feelings from coming out. That she wanted to see people was a clear sign that she felt stronger. He drove past the airport on the way to their home in Degernäs.

'I'll check with Charlotte when I get to the station,' he said, smiling at her.

'I could have driven myself to the meeting,' said Mia. 'You have to stop babying me.'

'Says the woman who's done just that with me all these years because of my diabetes.'

She laughed. 'True. But you seem to have managed fine without my help.'

'How do you think I managed before I met you?'

He turned in toward the house.

'Not at all,' said Mia, kissing him goodbye, before she opened the car door and got out.

When she closed it, Per's mobile rang.

'Hey, it's Tobbe at Surveillance here.'

Per set the phone firmly between his chin and shoulder while he backed away from the house.

'Hi, do you have anything good for me?' he said.

'Yes, maybe. You know Mr T?'

'Our tech genius? Sure. Oh, don't say he's dead.'

'Dead? Why would he be?' said Tobbe.

'I don't know, it doesn't matter. What about Mr T? Does he want to stop being an informant?'

'My God, aren't you positive today? My guys out in the field just called. We have extra monitoring of Ibrahim and Omar . . .'

'Yes?' said Per.

'Ibrahim delivered a phone to Mr T. One to be unlocked,' Tobbe reported.

'Whose phone is it?'

'That we don't know yet. But Mr T confirmed the information. After my guys in Surveillance saw Ibrahim go in and out of his house, Mr T amiably answered their questions. He's going to inform us when he's unlocked the phone.'

Per yawned. He felt worn out. But the information from Tobbe was positive.

'Well thought out,' said Per. He was approaching the airport and could see a plane that was about to land there.

'He had a girl with him. The blonde – what's her name?' asked Tobbe.

'Klara?'

'Exactly. According to Mr T she didn't say much, only seemed to be tagging along. It was Ibrahim who had the phone.'

'Okay, did Mr T report anything else of interest?'

'No, but as I said, he'll be in touch when he's got the phone going.'

'Excellent. Thanks, Tobbe. The collaboration with Mr T is working well.'

'We'll let him carry on with his lucrative little business in return for him informing us if anything interesting shows up,' said Tobbe.

'Yep. Win-win,' said Per.

They hung up. Per drove past the Avion shopping centre. The phone pinged – Mia had sent a text. It was a photo of her scalp, which had some fuzzy hairs. The picture showed her laughing and that made Per smile. But then his thoughts were interrupted by an incoming call from Charlotte.

'Per, did you hear about Mr T and the phone Ibrahim turned in?'

'Yep, with a little luck it's Samir's phone that the guys want to get into.'

'Exactly,' she said. 'In addition to that, Carola at Forensics just called.'

'Yes, she's been looking for me too,' said Per.

'Carola wants us to come to the forensic medicine unit. She wants to show us something she's wondering about, something on Lena's body.'

'Exciting. Shall we meet there in ten minutes? Can you get there by then?' asked Per.

'I'm already here,' Charlotte replied.

They ended the call and Per pressed a little harder on the accelerator. He wondered about what his colleague had said. What could puzzle Carola?

He didn't find a parking place outside the forensic medicine unit, so he parked illegally and expected to get a ticket. He found himself acting like Charlotte. *If you have a boatload of money it's no problem, though,* he thought, almost running toward Carola's department.

Charlotte was sitting outside, waiting. Her black cardigan had a checked pattern on the collar that matched her scarf. Well-dressed, as always.

She stood up as Per approached her. He showed the picture that Mia had sent.

'She's on her way back from cancer,' said Charlotte.

'I hardly dare hope, but right now it looks positive.'

Carola opened the door before they rang the doorbell.

'You were quick, I must say,' she said, pulling up the mask that hung down at her chin and handing rubber gloves to them.

Carola took the lead and pushed open the door to the autopsy room. Lena's naked body was lit up by a strong lamp. Per never got used to seeing dead people on the bare table. Lena's toenails were painted a wine-red colour. The body was thin, the hip bones stuck out.

'Apart from the more recent injuries that were caused by your perpetrator, the body tells us that she lived with a violent man,' said Carola. 'Some of the injuries are older – bone fractures on the forearms and hands which are classic defensive injuries. The collarbone has healed after a fracture she got as an adult. It may be from a different situation, but considering her history then . . . Well . . .'

'We've brought the ex-husband into our homicide investigation. We'll have to see what that produces,' said Per.

Carola went on to reveal Lena's internal injuries from life with a violent man. There seemed to be no end to the misery Lena had experienced, he thought. How in the world could that have gone on without anyone around her noticing?

'You'll get a definitive, written autopsy report during the day,' said Carola. 'But I discovered something and was unsure whether it's interesting or not. You can see for yourselves here.'

She went over to one side of the body, raised Lena's forearm and showed it. Right below the inside of the elbow was a mark that appeared to be drawn there with a blue ballpoint pen. It was like a V, and rather large – it couldn't be missed if you lifted the arm.

'The ambulance personnel who drove her body said that the mark was on the arm when they received her, but that they didn't think more about it then.'

Per leaned forward toward the arm and brought his index finger over the mark. 'She may have drawn it there herself. Nothing strange.'

Charlotte took a picture with her phone, as Carola moved away from the body, took off the rubber gloves and discarded the mouth protection.

'I took the liberty of calling the shelter where she stayed a few nights,' said Carola. 'What I wanted to know was whether they'd seen the mark on her during the time she was staying there. Lena was wearing an oversized T-shirt, but the director hadn't seen anything on her arm then, when she was alive.'

Per's pulse rose a bit.

'So she may have been marked by the murderer?' said Charlotte, seeming inappropriately excited by the information.

'Could it stand for a name? The ex-husband's name doesn't start with a V, nor the daughter either,' said Per.

'Yes, perhaps the murderer marked the victim with their own initial,' said Charlotte.

'That's one theory,' said Per.

'If I may interject,' said Carola. 'My guess is . . . Well, to me this is a V-mark as in "check" – something you check off as finished. I may be way off base, but that's the way it feels.'

Per raised his eyebrows. It was a wild guess, but there was something there in what she said.

35

SATURDAY, 3 SEPTEMBER

Charlotte placed herself last in line for the cake. A pink princess cake. Anna had chosen it, which was a little ironic because she was the one person on the team who never ate sweets. The lovely weather outside allowed for open windows in the break room at the police station. The cake was perhaps a way to perk up the team, which was working at full strength on a Saturday, or to welcome Alex. She didn't know.

Besides the usual briefing, a lot of internal information had been presented to the group earlier that Saturday morning. Charlotte already knew that it would happen, but it was still interesting to see how her colleagues reacted. First, everyone was told about Kennet's sick leave and that during that time Per would take over his position as regional chief of police. Then, when it was announced that she would step in as acting chief inspector for Major Crimes, Kicki mostly sat quietly, but the others seemed satisfied with the temporary solution. Mostly they were impressed that Kennet had managed to arrange an external extra resource in the form of Alex from Gothenburg. That was virtually impossible within the organization. And then they were relieved when Kennet said that they should work as usual until the murder of Lena Bengtsson was solved. That part was a bit trickier for Charlotte. So far she'd kept her distance from Alex, who hadn't been in the police station since he came to Umeå three days earlier, but she wouldn't be able to do that any longer.

'This was very nice,' said Alex in his broad Gothenburg dialect, extending his arms to everyone who was there to welcome him. Charlotte saw him in the corner of her eye and focused on taking a piece of cake. She tried to make herself less visible by keeping her head down. His Gothenburg accent alone, which echoed throughout the break room, did something to her. Her heart felt it immediately and reacted accordingly.

'What a good group you have here,' he said loudly, and everyone's eyes were directed to the new guy. Except Charlotte's. She tried to hide her nervousness by eating the whipped cream on the cake.

Alex had an ability to take over a room and he was immediately welcomed into the group. It wasn't exactly the same reception that she had got as a newbie. Charlotte was the only one who avoided greeting him. Reluctantly she turned around when she could no longer play with the cake, and inspected him discreetly as he shook hands with everyone. Alex had beard stubble, blond strands of hair that looked rough. Or, she *knew* they were rough. Charlotte preferred him clean-shaven. But the smile was the same. The happy eyes too. The cross that he always wore around his neck glistened. She wondered whether he still said grace before he ate. There were some new tattoos on his arms, she saw. They were covered with symbols and images.

After what felt like an eternity, Alex directed his gaze at her.

'Well, hello there, little lady, it's been a long time,' he said cheerfully and walked straight toward her. Charlotte clenched her jaw so as not to hiss at him. Who was he to call her 'little lady' in

181

front of the whole work team? Even if they would keep working in their old roles a while longer, soon she would be their boss.

'Yes, it has been,' said Charlotte, giving him a weak kiss on the cheek out of old habit.

'So we're still cheek kissing? Norrland hasn't taken too strong a hold on you yet,' he said, and Kicki laughed loudly.

Actually, Charlotte wanted to get back to work as quickly as possible and put an end to the rounds Alex was making in the break room, but at the same time this was perhaps Per's last chance to have coffee with his colleagues before he went over to the other side of the glass bridge. To the real bosses.

'How's it going with . . .' Alex snapped his fingers while he searched for the name.

Charlotte gave him time to remember. Tried to seem unaffected by his proximity to her.

'Your daughter? What's her name again?'

'Anja.'

'Yes, how is Anja doing?' he asked, taking a piece of cake for himself, which was a little too big, in Charlotte's opinion.

'Things are just fine with her.'

Alex smiled and awaited a more exhaustive response.

Charlotte noted a crocodile running along his forearm. When she first met him at the police academy, he mostly had tattoos on his upper arms. Now they were everywhere, right down to his hands.

'Well now, that one's new I see,' she said, pointing at the reptile.

Alex pulled up his shirt sleeve, showing more of his arm.

'Several new ones, and a scar,' he said, pointing at his elbow.

'Oh boy. A hoodlum or an accident?'

She thought about Alex's history as a policeman. He never hesitated to engage in hand-to-hand combat. That produced respect, despite the fact that he wasn't very tall. There was something about his energy that meant that most people backed away from a confrontation with him.

'Knife, hoodlum, very angry,' said Alex, laughing. His blue eyes were small but showed exactly what he felt.

Alex was fearless, an unconventional thinker and talented. He'd worked several years undercover, infiltrated the toughest gangs. She knew no one else like him. Even if Alex ploughed ahead like a bulldozer out in the field, he was always nice about the hard things, and seldom crossed the line. At least as long as it wasn't necessary. Soon she would be responsible for and supervise him. Good Lord, how would that go?

He stabbed the cake knife into the marzipan, cut a suitable piece and set it on her empty plate. Charlotte smiled and cast a glance at his necklace again. Still religious then.

She reached for a napkin on the table, unconsciously let her arm graze Alex's. The aroma of sweet cake was mixed with his cologne. She looked at him. A man in a dress shirt with a riot of tattoos and a religious soul.

But then her thoughts were scattered when Anja rang.

'Hi, honey. Sorry I hadn't called back. It's completely intense here.'

Her daughter laughed. 'I've just sent in my application to the police academy – the one we were going to fill out together yesterday.'

Charlotte put her hand on her forehead. 'But of course! I'm a worthless mother, sorry.'

She walked away from Alex, who listened unselfconsciously.

'Did you apply to Stockholm or to Umeå?'

'Both.'

'Have you told your father?'

'Hardly, he'll probably have a nervous breakdown.'

'So now both you and I are lying to him? He has no idea that you've dropped out of the pre-law course?'

'Mum, we have no choice. If I say anything before I know whether I'll be accepted he's going to nag a hole in my head. I can't bear his outbursts.'

Charlotte laughed. Anja felt exactly the same as her. Carl was a person who created chaos and drama when things didn't turn out the way he wanted. His daughter's plans to become a police officer would happen over his dead body, because it didn't suit his life. And he completely ignored what made Anja happy; it was all about him and his feelings. Exactly like when he was notoriously unfaithful during his marriage with Charlotte.

She was about to ask Anja if she wanted to come up to Umeå and visit, when everyone's phones started ringing at the same time in the break room. Charlotte looked at hers. An alarm had gone out. The emergency response centre had sent all available patrols out to Rådhus Square.

'Sorry, Anja, but I have to hang up. Things are happening here,' she said, clicking away the call.

Per and Alex came running toward her.

'Of course a lunatic would show up on the square with a bomb vest today,' said Per.

'Charlotte and I can take it,' said Alex.

'The hell you will – I'm still the head of the department,' said Per, rounding up the group.

36

Ibrahim stared at his leg, shaking it in an attempt to put out the flames. He screamed but nothing was heard. Nothing came out of his mouth, no matter how much he exerted himself. Even though the whole square was full of people, no one saw that he needed help. The foot with the tennis shoe was twisted in an unnatural position. He rolled over on the dry ground, got dust in his eyes, in his mouth. Pain passed over his body like the lash of a whip, driving through bone and marrow. Someone called his name – he heard it at a distance.

'Ibrahim!'

He tried to answer, but his voice was gone. Struggled to see, but couldn't open his eyelids.

'Ibrahim!'

With a jerk he sat up and felt a pair of arms around his body.

'You're dreaming. You're dreaming.'

His heart was pounding in his chest; he was staring right into a wall. He was in his bedroom in Umeå. Daylight streamed in through the window and Klara held him from behind in an attempt to calm him. He heard her sobbing, felt her thin arms. He was completely soaked with sweat. His muscles tensed.

'Damn, what a dream,' he said, his back meeting the damp sheets when he lay down again.

'You're scaring me,' said Klara. 'Where were you?'

Ibrahim had to think about it. He focused on a stain on the ceiling, his brain still in shock. Where had he been?

Raqqa in Syria.

He tried to hold on to the memory of the square, stared up at the ceiling and concentrated. But it got blurrier and blurrier, as if it was fading away with every breath.

Klara lay down with her head against his chest. He felt her tears against his skin.

'What were you dreaming?'

Ibrahim placed his hand on her head. 'That a bomb exploded and I was burning, that I lost a leg,' he said, holding up his leg.

'Where was that?'

He listened to his own breathing. His mouth was open and he tried to moisten his dry lips, but there was no saliva left.

'In Syria. Really crazy, because I only have vague memories from home, but everything was so clear in the dream. It's like that every time. The shops, the smells, the sound of native music, everything was there before it exploded.'

'Was your family there in the dream?'

He thought about it. Searched his memory.

'No, I don't think so.'

'We've slept away the whole morning,' said Klara, creeping closer.

Klara's phone pinged and she reached for it. She looked at the screen and sat up immediately.

'But what the hell . . .' she said, sounding shocked. 'My sister sent a Snap, look!'

Ibrahim read.

Where r u? There's a lunatic on Rådhus Square who's going to blow himself up! Where r u???

37

Charlotte took the protective vest, putting it on as she ran down the street toward Rådhus Square. The alert about a suicide bomber in the middle of town had gone out at 12.34 p.m. and the place was surely full of people off for the weekend who had ended up in the middle of the chaos. Now the area was being cordoned and the bomb technicians, National Operations Agency and intelligence service had been contacted. All the police districts in the country had trained for this scenario, but no one wanted to experience it in reality. Charlotte fell in behind four heavily armed officers from the SWAT team who were moving from Skolgatan down Rådhus Esplanade. The reinforcements, which were constantly arriving, were heard over the whole city. A helicopter buzzed above.

With an expert movement she released the safety on her service revolver; she was ready.

'Charlotte! No damn way you're going in there first,' Per said behind her. He took hold of her arm and held it so hard that it hurt.

Charlotte was forced to stop.

'Think about Anja,' he said, his face close to hers. Shouts and commands echoed around them. Weapons were ready to fire. Charlotte was breathing rapidly under the heavy vest. They stood under cover of the facade of the Utopia shopping centre. Through the glass windows she could make out the man with the bomb vest.

He had moved, turned his body toward them. Arms outstretched, a detonator in one hand. Jeans, black hoodie, sneakers, green vest. Charlotte took a few quick steps forward, raising her gun.

'Damn it!' said Per.

If the bomber detonated himself now she would be injured, perhaps die, but there was no stopping her. Charlotte couldn't stand waiting. She was drawn to the explosives, stopped when she had a free view and scanned him. He didn't see her, instead he had his gaze fixed on the ground ahead of him. She knew very well who he was. They'd been searching for him for a week. Sweat was running down Samir's temples; he was mumbling and screaming something at regular intervals that she couldn't make out. His legs were spread wide, his eyes stared down at the asphalt in front of him. Sometimes he staggered.

She didn't understand. Why would Samir want to blow himself up?

'There's something that doesn't add up here,' Charlotte said loudly.

Per held on to her vest, preventing her from moving any closer.

'Yes, Samir intends to blow himself to bits,' he said, pulling her carefully backwards.

'But why? There were no indications that he'd been radicalized or anything along those lines. He's a suspected murderer, but not this.'

Per nodded. 'It's strange, but what do we know? He may have passed under the radar.'

Charlotte's jaw was clenched. 'In that case why hasn't Samir already done it? The square was full of people when he stepped out, and now he's standing there alone.'

'I know, that struck me as odd too. Maybe he regretted it, didn't want to finish the deed,' said Per, turning around. 'We have to wait for the interpreter who's on their way.'

'I want him alive. If Samir dies he'll take with him the answers to lots of questions in our investigation,' said Charlotte, aiming her gun at the ground. Her body was tense but the hands that held the SIG Sauer were relaxed. She had trained for this, not to fire shots by mistake in stressed situations. The weight from the vest compressed her spine; the scoliosis hurt. She turned her neck to loosen the bindings. Then she let her back meet the facade, leaning slightly forward. She was forced to try to lower her pulse.

Per kept holding on to her vest while he talked with a man from the SWAT team. Charlotte's gaze wandered; she was looking for something but didn't know what. Further away, by the statue on the square, a man was standing still. He looked to be in shock; a person tried to pull him away but he didn't seem able to move.

Per let go of her. He didn't say anything but his look was clear. The order was to stay put. He went back to the response team leader. The bomb group was ready; through the earpiece he could hear their dialogue. They were talking about a simple bomb construction that anyone could build by following instructions found on the internet. Per looked at a screen they had placed further away – presumably displaying the bomb technicians' close-up images of Samir's vest.

Charlotte observed Samir. He'd been in motion during the whole course of events, but now he stood quite still.

She waved at Per to come over. He trotted toward her.

'Something *is* wrong,' she said again. 'Check his eyes – he's afraid.'

One of the men from the SWAT team turned his attention to her. 'We saw that often when I served in Afghanistan. Suicide bombers who changed their minds, who were interrupted and started to distance themselves. But sometimes they were blown up anyway by someone else who detonated the bomb via mobile. The terror in their eyes when they understood what it meant to blow yourself to pieces – you never forget that.'

Charlotte looked up at the tall man. His face was well covered by a helmet, protective goggles and black mask.

'It's even stranger that it hasn't exploded yet,' said Per, and Charlotte agreed.

'Samir seems to be acting alone, otherwise he wouldn't have been alive this long,' the man from the SWAT team said.

Charlotte put the gun back in its holster and took a couple of quick steps toward Samir. She knew that he understood certain words in English. If he changed his mind and was acting on his own, it might be possible to reach him. She held up her hands to show that she wasn't holding a gun. Her colleagues' shouts were heard in the background. Samir raised his eyes from the ground, staring at her. His nostrils widened from breathing, his chest raised and lowered at a rapid tempo. The white of his eyes were bloodshot, his lips dry and his hands shaking. He had peed himself.

'Samir, we can help you,' she said in English. 'The bomb technicians can take off the vest without anyone being injured.'

No reaction. Behind Charlotte colleagues were screaming at her to back away.

'Samir? Do you understand me?'

Still no response.

'Hello, do you understand me?'

Two steps forward. Charlotte screened off everything else, inspecting Samir's face, searching for signs that he would let the bomb explode. The hand that held the detonator started shaking heavily. It lowered when his muscles wouldn't stay in the same static position. Samir struggled to hold it up. Now she was standing closer, she saw his unfocused gaze, his eyelids drooping down, as if he wanted to sleep.

'Samir!' she screamed at him. 'Samir!'

She took two steps back. He appeared to be about to collapse. When his legs folded under him she turned around and screamed out loud.

'He's losing consciousness – take cover!'

She ran from Samir.

Just as Charlotte heard the powerful explosion, her body was lifted from the ground. Every part of her felt the pressure wave.

When the boom had settled down, she had asphalt against her cheek, against her hands. There was a faint ringing in her ears, feet running toward her. The dust made it hard to see and she blinked to get it out of her eyes. Something wet was running down her neck. Per's face showed up close to hers.

'Charlotte! Hello? Say something,' she heard as if from far away.

She opened her mouth to speak but it felt like she was eating sand.

Instead she tried moving her arms, and they functioned. Her legs also reacted when she raised her upper body. Her head was pounding. Per's voice came from somewhere else even though he was right beside her. She felt her body. Where did it hurt? Mostly in her head and eyes. Per's hands under her armpits. She was helped up to her feet. Her legs were shaky but with no pain. She seemed more or less uninjured despite everything.

'My God, woman,' said Per, hugging her. Now his voice could be heard more clearly. 'You managed to run pretty far before it exploded. Thank goodness.'

Immediately she was taken care of by ambulance personnel who hissed at Per.

'She may have neck or back injuries. You can't just stand her up.'

Charlotte meant to protest because she herself wanted to get up, but let it go.

She could only look at the dust and chaos around her.

38

Erik got back in his car outside the barricades. His heart was beating like a hammer in his chest. He took several deep breaths. Leaned his head against the neck support. A few more seconds and he couldn't have taken cover. What a fucking thing – he could have been dead now. It felt as if the blood in his body had turned into a tsunami that surged through his veins. He could really feel it pulse.

When the phone rang, his thoughts were interrupted. He thought it must be Helen who'd heard about the incident.

But when he answered, it was the neighbour's voice he heard in the car's loudspeaker.

'Hi, Erik, I just wanted to check that you're okay.'

'I was there, very nearly got killed. But I'm unharmed.'

Silence at the other end. Erik's hands were shaking. He wanted to get the adrenaline to settle down.

'How about you?' he asked when he remembered that the neighbour had also been in town. They had met of course on Rådhus Square shortly before the chaos broke out.

Erik brought his trembling hand toward the car key and turned it.

'I'm doing fine, I had just left the square,' said the neighbour. 'What a hell of an explosion!'

'Jesus, yes,' said Erik.

'On the news they're saying that no one seems to have been injured except the terrorist,' said the neighbour.

'That's good,' said Erik, starting to drive. Several people were standing on the street, waiting to get to their cars. 'Listen, I have to get hold of Helen and tell her that I'm okay. Talk to you later.'

They hung up.

He called her number but only got voicemail, so he tried again. His ear was ringing. A light, thin, piping signal from the explosion. Damn, she should be at home. What was she doing? Erik had to exert himself not to call a third time. He wanted to go home, but traffic was backed up everywhere.

Erik turned on the radio to listen to the news. All channels were talking about the suspected terrorist attack. The police were taciturn and said it was not yet known if it had been organized or if the perpetrator was a lone radical. No terrorist group had taken credit for the suspected attack, according to the media.

He was about to call Helen's number for the third time when she finally called back.

'Hi, were you in town when it exploded?' Helen asked. She sounded worried but he didn't trust that this was a correct analysis of the situation.

'Yes, it was a very close call. A miracle that I survived,' he said, embroidering a little more than necessary.

'But you're okay?'

His muscles relaxed when he heard the gentle tone in her voice. Now his hands were shaking less. His pulse was slower.

'Yes, and I'm on my way home, but there are traffic jams all over the city.'

'When, do you think? That you'll be home, that is?'

Now she seemed stressed.

'No idea. I'll have to see how the traffic works out.'

'Okay,' she said and ended the call.

193

Erik sighed. Why did she want to know when he would be home? Would she be at another secret meeting? Should he confront Helen? Put her back against the wall, reveal everything he knew about that Nokia phone, about the calls at night, about the secret meetings in the Volvo. He hadn't yet dared bring up the call from her boss, that she hadn't shown up at work. He ought to force her to tell. But something told him that he should lie low a little longer, bide his time. As soon as he got into the Nokia, he would get more information and know what was best to do.

39

Charlotte stepped out of the lift first, with Per and Kennet behind her. The offices of Major Crimes had been transformed into a command centre for all departments involved in the investigation of the bombing. The tip line was set up in a separate room and was ringing constantly, the Security Service occupied every available surface and in reception journalists were waiting for a press conference.

Charlotte wanted to lie down for a moment, rest her head, which felt as heavy as a medicine ball. Ola came toward her and when she saw him her emotions welled up to the surface. He led her to the kitchen, where there was still leftover cake from that morning. No one seemed to have time for coffee. As soon as they went in there, she leaned forward and vomited into the wastebasket. Coughed out the last of it, spat. The smell made her recoil and back up a few steps. She reminded herself not to forget to take out the bin bag, wiped her mouth with the palm of her hand and then rinsed it off in the sink. After that she turned around, placed both hands on the counter and leaned her rear end against the kitchen drawers. Ola stood beside her, caressing her cheek. Alex looked into the kitchen but turned around when he saw them.

'Why do I expose myself to such dangerous situations?' she asked.

Ola shook his head. 'I have no idea. Maybe you want to prove something to the rest of us. That you're capable, or that you're not a coward, I don't know. You just throw yourself in without thinking.'

'My therapist has to work on that with me, because there's no logic in my behaviour,' she said, looking up at the ceiling. Blinked away the tears. 'There's something incorrect with me.'

She met Ola's gaze.

'Incorrect?' he said, smiling.

Charlotte laughed, placing her hand to his neck. 'Anja called and cried earlier. She was so incredibly angry. I got a lecture from my eighteen-year-old daughter.'

'You'll no doubt get one from others too – both Kennet and Per.'

'And from myself . . .'

Charlotte leaned her head against Ola's chest.

'I can't stop myself when I'm there, in the moment. It's like a drug. My whole self is drawn into the situation. Do you think that's suicidal behaviour?'

She was embraced by Ola and put her arms around him. Took in his scent and knew that she was soiling his white shirt with make-up that had run. His muscles moved, she felt them, and he let her stay there a while.

'Three hours have passed since it happened. Give yourself a little time,' Ola said when at last he let go of her. 'I have to work, but call if you need to. I'll be in the building.'

Ola gave her a gentle kiss on the mouth and grimaced. *The smell*, she thought.

'You won't get a lecture from me because others are going to do it.'

'You just gave me one,' she said, smiling.

'Good, so that's done. See you at your house later, once we have time,' he said and left her in the kitchen.

Charlotte filled a glass with water, tossed in an effervescent pain reliever. The doctors had talked about a concussion. That seemed to be true.

Alex came back into the break room. He stopped a short distance from her with his hands in his jeans pockets.

'How are you feeling?' he asked.

'Dizzy, and I have a headache,' Charlotte replied.

'Nice, but you ought to be locked up anyway, for your own safety,' he said, smiling.

'My thoughts exactly. And my daughter's,' she said with a laugh.

Alex stood there, running one hand over his blond hair. His fringe was to the left and was longer than the rest of his hair, which was cut relatively short on the sides. His gaze was gentle. Charlotte still remembered his skin and scent and had to force herself to act cooler than she wanted. She turned her back to him and washed her hands in the sink.

'Are you two coming? It's time for a briefing,' said Per, knocking twice on the doorframe. He observed them for a moment and Charlotte suspected that he was wondering about their relationship. But he didn't ask. And what would she have answered? Sure, we liked each other and previously had some good sex.

She finished the water with the tablet and went over to the others with Alex at her heels. He was smirking behind her and she hated that.

Their usual room was too small for all parties involved, so instead the conference room was used for the briefing. Charlotte preferred not to meet anyone's gaze when she went in there, aware of what they were thinking. *Irresponsible.* And she was going to be boss.

'Nice that you could come,' said Kicki loudly.

Heads were turned to Charlotte and she got applause from some in the room.

'I'm glad you're okay,' said Anna.

Charlotte sat down at the front and Kennet started the meeting by immediately giving the floor to Fanny Nyberg from the Security Service in Umeå.

'It's been over three hours since Samir blew himself up and no terrorist group has claimed responsibility for the act.'

'No, who the hell takes credit for a failed attack?' said Kicki.

Fanny let the comment pass without saying anything. She seemed uncomfortable, picking at her fringe the whole time. She was unusually short in stature. But Charlotte looked up to her, as she was the most interesting person in the whole building. One day she would invite Fanny over to her house.

'We see no indications that any of the terrorist cells here in the north have been activated, so from our side we recommend that you work broadly and without preconceptions. Samir may have been radicalized through the internet, that's always possible, but it may also have been something else that triggered him. The bomb technicians are working on-site right now, but, in brief, we can say that this was a classic pipe bomb with three connected pipes. Not much is left of it, although we can see that the recipe for the explosive he used is easy to obtain, for example, via the dark web. Anyone at all can order the ingredients for this type of bomb on the internet.'

Fanny made a brief pause, turning off the ceiling lights before she continued.

'We know that Samir had a detonator in his hand, but the bomb was also connected to a mobile. At the present time we don't know what made it detonate – the mobile or the trigger.'

'A rather important detail,' said Per. 'If it was a mobile, some-one else may have set off the bomb. Then he wasn't acting alone.'

'Exactly. I'll come back to that,' Fanny replied. 'We've gone through the video material from the incident and can state that Samir was screaming short phrases, sometimes incoherently.'

Fanny started a video sequence that was shown on a white screen on the wall. Charlotte was thrown back to Rådhus Square.

'Here comes Samir on foot – see how he's moving. As if he's drunk. He seems confused,' said Fanny, letting the video continue for a little longer. 'Now we see how it's almost as if he realizes what he's carrying, and in that moment . . . Watch . . . Here comes the terror.'

Fanny started the video again and Charlotte agreed. Samir discovered the bomb and what he was holding in his hand when he came out on the square. He started shouting, although at the time no one understood what he was saying. But now the interpreters had been put to work.

'"You swine," he says repeatedly,' said Fanny, stopping the video and fast forwarding a little. 'Other phrases that are repeated are "Help" and "Allahu akbar". You all probably know that the latter roughly means "God is great". It's a powerful expression that is used by Muslims on various occasions and in many prayers. It's actually a tribute to life. But, as you know, the phrase is also used with certain brutal crimes, which has given it an unjustly negative sense.'

'So, is he asking for our help or for Allah's?' asked Charlotte.

'That remains to be seen and depends on what you find in your investigation. We also have to assume that Samir wasn't wearing the vest voluntarily, given that he seems to only realize what he has on there and then. The terror in his eyes seems genuine. Were there any threats being made against him?'

Charlotte's jaw clenched. 'Where shall we start? There are people all over Umeå who hate him. He wasn't a very nice person.'

Fanny continued talking about the bomb, the vest and Samir. Charlotte's thoughts wandered away and she thought about how drugged he appeared.

'Where did he come from? What do we know?' asked Per.

Fanny pointed at the screen. 'At first we believed he got out of a car that dropped him off, but if you look here . . .'

She indicated a point behind Samir, a place by the facade of the chain store where the surveillance camera didn't reach.

'We discovered a sleeping bag on the ground around the corner there. So far we haven't managed to link it to any person. It's now with Forensics for DNA testing. But we think he came from there, because several witnesses report having seen a person lying there all morning.'

'In the sleeping bag?' Per asked in surprise.

'Yes, completely covered up. And note that it's impossible to see it via any cameras. It feels too coincidental to be unplanned.'

'Was he lying there waiting for the right moment? With the bomb on him?' asked Charlotte. 'Hidden in the sleeping bag?'

'That's our theory, or that someone placed him there.'

'It's the middle of the day on a Saturday, in a town full of people, and no one was bothered about a man lying there in a sleeping bag?' said Kicki.

'That's what society looks like today,' said Per.

'Have we managed to take any samples or examine the body?' Charlotte asked. 'When I tried to reach him he actually seemed completely out of it.'

'Not yet. The body is being . . . gathered up. Parts . . . are scattered. You'll have to give me and my colleagues time.' Fanny looked at Per. 'I'm done. If you have any questions or thoughts, you just need to speak up now,' she concluded, smiling cautiously at the group, and tugged on her fringe.

Per took over. 'I'll be at the press conference in a moment, but I want you to collect all video material you come across from private individuals and surveillance cameras all over central Umeå. We know that Samir ran from the place where Lena was found. What does that mean?'

Charlotte raised her hand.

'Yes?' said Per.

'Could Samir have been in conspiracy with Lena's murderer? What are the odds that he happened to be running right there at exactly that time and then later is blown up on the square? Why? Did he know too much?' she asked.

'As I said, we have to work based on various theories. That is one of them.'

Anna too raised her hand. 'Perhaps this isn't the right forum,' she said. 'But I'm in the process of checking up on Lena's ex-husband. If he's been in Umeå or has an alibi for the time of her murder.'

'Super, I don't want you to drop that ball. The ex-husband is the only person we *know* with certainty who has a motive to kill Lena. Could he have hired someone to do the killing?' said Per, looking out over the group. 'I also want you to question Roger Ren. He has threatened to kill Samir on an internet forum and expressed a desire to take revenge on the guys who robbed his son. Follow that up immediately.'

'I'll get on that,' said Kicki.

'Good. We're taking witness statements on Rådhus Square, but I want to know everything about Samir – for example where he's been staying the past week when we've been looking for him. We'll start with the sleeping bag, where we suspect that he came out with the bomb, and work backwards. His phone was destroyed with the explosion, but everyone leaves digital traces behind them. I want all of it. Before we go home this evening we must know Samir's shoe size, what he had for breakfast and who he associated with.

The camper he was staying in must be picked apart . . . You get the picture.'

He made a short pause when Kennet, who was standing silently and listening, got a phone call and left the room to answer.

'Work all your sources and informants, get them to talk,' Per added.

Anna had one more question and indicated that by holding up her pen. 'What do we do with Samir's buddies, Omar and Ibrahim? Shall we bring them in again?'

'Good question,' said Per. 'I think we'll get more out of them if we increase surveillance instead. I want a wiretap and for Surveillance to follow every step they take. Or else, bring in Ibrahim again. He'll talk a little, anyway.'

Kennet came back into the room. 'Excuse me for interrupting. Carola is down at Rådhus Square and can't get hold of you.' Kennet handed his phone to Per.

'Okay, you all know what you have to do,' Per said to the others.

He asked Charlotte and Alex to follow him out. When they were alone, he put on the speakerphone so that all three of them could hear.

'We hear you now, Carola. What have you found?'

'Parts of Samir which are of interest for one of your investigations.'

'You're speaking in riddles,' said Per.

'Come back to Rådhus Square,' she said. 'You must see for yourselves.'

40

Klara's throat tensed from the exertion as she screamed at her father. Her eyes flashed with hate, she felt it herself. What happened had shaken up everyone in Umeå, and an ordinary Saturday had become the worst day of her life.

'You can't keep me from leaving the house! You don't understand a thing!'

Her whole body felt like a powder keg about to explode. There was pounding in her temples, her heart, in every vein.

'Your boyfriend's buddy just blew himself up on Rådhus Square – you're not going anywhere! You're not meeting Ibrahim, is that understood?' her father shouted, and the words struck her like a baseball bat on the neck. The tears welled out.

'You're so damned racist!' she said, throwing the jacket she was holding. 'Ibrahim would never do anything like that, and Samir isn't his friend!'

Her father was blocking the front door and her mother was in the kitchen. Klara's breathing was heavy and rapid. Thoughts were whirling around in her head.

'Klara, you must understand that now is not the time to see Ibrahim,' her father continued, gesturing with his arms. 'Don't you think that the police will be looking for everyone who has anything to do with Samir? Do you want to be interrogated too? Get your name in the police database as the girlfriend of a suspected terrorist?'

'But Ibrahim isn't a terrorist!' Klara shouted. 'You've met him. He has nothing to do with this! Are you completely retarded or what?'

Her mother came out of the kitchen and leaned against the doorframe.

'Honey, we like Ibrahim. But right now you must take a step back until the police conduct their investigation. Wait. Be smart. If it turns out that he didn't have anything to do with the explosion, then you can see him again.'

'You're not leaving the house this weekend,' her father concluded, a bit gentler in tone. 'What if something else happens . . . Neither of you girls may leave the house.'

'But now is when he needs me,' said Klara, before she turned and ran off to her room, where she threw herself on the bed.

Her body was shaking as her emotions took over. She held hard on to the pillow and pressed it against her face. They didn't understand. The only thing she wanted was to see Ibrahim. He must be scared to death. Klara took out her phone, but when she entered his number she went straight to voicemail. Then she sent a message on Snapchat. No response. *Have the police already brought him in?* Klara rolled over on to her back. Everything was falling apart. First the robberies and now the attack by Samir . . . She sat up and reached for the toilet paper roll on the nightstand, blew her nose and pulled her hair back, tied it up in a twist. When the phone suddenly rang, her heart jumped from expectation, to be disappointed a moment later when she looked at the screen. It wasn't him.

'Hello,' she answered the unknown caller.

'Hi, this is Mr T. I can't get hold of Ibrahim, but you can tell him that the phone you came in with is harder to unlock than I thought. It's going to take longer.'

'How did you get my number?' she asked.

The man laughed. 'Just tell him.'

Klara hung up. She didn't care about Erik's damn Nokia phone now.

The doorbell rang and she stiffened. Ibrahim?

She ran out into the hall, but stopped abruptly. Two police officers were standing there.

'Hi, Klara, we're looking for Ibrahim. Can you tell us where he might be?'

'No, I don't know. He's not here anyway.'

'When did you last see or hear from him?'

'Today. I was at his place earlier, but since then I haven't heard anything, not since the explosion . . . Yes . . .' She swore silently to herself. It sounded like Ibrahim had something to do with the attack. 'I mean, he was with me when Samir . . .'

'Is it okay if we look around a little?' the police asked her mother. She shrugged her shoulders, looked at her husband.

The uniformed men came in with shoes on. They moved through the living room, the kitchen, the bathrooms, the top floor. Smiled amiably at the family while they looked in Klara's room, then continued to Svea's. Both bedrooms were on the ground floor, but her little sister's door was closed. As one of the policemen reached for the handle, Svea opened the door.

'May we take a quick look? We're looking for someone,' the policeman said.

'Listen, he's *her* boyfriend. He doesn't come into my room, that terrorist jerk.'

Klara was breathless with shock.

'Ibrahim has never been in here,' Svea continued. 'He's a waste of space.'

The policemen ignored her and took two steps forward.

Svea extended her arm. 'See, no terrorist here.'

Klara shook her head. Now Svea's real thoughts about her boy-friend had come out.

The police looked quickly into her little sister's room and then went back to the hall.

'Ibrahim isn't suspected of a crime, we just need to speak with him. Can you call this number if he makes contact with Klara?' one of them said, handing a business card to her mother who took it, straightened up and raised her chin.

'Absolutely.'

After the police left the house, Klara went back to her room. Her heels pounded on the wood floor and she slammed the door behind her. It felt like she was burning up.

Svea called from her room. 'Can you come here, Klara?'

She didn't intend to go to her, she would never talk with her sister again. *Cowardly traitor*, she thought. As soon as Ibrahim was in a pinch, she betrayed him.

'Can you come here, you pea brain?' said Svea in a low voice from the doorway.

Klara glared at her, showing her contempt. 'You pig,' she said.

Svea started making strange faces, gesturing wildly without saying anything. Klara got up from the bed and stared at her sister, who had just said such terrible things about Ibrahim.

'Come on,' Svea whispered, taking hold of Klara's arm and dragging her out of the room and into her own.

Ibrahim was sitting in the corner behind the door.

41

Per got out of the car before his colleagues and looked in at them from the driver's side door.

'Are you coming?'

He saw Charlotte open her eyes. She had let her head rest against the neck support during the short drive to Rådhus Square. There were stitches on her forehead and she seemed to be in some pain. Per had asked her to go home, mostly because that was what a boss ought to say. He knew she would never do it. It was already 5.04 p.m., but this work shift was far from over.

Charlotte slowly got out of the car. *She must feel the pressure her body was subjected to,* Per thought, and watched as Alex helped her put on her jacket. He suspected they'd had some sort of relationship previously and that worried him. Things could get messy with Ola.

A pack of journalists ran toward them, shouting questions that echoed between the buildings. Per raised the plastic tape and let Charlotte in first.

'You'll get all the information at the press conference in about an hour,' said Per. It had been postponed several times since the explosion. The clicking sound from cameras was something he never got used to.

'Charlotte, how injured are you?' asked one of the journalists.

'Not as badly as the perpetrator,' she replied, and was met by gaping mouths.

'Yes, what should they say to that?' said Per as they walked to the square. The people who had access were working feverishly, but a strange silence prevailed.

'I think everyone is still in shock,' said Charlotte, as if she'd read his mind.

'It could have ended very badly,' said Alex, looking around. 'It was the busiest time on a Saturday. If the explosion had come a few minutes earlier, we would have had more body parts to scrape up from the ground.'

Round about the square were small, yellow signs with numbers. Locations of evidence. Body parts. From pure instinct Per raised his hand toward his nose. Iron mixed with something sweet. The stench from body fluids. He squinted at the sun; the sky was clear blue. Birds were chirping. The contrast to what was on the ground was striking.

He saw Carola and her team leaning over something. Parts of a torso.

'My God,' he said at the same time as Charlotte called to Carola.

They were not allowed in further without guidance because Forensics was busy securing evidence.

'Carola looks like an astronaut,' said Per in an attempt to lighten the mood. Right now she was dressed in a completely white coverall, from top to toe. All that was visible were her eyes through the protective goggles. The coverall rustled as she came walking toward them. She stepped over evidence item number eight. From what Per could see it was half a hand. The redness that had sprayed out on the ground had started to dry. An overturned baby's buggy was the same colour. Stained with blood.

'This is macabre,' he said, still with his hand over his nose. He looked at Alex, who didn't appear to suffer noticeably from what he saw.

Carola stopped a few steps from them. She looked in her report, browsed among the papers. Then she brought her goggles over her head, which was also covered in white fabric.

'Come here and you'll see,' she said at last, showing the way. They had to keep to the outside of the pathway where most of the markings were. She stopped across from the main entrance to the Utopia shopping centre. Evidence item number five – a whole arm that had been torn off at the shoulder. Per turned around, away from the evidence; the contents of his stomach wanted up.

'If you're going to vomit please do it in this,' said Carola, extending a bucket. Charlotte took it first. Per leaned forward instead. Closed his eyes and took a few deep breaths. He would prefer not to vomit at the crime scene. Sweat was seeping out from under his T-shirt. When he heard Charlotte vomit, he clenched his jaw, swallowed repeatedly. Per wondered if her reaction was due to the explosion or to what they saw around them. She needed to rest. Alex on the other hand offered a little smile and had put his arm around her lower back; it looked as natural as anything. *He seems to be made of steel*, Per thought.

'Yes, this is not a fun crime scene,' said Carola.

Per looked at Charlotte. Standing in the middle of the mess reminded him of how close she came to dying with Samir. It was actually a miracle that she hadn't been more badly injured.

Finally his stomach calmed down a little, but he still kept his gaze upward, looked out over the square. Umeå, his hometown, was shaken and deserted. Cordoned off. The airport was closed down, awaiting information from the Security Service. A feeling of sorrow struck him like a clenched fist in the stomach.

Charlotte pressed two fingers on the gauze that covered her head wound. Her nails, painted black, glistened in the sun. She threw out her hands like an Italian when Carola stopped in front of a body part that a few hours ago had belonged to Samir.

'I can't take any more,' she said.

'Check this out,' said Carola, ignoring Charlotte's comment. She sat down in front of the severed arm, which seemed to be intact, and carefully raised it. Per forced himself to crouch down beside Carola and look.

'Do you see the sign on Samir's forearm?' she said, pointing.

'What in the world?' said Charlotte as she covered her mouth.

'It's a mark similar to what Lena had on her arm, in the exact same place,' said Per, feeling his pulse rise even more. Charlotte took out her phone and took pictures of the mark.

'V, blue ink, same size. It can't possibly be a coincidence,' she said, seeming to have forgotten how bad she'd just been feeling. 'So, was it Samir who murdered Lena, or is he a victim of the same perpetrator?'

'Why would Samir murder Lena and then blow himself up on the square? This sign that's on both victims obviously means the crimes are connected,' said Alex.

Per agreed with him.

Charlotte turned to Carola. 'You've worked in Umeå a long time and seen a lot of things. The mark on Lena felt random, but now there are two dead persons with the same sign on their arms. Can you recall ever seeing anything similar?' she asked.

'No, never. But I'll ask around among my colleagues.'

'Thanks.'

'The marks on their arms is our best lead right now,' said Per. 'We have to find out if there are any other similar cases in Sweden.'

'If there are others, this is just the beginning,' said Charlotte.

42

Ibrahim took a bite of the sandwich that Klara's sister brought to her room. His favourite: egg with salt. The floor lamp in one corner was the only light in the room. The darkness outside the window was hidden by the blind. Klara sat next to him with her back against the wall. Her light hair was loose and hung down over her shoulders.

When Klara's parents came and picked her up after the initial news about the bombing, he didn't want to stay at home, but instead be with Klara. So he'd gone to her house, but overheard the argument they were having about him. The shouting. So he didn't ring the doorbell but instead knocked on Svea's window and was let in that way.

Klara looked at him. 'How are you doing?'

He did not meet her gaze. 'Bad. I don't know what I should do,' said Ibrahim, sounding more desperate than he wanted to.

'You should do what's right,' she replied.

He snorted. *Easy for you to say*, he thought, but didn't want to be mean to her. Ibrahim was afraid of losing Klara; without her he was nothing. She was perfect, like a dream. He had followed his father's advice and got a smart girlfriend.

'If you're innocent and don't know anything about Samir's explosion, you have to tell the police that,' she continued.

Suddenly a knock on the door was heard.

'Hello, what are you doing in there?' the girls' mother asked.

Ibrahim stopped in mid-motion and stared at the door. The parents couldn't know that he was there – they would call the police. He wasn't ready for questions.

'We're just talking. She's sad,' said Svea.

Their mother didn't say anything. The door was locked. If she discovered that she would be suspicious. 'Okay,' she said at last. 'We're going to bed. Wake me if you want to talk, Klara.'

'I'll take care of her,' said Svea. 'She's eating her sandwich now.'

Ibrahim breathed out and finished the rest, wondered how he would go to the toilet without being discovered.

Svea sat down on the bed, right in front of him. Klara moved and joined her, took his hand, her skin soft around his fingers. The whole situation was strange, and not just everything with Samir and Omar. Svea's room was full of colours: pink, blue, green, white. And Klara looked like an angel in the midst of it all. Innocent. After living most of his life in slums, among drugs, criminals, violence and evil, he was now sitting in a room in pastel shades that smelled of violet. With him were two girls who knew nothing about life. Ibrahim thought about the girls he'd met on his journey here. Sex slaves, ISIS women, oppressed and oppressors. Victims and perpetrators. All packed together in refugee camps that were like one big bin with people no one wanted to know about.

Ibrahim had managed better because he was male and had protection from Samir and Omar. They had always been together. When they came to Sweden, Ibrahim chose a different direction in life to honour his parents. He went to therapy, sorted out all the trauma – while Samir and Omar numbed their feelings with drugs, which in turn led to more violence and shit. Ibrahim thought about Raqqa, which once again had become a blurry memory. The nightmares he had at regular intervals were awful. Omar and Samir

212

experienced similar things. Their brains processed the awful experiences while they slept.

'Can you tell us what you know about Samir?' Klara asked. She laced her fingers in his.

He turned his eyes away. What should he say?

'You don't understand. Your lives have always been simple. How can you understand?'

'Try us,' said Svea.

Ibrahim inspected the girl he would never leave. He opened his mouth to say something, then changed his mind.

'Ibrahim, we won't go to the police if you don't want that, you can trust us. But you have to tell us what you know, so that we can decide together what's best for you.'

Klara sounded determined. Almost adult. Like a worried mother.

Ibrahim was tormented by feelings of guilt. He had betrayed his brothers – the ones who had taken care of an orphaned child in flight. At the same time Ibrahim's view of people had changed more and more. It went in an entirely opposite direction compared with Samir's. His buddy hated, was driven by revenge, and the security that Ibrahim had felt around him for years now felt more like fear. Those emotions were hard to handle and something that Klara would never understand. She was afraid of spiders.

He had told the police about the robberies. Tried to do the right thing. Wanted to do the right thing. But that was before Samir was blown up. To be classed as a terrorist was quite a different matter. What happened to Samir created a different fear, uncontrolled. Omar was calling him constantly. In his messages he wrote that they had to run, leave the country. But Ibrahim was tired of fleeing. He had no energy left.

He met Klara's gaze. It felt like he would drown.

'Samir is a . . . *was* an evil bastard,' said Ibrahim. 'But that evil rescued me several times. He was like a brother, both him and Omar. We became a family, do you understand? It was our way to survive. I've been protected in flight, by Samir's anger . . . It's hard to explain.'

'In what way were you protected?' Svea asked.

Ibrahim did not take his eyes off Klara. 'This is what I mean,' he said, irritated. 'You can never understand.'

Klara took his other hand. 'You don't need to go into details. Samir rescued you from awful things – that means you're in debt to him. But if he tried to kill people by blowing himself up, you have to tell us. That's the right thing to do. Think if there's an explosion somewhere else, if Samir is part of a network of others who will do that too. Do you understand?'

Ibrahim ran his hands through his hair. Stopped at his temples, pressed his head down toward his chest and closed his eyes. His phone was turned off; he knew that the cops were trying to trace him, that his foster parents were calling, Omar was calling, every damn person was calling. He didn't want to talk with anyone before he'd worked out everything in his head.

'I don't think there will be any more explosions. Samir wouldn't blow himself up and do such a thing.'

'How do you know that?' said Svea. 'What if Samir was part of a group? One of those terrorist cells.'

'I would have known,' said Ibrahim. He shook his head at what he could say. 'Well, this isn't easy,' he said, getting up from the bed. He sat down on the floor, which he was used to doing. 'Do you remember that woman who was found under the Teg Bridge? She—'

'Did Samir kill her?' Svea interrupted and seemed almost exhilarated.

Ibrahim got angry. 'Do you want to know or make things up?'

214

'Okay, sorry.'

'Samir, Omar and I were there, by the pier, when someone in dark clothes came carrying something big. We were standing pretty far away, talking about robbing that person because we were the only ones there. No one would see us.'

Ibrahim paused, searching for memories from that night.

'We started walking in that direction to meet the guy who hadn't seen us yet. Suddenly that person stopped by the edge of the pier and set something on the ground. It looked like a big bag or something. At first we didn't understand what was happening. It was like a movie. And Samir recorded it all with his phone.'

Ibrahim paused again.

'When the person ran away we went up to the edge of the pier to check it out. We'd seen how he pushed that big thing into the water and got curious. And that . . . well . . . Damn, it was her. The woman that the police found the next day.'

'What?' said Klara.

Ibrahim scratched his forehead. When he said it out loud, he heard for himself how sick it sounded.

'She'd got stuck on a hook and was lying with her front side down in the water. The only thing that stuck up was her rear end. In her back pocket there was a phone. We took it.'

Klara stood up. She held both her hands over her mouth.

'My God,' said Svea.

'Why didn't you rescue her?' said Klara, sounding accusatory.

'She was already dead,' he replied.

'Who does something like that? Leaves a dead person there and takes their phone?' said Svea.

Ibrahim sighed. 'I know,' he whispered.

The shame weighed heavily on him. He looked at Klara, who was looking at her hands. Maybe he would lose her now.

'Maybe the woman would have survived,' said Klara.

215

'She was already dead,' Ibrahim repeated softly, but noticed how bad that seemed. 'So we didn't do anything else . . . Samir took the phone. I intended to call the police but didn't dare. Someone had murdered her. We would've been blamed for it if I'd called. Refugee guys, you know.'

Klara brought her hand across her cheek. Wiped away the tears. 'Who was it who dumped her?' she asked.

'No idea, it was dark. The person's face was covered with a ski mask.'

'But you didn't see what he looked like at all?'

Ibrahim shook his head. 'His face was covered, and his build was normal, fairly short.'

'So that was how you got that Samsung phone I found in your room?' Klara asked. 'You were telling the truth.'

'Yes, or rather . . . Samir took the phone from the woman's back pocket. Then he told me to hide it. He wanted to find out who the murdered woman was – we were going to take the phone to Mr T. But I never had the chance to do that, because you found it in my room.'

'But say something,' said Svea, staring at Klara, who sat completely silent.

Ibrahim sought her gaze, wanted forgiveness.

'What did you do then?' she asked curtly.

'Samir had filmed it all and wanted to extort the murderer for money. But to do that he needed to know who it was. So he ran after them, to find out more.'

'What happened then?'

'We never saw him again and he was blown up on the square.'

'What?' said Klara.

'Omar and I called him lots of times but only got to voicemail. We thought he'd either left town, fled for some reason, or that the

216

blackmail was successful and he wanted to keep the money for himself. We started thinking every conceivable sick thought.'

Ibrahim bent his neck. He drew his legs up toward his stomach and let his elbows rest on his knees. Folded his hands.

'Why don't you tell this to the police?' said Klara, raising her voice. 'If Samir followed the person who dumped the woman, maybe the murderer got hold of him.'

Ibrahim raised his head and looked at her. This over-confidence in the police was sweet, but misplaced.

'At first I didn't dare because I didn't want to take the blame, and now . . . There's a crazy murderer out there, maybe people think it's me – or else the murderer knows what I saw.'

He closed his eyes.

'I'm afraid, do you get that?'

Ibrahim was ashamed at how weak he was. As a man, you should never show fear. That was the most cowardly thing of all.

Klara threw herself from the bed and down on the floor. She straddled him and wrapped her arms around him. Held him.

'Omar and I suspect that we're being followed. Some cops are watching us.'

Klara released her hold and put her palms on his cheeks. Ibrahim felt how the tension released in his muscles. Klara removed the anxiety like a drug. She looked into his eyes. Kissed him on the forehead, on the nose. Whispered.

'You must tell this to the police. Trust me. There's no other way out, if you don't want to run again.'

217

43

Sunday, 4 September

Erik sat upright in bed, leaning against the headboard. It was just past midnight and Saturday had turned into Sunday. His pyjamas were freshly laundered, with a scent of fabric softener. Helen was brushing her teeth in the adjoining bathroom. He heard the water running from the tap and reached for his phone on the nightstand to check through the usual – what he hadn't got around to during the day. The explosion created drama everywhere, of course – on TV, in the newspapers, among friends . . .

Erik heard Helen turn off the tap. He waited for her to come into the bedroom, but the door remained closed. Not a sound was heard from the bathroom.

'Helen? Is everything all right?'

No response.

Erik put his feet on the wooden floor. He took the few steps needed to reach the bathroom door and placed his head against it to listen. This wasn't the bathroom where he'd found the hidden Nokia phone the first time – it had been in the laundry basket down in the kids' bathroom. He wondered if the phone guy Klara knew would find anything on it.

'Helen?' he said again.

'Coming,' she answered at last. Her voice seemed stressed.

The toilet flushed.

He went back to bed and she came out in her blue nightgown. Her hair was gathered in a twist on her head and she pulled the sleeves on the nightgown down as far as possible. Helen sat on the edge of the bed and picked up the cream she always used before bedtime. A chemical odour spread in the room as she applied it. Her movements were slow. It took an awfully long time before she finally put her legs in the bed. She placed the blanket over her body and stared up at the ceiling.

'What's going on with you?' asked Erik.

She turned her head to him. She had loosened her curly hair, which now covered the pillow. She looked tired. 'You know, the usual.'

Erik clenched his jaw. 'We need to talk. You don't seem to be doing okay,' he said in an attempt to open up.

'What do you mean?' she said curtly, looking up at the ceiling again.

'A few days ago your boss called and asked about you. Apparently you hadn't shown up at work. What was that about?'

Helen reacted immediately. She sat up in the bed and pulled the covers up to her throat.

'Did they call you?' She seemed scared.

'That's right. Last Thursday, I think it was. What were you doing?'

She breathed in through her nose. 'What was I doing last Thursday . . .'

Erik sat up beside her. 'Yes, where were you then, Helen?' This time he sounded more accusatory than he'd intended.

'What does it matter?'

Erik was surprised at her forceful reaction. So unlike Helen, who was always balanced. She could at least try to lie her way out of the situation. He was worth that at least.

'That's just what I mean – you're acting strange. What are you up to?'

He pulled back the covers and got out of bed. Helen followed him with her gaze, but stayed put, not moving.

Erik had to bite his lip hard not to reveal that he'd found the Nokia and seen that she'd had secret meetings. He wanted to keep that to himself and continue following her. Once he had evidence he would tell her, expose her in the hope that it would get her to stop. However awful the truth might be, he would always love and protect Helen.

'Have you started hanging around with the wrong people again?' he asked cautiously.

'What? I just overslept.' Her voice betrayed her. She was obviously affected by the questions.

'Overslept? It was the middle of the day,' he said gently.

Erik went over to her side of the bed and sat on the edge. Her cheeks were red. The redness spread down across her throat, as always when she was angry or stressed.

'You understand that I get worried, right? When we met, you were hanging around with dangerous people. Right-wing extremists. You were just as full-on as your dad, Helen. How do I know that you haven't drifted there or are seeing him again?'

'Stop!' she screamed and tried to get up, but Erik had placed his arm across her stomach. He wanted to get her to understand just how worried he was.

'Is that what it is? Am I right? Are you associating with your dad again? Are you? He's dangerous.'

Helen took a deep breath and brought her hand to his arm. Stroked it carefully. It was like turning a coin. From angry to considerate. Erik wanted her love, he longed for it. But the change in her mood made him even more suspicious.

He stroked away a lock of hair that had settled over one eye. Helen's strong reaction was a sign that he was on the right track. She was behaving like someone who was guilty.

He removed his arm so that she had room to move, but she was completely still and stared at him as if she was waiting for him to act in some way. But Erik simply stayed seated on the edge of the bed, with his back as bent as his self-confidence. The attempt to get her to open up had failed.

Helen took a deep breath before she wriggled past him on the bed and went toward the door.

'Where are you going?'

'I forgot something,' she said and left the room.

Erik glanced at the nightstand where her phone still was. The usual one that she used openly. After glancing at the door he quickly picked up the phone and unlocked it with the code he knew from before. They'd always had full transparency between them and easily got into each other's phones. There hadn't been any secrets between them. Until now.

He went into her text messages. At the top was what Erik had feared, a text from her dad.

Well done, honey.

She had answered with a heart and there was nothing saved prior to that.

44

Charlotte was wakened by Ola's laboured breathing when he came into the bedroom. She turned around in bed and in the corner of her eye saw him grimace and wipe sweat off his face with a towel. She pulled the covers over her arms and crept in under them so that only her head was sticking out.

'Have you already been out for a run?' she asked.

Ola was breathing heavily. 'Yes, couldn't sleep.'

'But it's Sunday morning, dude,' she said, raising the covers. Showed him her naked body. Although Ola was already on his way out of the room.

'It's not that early,' he said and left her.

Cool guy, she thought and stretched. Her body ached from the exertion, but she let every muscle come to life. Charlotte turned her head to the window, resting her gaze on the water outside. A few scattered leaves fluttered around in the wind. That was one thing she didn't like about Norrland. Autumn would come early.

She pulled back the covers and got up, went naked to the bathroom. The stripes from the summer's sunbathing were starting to gradually fade. Charlotte wrapped her bathrobe around her and sat down on the toilet seat. Her fingers picked at the bandage on her forehead. It felt tight and hurt. The day before Per had ordered her to go home and rest. At last, after the second visit to Rådhus

Square, Charlotte had obeyed like a well-trained dog. And her head probably had needed a time-out. It was pounding less now.

When she was done she came out of the bathroom and picked up her phone. It was 10.43 a.m. *Not ideal*, she thought, and noticed that no one from work had called. She knew what activity was going on at the police station and it was worrying that they didn't seem to need her there. Either the investigation was at a standstill or else they were getting along fine without her.

'Ola, have you heard anything from the station?' she called. 'Has anyone been looking for me?'

He was in the kitchen. She could smell the coffee.

'Yes! Although I didn't want to wake you!'

'Oh, holy moly,' she said loudly, striding down to him from the top floor. Ola was holding one hand against the kitchen island and stretching his thigh. His face was still shiny.

'So what did they say? Did anything happen I need to know about?'

'Yes, but nothing they can't manage without you.'

Charlotte put her hands in the pockets of her bathrobe, pressing them down.

'You should have woken me, you know that,' she hissed and took her coffee cup, set it in the machine and pressed on the button to start grinding the beans.

'You needed to rest,' said Ola, changing legs to stretch.

'Who was it who called?'

'Alex, the new guy. He wanted to tell you something about a hunting vest that Samir was wearing.'

'What? And I have to drag that out of you?'

She waited for the coffee to be ready. The pleasant Sunday lethargy had been replaced by anger.

Ola seemed not to understand his offence. Calmly he sat down at the kitchen table and took a sip from his cup.

223

'Chill out, lady,' he said, sounding like a pimply teenager.

'Chill?' she said. 'Who are you?'

Without awaiting a response she left the kitchen with firm steps and went upstairs. Sometimes she wished Ola were back in his own apartment. The one he never stayed in any more. She closed the door to the bedroom and called Alex, who answered immediately.

'G' morning, honey bunny,' he said happily.

'Yes, it seems to be the day when I'm a honey bunny who should chill,' she said seriously. Alex was used to her sarcasm and laughed out loud. It was a long time since she'd heard that phrase. 'Honey bunny' was what Alex called Charlotte the first time they met. He came up to her at the police academy and said just that. In his Gothenburg dialect too, which made it extra charming. Back then she hated it, thought it was bad form when they didn't know each other. She was already with Carl at the time. But Carl loathed her choice of profession; they argued so much about it that they broke up for a while. That was when Charlotte and Alex started talking with each other at the academy and gradually that turned into drinking wine together at the local bar. The sex started right before the Christmas break and at that point the term of endearment was simply charming. They kept at it for six months. Six magnificent months before she realized that Alex would never love her most, and Carl came back into her life.

'Ola said that he wanted to let you sleep when I called earlier. He was worried that you'd over-exerted yourself yesterday, considering your concussion. Good idea, I think. But all the better that you finally called. I've already informed Per, and for your information I've found out facts concerning the bomb that Samir was wearing. The vest it was in is rather unusual.'

Alex paused and Charlotte could hear that he was shuffling papers. He was at the station, and phones were ringing in the background. She took the opportunity to drink her coffee while she was getting dressed.

'Samir was wearing a hunting vest,' Alex continued. 'This particular brand is uncommon. Exclusive. Something you ought to know about.'

He seemed to await a laugh from her but she was too curious to play along.

'I'm not quite sure how the name of the brand is pronounced, but the vest is evidently the most expensive on the market and is only sold in one hunting store in the whole Nordic region. On Kungsgatan in Stockholm.'

Charlotte brought the phone into the bathroom so that she could put on make-up and talk at the same time.

'My guess,' said Charlotte, 'is that Samir either stole it in a robbery, or else our murderer is a hunter.'

'Presumably the latter,' said Alex. 'Your extremely good colleague Per had a chat with Ibrahim just this morning. The guy has told us some important things that he's seen and didn't dare talk about earlier.'

'Like what?' she said, stopping putting on make-up.

'He told us something that was of interest and which rules out Samir being the perpetrator in the homicide investigation . . .'

Alex seemed to be doing something while he talked.

'What did he say?' said Charlotte.

'I can't tell you over the phone. Per will have to bring it up with you anyway.'

'Alex, I've been sleeping for twelve hours, not for twelve days! Why hasn't anyone called me about this?'

'Orders from the boss. You were injured yesterday, you know. They're protecting you, pea brain.'

'A honey bunny with a pea brain who should chill. This seems to be turning into a good day . . . Tell Per that I'm coming in soon and then I want a full report.'

225

With rapid movements she put on the finishing touches, picking up her handbag too. The silver Dior brand glistened when the sun hit it right. She went down to the hall, first pulling on her Stinaa.J boots but changed her mind, instead choosing the ugly police boots.

Ola came up to her, still sweaty.

'Oops, already on your way. I intended to ride with you.'

'Too late,' said Charlotte, giving him an air kiss before she opened the door.

As she was getting in the car Per called.

'Why haven't you informed me about Ibrahim?' she said in an irritated voice.

'Hello to you too, Sleeping Beauty.'

'What did he say?'

While Per reported what Ibrahim had told him, she stopped at a cafe and bought a breakfast sandwich. Charlotte listened as he told her how the trio had witnessed a masked person throw Lena over the edge of the pier on Saturday night a week ago. How Samir took a video of the incident and ran after the murderer to get an identity for extortion purposes. That Samir had taken Lena's phone and asked Ibrahim to hide it.

When he was done she got in the car again and put the phone on speaker.

'Why didn't Ibrahim tell us this earlier? Why only now?' she asked.

'He was afraid,' Per replied.

'Then we know fairly certainly that Samir didn't want to blow himself or anyone else up. In all likelihood, he was in over his head and made a mistake. The murderer killed him so as not to be exposed or extorted.'

'That's the theory we're working with right now. Samir followed Lena's murderer and never came back. No one had seen him since then, not until the incident in Rådhus Square,' said Per.

226

'But why blow him up?' she said. 'That seems unnecessarily difficult and risky.'

'I agree.'

Charlotte stopped at a red light. Per's voice echoed in the speakers, and she lowered the volume.

'So Samir could have been the victim of the same perpetrator that Lena . . . Do we know if all of his teeth were intact before, that is?'

'Yes, his teeth were in place, so to speak,' said Per and then changed the subject. 'You and I are going down to Stockholm. We have to find out more about the threats against Lena from the ex-husband in Solna, investigate if there is a connection between him and Samir. We also have to talk with the people at the hunting store, see if we can figure out who bought the vest. If it even came from there.'

Charlotte signalled left and turned.

'Good. We can stay in my apartment on Floragatan. I have to check on it anyway.'

'Then the boss will be happy, fewer expenses. Or wait, I'm the one who's the boss, soon,' said Per, laughing. 'It will be a quick trip to Stockholm. We'll take the flight this evening.'

'Can the investigation manage if we both go down there?'

'The answer is spelled *Alex*,' said Per.

There was a toot in the car speakers. Unknown number.

'Per, I have to take this. See you in ten minutes. Bye.'

She switched to the other call.

'Charlotte von Klint, Umeå police.'

'Hi, this is Mr T.'

'Hi,' she said to the informant.

'Listen, that Nokia phone that the foreign guy and his Swedish girlfriend turned in . . .'

'You mean Ibrahim and Klara? Have you got into it and found out anything?'

'Yes, both. There's something shady about it. Presumably it's a burner, because there's only a single number entered. That's all. No texts, no pictures or other contacts . . . nothing. Only incoming and outgoing calls come in through the saved number, but I can't find who it goes to.'

'What do you mean? It's impossible to trace?'

'No, I haven't been able to. The number may lead to another prepaid phone. I've called a couple of times but it's always turned off.'

Charlotte thought about the phone that Samir had taken from the murdered Lena and which Klara had found in Ibrahim's room. The one with the crocodile-hide case, which they believed belonged to Adrian but turned out to be Lena's. And now Ibrahim had turned in another phone to Mr T to be unlocked. A Nokia. Where did it come from and whose was it?

'Send the number to me and I'll see if we can do anything.'

'This is fucking shady, or maybe not,' said Mr T. 'Burners are everyday fare for criminals. Anyway I thought you needed to know this considering everything that's happened. I'll give the phone back to Ibrahim and say that it was empty, that there wasn't anything on it. He won't get the information you've got.'

'Okay, good thinking. Thanks for your cooperation. Can I call you if we need more help?'

'Sure. Considering that the guy is buddies with Samir who blew himself up, I'm more than willing to cooperate. We have to fight terrorism together.'

Charlotte turned into the police station car park. Thought about what she'd just found out. She believed Ibrahim's story about what had happened with Lena and Samir. That the guys had seen her being dumped by the pier, after which Samir followed the perpetrator to then disappear until he showed up on Rådhus Square. There was nothing for him to gain by lying, and from what they could discern from Ibrahim's phone calls and texts, he was telling the truth. He seemed to want to do the right thing and what he said matched up with their evidence. But this new mobile phone that had shown up was interesting. Per hadn't received any information about it from Ibrahim, who nonetheless had now opened up and told them everything he knew. Why had Ibrahim and Klara taken the phone to Mr T?

45

Erik put his hands in his jacket pockets. He was standing outside the Teg Central School, waiting for his daughter. Elsa was playing with some friends in the gym which was open for use on the weekends. The air was chillier than it had been in a long time. The artificial turf on the soccer field was green and the trees still had some time to go before they would be beautifully painted in autumn colours.

He yawned, covering his mouth. The discovery that Helen had contact with her right-wing extremist father had kept him awake for the rest of the night. The thoughts gnawed at him, chewing up hope. She was back in that mess. Erik had been shocked but not surprised. It was as if everything he'd struggled for had been taken away. He leaned against the fence that separated the schoolyard from the soccer field, crossing his legs.

Another dad was standing a short distance away with a plastic bag in his hand. Erik smiled cautiously at the man when their eyes met.

'She forgot her gym clothes,' the man said, holding up the bag.

Erik laughed. 'I'm waiting for my daughter,' he said.

The fence was his spot. If he stood here Elsa knew where to meet up afterwards. He took out his phone to send a text to Helen, wanted to see if she would answer. She was grocery shopping with

Liam, so Erik asked how things were going at the store. The answer came immediately.

Good.

Erik looked at the phone. Her tone was so curt. He checked where her phone was. At the right place.

The man with the bag came closer to Erik. Friendly blue eyes, wax in his hair. Well-groomed.

'Hi, I'm Roger Ren,' he said, extending his right hand.

Erik shook hands with him. There was something familiar about him. They'd met before, he believed.

'Erik Stenlund,' he introduced himself.

Then they stood silently for a while. The wind made the leaves rustle.

'Have you heard whether there have been any problems with robberies at this school?' Roger asked. 'My youngest goes here.'

'Not as far as I know. On the other hand we have some problems with that at the high school where I work. It feels like it's a growing problem and starts at a younger age.'

Roger looked toward the brick building. 'That's just awful. What school do you work at? Are you a teacher?'

'Hell no, I'm a counsellor at the Dragon School,' said Erik, scraping the ground with his shoe. He was waiting for the ringtone that would mean that Elsa was on her way.

Roger took two steps forward.

'My son was recently robbed by an immigrant gang.'

Erik blinked. 'Oh, how is he doing?'

'Under the circumstances, lousy. The police aren't doing anything either. Immigrants are a protected species, it seems.'

Erik glanced at Roger. Where had he met him before?

'I don't think they are. But the police can hardly bring in people willy-nilly. They must have grounds for arrest and custody. All residents in our country have that right.'

Roger looked up. 'Residents? This is about criminal immigrants. Would you feel the same if it happened to your daughter?' he asked, pointing to the gym where Elsa was.

It felt as if Erik had travelled ten years back in time and was talking with Helen's father. The same opinions.

'I don't know, but as a counsellor I find out a lot about the refugees who go to our school and the majority are good people who've been harmed. They have often experienced very difficult things.'

'That's exactly what makes me so angry!' Roger said, raising his voice. 'That they can do what they want and then get away with it because they must be protected. But what about our young people who encounter them? Who protects them?'

Erik patted Roger on the shoulder and smiled at him. 'It's a complicated question. There is truly no excuse for robbing anyone. That's how it is. I'm sorry that it happened to your son and I truly hope the guilty parties are punished.'

Now Erik looked over toward the gym, wanted to be rescued by his daughter. But Roger didn't give up.

'You're one of those people who make it easier for the immigrants to rob people by indulging them. Nah, lock up or send back every single one who commits a crime. It's impossible to mix people with such different views of human worth.'

Erik didn't say anything, just kept looking for Elsa.

'I may have to move out of Sweden soon, when the immigrants take over,' Roger continued. 'I say to my kids that they're going to have to flee the country when I'm dead.'

Erik crossed his arms, straightened his back. What kind of father was this?

'You can't go around believing that all refugees want to harm you,' said Erik, once again scraping in the gravel on the ground

232

with his foot. 'You can't blame a whole group of people simply because of the actions of a few scattered individuals.'

'If my son doesn't get justice, I'm going to get it for him,' said Roger, waving at a girl who came running.

Erik looked at him. What did he mean by that?

46

Charlotte entered the airplane before Per. It wasn't dark out yet, fortunately, because she really didn't like to fly at night. Blindly. Not seeing what kind of weather they were in. The flying ban had been lifted only a few hours earlier and this was the first plane to take off after the explosion the day before.

In one hand she held her carry-on bag; in the other was the ticket she was looking at.

'What seat do you have?' Per asked behind her.

It turned out that they would be sitting next to each other. She put her bag in the overhead locker and sat down. Found the seat belt and tightened it as hard as she could. She took a deep breath and looked straight ahead. Her heart was pounding in her chest.

Per turned to her. 'Do you have a fear of flying?' he asked.

She nodded. 'Loathe it.'

'But you travel to exotic places all the time, how do you cope?' said Per.

Charlotte followed the others boarding with her gaze. With several flights cancelled, the plane was full. She inspected every person who went past. Scanned them for suspicious behaviour.

'I fly in private planes or business class. The further forward you sit, the less turbulence you feel.'

Per put on his seat belt. When all the passengers were finally ready, the captain's voice was heard in the loudspeakers.

'Was that why you had a glass of wine at the airport?' said Per. 'It's going to—'

'Quiet!' Charlotte interrupted him. She wanted to hear the captain, who was talking about good weather for flying and landing within an hour. When he was done she turned to Per again. 'Yes, what did you want to say?'

'It's going to be fine,' he said.

'You don't know that. So how does it feel to leave Mia by herself at home with the kids now?' she asked to change the subject.

'Well, this is the first time since her diagnosis. But she's stronger and will get help with Simon and Hannes from her friends,' said Per.

Charlotte nodded but felt like a poor friend to his wife because she didn't have time to be there for her herself. But in the next moment she had something else to think about. Because when the plane rolled out toward the runway, her muscles tensed. Her nerves became like uncooked spaghetti – hard and fragile at the same time. Charlotte looked at the upright tray table in front of her. Followed its edges with her gaze. She took in air, held her breath, counted to three and slowly breathed out, while her eyes continued to trace the upper edge of the tray until she came to the corner. Then she repeated the same procedure but now let her gaze run along one side of the tray. As the plane accelerated she slavishly continued her controlled breathing and thought exercise, and didn't deviate from it when the wheels left the ground, which kept her panic in check.

The cabin shook and she closed her eyes, felt cold sweat seeping through her shirt. Her nails were pressed against the armrest. Her jaw was firmly clenched. She breathed rapidly through her nose. But then the plane settled and levelled out. Charlotte took as much air into her lungs as she could and opened her eyes. Saw white

235

clouds close to the window. They were about to break through them. Per held his hand on her arm. She hadn't even noticed that he'd placed it there.

'Are you going to be afraid during the whole flight or is it take-off that's worst?'

Without relaxing she looked at him. 'The whole trip. But if there's no turbulence I can talk. Otherwise it will be an hour of total anxiety.'

'It's hard to understand how it feels when you're not afraid of flying yourself,' said Per.

The sign with the safety belt was turned off and the flight attendants started to work. Charlotte pulled on her belt. With strong turbulence anything at all could happen.

'I'm in therapy and I've been given exercises to do when I fly. But it's so deep-seated in me,' she said, opening her jacket a little.

'Do you want anything?' Per asked when the beverage cart came up to them.

'Wine.'

'Wine?'

'Yes, for my nerves.'

'Do you always drink when you fly?'

'Yes, if it's not a morning flight or if I'll be driving. Then I have to live with the fear.'

He made sure that she got her red wine and she poured it in the plastic cup, drinking half in one go.

Per laughed. 'Charlotte von Klint, you are an extremely complex and interesting person. You can barge straight ahead, without hesitating, to a man who's wearing a bomb vest, but you're scared to death of losing contact with the ground.'

'Research should be done on me,' she said, laughing while she took another sip, awaiting the calming intoxication that would soften the uncooked spaghetti.

236

The full plane prevented them from talking about the cases. Instead they made plans to have dinner at Per and Mia's the next weekend. If work allowed it.

When the wheels of the plane landed again on solid ground Charlotte was slightly tipsy and in a considerably lighter mood. Both of them turned on their phones. There was pinging all around the cabin, but Per and Charlotte got the most pings.

'So what is it now?' he said, reading his messages.

Charlotte looked out of the window. Arlanda airport was lit up. She hadn't been in Stockholm for several months and hoped to have time to see Anja too. Her daughter who apparently wanted to be a police officer.

She looked through her messages. One was from Alex.

Exactly how drunk are you after the flight? ;-) I've sent the autopsy report to you and Per. Samir had traces of Rohypnol in his blood.

Charlotte showed the text to Per, who nodded seriously. 'Rohypnol in the blood,' he said. 'Just like Lena.'

47

Per had rented a car at Arlanda and now they were on their way to see Lena Bengtsson's ex-husband, who lived in Solna. The same man who had stood in the forest and spied on Lena and her daughter after the divorce.

It was dark out and it was really a bit late to go to the ex-husband's home on a Sunday. Per wondered what type of man they would meet. Anna had dug into his life; on the surface everything looked perfect apart from the assault conviction.

'It will be interesting to see what kind of person Bengtsson is,' said Charlotte as if she'd read his thoughts.

She took out Anna's report and read aloud from it while Per drove. Considering the wine she'd had, Charlotte really shouldn't be working, he thought.

'Previously the ex-husband earned over three million kronor a year as CEO for a company that sells heat pumps. According to Anna, Lars Bengtsson was not well liked as a corporate leader and when he went to prison he was fired by the board. Most people seem to be afraid of him. A few use the word "narcissist". What do you think, Per? Such a personality type probably has a hard time being abandoned. They take it as an insult.'

'In any event he agreed to see us without any counterclaims,' said Per, 'except that his attorney must be present. Maybe out of simple curiosity, to find out what happened to his ex-wife.'

Per guided the car between the lanes of Stockholm traffic heading into the city.

He and Charlotte made small talk about the case on the way. It had been several years since Per had been in the capital. He preferred Norrland, but as they travelled south on E4 he still looked forward to his brief visit to Stockholm.

After half an hour he stopped the car outside the ex-husband's two-storey house.

'We're here now,' said Per, turning off the engine. 'Lars has a nice place, but was sentenced for aggravated assault. Wonder if the neighbours know.'

'In Stockholm you don't keep track of your neighbours,' said Charlotte. 'You say hello and talk a little, but my experience is that you don't get involved.'

The temperature outside was warmer than in Umeå, so Per didn't bother to put on his jacket for the short walk to the front door. The granite slabs on the ground were lit up by path lights on either side. The plastered white facade was well illuminated. Per wondered who paid the bills for the house while the ex-husband was in prison. He was just about to press the doorbell when the door opened.

'Hello! Welcome!' the ex-husband said, smiling broadly.

Per had seen a photograph of him but reality reinforced the image. He was of medium height, with short, well-groomed, ash-coloured hair. Brown eyes that drooped down and made him look sad. Narrow face, thin lips and slumped shoulders. It was hard to imagine Lena's ex-husband as violent.

He asked them to come in. Pointed to a woman who met them in the hall. She introduced herself as Lars's attorney.

The inside of the house was hardly modern, but not old either. Per took off his shoes and noted that Charlotte followed his example this time and did the same.

They were shown into the kitchen and sat down at a white table. The ex-husband was calm. He looked neither stressed nor worried. They knew from the daughter that he had a new wife, but she didn't seem to be at home, or else they were separated. Per hoped the latter.

Charlotte told Lars why they were there and Per let her take charge because she would soon take over his role.

'So Lena is dead?' said Lars, leaning forward to Charlotte over the kitchen table, which was set with a thermos, cups and a plate of pastries. It reminded Per of conference room coffee breaks.

'Yes, we're sorry,' said Charlotte.

The ex-husband nodded, looking down at the table. 'Our daughter, how is she doing?'

'Emelie is grieving.'

'Can you tell her that I want to see her?'

'We'll do that,' said Charlotte. 'Can you tell us why you divorced Lena?'

'Divorced her? It was Lena who left me. I didn't understand a thing when it happened.'

'We've understood that your marriage was rather violent.'

'Who said that?' asked Lars.

'There is documentation,' Charlotte replied.

'Not at all. Lena reported me once but retracted her police report when she realized that she was wrong.'

Per's phone vibrated in his pocket but he ignored it. Instead he took a cup and poured coffee for himself. He looked at Charlotte who was shaking her head at Lars's response. Then Per met the ex-husband's sad eyes. Lena had retracted her report out of fear, nothing else, the daughter had told them.

'What did you feel when Lena wanted a divorce?' asked Charlotte.

Lars's gaze was back on the table. 'Sadness,' he answered.

'We know that you made life rather difficult for Lena after the separation. For example, you threatened her. Was that your way of showing how sad you were?'

The ex-husband pursed his lips. 'Is that what you think? That I've been sitting here planning her death?'

'Did you?'

'What do you believe?'

'We don't believe anything, we look for facts,' said Charlotte.

'You know that she was mentally unstable, right? That was why she reported me. I was innocent. She was jealous of me and my success, and wanted to get revenge.'

Classic narcissist, thought Per.

'But you just got out of prison, where you were serving a sentence for the aggravated assault of your new wife,' said Charlotte, looking around.

The man laughed and leaned backwards. His hair glistened in the sharp light from the ceiling. 'I was wrongly convicted. She made it all up. The Swedish legal system is a scandal.'

'What were you doing the night between the twenty-seventh and twenty-eighth of August?'

The ex-husband took one of the store-bought cinnamon rolls that were on the plate, broke off a piece and stuffed it in his mouth. He took out his phone and opened the calendar.

'Let's see now,' he said.

Per took a sip of coffee, which tasted bitter. He also heard Charlotte's phone vibrating – someone was trying to reach her.

'Yes, damn it, that was the night,' the ex-husband said, smiling. 'I was having sex with a very attractive woman from Kista.'

'Where did this happen?' said Per, hoping to avoid hearing further details.

'At her place. But we met on Söder, at a bar there.'

'Does this woman have a name and number, so that we can check your alibi?' Charlotte asked.

The ex-husband started poking at his phone again. 'Now you're in luck. I don't usually ask for phone numbers after a one-night stand, but this time I did because she was so amazing.'

He wrote down the information on a piece of paper and then turned to Per. 'Now then, we've cleared up the suspicions against me. How did my Lena die?' said Lars, fixing his eyes on him.

'You do understand that we're going to check your alibi, as my colleague just said?' Per asked.

The ex-husband nodded. 'Be my guest. So what happened with her?'

'Unfortunately we can't go into that, but she was severely assaulted.'

'And you suspect me? I don't assault people.'

Per laughed.

'Listen now,' the ex-husband said with his gaze fixed on Per. 'I didn't murder her, but in my opinion, Lena got what she deserved. She was a bad person. It's not a crime to think that. When she left me, she took our kid with her, wanted sole custody, and slandered me as a violent lunatic. Ironic that she encountered a real one.'

Per thought about the conversation they'd had with the daughter. She had described a man who didn't hesitate to use violence, and what Per saw in front of him was a person who totally denied everything he subjected his partners to. He sat there like a well-brought-up schoolboy with sad eyes.

'Did you want joint custody of your daughter?' asked Charlotte.

Lars brought his hand over his head. 'I did everything for Lena. But it wasn't enough. And I would have been an amazing father, if I'd had the chance. Now my daughter is grown up and doesn't even know me.'

That was not an answer to Charlotte's question. Per looked at her; her jaw was clenched.

'Tell us about your life together with Lena.'

'I had a good job, earned an incredible amount of money. We lived in a nice house in Täby. Lena could study, while I paid all the bills and spoiled her. Do you understand? And my daughter got whatever she pointed at, even after the divorce. Isn't that nice? But I didn't get to see her because Lena . . . And did I argue about that? No. I did everything she wanted. I tried to explain that, although she didn't want to listen.'

'But if it was so good, why did she want to leave you?'

'Because she was an ungrateful fucking whore who brain-washed my daughter.'

There was a glimpse of the man that Lena had been afraid of, thought Per.

'Your daughter is an adult now and makes her own decisions,' said Charlotte.

Lars got up and took a few steps. Per and Charlotte followed him out of the kitchen.

'You wanted to know if I killed Lena,' said the ex-husband. 'The answer is no. If you want to take it further, speak with my attorney.'

He held out his arm and led them back to the hall. The attorney gathered up her papers behind them. She had been unusually quiet, but her client wasn't charged with any crime.

'When was the last time you talked with or saw Lena?'

'Maybe two weeks ago. The bitch refused to open the door when I was going to leave a present for her. She had a birthday, you know.'

'When was that?'

'Before she went to Umeå. I placed the package outside the door. I'm a good person, you see. Not the way she depicts me.'

'What did you get for her?' asked Charlotte.

Lars laughed. 'That has nothing to do with you, that's between me and her . . . Or was,' he said, making a gesture toward the front door.

When they'd left the ex-husband's house they walked in silence to the car.

Per entered the number of the woman in Kista, but only got a voice message that it was no longer in service.

'Either he's lying or else the woman has changed numbers. We have to check up on that,' he said.

At the same moment Per's phone rang. It was Alex, who presumably was the one who had tried to reach him and Charlotte during the interview.

'Hi, Alex. You're one persistent Gothenburg guy.'

'Hi there. Yes, you were hard to get hold of, anyway.'

'Can you check on a phone number for us?' asked Per.

'Uh, of course. Just send it over. But there's something you need to know that showed up just now. That was why I tried to reach you.'

'What?'

'There's another victim.'

48

Per parked the car and got out on Floragatan, the street where Charlotte's apartment in Stockholm was. He looked up at the facade. White stone with stucco, imposing wooden door in the entrance and a flowerbed that framed the building.

Alex hadn't called back yet about the number they'd asked him to check on, but the big news was that there was another victim. He would email all the information and Per obsessively checked his inbox.

'Are you coming?' said Charlotte, entering the code to the outside door.

'Do you have anything edible?' asked Per, following her. 'It's ten o'clock and we'll probably have to work a little before we go to bed.'

He stood behind Charlotte while she pressed the button for the lift, which rattled noisily on its way down to the ground floor. The iron grille looked worn and at least a hundred years old.

'We'll order take-out – there's a neighbourhood restaurant nearby that delivers,' she said as if it were the most obvious thing in the world.

The lift slowly glided downward and once it arrived, stopped abruptly. It was small and they had to crowd together to make room.

'Now we've talked with the ex-husband, anyway. We'll have to see what that produces,' said Charlotte, setting her handbag on top of the carry-on. 'Tomorrow we'll go to the hunting store on Kungsgatan and hopefully find out who bought the vest Samir was wearing, if it was even purchased there, and then we'll go to Lena's apartment and see if we find anything that can help us move forward. Have I missed anything?'

Per shook his head.

The lift took them to the top floor of the building. Her door was the only one on that floor and was directly connected to the lift. Three locks had to be opened before they were inside. Charlotte turned off the alarm and hung up her jacket. Then she took a hanger and reached out to take his. She took off her boots and put her feet in a pair of ballerina shoes that were on the hall floor. Per entered in socked feet.

'Have a seat, I'll order some food,' she said, disappearing up a stairway to the left.

Per moved further into the apartment. Straight ahead was a large living room with an open fireplace. The furniture was a mixture of modern and old-fashioned. The parquet floor creaked under his feet; lamps were turned on in several places. *She must have everything on timers,* he thought, turning into another room to the right. There was a dining room table with twelve chairs and a large candelabra in the middle. Per kept going. It was like a labyrinth of rooms. The kitchen looked recently renovated, and clean. He looked into an adjacent room, which was girlish. Must be Anja's.

'Do you like my apartment?' Charlotte asked, who appeared behind Per and brought him back to the room with the dining room table. There she spread out the investigation material.

'What can I say? It's big,' he said with a laugh. 'What's on the upper floor?'

'My bedroom, bathroom, office, balcony . . .'

246

'How big is this place anyway?'

'Two hundred and fifty square metres – too big, really, but . . . well . . . The food is on its way. It will be here in about half an hour.'

Per nodded and looked at the chest of drawers on one side of the room which was covered with framed photographs of Anja. There were also pictures of who he assumed were Charlotte's parents and others who seemed to be girlfriends.

Per sat down at the table. Charlotte turned on the chandelier in the ceiling. He started at the powerful illumination; it was as if a sun had been lit. Then he checked his email again.

'Now we've got more information from Alex. He has mainly called around to medical examiners in other cities to see if they've taken in deceased with teeth extracted, or with a V-mark on the arm.'

Charlotte listened attentively.

'According to Alex, a homeless man was found badly beaten in Stockholm . . . What does he say . . . ?' Per searched in the email. 'Yes . . . two years ago. The victim had twelve teeth extracted, although the cause of death itself was overdose. It was investigated as homicide or contributing to another's death, but the case got no further resources and is still unsolved.'

'Overdose of what?' asked Charlotte.

'A combination of Rohypnol and alcohol.'

'Rohypnol, like our victims,' she said.

'Exactly. Here we have a specific pattern, especially with the teeth being extracted. It may possibly be the same perpetrator as in Lena's case, but of course it's too soon to say,' said Per as Charlotte went out into the kitchen. There was rattling in the drawer as she took out cutlery. Then she came back to the room and set the table.

'Although the question is why Samir's death was different,' said Charlotte, disappearing out to the kitchen again. 'Why was he blown up?' she called from there. 'From what we can see in the video, his teeth were intact when it happened.'

Per fixed his gaze on a painting and thought about what she was saying. Perhaps the murderer had changed their approach.

'Can we meet the detective chief inspector in Stockholm?' said Charlotte from the doorway.

'Yes, I'll try to arrange a meeting tomorrow,' he replied. 'Alex also attached the scanty investigation about the incident.'

'Was there a V on the arm?' she asked.

'Nothing that seems to be documented in the file,' said Per while he read. 'Although that doesn't have to mean that the victim in Stockholm lacked such a mark.'

Charlotte took out a bottle of red wine and placed two large wine glasses on the table. Then she went over to the fireplace in the adjoining room and brought it to life. The open plan meant that Per could watch what she was doing.

'Must have a little fire when I'm here,' she said. The subdued light from the next room spread to the dining room, and the logs crackled pleasantly. He understood why she was comfortable here. The apartment was large, but all the rooms hung together somehow.

Per looked at the clock, which showed 10.32 p.m. It was too late to call the detective. They would have to wait until tomorrow.

'It doesn't feel good that yet another victim has turned up . . . So we have Lena – a woman who was on the streets of Umeå as homeless but wasn't. She was found with all her teeth extracted and with a V-mark on her arm. She had Rohypnol in her blood and had probably been held captive. Then we have Samir, a criminal with no fixed address, who we suspect took up the chase after Lena's murderer. He was blown up, also with Rohypnol in his blood and a V on his arm. And now we can add a homeless man in Stockholm who was found two years ago with almost half of his teeth pulled

248

out. Cause of death: overdose with the same drug. What are we dealing with here?'

The doorbell rang, but Charlotte didn't move from where she was.

'Do we know if Samir had the mark on his arm before he disappeared without a trace that Saturday night?' she asked.

The doorbell was heard again and Charlotte went to answer it while Per kept talking.

'We asked Ibrahim and according to him it wasn't there the last time he saw Samir, not as far as he noticed anyway . . . So Samir must have got it during the week he was missing, from the murderer.'

Per realized that this confirmed their theory.

He expected that the food would be delivered in the hall. Instead a man came into the room with a chef's apron under his jacket. Charlotte followed, placed a hand on his shoulder and introduced the men to each other.

'It's been a long time, Charlotte. We've missed you,' the chef said, taking out several containers of food. Per counted five of them. He watched while the man carefully laid out baked potatoes, veal fillet with red wine sauce and vegetables on their plates. The chef set a spoonful of sauce on the meat and placed two cloth napkins on the table. Finally he picked up two smaller containers.

'Your dessert,' he said, looking satisfied.

What is this? thought Per. *What happened to delivery to the door?*

Charlotte paid with Swish on her phone, thanked him and followed the man out. Per took the opportunity to pour wine and check his blood glucose. It was too high for him to be able to eat, so he would have to inject himself in the stomach, again. The thigh would have been preferable, but he didn't want to unzip his trousers in front of Charlotte, who came back into the room. Instead he put the syringe right above his navel and it stung.

His thoughts were whirling around the summary that Charlotte had made. He was becoming more and more convinced that they were dealing with one and the same murderer.

His musings were interrupted by the phone.

'Who's calling this late?' he said, taking a look.

Alex.

'Hi, Charlotte and I are here,' Per answered, putting the call on speakerphone.

'Hi, Lottis and the boss,' said Alex, and Per smiled at Charlotte's nickname. They must have been more than colleagues, he was even more certain. The only reason that Per didn't ask her flat out was his fear of the answer. If it was yes, he had a responsibility in how the matter should be handled. Right now he was playing ostrich.

Charlotte took a sip of wine and sat down at the table.

'Hi,' she said. 'How's it going?'

'Good, we're working away here while you're enjoying yourselves in the big city.'

'If talking with a genuine narcissist in Solna counts as a pleasure then we're guilty as charged,' said Per, taking a bite of food. 'Tell us what's happening with you.'

'Lots of things are happening here,' Alex said quickly. 'We'll start with Lena's ex-husband's alibi. The phone number he gave you previously was to a woman in Kista, but she recently changed numbers. I'm in the process of looking into that now.'

'Do we know anything new about Roger Ren, who made threats against Samir on the internet?' asked Charlotte.

'Not yet, but it's under investigation.'

Per looked at Charlotte before he answered Alex. 'Good. But if he has a watertight alibi, we shouldn't waste any energy on that track. And find this woman in Kista.'

'What else? You said that things were happening?' said Charlotte, sounding impatient.

'I thought you would never ask, Lottis.'

Per saw that Charlotte was offended but not irritated.

'Your colleague Kicki asked if we could go out and have a beer sometime,' said Alex, and his laughter echoed out of the phone on the table.

Per didn't know what to say. Was he teasing Charlotte or was this some kind of inside joke between them?

She didn't touch her food but held on to the wine glass, leaning back with her feet on the chair beside her. More relaxed than he'd ever seen her in Umeå.

Charlotte leaned forward to get close to the phone.

'I'll pray for you, Alex,' she said, ending the call.

'What was that about?' asked Per.

'Nothing.'

'Why should you pray for him if he has a beer with Kicki?'

She dived into the food, her gaze mischievous. This was a different Charlotte than he was used to.

'I can just as well tell you now, because you're going to notice it soon anyway. Alex is deeply religious – I mean, for real. He says grace before meals, he goes to church and is a real charmer besides. You're going to have your hands full with him.'

'*You're* going to, not me,' said Per, enjoying talking about things other than murder and misery. Even if she hadn't answered his question.

49

MONDAY, 5 SEPTEMBER

Ibrahim looked at the cars driving past. It was lunchtime and he was already done with class for the day. Klara was off too, as her teachers had a training day, so now the two of them were sitting at the Nybro bakery cafe having coffee and pastries. The outdoor seating was open but the cloudy weather kept them inside. It was easier for them to meet again, because Klara's parents no longer suspected Ibrahim of involvement in the explosion.

'Thanks for paying,' said Klara. 'My wallet's at the Stenlunds'. I forgot it when I was babysitting there for a while last Friday. I have to go get it.'

He snorted at her. 'You said you wanted to treat me because we were going to celebrate something, and now I'm the one who has to pay for the party,' he said sarcastically.

She stuck her tongue out at him. 'I'll pay you back in kind.'

'What do you mean by that?'

Klara laughed. 'That means you pay someone back, but not with money. That can mean lots of different things.'

He shook his head. 'I don't always get what you're saying.'

'Really?' said Klara, before she changed the subject and started to speak in a more serious tone. 'Anyway, it's worth celebrating that you have a chance for a lighter sentence for those robberies.'

Ibrahim took a large piece of princess cake and nodded. It was a simplified version of things, but he didn't want to argue.

'Is that why you wanted to treat me to coffee? I'm not dismissed from the homicide investigation yet, so maybe there isn't that much to celebrate.'

Klara leaned forward across the table. Whispered. 'No, we're celebrating that you passed the SFI course. You'll easily get into high school now – the term has barely started.'

She was happier than he was about his study successes. For himself, the events of the last week sat like a machine gun poked in his chest. Samir was dead and Omar had left Umeå. He was without them for the first time since his family had died. He was suspected of murder too. Ibrahim had dreamed of being free from Samir and now he was, he couldn't be happy.

'What's going on with you?' said Klara.

He shrugged. 'Don't know. I have a funny feeling, feel like I'm being watched. Omar said the same thing.'

'I'm sure it's nothing.'

'Do you see the man over there?' he whispered, leaning forward. 'I've seen him several times. He's everywhere I am.'

Klara turned around and looked. She thought he was exaggerating; that man looked like a father of small children and like he worked in an office. Very dull. Why would he follow Ibrahim?

'And the police asked strange things about Samir, for example if he had some mark drawn on his arm before he disappeared.'

Klara's eyes got bigger. 'You didn't tell me that. What kind of mark?'

'They didn't say why they were asking, but they showed a picture. It looked like a V, drawn with a blue pen. The police wanted to know if Samir had something like that on his arm. A really shady question.'

'I agree,' said Klara. 'Did he?'

'No, I've tried to replay our last encounter over and over again in my head. I know that he didn't. The question is, why did they want to know that?'

'Maybe because someone who's been robbed saw a mark like that on the robber,' said Klara, going around the table and sitting down beside him. 'Don't worry about it.'

She was right, thought Ibrahim, it might be that simple. He felt her hand on the inside of his thigh. Her back swayed, she pouted her lips, tousled her blonde hair. He laughed at her exaggerated tricks.

'There now, good . . . Smile, damn it,' she said and kissed him.

His body wakened to life from her eagerness. He looked to the side, aware that they weren't alone at the cafe, and carefully pushed her away.

'Okay, okay, I get it,' he said with a smile. 'Calm down, otherwise we'll have to go home and screw.'

Klara grimaced. 'Meh! I hate it when you talk like that. It's crude. It sounds like you're just going to use me, like, without caring.'

Her sweet comment made him burst into laughter. *If you only knew how men talk*, he thought.

'So what do you want me to say?'

Klara squirmed. 'I don't know, something sweet. Like that we should go home and . . . cuddle?'

The machine gun in his chest was replaced by a bubble in his stomach. His laugh echoed across the cafe.

'You're never going to get me to say that. Cuddle. Not a chance. Give me a different word, a good word.'

'How about "go to bed"?' she suggested. 'But that's so common, really boring.'

'Sounds like you're just going to sleep,' said Ibrahim.

'Better than screw, which is crude.'

Klara appeared to think while she took a spoonful of his cake. 'Okay, this then,' she said. 'Dance. Shall we dance?' She held out her arms and smiled broadly. Super-satisfied.

Ibrahim pulled her to him. Kissed her head. For a few minutes she had put him in a better mood. With Klara life was simpler. Nicer.

'"Dance" works. Want to go to your place and dance?'

They forced down the last of the treats and went toward the exit. On the way there they walked past the man Ibrahim thought seemed suspicious. He didn't even try to conceal that he watched them.

The machine gun in his chest was back.

Who was that guy?

50

Liam and Elsa got out of the car. They'd had an unusually short school day for a Monday. Something with the teachers, Erik didn't really know. He himself stayed in the car outside the house. He'd got the Nokia back from Klara and now took it out of the inside pocket of his jacket. Looked at it anxiously. The phone guy hadn't found anything usable. Completely blank, he said. No numbers, no calls made. Erik didn't understand a thing. Helen was in contact with her father again, and lied about it too. He thought about the message her father had sent to her usual phone. *Well done, darling.* What did that mean? What had Helen done? And Erik's best lead had been that extra phone. Had he been imagining things? Made too big a deal of it? But if the Nokia phone wasn't used, why did she hide it?

Erik left the car and went into the house. In the hall he hung up his jacket and stopped. The children were sitting in the kitchen right ahead of him. Liam was munching on an apple and doing his homework. Elsa sat bent over a colouring book and took no notice of her father.

'Mum's home,' said Liam.

'What? Already?' Erik was sincerely surprised. 'Where is she?'

'The bedroom, I think,' said Liam.

Erik had the Nokia with him in his jeans pocket. Now he needed to put it back in the right place in the laundry basket. It was hard to let go of the thoughts of Helen's strange behaviour lately. The meetings with the person in the Volvo that he couldn't trace. The contact with her father and the calls at night that the neighbour had told him about. *I must confront her*, he thought, and placed himself in the doorway to their bedroom.

Helen was lying on the bed with her clothes on and her back to him. What was she doing there? It was just after one o'clock in the afternoon.

'Are you sleeping *now*?' he asked.

She neither replied nor moved.

'Why are you home in the middle of the day?' said Erik, still standing by the door. He had a need for distance. Being close to Helen got harder and harder, the more strange things kept appearing.

'Why are you home yourself?' she asked.

'Have you talked with your boss, who was looking for you last week? You have to call her if you're not working,' said Erik.

Helen turned and looked at him. 'You're suffocating me, Erik. Leave me in peace for five minutes!'

'What? Are you angry?' he asked.

'No.'

'So why are you shouting?'

Helen sat up. 'I'm not shouting,' she said, getting up from the bed. Erik placed himself in her way as she was about to leave the room. She looked at him but didn't say anything, simply stood there waiting for him to move.

At last Erik let her leave the room and went to the laundry room, where he stood with both hands on the washing machine and bowed his head. Thought. He needed to do something, but what? Should he call the police? Although what would he say? That his wife had contact with her father again and that she had secret meetings with people? They would laugh at him.

Erik turned his gaze to Helen's piles of clean clothes on the counter. Everything looked neatly stacked. And so it was all over the house. The way Helen liked having it.

'Dad!'

Liam's call interrupted his thoughts.

'Yes?' Erik answered.

'Dad, come here!'

Erik went to the kitchen. 'What is it?' he asked, suddenly discovering that his son had a knife in his hand. 'What are you doing with that?' Erik took two steps forward. 'Children shouldn't play with knives,' he said.

'I'm just cutting a slice of apple,' said Liam, holding it up.

Erik took the knife from him, well aware that his son was old enough to handle it. But knives had an unfortunate history in the family; Liam had cut his arm when he was little.

'What did you want?' asked Erik.

'Can you check my homework?' his son said.

Erik nodded. He fixed his gaze on Elsa, who was still completely engrossed in her colouring book.

'How long is Mum going to sleep?' Elsa asked, taking her eyes off the colouring book.

'She's not sleeping. I don't know what she's doing.'

'Where is Mum going?'

Erik looked questioningly at Elsa. 'Mum's not going anywhere. Where did you get that idea from?'

'She packed a bag yesterday,' Elsa said defiantly.

51

Charlotte looked to the left and stopped the car at the red light. There was Humlegården, considered one of the most dangerous parks in Stockholm after dark. She signalled right, turned on to Linnégatan. They had just been at police headquarters and met the person who'd led the investigation of the homicide in Stockholm two years earlier. But he didn't have much to add to what was already in the report.

'Do you think we're dealing with a serial killer?' she said, but sounded just as doubtful as she felt.

Per took a deep breath and exhaled through his nose.

'We need to find out if our new homeless victim had a V-mark on him,' she added.

Per nodded. 'I'll ask the perpetrator profile group to compile a new profile of our murderer.'

'Is this a person who travels for work or does the perpetrator live in those areas?' asked Charlotte. 'We're talking Stockholm and Umeå. The victims are vulnerable, homeless. Something triggers violence. The teeth may be trophies that are kept. And the violence seems to escalate – it gets more extreme.'

Charlotte tried to understand. She turned down into her favourite car park on Linnégatan in the vicinity of Stureplan.

She had spent many nights there when she was young at the trendiest bars. Nowadays more and more criminals hung out there to rub elbows with the in-crowd and that had made the area much more dangerous. But the glamour around the district still remained.

'The most important thing now is that we keep this away from the press,' said Per. 'Otherwise we'll create panic and that will hamper the investigation. Then we must find DNA or other linking evidence. All we have right now are theories.'

'First and foremost we must have a perpetrator,' said Charlotte, parking the car. It was time for lunch at Taverna Brillo. She would treat Per to their vendace roe pizza.

'We'll just have a quick bite, then go to the hunting store and Lena's apartment,' said Per as they left the car park on foot.

Charlotte met several people she knew on the short walk to the restaurant. Stopped, smiled, cheek kissed, introduced Per, who responded politely. A woman who was an old classmate from Lundsberg. One man was an acquaintance she'd met several times with Carl. The person she was happiest to see was a woman whose daughter had been in the same class as Anja.

'That's a lot of cheek kissing,' said Per as they walked on.

'The interesting thing is that I've weaned myself from kisses during my time in Umeå. I tried to hug the first woman, did you see that? She got extremely uncomfortable.'

Then Charlotte had to continue the greetings as they stepped into the restaurant – the staff knew her and they were shown to a centrally located table. Once they'd sat down, Per looked around.

'Look, there's a woman who's on TV. What's her name? From *News Morning* on TV4.'

Charlotte glanced discreetly over her shoulder. 'Jenny Strömstedt.'

'Yes, of course, that's her.'

Two glasses of bubbly were placed on the table.

'This is on the house,' said the waiter.

'Thanks, dear, but I'm driving today,' said Charlotte.

She'd forgotten what it was like to go out in this neighbour-hood in Stockholm. It was like her own patch. Familiar, where she felt spoiled. They ordered their food and ate without talking work in the crowded restaurant.

'Hey, Charlotte!'

Both of them looked up at the same time, mid-bite.

Damn, she thought and stood up. *More cheek kissing.*

'Hi, Marie,' said Charlotte, sitting down immediately. Demonstratively.

'What are you doing in town?'

'Working.'

'Ooh, exciting. To think that you became a police officer. We never predicted that when we were young,' the woman said, laughing out loud at herself.

Charlotte had a smile on her lips but inside she felt anything but friendly. That woman was part of her former circle of friends and one of those that Carl had the bad taste to sleep with while they were married. Marie still didn't know that Charlotte was aware of that. And Charlotte didn't care to have that conversation. In Umeå she was shielded from all the women he'd slept with. Money and power attracted people who were climbing the social ladder, the ones who stepped on others to move upward. Carl had finally worked his way really high up, and he had exploited many to reach that goal.

'May I sit down a moment?' her old acquaintance said, sitting down. 'Who is this handsome fellow?'

Charlotte noted that she wasn't even looking at Per.

'This is Per Berg, my colleague with the Umeå police.'

He extended his hand, but she was already leaning toward Charlotte.

'So what about Carl? Do you miss him?'

Charlotte closed her eyes for a moment. The woman was just as brash as she'd always been. 'No, I've traded up.'

'What? Who? Anyone I know?'

'He's from Umeå.'

Her old acquaintance burst into laughter. Charlotte sighed and took a bite of her pizza. Prayed to higher powers that the woman would catch sight of someone else and leave them.

'By the way, what's going on with that explosion in Umeå? Do tell!' Her eyes widened, as if it was obvious that she would get gossip from a police investigation.

'We can't say anything about that,' said Per, leaning forward. 'Hi, as Charlotte said, my name is Per. We're having a working lunch and need to talk privately.'

He extended his hand again and the woman responded to the gesture with a brief handshake. But she got the hint and stood up.

'Charlotte, don't be a stranger. Call me. Ta-ta,' she said, going to the nearest table with a celebrity. *Poor Jenny Strömstedt*, thought Charlotte.

'My God, how can you live here?' said Per.

She took a sip of water and placed her hand on his arm. 'I don't any more. But you know, I have many friends who aren't like her. She's actually the worst of them all. False, calculating, manipulative and heartless. CEO of a recruitment company and sleeps with other women's husbands as if they were trophies.'

Per nodded at her comment and looked at the woman who had just ignored him. Charlotte straightened her hair and found that she had missed what was so obvious here in Stockholm: what played out at the restaurant, the demonstration of who knew whom. Who was the most famous, notorious or recognized – a ranking of human value took place that was quite natural in the middle of lunch. Here she knew her place in the hierarchy, which was preordained by surname, money and contacts. In Umeå she became a different person in the eyes of others. It wasn't obvious who she was there. She missed the social scene in Stockholm sometimes. Even though she hated it too.

'Shall we go?' said Per, scattering her thoughts.

'Yes. I'll get the bill.'

As Per got up, he got a text message and stopped.

'What does it say?' asked Charlotte, tossing her handbag over her shoulder.

He handed his phone over to her.

Västerbottens-Kuriren covered the screen. There was a picture of Lena and a big headline.

The Murdered Woman Under Teg Bridge: Not Homeless

The lead started with: *This was the victim's life before the murder.*

Charlotte sighed deeply. 'How many leaks do we have within the police?'

'They write that she'd been drugged with Rohypnol. But they don't have the most important details: the teeth and the V-mark,' Per whispered.

'It's only a matter of time. We must get further in our investigation before it's all in the news.'

They left the restaurant and aimed for Kungsgatan, where the hunting store was.

'Keep your fingers crossed that we get the name of whoever bought the hunting vest that Samir carried the bomb in,' said Per, turning to Charlotte. 'If the murderer finds out that we're close to

263

a resolution, there's a risk that person will destroy any evidence. For example, the victims' teeth.'

'Or even worse,' said Charlotte. 'The stress of imminent exposure may lead to more victims. The perpetrator may feel that the only way to remove the mental strain is by killing again. The spiral of violence won't end until we stop it.'

52

Klara looked at Ibrahim, who had gone with her to the Stenlunds' to pick up the wallet she'd left there. It was the reason he had to pay for coffee earlier. He wasn't rich in money, but was in other things, she thought, giggling to herself.

'What is it?' asked Ibrahim.

'Nothing, here it is,' she said, pointing at the Stenlund house.

They had taken the bus but had to walk the last bit up to the Stenlund family's home.

'Why didn't we take your moped here?' asked Ibrahim.

'I'm actually thinking about selling it. I never use it, it just stands there outside the garage. I like cycling.'

He shook his head as if he didn't think that was a good idea.

'It looks like they're at home anyway,' she said. She rang the doorbell.

'Come on in!' Erik's call was heard from inside.

Klara opened the door and they stepped into the hall.

'Hi! I left my wallet here and was just going to pick it up.'

'Hi, Klara. Come in,' said Erik. Klara thought he seemed a bit low.

He was sat down at the kitchen table where Helen was having a cup of coffee. She neither looked up nor said hello. It was as if Klara wasn't there.

'Have you seen it? A red wallet with a big wad of cash in it. It's very heavy,' she said in an attempt to get a reaction from Helen. But she just stared straight ahead and slowly brought the coffee cup to her mouth. Ibrahim stayed behind in the hall.

'Have you looked in the living room?' asked Erik.

'I'll check there.'

Klara scanned the room, searching for red. She raised a few pillows, but no wallet. Where had she put it?

She heard Erik invite Ibrahim into the kitchen and felt happy that someone was showing him a little friendliness. Then she went into Elsa's room, where the daughter in the family was drawing in what looked like a workbook.

'Have you seen my wallet?'

'No, check in Liam's room. He takes things,' said Elsa, sounding sincerely angry at her brother.

Klara didn't have time to work out what had happened between the siblings, so she continued to Liam's room. He was sitting with his back to the door playing computer games. Klara took the earphones from his ears. He shrieked in surprise.

'Easy, it's just me,' said Klara. 'Have you seen my red wallet anywhere?'

'What, in here?'

'Somewhere in the house.'

'Nah. Have you checked Elsa's room?'

'I just came from there,' said Klara, looking around. She was rarely in here during the day. 'You have a really nice room.'

Liam sat with the controller in his hand, but had stopped playing and looked at Klara.

'It was cleaning day yesterday,' he said, sounding just as low as Erik seemed when she arrived.

Klara noted that the bed was made. There were fewer things on the bookshelf than she remembered and it felt like it had been tidied up by a manic grown-up.

Helen, thought Klara, shaking her head.

'Okay, you can call or text me if you find it,' she said, pointing to his phone. He picked it up and entered her number as she rattled it off. 'I'll check in the kitchen too. It's here somewhere, I know it.'

Klara tousled Liam's hair, but when she left the room he still looked serious.

She went out to the others. Her jacket was making her sweat, and her back itched.

'Did you find it?' asked Erik.

'No, and we have to go,' said Klara and continued toward the hall.

Ibrahim was leaning against the doorframe into the kitchen. He had his coat on, but had taken off his shoes. He looked tensely toward Erik and Helen.

'Shall we go?' she asked, pulling on his jacket, but he just stood there. His mouth hung open.

'Hello?' she said, putting on her shoes. 'Are you coming or not?'

He turned around, stared at her.

'Ibrahim, what is it? You look like you've seen a ghost.'

53

Per inspected the sign for the hunting store. He stepped in after Charlotte and was met by the smell of leather, metal and forest. The parquet floor creaked under his feet; rugs covered parts of the wood.

This was a world quite far from Per's. Hunting apparel, mostly in shades of green or brown, was hanging along the walls. Except for traces of orange and dark red, bright colours seemed to be banned. A glass case stood by the entrance, full of antique revolvers. On a counter were cans with bird motifs that he guessed contained ammunition for duck hunting.

One part of the shop had gear for dogs, another was full of boots. Charlotte disappeared into an adjacent space – she seemed to know where she was going. Per latched on and stepped into a kind of war room. Guns everywhere. The walls were covered with rifles, and they were in stands in the middle of the floor, others in glass cases. Per realized that he was reacting like an amateur when Charlotte punched him in the side.

'You have to blink, Per, otherwise your eyes will dry out.'

'I'm a policeman and I've never seen so many guns in one place.'

'This is a hunting store,' she said. 'Haven't you ever been in one before?'

'Not really.'

Per turned around when he heard a deep voice.

'Hi, Charlotte, it's been a long time. How are you and your amazing daughter doing?'

More cheek kisses.

The man extended his hand to Per and introduced himself as Robert, the store manager. *Someone who says hello at least*, thought Per.

'Are you happy in Umeå?' asked Robert. 'It's a beautiful city.'

Charlotte replied and her Östermalm accent was distinct; what was soft had once again become razor sharp. The short time they'd been in Stockholm had given him a completely different image of her life here. If she was a celebrity in Umeå, she was royalty here. Everyone wanted to greet her. His respect for her as a person was reinforced. Who could resist that to become a police officer? Say to hell with what's expected and follow their dream? And everyone somehow seemed to buy her choice of career, even if they talked about it as a phase she had to go through.

Robert spoke with the same well-articulated language as Charlotte, and Per inspected him. The man was at least two metres tall. Thick, dark beard, merry eyes. Shiny brown hair with streaks of grey.

Charlotte picked up a gun from the stand in the middle of the room.

'Is this new?' she asked eagerly.

'Of course,' said Robert, happily rubbing his palms together. Per raised his eyebrows. *Does Charlotte hunt?* he wondered, but didn't ask.

He listened while they talked about guns, hunting and other uninteresting things, but got tired at last and went back to the other section and started looking for the type of vest that Samir had worn. He heard Robert's deep voice before they left the arsenal.

'So what can I help you with?' the store manager said, still smiling. He was clearly the most pleasant of her acquaintances so far.

Per took out the picture of the vest that he'd got from Alex.

'You've sold one of these, do you remember that?' he asked.

Robert cast a quick glance at the picture. 'Oh yes, that's the best one on the market. A little too pricey, even for our customers – sells mostly in Europe. A couple of years ago we ordered three of them, mostly just to have them in stock. All three were sold.'

'Do you know who bought them?'

Robert laughed loudly. 'I got one myself immediately. Staff discount.'

More laughter. Per liked Robert.

'One of the buyers was an elderly gentleman by the name of Fredrik Adolfson, maybe about six months ago. Unfortunately he's in hospital now with cancer.'

'Do you have a number for him or his next of kin?'

'My goodness, yes. I visited him at the hospital three days ago.'

'Do you know if he still has possession of the vest?' asked Charlotte.

'Yes, it was actually on a hanger at the hospital. According to his son, he wore it every day before he had to be admitted.'

Per wrote on his notepad and got a number from Robert. If it was correct, then the old man wasn't their perpetrator and could be checked off. They also took information about what Robert himself was doing over the past two weeks and Per didn't think the store manager had anything to hide.

'The third vest then, who bought it?' asked Charlotte.

'Hmm, it was sold by one of my employees. Wait here and I'll get her, she's in the office.' Robert went away.

'He's a likeable guy,' said Per.

'Who? Robert? Yes, he's great.'

'Old friend?'

'Friend of the family. Ladies' man, consumes everything that comes his way,' said Charlotte, laughing.

Per smiled when Robert came back. He could picture how the store manager let the women test fire his guns, how they stood close to each other, aimed.

'Yes, here she is,' said Robert and introduced a young woman before he left them to take care of a customer.

Charlotte showed her the picture of the vest, explained what they wanted to know and the woman nodded.

'I remember her fairly well.'

'Her?' said Per, fixing his eyes on the store clerk, who looked puzzled.

'Yes, it was a woman, however unusual that sounds. That's probably why I remember her, and because she had such anxiety about deciding. She was here for at least an hour and dithered between different vests. It had to have several pockets – she was looking for something quite specific. I never thought she would pick the most expensive one, but she did.'

'Can you describe what this woman looked like?'

'Uh . . . No, not exactly. She was ordinary. Blonde.'

Per looked at Charlotte.

'Do you remember what her face looked like – any particular features?' she asked.

The store clerk shrugged. 'No, except that she was very tanned. As if she'd been on a beach holiday or something. Otherwise I don't remember much about her appearance – it was like I didn't think about it.'

'When was this?'

'A long time ago, maybe two years? Just after we got them in stock. If you want a name I'll have to go back and check the card purchases manually, although that can take a while.'

'Call us when you've done that, preferably as soon as possible,' said Charlotte, handing her a business card.

They left the hunting store.

'A woman,' said Charlotte, sounding just as surprised as Per was.

'A blonde besides . . .' he said. 'In Sweden, that could be just about anyone.'

54

Charlotte turned the key to Lena's apartment, continued to the upper lock and then the one above that, after which she and Per stepped inside. The police had already searched it, but they wanted to see if anything had been missed and form a better understanding of who Lena had been before she ended up under a bridge in Umeå. Could the murderer have been stalking her? They searched for anything that might lead them closer to their perpetrator.

To the left in the hall was an alarm box, which was turned off. A camera was aimed toward Charlotte from the upper corner on the wall.

'She evidently felt threatened by her ex-husband,' she said to Per.

Stepping into a dead person's home was always uncomfortable, Charlotte thought. You were violating a private space.

She took out her rubber gloves and entered the nearest room, which was the kitchen. Lena seemed to have cleaned before she went on the business trip. Charlotte opened the dishwasher. Empty. Turned on the tap in the sink and turned it off. The cupboards were pine, the walls white and a glass cabinet was placed by the round kitchen table on which there was a sewing machine. Four chairs. The whole style exuded IKEA.

There were some pictures on the refrigerator door. The daughter, an older woman who perhaps was Lena's mother. Nothing that stuck out.

Per called from another room. 'Check in the bedroom.'

The apartment was larger than she thought. Charlotte passed two bedrooms that seemed to be for guests. A small bathroom. Lena's living room with picture windows offered a lovely view. The couch would fit more than ten people. Blankets were neatly folded on it. On the low coffee table were two empty wine bottles and a half-empty glass of wine. The drinking must have started before she left, thought Charlotte, looking at the bra hanging over one edge of the couch.

When she turned to the left she came into Lena's bedroom. There was an adjacent bathroom, in which Per was rooting through the medicine cabinet. He showed what medication he'd found, which fitted with her bipolar diagnosis.

'According to the daughter, Lena had been taking her medication recently. The question is what made her stop when she was going to Umeå. See if you can find anything in the bedroom,' he said.

Charlotte turned toward the bed. By the nightstand there was an alarm box from a security company. She had a similar one at home. With it you could turn the alarm off and on from inside the room. When she continued looking around she discovered a camera in one corner and a TV screen right in front of her. It wasn't there to watch movies in bed, but instead to monitor the apartment. Per had turned it on and the black and white images on the screen showed all the rooms except the guest bathroom.

'The apartment is equipped like Fort Knox,' said Charlotte. 'The people at the shelter did say that she felt pursued and thought someone was after her. Maybe this was what she meant? That is, the ex-husband? Lena was afraid of him. Even if he'd met someone new, and things had calmed down a little, she may have stopped taking her meds because of stress over something he did.'

Per came out of the bathroom and they continued searching through the apartment for clues, but all they found were signs of a life lived in fear.

Charlotte stepped into Lena's office – a small room centred around the desk. A cord for charging computers stuck out from one side of it.

'Surely the police haven't confiscated a computer?' she asked.

'No, I don't think so.'

She thought that it must be in Lena's car, which had still not been located. Charlotte went back into the kitchen and flipped through the post that was in a pile on the table. A handwritten letter stuck out. The opened envelope that seemed to belong to it hadn't been posted; there was no address, only Lena's name was on it. Charlotte called to Per.

'It's from the ex-husband that we just met. He asks for the daughter's contact information, harsh in tone but not threatening. Nasty person, when you know what he's done. Although this must have been photographed with the other evidence,' she added.

'Maybe this could explain the empty wine bottles in the living room. One glass but two bottles,' said Per. 'And then the drinking led to her missing medication and it became a downward spiral.'

Charlotte searched through the rest of the post. Bills. They knew that Lena had no financial worries.

'That present the ex-husband talked about, what do you think it was?'

Per looked around. 'There was something in the hall, on the hat rack.'

They went toward the entrance. Sure enough there was an object that looked like a photo album and Charlotte took it down.

'The sort of thing you had years ago, with photographs that you can touch,' said Per.

Charlotte started browsing through the pictures of the ex-husband and Lena. They looked young. Happy. In one of the pictures Lena was very pregnant.

'There's nothing threatening here, but Lena must have perceived it that way,' said Per.

'Yes, that may be so. But he gave it to her a few days before she left. Maybe he knew how she would react to the photo album.'

Before Per could answer her, his phone rang. Out of routine he put it on speakerphone. It was Alex.

'Well, you're going to get some information that you're not going to like.'

'What do you mean?' asked Charlotte.

'I think we have to assume that we're dealing with a serial killer. Everything indicates that,' said Alex.

'We've thought about that too,' said Per.

'It appears that we have as many as four victims,' said Alex.

'What?'

'I've done a little investigating and just had a call from a colleague in Malmö. There we have yet another similar victim. A homeless man they suspected lost three front teeth just before he died.'

'When was this?' asked Per.

'Just over five years ago. The incident was written off after investigation as overdose because the man was a known addict. He had large quantities of Rohypnol in his blood.'

'Were the teeth by the body?' asked Charlotte.

'No.'

'I'll be . . .' she said.

'According to the officer the investigation was closed because there wasn't enough to go on, beyond the three missing teeth,' said Alex.

'Did the man have a V-mark on his body?' asked Charlotte.

'No information about that.'

'In that case the violence has truly escalated with the years,' said Per. 'What do you think about this: the murderer has changed his approach. Maybe "just" extracting the teeth is no longer enough. More spectacular things are needed to achieve satisfaction. Samir was an experiment that fell into the perpetrator's lap. His death seemed staged, almost like something set up for a movie. Send him out with a bomb vest. Create drama and get us to believe it's terror-related.'

'Sounds like a credible theory,' said Charlotte.

'Anna reported that we'll have a new profile of our suspected serial killer tomorrow,' said Alex.

'Okay, good,' said Charlotte, feeling that the word itself was hard to take in. 'What if we're searching for a female serial killer? Because a woman bought the vest, I mean. In that case it's extremely unusual.'

'Statistically the chance is zero, but let's keep an open mind and follow the evidence,' said Per.

'Could there be two perpetrators?' said Charlotte. 'The woman may be an accomplice.'

Per looked at her with surprise. 'You're right about that.'

'Are there more homeless victims out there that no one has bothered about?' said Alex, who was still on the phone.

'And when will the perpetrator strike again?' Charlotte replied.

Per looked at his watch. 'We have to get moving to the airport – our flight departs in two hours.'

55

TUESDAY, 6 SEPTEMBER

Ibrahim sipped the morning tea that only he drank in the family he lived with. The others preferred coffee, but he thought it was bitter. He scrolled on his phone, would soon be going to school. As usual he woke up first; he always did when he didn't sleep with Klara. Now she was at her house and he was here, on orders from her parents. They thought that it was fine for him and Klara to see each other but that they should sleep separately.

Klara usually got up at seven thirty, so he would have to wait an hour and a half until he could call. He poured more tea and thought about Omar. His friend was wanted by the police for the simple reason that he had fled and behaved like a guilty person. Or yet another victim.

Ibrahim no longer knew what to believe, but it was unpleasant. He'd tried to get hold of Omar for several days but came to the same voice message every time.

The number you are calling is no longer in use.

When he went to the campground and searched it was fruitless. The camper Omar was living in with Samir had been impounded. Ibrahim was still a suspect in the murder of the woman, but it didn't feel like the police were after him. On the other hand, he still had a sense of being watched. The man from the cafe showed up in his dreams. Sometimes the stranger was with him in the square in Raqqa, laughing at Ibrahim when he was lying injured on the ground. It felt like he never got to rest from this shadowy person, who actually was not threatening, just present and observant.

Ibrahim had been assigned a case manager from the juvenile unit for robbery by a person his age. He had admitted being guilty of participation and agreed to do a so-called mediation, where he would apologize to the young man and explain why he'd done what he did. Right now the ball was with the victim's family, who could no longer get rectification through Samir. But there were still two people for them to meet. Ibrahim hoped that the mediation would calm the boy's family.

His thoughts were interrupted when he heard someone slip into the bathroom. Apollonia and Martin were evidently waking up, and Ibrahim took three steps to the coffeemaker and turned it on. The machine started gurgling at once. This was a routine he followed every morning when he slept at home. Make coffee for the family. A way to give back.

Martin came into the kitchen in his black bathrobe. His hair was sticking out in all directions. 'Good morning,' he said, patting Ibrahim on the back as he went past.

'Morning,' said Ibrahim, putting his teacup in the dishwasher.

'No Klara today either?' asked Martin.

'No, her parents aren't quite convinced that I'm not a criminal. But of course I am, kind of.'

Martin laughed. 'You're doing the right thing, Ibrahim, by taking responsibility for your participation in the robbery and what you did to that young guy and the older man. You can be proud of that.'

Ibrahim leaned against the kitchen counter. 'Klara's parents don't think so.'

'Give them time. The whole city is in shock. You'll probably have to expect a bit of a rough time ahead just by being a new arrival.'

'Should I take the blame just because I'm an immigrant?'

'No, of course not. But people are afraid. And you represent what they're afraid of. But it will settle down after a while.'

'Although if someone like you, a white Swede, kills someone – then you don't become afraid of all white people, do you?'

Martin laughed again, not least at Ibrahim's description of him.

'That's right, it's like that. Unjust, but true. Maybe it's because we Swedes know so many other Swedes, but are bad at socializing with people from other cultures. Although I don't know . . . It's . . .'

Martin didn't finish the sentence, but Ibrahim thought about what he'd said.

'In a way I'm glad that Samir is dead. It gives me . . . what's it called . . . when you can rest from everything . . . Get more time?'

'Recovery?' his foster father asked.

Ibrahim laughed. 'What does that mean?'

'Or do you mean breathing room?' Martin suggested.

'Yes, maybe. Samir always demanded total loyalty. Now for the first time I can live my life the way I want to.'

Martin took out a cup, filling it with the bitter poison. 'I believe you're going to miss him sometimes. He was an important part of your life before you came to us. Without Samir, maybe you wouldn't be alive today. But I understand what you mean.'

Ibrahim crossed his arms. It was starting to be too cold to go around in a thin T-shirt. He had goosebumps. Martin stood bent over his phone, reading something.

'Your case manager is working on scheduling a mediation with the boy and his family,' he said. 'Have you ever met them? Maybe at the police station?'

Ibrahim shook his head. 'Just the boy, at the robbery, not the parents.'

'The boy is willing to meet you, your case manager says. The mediator has been in contact with social services and the prosecutor and everyone is positive about it. They're trying to include the father – apparently he's the only one opposed to the idea.'

'Does he have the right to do that? It's all about what I did to the son, not his dad.'

Ibrahim wanted to meet the boy they'd robbed. Explain why. Apologize.

Why was the father standing in the way? Shouldn't he want his son to hear an apology from one of the robbers?

Fucking ego, thought Ibrahim, and looked at the clock.

One more hour until Klara would get up.

56

Tuesday morning was a slog, but Per walked quickly toward the briefing room where the perpetrator profile unit would present what they had come up with. In his hand he was holding a juice box. His brain was on half-speed; he was breaking into a cold sweat and hoped that the sugar content would be enough to restore his balance. He and Charlotte had landed in Umeå late the night before, and he had to get up at the crack of dawn to drive his son to hockey practice, and he would soon dump his son's equipment in another ice rink where the team would train later in the day. The logistics from hell, as he liked to call it.

Per stepped into the briefing room and saw that Charlotte was already seated with Kicki, Anna, Alex and Kennet. Those with a need to know – no one could leak to the media now. Charlotte looked up when Per cleared his throat. Her eyes teared and she tried to suppress a yawn.

'Sorry,' she said with a laugh. 'It was a late one last night.'

The woman from the perpetrator profile unit who would be making the presentation stood up alongside Per.

'Yes, thank you, my unit has worked intensively the past twenty-four hours to get a more detailed understanding of what kind of person we're dealing with here. The course of events is worrying to say the least,' she said, placing a folder on the table in front of her. 'We are now convinced that you are on the trail of a serial killer. Most likely a male. He's white, between thirty-five and fifty-five and—'

Charlotte interrupted her by raising her hand like an eager school pupil and started talking before the woman had time to react.

'But, if we follow the leads, it was a woman who bought the vest that Samir was wearing when he was blown up. Could this perhaps be an exception from the statistics?'

'Yes, anything is possible,' the woman replied. 'The victims have been drugged and beaten and are therefore easier to handle. That may suggest a woman. But let me present the results in their entirety, then you can ask questions. I'm going to refer to the perpetrator as 'they'. Okay?'

Charlotte nodded, smiling a little awkwardly. Kicki's sigh was heard across the whole room.

'What you're dealing with here is a person who suffers from an anti-social personality disorder. A psychopath with sadistic tendencies.'

'Yay,' Anna said quietly.

The woman proceeded to read from a document. 'The person you are seeking has difficulty expressing empathy. They may be perceived as emotionally cold, but presumably have learned to function in social situations and act in a way that appears normal. This is behaviour that does not come naturally to your perpetrator, but is instead practised. Basically they are completely free from deeper feelings for others.'

The woman looked up at the group, who sat quietly, before she continued.

'This person has a hard time holding down a job – either they are unemployed or often change jobs. They don't really fit in and after a while become incapable of maintaining their pleasant facade. It starts to crack and then collapses.'

The woman took another pause. Per thought that this was both interesting and frightening at the same time.

'There is an enormous need for control here. As long as everyday life flows according to plan, the person can function normally. When that's not the case, then it starts to boil. It's like shaking a bottle of carbonated beverage; the more you do it, the stronger the pressure and . . . Well, I'm sure you understand?'

Everyone in the room nodded. There was silence for a moment while the woman browsed through her notes. Per's thoughts went to the people they'd met during the investigation. *Who fits this description? Roger Ren? Lena's ex-husband?*

'The perpetrator kills when they are under stress or pressure, when they're feeling bad about something that's going on in their life. So this person may have been fired, abandoned, someone may have died. In other words, this is about events in life that stir things up.'

Per saw that Charlotte was taking notes.

'Extracting the teeth of their victims is a way to denigrate, demonstrate power, create fear and injure. It's a fantasy that is put to work. Then the technique has been refined through experience and audacity. One of your victims here in Umeå, the woman under the Teg Bridge, was held captive, while the others seem to have been attacked at the place where they were later found dead. Maybe the perpetrator wanted to be able to work in peace. Not be stressed, take their time. Work methodically. Planned.'

'So, like with Samir?' said Charlotte.

'Exactly, the same thing there. The person enjoys doing what they do, and the longer it takes, the more enjoyment, so to speak. Thus the captivity.'

The woman looked out over the room and was once again met by silence.

'That's how they're going to work going forward,' she added. 'The violence escalates with each victim too. It won't stop until this person is arrested.'

Per wanted to ask about timelines, but waited.

'Note that the majority of your victims have been found under bridges. Not all by the water, like the woman under the Teg Bridge, but that was why she was dumped there, even though the crime occurred somewhere else. Bridges thus have significance for your perpetrator. Although what happened later with the refugee guy is a deviation from their approach.'

Pet clenched his jaws. Damn, how could they have missed that detail? What she said about the bridges was correct.

'Blowing a person up may have been a way to try to lure the police on to the wrong track,' the woman continued. 'But the perpetrator may also have started exploring new ground. The murder of Samir seemed staged. However, the fact that Lena wasn't homeless ought to have shaken them up. A mistake was made. And that's to your advantage.'

'Hopefully the Mermaid was the beginning of the end,' said Per, thinking of Carola's description of Lena when she was found in the water.

'So what has the perpetrator done with the teeth?' asked Charlotte.

'No teeth have been found at any of the crime scenes, so most likely they've been saved. As trophies, mementoes. But as you surely know, extracting all the teeth of a grown person is not the easiest thing to do. It requires technique and the right equipment.'

'Could it be a dentist?' asked Per.

The woman cocked her head and shrugged. 'I'm doubtful that this person has completed that level of education. Perhaps may have started it, but didn't finish.'

'So what have they taken as a trophy from the murder of Samir?' asked Per.

'That we don't know. Samir was pretty well torn apart by the explosion. You should focus on the mark on the arm, however. There you have a common denominator, along with the drug.'

'Does the perpetrator live here, or how should we search? The victims are scattered across the whole flipping country,' said Anna.

'Yes, that's a problem. In geographical terms these crimes are hard to execute. Travelling around, for example in a job as a salesperson or something similar, doesn't fit into the profile. The perpetrator seeks security, routines. But like I said before, this may concern a person who hasn't been able to hold a job for a long period, and maybe for that reason has moved around.'

'So the lunatic is living here in Umeå now?' asked Kicki.

'Yes, or visiting someone here. For a length of time. A relative, or someone who offers a longer, more or less secure stay. I would check rental cars and hotel bookings.'

'We've done that, with no result,' said Charlotte.

'If they now need to kill again . . .' Per asked. 'When do we risk finding a new body?'

'A long time passed between the three first victims that we know about, in Malmö, Stockholm and Umeå. What is worrying is the extremely short time interval between Lena and Samir. Either the perpetrator will strike again within a few days, or else in several years and presumably in another city.'

'What do you think about the V-mark? What does it mean?' asked Per.

'Our theory is that the person checks off the victims when they are finished with them.'

'But why hatred of just the homeless?' asked Charlotte.

'It could be something from childhood, an incident or a trauma. But it could also be as simple as finding that they are gratifying victims. No one misses them right away. The cases are often investigated carelessly by us and are easy to classify as overdose, as you've seen. That's probably why they drug their victims with Rohypnol.'

'Can we go back to Samir and that completely different type of violence?' asked Charlotte.

'Absolutely. First and foremost it requires patience to plan such an advanced event. Making a bomb is simple enough these days, as you know. Any criminal can find out how to do it, for example with acetone peroxide,' the woman said, and Per could only agree.

'Although that substance easily becomes unstable,' Charlotte objected. 'It can't be stored for a long period because it decomposes and risks exploding on its own. The explosive that was used on Samir is more advanced. How did the person acquire the ingredients and recipe?'

Per looked with surprise at Charlotte. Here was knowledge that hadn't come out earlier.

'That's correct,' the woman said. 'Everything indicates that this was a more advanced explosive. The perpetrator has spent time on it. In combination with the procedure – holding Samir captive, putting him in the vest and taking him to Rådhus Square without being discovered – it means that we have every reason to assume that this person not only possesses an extraordinary capacity for control, but that they are also very intelligent.'

'That's just great,' said Per to himself.

'The stress because of the mistake with Lena, along with the rush of having performed the bombing, presumably is going to increase the need for violence and control even more. That makes this serial killer very dangerous.'

'Lovely,' Charlotte said sarcastically.

'And perhaps careless?' asked Kicki.

'Yes, we can hope so,' said the woman.

'Have we found out if it was a mobile or the detonator that made the bomb go off?' Per asked his group.

'A phone,' said Anna. 'You should have received a report on that in your inbox before the meeting.'

'And that's completely in line with the assumption that we're dealing with a serial killer, not a suicide bomber,' the woman said a little sarcastically. 'By extension, this means that the perpetrator didn't want to kill innocent people, just Samir, who they presumably saw as homeless. Otherwise the bomb would have gone off when the square was still full of people.'

'Shouldn't we try to warn our homeless somehow?' said Kicki.

'That's a tricky question,' said Per. 'The risk is that at the same time we'll have the media rooting through all the evidence. The teeth and the mark on the arm must be kept away from them at the present time.'

Kennet took the floor. 'The perpetrator hasn't left behind any trace of DNA at all. That must mean that the person is extremely knowledgeable in that area too.'

'You're dealing with a perfectionist – nothing is left to chance,' said the woman who thereby concluded the review and thanked them for their attention.

Per praised the quick work and let her leave before he continued the briefing with the group.

'As far as Lena is concerned, we're working based on the assumption that she was abducted the same day she left the shelter. Everything that happened to her that day is of interest – where she went, what she did, etcetera.'

Alex continued. 'If we get a report in of any missing person, we must act immediately.'

288

'But the murderer may also have left Umeå,' said Kicki in a hopeful voice.

Per nodded, turned around and looked at the whiteboard with the victims. He had no idea whatsoever who the perpetrator was. He couldn't even venture a guess.

'None of our informants know of any criminal gang that still sells Rohypnol in the area,' he said. 'But I'll be damned if someone here in town isn't pushing and that person has information about who is buying. And that blonde woman who bought the vest in the hunting store – who is she? Prioritize that. Work from inside the hunting store and out.'

Alex raised his hand, at the same time as he glanced at his phone. 'It's been confirmed that the victim in Stockholm also had a V-mark on one arm. It wasn't noted in the preliminary autopsy report, but was included in the final one that I took out of the archives.'

'Okay, well done,' said Per. 'That confirms our suspicion. The same perpetrator.'

Anna's chair scraped on the floor as she stood up. She was unusually dressed up, her exercise clothes replaced by a wine-red suit that matched her always rosy cheeks. Anna went up to Per with an iPad in her hand. From it she showed images on the TV screen of the explosion at Rådhus Square.

'Kicki and I got the task of analysing Omar's, Samir's and Ibrahim's social media at an early stage in the investigation of the robberies in town. We looked through hundreds of images and didn't see it then, but . . .'

She pointed at one of the photographs on the screen.

'I just discovered that we weren't the only ones keeping track of those guys. Do you see here, someone is standing a short distance away, taking pictures of them with a cap pulled far down?'

Per inspected the photograph carefully. The gang was hanging outside the deli by Strömpilen. A short distance away from them a person was standing there. It was hard to see the face but Per recognized him by his clothing.

Roger Ren. Adrian's father.

57

Charlotte felt nauseated. Per's drive to the ice rink was anything but calm. She was worried that he would have a heart attack from all the stress.

'Is Roger Ren our serial killer?' Charlotte asked as the car stopped abruptly. She had to take deep breaths.

'He's white and the right age,' said Per. 'He has extreme opinions about immigrants and has threatened Samir on an internet forum. But we must find out if there's more that agrees with the perpetrator profile. I just have to do this before we go to see Roger. Come in with me.'

They were about to get out of the car when Alex called. Charlotte wondered whether he'd had that beer with Kicki, but didn't want to ask when Per was around.

'New information about the investigation,' Alex said without saying hello.

'Okay, let's hear it,' said Per, getting ready to open the car door.

'Lena's ex-husband in Solna has an alibi that holds up. I got hold of the woman he claimed to have met.'

'Really?' said Charlotte. 'What did she say?'

'She's changed numbers a couple of times. The reason is that a man she met on Södermalm started following her and became unpleasant.'

'Lena's ex-husband,' said Per.

'That's it, but she also confirmed his story. They met at the bar the night in question and went to her place and had sex. So the ex-husband's alibi for the weekend of the murder is valid.'

Per sighed.

'It all feels extremely unfortunate. Lena lives under a death threat from her husband, gets out of it, and then falls victim to a serial killer. What are the odds of that?' said Charlotte, glancing out of the window at the big building.

'Then we can dismiss him as our perpetrator,' said Per, ending the call.

They got out of the car in silence. Charlotte was thinking about the ex-husband; she would have liked to frighten him a little, but now they had to drop that lead. Together they went through the glass door into the building and she coughed from the stench in the ice rink, Per's new home. The odour of sweat was intrusive.

'Wait here, I'll be right back,' said Per, disappearing down the corridor.

Doors along the walls opened and closed, hockey players of various ages stepped in and out – some with cages on their helmets, others without. Per had to get something and Charlotte was forced along to help carry. She didn't love this environment. She hadn't been to a hockey match a single time in her entire life. Just soccer, once.

'Charlotte, can you come here?' Per called, peering out from one of the rooms.

She walked soundlessly on the rubber mat in the middle of the corridor, tied the belt on her coat tighter around her body to keep out the cold. An adult player moved politely toward the wall to let her pass. He looked like the Hulk with all his protective gear, and without a cage on his face, rather good-looking. Unshaven. Smelled like an ape. He smiled at her.

292

'Are you picking someone up?' the hockey guy asked, taking off the enormous glove and extending his right hand. Charlotte hesitated a little too long.

'Some*thing*,' she said, reluctantly extending her hand, and looked up at the man.

'There may be a smell from wet gloves but it's clean,' he said, showing his white teeth.

'Okay,' she replied, feeling how her cheeks started to heat up.

'My name is Christian. See you,' he said self-confidently and staggered away on his skates toward the ice. Before he disappeared, the hockey guy turned around and met her gaze.

Perhaps a person should hang out here a little more, she thought as Per handed over two hockey clubs and a helmet with cage.

'Here,' he said, coming out carrying a big holdall full of things. His breathing was laboured.

'It really stinks.'

'Wait until it's sitting in the car fermenting,' he said, walking quickly toward the exit.

'Who was the hockey player I met?'

'One of the A-team players in Björklöven. Defence.'

If she overlooked the smell there was something extremely manly about this equipment. The insight surprised her; most of her dates in Stockholm had been with men in suits. Charlotte shook her head at her own musings. They made her lose focus from the investigation.

Per quickly stowed the gear into the back of the car and got into the driver's seat alongside Charlotte, who had slipped in on the passenger side. He started the car and drove in the direction of Roger Ren's house.

'Shouldn't we unload everything first?' said Charlotte, rolling down the window to get a little fresh air.

'We'll do that on the way back. Roger is home now and we don't want to miss him. I just had to pick up the gear for the next practice, which is at a different arena.'

Charlotte didn't understand a thing about this transport of hockey equipment and let it be.

A truck came up on the road in front of them and Per moved close behind.

'You have to stop stressing,' said Charlotte.

'I'll soon be sitting in Kennet's chair, then it will be calmer,' he said, coughing.

She looked out of the windscreen. Her thoughts went back to the men. Alex, Ola and the hockey guy. Three completely different personalities who all attracted her. Outside the window the green leaves of the birch trees were blended with yellow, lit up by the sun which was still able to warm them.

When they stopped outside Roger's home, Adrian came out of the door. He waved at them, passed the car and turned toward the street, no doubt on his way to school. Roger also came out on to the steps and welcomed them – surely in the belief that Charlotte and Per had news about the investigation of the robbery of his son, not to talk about the murdered Samir.

Inside the house it was tidy but not sterile. Charlotte took off her boots and entered in socked feet so as not to irritate Roger unnecessarily. He offered them coffee and when all three were sitting around the kitchen table, Per took it from the beginning.

'As you know, we are no longer investigating the robbery because the suspects are under the age of eighteen.'

Roger set his coffee cup down so hard that it spilled. 'I've received information that you want to conduct some damned mediation. What kind of justice is that? I thought in my eagerness that you were coming to give me some positive news for once.' He leaned forward over the table.

Charlotte looked first at him and then around the kitchen, searching for something that could expose Adrian's father as their serial killer.

At the same time Per set out the pictures they'd received from Anna in front of Roger.

'What's this?' said Roger, leaning backward.

'You've been following the boys. Why?'

'Why the hell do you think? Aren't you a policeman?'

Per smiled faintly. 'You have motive to injure them . . .'

Roger leaned forward again and fixed his eyes on Per. 'Yes, I've been keeping track of them. Before Samir did the whole city a favour by blowing himself up. My plan has been to follow and catch them red-handed when they rob some other wretch. Document it all with video and photos and then go to you. You are completely incapacitated.'

'That doesn't give you the right to take the law into your own hands, does it?'

Roger laughed. Charlotte tried to see the personality traits in him that tallied with their profile.

'I haven't done anything illegal, simply watched . . . Or wait, do you think that I . . . ?'

He stood up. Shook his head. 'Here a terrorist act has been committed and you think I had something to do with it? How incompetent are you?'

'Are you a hunter?' asked Charlotte.

'I'm from Norrland. What do you think? The wife and I both hunt. We have guns locked up in the garage, in accordance with all the regulations. You're free to examine them if you want.'

He seems willing to cooperate, she thought.

'What were you doing the night between the twenty-seventh and twenty-eighth of August?'

Roger's cheeks turned red, but he demonstrated a calm exterior. 'I was out with some colleagues in town. There was a launch that weekend and we had a few beers that evening.'

'You know we're going to check on that,' said Per.

'Please do. I was in their company until three o'clock in the morning.'

Charlotte knew that the team had already checked his whereabouts on the night in question. But she also believed Roger. He was a frustrated father who hadn't got the justice he wanted for his son. Besides, he didn't stand out as a sadist with a need for control.

'Samir is dead. What do you think about the other two?' asked Per.

Roger poured more coffee for himself and then looked at the pictures with a grim expression.

'What do you mean? I want to watch them until they rob again. But Omar seems to have vanished and the other one wants to apologize. Don't know if I want to make it so easy for him.'

'Why not? Maybe it will be good for Adrian to meet the perpetrator who wants to confess and say he's sorry.'

'Adrian is still afraid. He doesn't leave the house after dark. And you surely understand that's rather limiting when you live here. Soon the sun will hardly come up during the day. Why should those two get to live their lives as if nothing has happened?'

Charlotte noted that the hostility to immigrants had been seriously toned down. But then it wasn't the same thing to write what you felt behind a computer screen as to have to explain yourself to the police.

Suddenly she got an idea. 'Roger, you were taking pictures of the guys before the explosion. Might we be able to look at them?'

'Why?'

'We're trying to map out Samir's final days of life. You may have material in your camera that can help us in the investigation.'

Per nodded in agreement.

'I'll get the computer,' said Roger, leaving the kitchen.

'That was a good idea,' Per said to Charlotte.

They sat quietly until Roger came back with his laptop. He opened it, gathered his pictures and sent them to Per via a link.

'When did you start watching them?' she asked.

'Right away, the day after the robbery, when I understood that you weren't going to arrest any of them. Then Samir disappeared. Just like that. But for Omar and Ibrahim, it was business as usual while Adrian lay at home in a fetal position. Unfortunately they kept a low profile and didn't rob anyone. Mostly they seemed stressed.'

'Are you a doctor?' said Per, who knew very well what he did for a living.

Roger nodded.

'How long have you worked in Umeå?'

'I've been at Norrland University Hospital for fifteen years.'

Charlotte thought that this didn't tally at all with their perpetrator profile. Although on the other hand he ought to know a thing or two about DNA.

'Do you encounter Rohypnol often at the hospital here in Umeå?'

'What that murdered woman was drugged with? I read about it in the newspaper,' said Roger. 'The answer is no, not often nowadays. There was more previously. The immigrants push a lot of pills, but not that drug.'

'If you encounter a patient who has ingested Rohypnol, can you give me a call?' said Per.

Roger nodded. 'Damn, you really seem understaffed, needing my help with everything.'

Charlotte's phone rang, so she excused herself and left the kitchen. 'Hi, Anna.'

'Hi, something has come up concerning the extracted teeth. We've consulted several dental clinics about whether anything unusual has happened recently.'

Charlotte saw Per stand up from the table in the kitchen. It sounded as if he and Roger had switched to talking hockey.

'Yes?'

'We got a little bite from the Idun dental clinic on Rådhus Esplanade. Weirdly close to the place where Samir exploded,' said Anna.

Charlotte pressed the phone to her ear. 'And?'

'The boss there said that she had reported a theft to the police. Equipment was missing – someone stole tools from the clinic. An internal investigation is ongoing. May be of interest for us, I think.'

'Then you're thinking quite correctly. Well done,' said Charlotte, feeling a little hope again.

58

Ibrahim was lying in bed at home. Tuesday had gone by quickly, he thought. It was almost eight o'clock, and the darkness outside just got thicker and thicker. The short days in this country were still a challenge, but Apollonia had at least put a floor lamp in his room which gave a warm glow. Ibrahim lay on his back, tossed a pen up in the air and caught it on the way down, and then started over again. His thoughts were whirling.

He had ducked Klara's questions after the visit to the Stenlund family, when she was looking for her wallet. Chose to laugh at her when she asked what was going on with him. Joked away her question as imagination on her part. But he'd seen something in Stenlund's kitchen that made him cold.

Klara wanted to hang out as long as they could after school, but Ibrahim was tired and broke off the day with her earlier than usual – blamed it on his foster parents, but in reality he was the only one at home. The family was at some road meeting with the local council, he didn't really know what it was about. They wouldn't be home until nine o'clock, so until then Ibrahim was alone with what felt like a big hole in his gut.

He got up, set the pen on the bed and grabbed his phone before he left the room. In the kitchen Ibrahim opened the refrigerator, looking for something edible and found two containers of leftovers. He picked one of them without checking what was in it, got a plate and poured out the contents. Cod and mashed potatoes. That worked. He set the plate in the microwave and started it. Then he leaned against the kitchen counter and scrolled through his phone.

Ibrahim had just found out that the mediation with Adrian was going ahead. His father had agreed at last, so it was scheduled. *That's something, at least*, he thought.

During the evening he had also brooded about Omar but was no longer trying to reach him. He'd given up on that. Ibrahim knew that his buddy had left Umeå. When he asked around at the campground during the day, a guy told him that Omar had split for Finland.

He thought about the fact that he was without Omar and Samir. This freedom was new; he was no longer forced to rob or hurt others, and instead he had a chance to create a life of his own. Nonetheless that strange absence was still there. From now on, he had to solve his problems himself.

The microwave beeped and Ibrahim took out the food, just as he got a Snap from Klara that showed her happy face and sent a message where she asked what he was doing.

How should he answer? He took a picture of the food and wrote back.

Eating. You?

He took his plate to the kitchen table and dug into the cod. Klara answered with a photo taken from the front seat of a car.

Wallet found by Liam. Will be babysitting there tonight, maybe sleep over too. More money.

And then she sent an image with dollar bills.
Ibrahim stopped eating.

Why sleep over?

Erik will be away to buy a car and Helen I don't know.

Ibrahim thought about what he'd seen in the kitchen and about Helen's reaction. She hadn't taken her eyes off him. Everything matched up with what he'd witnessed by the pier that night. Was Klara babysitting for a murderer? Or was he imagining things?

He struck his head with his hands. He couldn't go around making vague accusations, he was already frowned on by the authorities. It felt like he was going crazy.

59

Charlotte eased the car into the parking space. It was early in the morning and there was a spot right outside the entrance to Elite Hotel Mimer, where Alex was staying for now. Per was at the hospital with Mia. They were hoping for a clean bill of health from her cancer today but had been called in, and that was always worrying. Despite that, Per didn't want the conversation with the director of the Idun dental clinic to wait, so Charlotte had been ordered to go there with Alex instead.

After pulling down the sun visor, she used the mirror to get her lipstick right. She smacked her lips and fussed with her hair, which was hanging loose, and even blow dried. Ola had whistled at her in the morning, asked about it, and Charlotte had replied that she had a lunchtime meeting with the council. Which was a white lie. Charlotte didn't really need to primp, but she did so anyway.

As Alex stepped out of the hotel, she honked the horn. He walked toward her Porsche. Marine blue suit. White shirt, no tie. On top of that he was wearing a jacket that was one of the ugliest she'd ever seen. Alex opened the passenger door.

'Well, thank you. Nice car,' he said casually.

'Hideous jacket,' she replied.

Alex laughed loudly as he got in and pulled out the seat belt. His narrow blue eyes seemed even bluer today. His hairline was high and the fringe combed casually to the left. His pointed chin with the little indentation was covered by beard stubble as always, but what Charlotte had fallen for, once upon a time, was the mischief in his gaze. And his tattoos. Normally she despised such things, but it suited Alex's character.

'So, you still drive your personal car on duty?' he asked.

'Not at all, but because I'm apparently your Uber I didn't make it to the station to change cars. But we're only driving a short distance.'

'It was just confirmed to me that Roger Ren's alibi holds for the murder of Lena. He was out partying that Saturday night with colleagues. There was apparently some heavy drinking which ended at home with one of them early Sunday morning. Besides, Roger was at a launch the whole weekend. So we can dismiss him as a suspect.'

'Okay, not good. Both Roger Ren and the ex-husband have alibis. Dead ends. Have you told Per?' she asked.

He nodded and she drove out on Västra Kyrkogatan and further on Storgatan. Alex sat with his phone, writing a text. Charlotte glanced at the screen.

'To your wife?'

'To my girlfriend.'

'Nice. How long have you been seeing each other?'

'Six months, maybe.'

'New, then. Is she a police officer too?'

Alex turned toward Charlotte to look at her. The sly smile was back. 'The only police officer I've had the pleasure of undressing is you.'

'Oh my, but that's past the statute of limitations now. A really long time ago,' she said, meeting his gaze. It was like being thrown back decades in time, when they were at police academy and couldn't get enough of each other. Finally he'd ended up in Gothenburg, his home town, and she in Stockholm. With Carl.

'What does your girlfriend do, if I may ask?'

'She's a minister.'

Charlotte snorted. First a bit quietly, but she couldn't hold back the bubble in her belly.

Alex turned toward her. 'Are you laughing at my girlfriend, Charlotte von Klint?'

'Sorry,' she said as she started to get hold of herself. 'Of course you're involved with a minister. The closest to God you can get in bed, I think.'

Alex looked at her with his eyes full of mischief, and Charlotte became uncomfortable. He challenged her.

'I'm glad you've met a person you like, Alex. If she, the minister, is the one who can get you to settle down, then I'm on her side.'

'Her name isn't "minister", it's Pernilla.' His smile was still directed at her. He seemed to want to tease.

'I couldn't compete with God, but Pernilla ought to be able to put up a fight,' said Charlotte, stopping the car outside the dental clinic.

Alex's deeply religious side was something she was both impressed by and loathed. His loyalty to something that for her was a fantasy, an illusion, was hard to understand. But that also made him desirable, which she knew was a cliché. You want what you can't have . . .

'You were the one who saw it as a competition, not me,' he said seriously as they got out of the car. 'God was never with us in bed. There, it was just the two of us.'

'Maybe it was like that for you. But it's like the man upstairs is with you everywhere – it felt like we were never alone. I was like your mistress,' she said, winking. She walked ahead of him, backwards, and then turned around in a pirouette, in an attempt to smooth over the serious conversation with levity. Even though a part of her felt jealous of the minister. And God.

Charlotte felt Alex's gaze burning on her neck as she took the lead and walked ahead of him into the dental clinic. She didn't want to go back to what had been. The attraction between them was extremely difficult. After all these years, she still wasn't prepared for it.

'Hi, we're from the Umeå police and are looking for the person in charge here,' she said, showing her identification to the young woman in reception.

'Yes, she's expecting you.'

Charlotte got the shivers from the place. The sound of drills working their way into enamel, the smell of fluoride. For some reason she always thought about childhood when she was at the dentist.

The young woman showed them to an office where a dark-haired woman with big brown eyes and a white coat was sitting. Alex and Charlotte sat down in front of her desk.

'I heard that you were a little curious about the theft we've had here at the clinic,' she said, turning the chair so that her legs had more room.

'Yes, and we would like to know if you suspect anyone on your staff,' said Alex.

'Well, I don't know. If my employees are interested in certain things, they can acquire them themselves through their own channels. They don't need to steal, if it's not because of the expense.'

'What kind of things are missing?' asked Charlotte.

'Oh dear, lots. We're taking an inventory right now, so we don't know exactly yet. But it basically concerns everything needed to perform oral surgery. For example, tools such as an elevator, which is used for simpler tooth extractions.'

'What about anaesthetics?' asked Alex.

'Strangely enough, no.'

'Have any of your employees behaved differently recently? Is there anything you've noticed?'

The director placed one leg over the other and thought. 'Hard to say if this has to do with the thefts, but there is one employee we're thinking about firing.'

Charlotte thumbed to an empty page in her notebook. Alex recorded the conversation. Sometimes Charlotte thought that recordings were tricky to use as an aid because you had to flip back and forth if you wanted to find details in the conversation.

'As I said, I don't know if this fits with the rest, but we have a hygienist whose performance is questionable. She doesn't show up for her shifts, she's careless with patients – it's gone so far that we threatened termination.'

'When did this behaviour start?' asked Alex.

'A few months ago, but it has escalated recently.'

Charlotte looked at Alex.

'Anything else?' she asked the woman.

'I don't know. She's pretty hard to work with, but she hasn't been here that long. Maybe a year and a half. Moved here from Stockholm.'

'What's the name of this person?'

'Helen Stenlund,' the director said.

Charlotte made a note of it. 'What does this Helen look like?' she asked, thinking about the woman who bought the hunting vest in Stockholm.

The director shrugged. 'Well, like many others, I was about to say,' she said, laughing. 'Blonde, curly hair. Medium height. Always tanned, like the Sun Doctor on TV4.'

That reminded Charlotte of the description they'd received in the hunting store.

'Do you have an address?'

60

Erik tore off the covers and set his feet on the floor. He hadn't been able to sleep more than an hour or so that night. Wednesday would be tough. He looked at Helen's side of the bed, which was empty and untouched. The pillow was cold when he put his hand on it. Erik looked toward the bathroom, but the door was ajar; Helen always locked it when she was there.

He got out of bed, stretching his arms to the ceiling. Yawned. Erik was worn out. His head felt like a medicine ball. The car shopping yesterday had gone well – the vehicle was exactly what he wanted and he would pick it up in the next few days. First he just needed to work out the financing with the bank.

Klara had been sleeping on the couch when he came home at two o'clock in the morning. Then he heard Helen put the key in the front door at four o'clock, lay there waiting for her to come into the bedroom, but she never showed up. When he went to look, it turned out that she'd fallen asleep with her clothes on in Elsa's bed. Presumably she'd been lying there for a while and then just happened to fall asleep. He knew exactly where she'd been – had followed her phone and in any event it had been where Helen said she would be: in Luleå, at a conference with colleagues from all over the country. Her workmates would sleep there, but

Helen couldn't bear to do that. She wanted to come home, she'd written in a text message. That was a ray of hope anyway in their otherwise difficult situation. Erik thought about what Elsa had said a few days before, that Mum had packed a bag. It was for the conference, of course. He'd searched for other signs of travel but hadn't found any.

With slippers on and still in his pyjamas, he went out of the bedroom. It was silent in the house. All that he could hear was the electrical sound from the refrigerator. Erik peeked into Elsa's room. Helen and his daughter were lying tightly entwined in the narrow bed. He looked at his wife. How would things go for them? Their lives had been perfect until he found the Nokia phone in the laundry basket and was forced to play detective, and now what he'd found had such consequences. All of her secrets, the sense of being a step behind, was a strain for him. The stress in his body manifested as sleeping difficulties, tightness in his back, a constant headache and racing pulse. Sometimes he thought insanity was near. Like when he found out that Helen was in contact with her father again. That was a heavy setback for Erik, who had once offered his soul to get her free from her father's grip, from his manipulation and brainwashing. Had it all been in vain?

He leaned his forehead against the wall; his teeth were clenched and he had to struggle to force them apart. It was only when he heard clatter in the kitchen that Erik took his head away from the wall.

Klara was still in the house.

When he moved in the direction of the clattering sound, he passed a mirror in the hall and looked at himself. Pale, dark circles under his eyes, thin as a hummingbird. His nerves were tense and it showed. He went into the kitchen.

Klara was frying eggs. Liam was up too but in his pyjamas, like Erik.

'Good morning,' said Klara, serving Liam.

'Hi, sorry about the overtime. I'm grateful you could be here and stay over.'

Klara looked at the clock. 'Are you going to school and work? Can you drive me?'

Erik sat down at the kitchen table. 'Yes, when do you start?'

'In an hour.'

'That's cool.'

Both his and Klara's phones pinged. He looked at the screen on his, where a newsflash was shown from a tabloid.

Murdered woman in Umeå tortured – found with all teeth extracted. Police seeking a serial killer.

'My God, how disgusting,' said Klara, looking at her phone.

'What is it?' asked Liam.

'Nothing for you,' said Erik, reading the news. His eyes scanned the text so quickly that he almost couldn't follow along. He read what the police had come up with. They had no suspect, but there were several victims in other cities. Teeth extracted from all of them.

My God, he thought and the pain in his head got even worse.

'How can we have a serial killer that pulls people's teeth out and a suicide bomber at the same time?' said Klara, shaking her head. 'It's not like we live in Stockholm. It's completely weird.'

Erik read further in the article. This would create more headlines until the murderer was caught. But the police didn't seem to have much to go on.

'I've heard that the detectives found a mark on Samir, the guy who died in Rådhus Square. That's apparently something they're looking into.'

Erik looked up at Klara. 'What kind of mark?' he asked.

'Something on the arm or whatever, I don't know. Ibrahim told me about it. The police asked him if Samir had one like that.'

Erik raised his eyebrows and looked at her. She had gone from talking about the murdered woman under Teg Bridge to Samir on Rådhus Square.

'It's probably a terrorist act committed by a lone madman,' Erik said, sighing. His headache was getting worse. He needed a pain reliever.

Klara shrugged and took a bite of her breakfast. 'I don't know, there was something about that mark anyway.'

'It almost sounds like a movie,' he said and Klara nodded.

Erik twisted his neck, trying to loosen the tightness, but nothing worked. It felt like someone had injected steel into his muscles.

'I'm not going out by myself until the lunatic is caught,' she said, setting down her phone.

When Helen came into the kitchen, Erik was dropping an effervescent tablet into a glass of water.

'Did you have a nice time yesterday?' he asked.

Her blouse was wrinkled after having slept in it. Helen nodded in response. He sought eye contact, but she avoided him. Once again Erik's teeth clenched like magnets. He closed his eyes to get control over his feelings and thoughts, wanted to cry to show Helen what she was doing to him. But the tears didn't come. All he felt was anger and fatigue.

'Have you read in the newspaper that there's a serial killer raging here in Umeå?' he asked, wanting to get her attention.

'What?' she said, sounding sincerely surprised. Almost afraid.

'Yes, read for yourself. Maybe you shouldn't go out alone at night any more.'

Helen took out her phone.

'I've promised to drive Klara to school, so I'll take her with me and drive in. Can you take Elsa and Liam?' he asked, finishing the contents of the glass, which fizzed and sprayed his nose as he drank. It tasted bad but hopefully it would help ease the brutal headache.

'Drive with Klara,' said Helen, going to the bedroom while she read her phone.

61

Charlotte had Per on speakerphone in the car. She and Alex were on their way to the Stenlund family's home. The information they'd just received from the dental clinic where Helen worked made her very much a person of interest.

'You'll have to talk with her. See how she acts when two police officers come knocking,' said Per. 'She is suspected with probable cause of several murders. I'll see that you get officers to do a house search and bring her in for questioning.'

'We need more information about this woman,' said Charlotte.

'I've asked Anna and Kicki to produce everything we need to know about her. We'll be in touch as soon as we can,' said Per.

'The newspaper article about a serial killer running loose pulling people's teeth out doesn't make things easier for us.'

'I'll take care of the media, you focus on the goal. But be on your guard . . .' Per said and then hung up.

Helen had quickly emerged as a suspect in their investigation. And that was probably lucky because all the others seemed to be a dead end. But Charlotte was far from convinced that this was the right track.

Charlotte turned on to the Stenlunds' street in the Böleäng neighbourhood and stopped the car a few houses away. Then she turned off the engine and looked at Alex.

'I understand that we can't skip leads, but doesn't it feel far-fetched that a mother of two children in Umeå would be a serial killer?'

'Let's overlook your gut feeling and consider what we know: Helen was living in Stockholm when the homeless man was murdered. Her boss confirmed that she worked there before she got her current position.'

'But we also have to find out where she was living when the murder in Malmö happened,' said Charlotte.

'Yes, although she also fits the perpetrator profile of a person who has a hard time keeping jobs. She's even close to being fired here in Umeå. Her appearance matches the description of the woman who bought the vest in the hunting store. All the victims have been drugged, maybe to facilitate dealing with them. And last but not least, Helen is a dental hygienist and knows how to extract teeth,' said Alex.

He leaned toward Charlotte in the car, seeking eye contact, but she opened the door and got out.

'When you put it like that . . . Well . . . We'll talk with her, then see what Kicki and Anna find.'

They walked in silence to the house. There was a car in the driveway. Charlotte started up the front steps, then stopped and turned around. Alex stood uncomfortably close by and she could feel his breath. Charlotte thought about Ola and moved another step upward, away from Alex.

'Now we go in,' he said.

'Let's do that,' she said, ringing the doorbell.

They waited for a moment before she rang again. Charlotte could see a figure moving behind one of the windows.

She was about to press the doorbell again when her phone rang. It was Anna.

'Already? That was quick. What have you managed to find?'

'Not much yet,' said Anna. 'But before you see Helen Stenlund you need to know something. She also lived and worked in Malmö when our first suspected victim was killed there. In addition, she lived only a few hundred metres from the crime scene. I'll keep digging, but be careful.'

Charlotte's pulse rose. It all added up, except that Helen was a woman.

They didn't have time to await a decision about a house search, as there was danger in delay. If Helen realized they were on her trail she might destroy evidence.

'Check if it's open,' said Alex.

Charlotte pulled down the handle and the door opened. She took a step in.

'Hello, we're from the police, is anyone home?'

Silence.

'Hello?'

Alex took a step past her.

'Hello, we're from the police. Is anyone home?' he repeated.

Charlotte placed her hand on her gun and undid the strap on the holster, pulled up the pistol. Listened. Someone was in here, but didn't want to make themselves known.

She aimed the gun toward the floor and went on in with Alex. They stopped at the kitchen. A smell of coffee. Breakfast food still set out. She cast a glance toward the wall. Gasped and stopped. Alex placed himself behind Charlotte. He looked first at her and then at the wall.

'Jesus,' Charlotte whispered. She took out her phone and took a picture of what she saw.

Alex followed her gaze again. Then he took two steps forward with his mouth open.

'Damn it, this can't possibly be a coincidence,' he said, cocking his gun.

For being deeply devout he swears a lot, thought Charlotte, who could not tear her gaze away from what she saw.

'They're exactly alike,' she said, going closer to the big board with white paper on an easel that was leaning against the wall. *Like a flipchart you use at meetings,* she thought. 'To do' was written in big letters above the names of the four family members and every day of the week. Some tasks were marked as complete with a V. Like they were checked off. Check. All written with a blue pen. 'Clean the toilets', followed by a V. 'Vacuum', marked with the same sign. Laundry, dust, mop floors, make dinner, clean cabinets.

'There's a V in front of every item,' said Alex.

'And it looks just like that on our murder victims,' said Charlotte.

'Helen knows we're here – she saw us through the window. I'm calling for reinforcements,' said Alex, going further into the house.

62

Klara was in the passenger seat beside Erik staring at her phone. Ibrahim had sent several messages on Snapchat the evening before when she had gone to bed, and asked how she was feeling. But now it was impossible to get hold of him. That made her wonder. He always got in touch in the morning when he knew she'd be awake. Hopefully nothing had happened to him. She looked out of the window – cars were lined up ahead of them at the red light. Blinking brake lights. She would probably be late to school even though she had got a ride from Erik. He drove calmly, almost too slow. As if he was afraid of something or waiting for someone. Warm air streamed from the vents in the car. Mornings had started to be a little colder. Everything outside the car was damp, shiny with dew.

Klara sneaked a glance at Erik. When she did practice-driving with her dad she held on to the steering wheel the same way Erik did. Like you do when you're a beginner, because that's what you learned at driving school.

She jumped when Erik pressed hard on the horn. The sound cut through the air.

'Come on – drive ahead, buddy,' he said to the car ahead that didn't cross the intersection before the light changed to red again.

You're the one who's slow, she thought, but didn't say anything. Erik honked again.

It would take time to get to school. On the radio they were talking about a traffic accident. Klara observed the people walking past their stopped car. Most were dressed for a colder season. She herself was wearing her thin blue jacket. A classmate rode past on a bike. Klara was stressed about not making it to her first class on time. Even though she had the best alibi in the form of the school counsellor.

'How is Helen doing?' she asked, to think about something other than missed classes.

Erik cast a glance at her. 'What do you mean?'

Klara shrugged. 'I just think she's been acting a little strange lately.'

'In what way?'

'I don't know . . . But the other day she called me and thanked me for being so good with the kids and wanted me to know that she appreciated my time with your family. As if I wouldn't be babysitting any more. Although a little later she asked me for help again as if nothing had happened.'

'That sounds strange,' Erik said in a tired voice.

'She sounded absent somehow. You and I can talk, but Helen is like a clam. She doesn't seem to like me.'

'You mustn't think that. Helen is a little strange right now. I agree with you on that. But that has nothing to do with you. She has problems with her father and isn't doing well mentally.'

Klara sighed. That explained Helen's strained actions. They had learned about mental illness in school, and many students also suffered from it.

Klara drummed her index finger on the phone resting on her thigh. Snapchat messages from several friends appeared. It was a daily routine to check in with each other on their way to school.

318

But still nothing from Ibrahim. The strangest thing was that he didn't appear on the map in the app. And they'd promised each other to always have it on.

Suddenly Erik turned the car abruptly and the phone slid down between the seat and her door.

'Damn it,' she said, pressing her hand down in the gap, feeling with her fingers.

Erik looked at her. 'Leave it be, I'll find it for you when we're there.'

'I can't find it, damn it,' she said, continuing to search for the phone.

'I can stop up here and help you,' he said, using the indicator.

'But then I'll be late. We're already late. I'm sure I'll find it.'

Erik pulled into a bus stop. 'It will be quick,' he said.

'I'm going to be late, will you give me an excuse?'

'Of course,' he said. 'I'll explain the situation.'

Erik stopped, let the car idle and got out of the car to go around to her side. Klara kept searching, running her hand the other way, right under the seat. Suddenly she felt something hard and she brightened up. *There it is*, she thought and pulled out a black velvet box. She smiled at Erik when he opened her car door.

'So you're a romantic? What have you bought for Helen?' she asked, picking up the box.

Klara's smile disappeared when she saw the contents. She looked up at Erik, who stood leaning over her in the car. Then he tore the box out of her hands. Swore. At first she didn't make the connection, but with every breath the insight increased. The panic.

By that time Erik had managed to go around to his side and jump into the car again. She heard the doors lock. Klara wanted to call someone but her phone was still lost between the seat and the door. She stared straight ahead. Couldn't breathe.

'You didn't need to fucking look!' Erik shrieked and drove off.

There was no jewellery in the box.

It was full of teeth.

63

Per hung up after talking with Alex about what they'd found at the Stenlund family home. They were on the trail of the murderer. He was being deluged with calls from journalists too. The leak about the teeth and their suspected serial killer was a serious setback in the investigation. The headlines were dark and big. He forwarded all calls to the public relations department, and Kennet helped out too. Per wasn't prepared for this part: handling journalists who wanted to know every detail in their investigation. Fortunately the media still knew nothing about the V-mark on the victims, but the stress made his glucose meter hit the roof, and in all the chaos he had to pick up Hannes from hockey as well. So that was why Per was in his car at ten o'clock in the morning, waiting for his son outside the Nolia arena.

Mia had got encouraging news about her cancer anyway. *What a relief,* thought Per. She didn't need more treatments. She would celebrate that during the day with friends.

He got out of the car and looked around for Hannes. Nearby the local council was constructing a big indoor facility for soccer, which would also house offices and a restaurant. The parents of the soccer kids were happy. They wouldn't have to stand outside and freeze. He had invested in snow boots and bodywarmers to weather the ice rinks.

His phone chimed. Mia this time. She was in a changing room in a store trying on clothes. The picture showed a red dress – the cleavage was deep but not conspicuous. Her collarbone stuck out. From a front seat he had witnessed how she was slowly fading away after the treatments, but now her smile on the picture was unmistakable.

There was a question too.

What do you think?

His heart warmed and he wrote back.

Buy it. Very nice.

She answered immediately.

It's a little expensive . . .

Buy it.

It didn't matter what the dress cost. Right now Mia could buy a new car if she wanted. In the picture, the sharp light from the store ceiling produced dark circles under her eyes, where she'd applied mascara today. She looked happy.

We have a table at Harlequin for lunch, but I read about your serial killer – just say if I should take the boys.

He answered at once.

I'll work out everything with the boys. Enjoy being healthy. Charlotte is eager to celebrate with you, be prepared ;)

A new message with a picture. Mia with a champagne glass in her hand.

> *She knew we were going to this store and made*
> *sure there was bubbly when we arrived! #crazy*
> *#10o'clockinthemorning*

Per laughed. He wasn't surprised after what he'd experienced in Stockholm.

'Hey, can you hurry it up a little?'

Per turned around and saw Hannes come half-running.

'How long a break do you have?' asked Per as they got in the car.

'I have class in ten minutes.'

'Why are you playing hockey in that time? Wouldn't it be better to do schoolwork?' said Per, sounding like his own father.

'I needed to practise shots.'

Per shook his head, didn't want to lecture his son today. He didn't have time. At the same time he was proud that the boy was so engaged.

'Do you want to hear something nice that I told Simon on the way to practice this morning?' he asked his son.

'What's that? Are we going to get a dog?'

Per broke into a smile. 'Your mother is healthy.'

Hannes looked at Per. 'What do you mean "healthy"? Is the cancer gone?'

He nodded and took his son's hand. Squeezed it. 'It hasn't spread and what was in her body is gone. The treatments have produced results.'

Per started the engine, turned on the heat, while Hannes sat quietly alongside him and stared ahead. Tears ran down his cheeks; his happiness was soundless.

'I know, son. She's out with her friends now, but we'll fix some good chow tonight and celebrate.'

Hannes nodded. Then he dried the tears and sniffed. Smiled. Per drove past the Dragon School where the boys would probably go later on.

'Can Mum watch my match on Sunday then?' his son asked cautiously.

'She would like nothing better.'

'Having Mum be healthy is better than a dog,' said Hannes, laughing, before he picked up his phone. Per knew that his son would call her and his eyes teared up too. He truly had to exert himself not to give in to strong emotions.

Hannes was busy talking with his mother when Kicki called Per and threw him back into work.

'Has something new happened?' he asked his colleague.

'Helen Stenlund,' said Kicki.

'Yes, what about her? Charlotte and Alex are there now.'

'There's something you need to know about her. It's a bit sensitive and must be handled confidentially. Can you come into the station? I'm calling them too.'

The phone beeped. Per checked who the other caller was.

Alex again.

'Yes, see you there in fifteen minutes. I have to go, I've got a call from Alex too.'

64

Charlotte turned her head toward a sound in the Stenlund house. It sounded like a child talking. She held the gun securely behind her. Alex had gone out into the hall to call Per, so she moved alone toward the sound that seemed to come from one of the smaller rooms. The home she was in looked like something out of an interior design magazine. Shiny, clean and tidy. Usually it was more common that they stepped right into squalor. The misery was probably on the inside of the people who lived here.

'Hello?' she called, making her way to the living room. The patio door was closed, but a window was open. On the far side was a rubber mat, outdoor furniture, plants.

Charlotte went further into the house, when suddenly a boy in pyjamas came running from one of the rooms. He stopped abruptly when he saw a stranger in the house and she quickly hid the gun in her waistband.

'Mum!' the boy called.

'Hi, I'm a police officer. Is your mother or father at home?'

He stared at Charlotte as if she were a vampire, but then pointed toward one of the rooms. She looked into it and saw various shades of pink. On a low bed a woman was sitting, smoking and talking on the phone while a little girl, perhaps six years old, was getting dressed. The woman whom Charlotte assumed was Helen, whispered into the phone, seemed to want to conceal her call. Charlotte turned toward Alex, showed him that she was going in.

'Hi, excuse me, I'm from the police,' she said. 'No one answered the door.'

Helen looked at her and ended the call immediately. Her eyes were red and swollen. She took a deep puff on the cigarette.

'I was on the phone and didn't hear you. What are you doing here?' she said without getting up. 'Has something happened?'

Charlotte noted a child's suitcase on the floor. The clothes in it appeared to have been thrown in carelessly.

'No, we're here to bring you in for questioning.'

Helen looked at her cigarette. Inspected it, blew out smoke.

'I was a smoker long ago, but quit when I met Erik,' she said as if she hadn't heard what the police officer in front of her had just said.

Charlotte didn't really know how to respond. Helen seemed out of it. Smoke circled up in front of her to vanish into nothing.

'He got me to quit. I guess that was good, but it's also the only good thing that came with him.' She didn't take her eyes off the cigarette. 'Apart from the children, of course.'

Charlotte took a step forward. Smiled at the little girl.

'Now I'm thinking about starting again, because I can,' said Helen.

Charlotte was joined by Alex, who placed himself in the doorway. The girl stared at the intruders and sat down close to her mother.

'What's this about?' asked Helen, looking at the police officers.

Charlotte considered what they'd seen on the wall in the kitchen. It was a turn she hadn't been prepared for and she decided to proceed carefully, continue on the planned tack until they got reinforcements.

'It simply concerns the missing items at your dental clinic. We're investigating that and need to ask a few questions.'

'What do you mean? Do you think I took those things?'

Evidently offended, thought Charlotte with regard to Helen's tone.

'No, I didn't say that. We're investigating and we'll be talking with everyone at your workplace,' she lied in the hope that it would get Helen to relax.

'I haven't stolen anything anyway. And I don't know who did it either.'

Charlotte looked at the little suitcase. 'Are you going on a trip?'

Helen didn't answer, simply put out the poison stick against a drinking glass that was on the floor. Charlotte's phone buzzed in her pocket, but she let it be.

'Are you police?' the girl asked.

Charlotte smiled. 'Yes, I am.'

The girl looked at the gun that was sticking out behind her jacket. Charlotte quickly covered it. 'Cool.'

'Helen, you need to go with us to the station so that we can ask a few questions.'

'Unfortunately that's not possible. The children and I have to leave.'

Helen moved with effort, as if her body ached. Charlotte noted a bruise on her wrist that extended past the sleeve.

The phone in her pocket rang constantly but she didn't want to interrupt to take the call.

'Where's your husband?' asked Alex.

Helen started fussing with the suitcase without answering.

'Daddy's at work. He and Klara left a while ago,' the girl who was dressing herself said.

'Who is Klara?' asked Charlotte.

'Our babysitter, of course.'

'What's her last name?' asked Charlotte, thinking that this was a person she wanted to talk with.

327

'Lundqvist,' Helen replied.

Alex noted the name on his notepad. It was the same girl who'd shown up earlier in the investigation.

'Why is that interesting?' asked Helen, looking at him.

'No particular reason. We're investigating broadly and unconditionally. Where does your dad work?'

'At Klara's school,' the girl said.

Helen stroked the little girl's back. 'He's the counsellor at the Dragon School,' said Helen.

Charlotte wondered how she could lead the conversation away from what was missing at the dental clinic to the cleaning schedule in the kitchen without arousing suspicion.

Alex crouched down by the edge of the bed. The girl was now sitting fully clothed with a jacket on. Helen stood up, closed the suitcase and called to her son.

'I saw your thorough cleaning schedule in the kitchen. Good idea, I'll suggest that to my girlfriend,' said Alex light-heartedly, sounding credible. 'Does it work?'

Helen's reaction was to light another cigarette. As she lit the cigarette, her hand shook. Like an addict on the way to getting clean.

'Sure,' she answered at last.

'I should have more chores on the schedule, I'll be six soon,' the girl said proudly.

'Congratulations in advance,' said Alex.

'Thank you.'

'Aren't you a little young to clean?' he continued.

'No, I help Mummy. It's easier for her then.'

Charlotte looked at Alex. They needed to bring Helen into the station and question her properly. She seemed about to flee.

'Excuse me,' said Charlotte, leaving the room. Outside she encountered the son again. He was still in his pyjamas and appeared to have been crying.

Charlotte went back to the kitchen and stood in front of the cleaning schedule. She called Per but didn't get through. Then she tried Kicki, who answered.

'Hi, this is Charlotte. We're bringing Helen into the station. She's getting ready to leave, she's packed a suitcase. How's it going with reinforcements?'

At first Kicki reacted with silence.

'Hello, Kicki?'

'Yes, they're on their way . . .'

'Good, we can't risk her leaving.'

'But you can't bring in Helen,' said Kicki.

'Why not?' said Charlotte, feeling irritated. 'Tell Per we're coming in with her.'

'Is her husband at home?' asked Kicki.

'No.'

'The children?'

'Yes.'

'Stay there, don't let her out of your sight. I'll call soon!'

65

Per's head and shoulders were out of the lift before the doors even completely opened. Hannes was back at school, Per's heart was pounding, and he almost ran into a colleague who had to back up two steps.

'Goodness,' the woman said, whose name Per couldn't recall. Right now there were people everywhere in the offices of Major Crimes.

He quickly mumbled an apology and hurried on. Kicki's call concerning Helen was worrying. What was it about? What did they have to handle confidentially in this sensitive part of the investigation?

When he got to his office he quickly threw his coat on to the visitors' chair – and missed. He then joined the others, where Kicki stood ready with a folder in her hand.

'Come with me,' she said, taking the lead.

'Kicki, we have reinforcements on their way to the Stenlunds'. What's so damned important that it has to be straightened out right now?'

'I know, but I have to discuss this with you first.'

They stepped into the briefing room, which was empty. Kicki closed the door behind them.

'What is it, Kicki? I have both Charlotte and Alex out in the field – are they in danger? You're making me a little nervous here.'

Kicki sat down at her usual place. *Creature of habit*, Per thought.

'Besides my job here at the police station I do volunteer work. At a women's shelter.'

Per raised his eyebrows. 'Okay?' he said, feeling even more irritation. 'You know that police employees aren't allowed to get involved in that type of organization. It can affect public confidence – it's been tested up here in the north.'

Kicki nodded. 'I know who the police officer you're referring to was and she still stands by her actions. But there was a heated debate both internally and in the media,' Kicki said self-confidently.

Per looked at her without saying anything.

'Yes, I know, conflict of loyalty, that's why I haven't told you,' Kicki continued. 'My involvement isn't okay according to my employer and that's why we're standing here, you and I, alone in a room. But now we have an acute situation that needs your attention.'

Per shook his head. *Jeepers*, he thought. He would be the one who would have to take that issue up when the case was solved.

'Right now, Helen Stenlund is about to leave her husband,' said Kicki. 'He is a notorious abuser of women. Erik has hit and manipulated her for years. The women's shelter has been close to getting her away from him previously, but she always changed her mind at the last moment.'

Per sat down. 'And you can't tell Charlotte and Alex that in person because that would be misconduct,' Per added.

'Yes, and because the women's shelter, at this very moment, will take her from Erik. The involvement of the police and the homicide investigation risk ruining that. Charlotte wants to bring her into the station and that won't work. We must get Helen away.'

'A homicide investigation must take precedence,' he said.

'Listen. Helen isn't our perpetrator. She's got her hands full surviving every day. I didn't connect Erik with the murders at all. To me he was just an abuser. But perhaps everything that led us to Helen is really about him. She probably bought the vest – could it have been a present for Erik? The dental equipment could easily have been taken by him at her work. They were living in Malmö and Stockholm at the time of those murders.'

Per exhaled heavily. 'So Helen is a victim in this? And Erik who's our perpetrator?'

Kicki nodded. 'At the women's shelter every day we hear stories from women who are living with brutal men. Erik is one of the worst I've heard about. He has total control over his wife. When I understood that the investigation was aimed at *our* Helen, the one we're helping at the women's shelter, then I felt panic. Per, we need to get her away from the home, without her husband having the slightest suspicion about it.'

Per stood up. 'Listen, if Erik is our perpetrator he'll go to prison for life. Then she'll be protected anyway. But until we know for sure, Helen and the children need to be kept in safety.'

'Yes, that's just what I'm trying to say,' said Kicki. 'The women's shelter is on its way to Helen's house to take her away from there right now. Let them do that. But we have to talk with Alex and Charlotte.'

'Just wait a little. What else do we know about Erik?'

Kicki held out a piece of paper. 'Not much more than this. Helen has been rather tight-lipped for some reason.'

Per read. Her notes were jotted down randomly. Erik, counsellor, nothing strange about finances or previous convictions. Seems conscientious. But did he fit their profile?

'He hunts too,' said Kicki. 'Like I said before, the vest Helen bought must have been a present for Erik. She's spoken about his hunting rifles. On more than one occasion he's threatened her with one of them.'

'Damn it, we didn't think of the husband. There wasn't a single warning sign about him before you stepped in and exposed who he really is.'

'Erik is a pig, no question about it, but if we're going to accuse him of being a serial killer, we must have watertight evidence before we even breathe a word about our suspicions,' said Kicki, and there was rattling on the table when her hands met the surface. The kind of bracelets that Charlotte called tingle-tangle.

'Find out more,' said Per. 'His childhood, employment history, if there are complaints from the school, everything.'

'Helen has bags packed and is ready to take off. What do I do?' asked Kicki. 'What do you intend to say to Charlotte and Alex?'

'I'll speak with the prosecutor. If we can produce enough to hold Erik then we'll do that. Bring Helen and the children to a safe place. Follow the women's shelter's plan, if she's finally ready to leave him now.'

Kicki nodded.

Per swore to himself. 'We're actually the ones who should offer her protection in this situation, but your solution is the most practical right now,' he said, but felt hesitation. 'And we must be able to contact Helen during the investigation.'

Kicki looked at her phone, which was ringing.

'Charlotte,' she said to Per.

'Okay, put her and Alex in contact with your team at the women's shelter. Solve it asap.'

66

Erik turned up the volume on the radio and turned down the heat in the car. This Wednesday was not working out as planned. He was driving on the E12, staying below the speed limit. The police speed traps were usually close together on this stretch and he didn't want to be stopped. He thought about Klara and looked at the place where she'd just been sitting. The box was still on the seat. Erik reached out his hand and touched the soft surface. The velvet was worn in places with some bare, black spots. He'd had it since he was a kid, a present from his mother. When he got it, it contained a necklace. It had been his finest possession as a ten-year-old.

Klara protested when he made her leave her seat in the car, but now it was finally calm. His thoughts were in better order when he was alone. His muscles were less strained, even if the tension in his neck was constant. The headache tablets didn't control the pain. Erik sang along anyway with the music, an old hit from the eighties by Ankie Bagger. When the phone rang his musings were interrupted and he turned down the volume.

'Yes, this is Erik.'

'Hi, this is Stina from the school. Are you coming in today? A student is sitting outside your door waiting.'

Damn it, he'd forgotten to cancel his meetings.

'Sorry, I have a doctor's appointment today. Apologize to the student. I'll be in tomorrow.'

His colleague sighed. 'I'll put a note on your door so I don't have to do your work for you.'

'What's the problem? Just do it, damn it!'

Silence on the other end. Erik was breathing more and more rapidly.

'Excuse me? This is why the staff don't like you, Erik. Your moods.'

He closed his eyes. Clenched his teeth. 'Was there anything else?' he said curtly.

'Yes, we've heard that you drove a Klara Lundqvist to school today. But she isn't here, according to the teacher.'

Erik slowed down. 'What?'

'Yes, her friends say she got a ride to school with you. But she hasn't shown up. Do you know anything about that?'

Erik looked at the passenger seat again. 'No, I dropped her off. She's probably there somewhere,' he said in an irritated voice. 'Have you checked with her boyfriend?'

'Not yet,' said his colleague. 'Well, she'll probably show up. Bye.'

Erik hung up and turned off the phone. He didn't want more calls from the school.

His hands gripped the steering wheel even harder.

He turned off the radio. The landscape changed during the drive. There was more forest. He had driven this road so many times that he could do it in his sleep. Erik was just wondering whether he should call Helen and check what she was doing, when a ringtone suddenly sounded in the car. He took his eyes off the road and looked at his phone. It was turned off. But it wasn't his phone that was ringing. It was Klara's.

He signalled and stopped on the shoulder. He bent forward and felt under the passenger seat. Klara's phone was still there and he managed to fish it out, still with his foot on the brake and the car in gear. He was not in an optimal place on the road and a car honked as it drove past, but Erik ignored that. Instead he stared at the number that was calling Klara's phone. He knew who it belonged to, even if she hadn't entered it as a contact.

Liam, his son. Why did he have Klara's number?

Erik looked at the phone until the ringtone stopped. Should he call home? He put the car in neutral, turned on the hazard lights and then sent a text from Klara's phone to Liam.

Can't answer right now, what did you want?

Erik needed to know why his son was calling the babysitter.

The police are here, can you come? I think it's scary and Mum is strange.

Erik stopped breathing, stared at the message. *What the hell?* he thought, drumming his index finger on the side of the phone. What should he do? What were the police doing there?

He continued pretending to be Klara.

Can't right now. What do they want?

Liam was quick with his reply.

Talk with Mum. And I don't know where Dad is, is he with you? He isn't answering.

Erik clenched his jaw and thought about his turned-off phone. The chaos continued.

> *No, I can't talk. Keep sending texts and tell me what's happening. I'm here for you.*

Liam wrote back that he would do that and Erik left the side of the road.

Fucking shit, he thought. The calm he had felt vanished, his muscles tightened up again and he heard his own breathing. He never got any peace. There was always something that had to be solved.

'Why can't people just do as I say?' he said out loud to himself. 'Why does it have to be so damned hard to understand?'

He pressed down on the accelerator but kept more or less to the speed limit as he drove on. After a while he turned on his phone again and called Helen.

No answer.

67

Charlotte listened to the new information from Kicki about the Stenlund couple, and then informed Alex about who Erik was. They asked the reinforcements to wait until they had talked undisturbed with Helen, and now both of them were standing in the kitchen with Helen, while the children had been sent to Liam's room to play video games.

'Do you know when Erik is coming home?' Charlotte asked her.

Helen rinsed off a coffee cup before she set it in the dishwasher. After that she lit a new cigarette.

'He's at work,' she replied, still on her guard. It looked like she'd been standing outside in freezing temperatures for hours; her muscles were tense, her movements stiff.

'Your contacts at the women's shelter will bring you and the children to safety. Until then we'll stay here.'

Helen sat down on the kitchen chair, brushing away a blonde curl that had fallen down over one eye. For a long time she sat silently before she said anything.

'You know.' Her back was bent. Tears were in her eyes, but she didn't let them fall.

'We know,' said Charlotte.

'We were going to do it today, but now . . .' said Helen.

'But now you'll proceed according to plan,' said Charlotte. 'We only need to ask you a few questions before your help arrives. You'll be taken to a place the location of which even we won't know. Your address will be protected and you'll get to take the children with you, at least to start with.'

Helen nodded.

Charlotte wanted to keep asking questions but could see that the woman in front of her was thinking about other things.

'How did my life get like this?' Helen said, sobbing, picking away the nail polish on a finger.

'This can happen to anyone who has the misfortune of meeting the wrong person,' said Charlotte. 'Right now it's important that you get away from Erik.'

'We're all packed. The children know what will happen. This time I'll do it,' she said, like a pep talk to herself.

'We have some more questions that concern our investigation. Can you answer those right now?'

Helen pulled her shoulders back. 'Okay, I'll answer as best I can.'

Charlotte made a sign to Alex to start recording the conversation. Now it was crucial to find out more about Erik's involvement in the murders.

Alex began. 'Did you buy a vest in a hunting store in Stockholm?'

'A vest?' she said, puzzled.

'Yes, one like this,' said Charlotte, showing the picture she had on her phone.

Helen took the phone and stared at the vest. 'What about it?'

'Did you buy it in a hunting store in Stockholm?'

Helen put out her cigarette and then fixed her gaze on the floor. 'Yes, I bought it for Erik. He hunts and wanted a special vest.'

'Do you have a receipt for it from the hunting store?' asked Alex. 'We need to have it.'

Helen looked questioningly up at him. 'Yes, I still have the receipt,' she said quietly. 'It should be in a binder in the office.'

'Was he happy about the vest? Has he used it often?'

A crooked little smile appeared on Helen's face. 'Erik is rarely happy, he takes everything for granted. He hung the vest up in the wardrobe, then I never saw it again. Not until today, when you showed it on the phone.'

She wiped her eye and Alex handed the roll of paper towels to her.

'Why are you asking about this?' she asked, holding hard on to the piece of paper towel with her hands in her lap.

Charlotte hesitated before she answered. She couldn't reveal their suspicions against Erik because he hadn't been questioned yet and the preliminary investigation was confidential. But she needed to get Helen to tell them what she knew.

'We have reason to suspect Erik of some very serious crimes.'

Helen looked with surprise at Charlotte and opened her mouth to say something.

'What kind of crimes?' she asked.

'Unfortunately we can't go into that, but there are things we're trying to figure out,' said Charlotte.

Helen was crying. 'Do you believe that he's the serial killer that's in the newspapers?'

'We can't say,' said Alex curtly.

Helen's arms fell against her thighs. 'God. Could you be mistaken?'

'We're at the start of our investigation, and need to ask you a few questions,' said Charlotte, knowing that she was making a mistake that almost confirmed Helen's words.

The woman before them sat silently for a moment and they let her take her time. It was a lot to take in.

'But he's nice to people . . .' Helen said at last. 'He's . . . good with the children. I'm the one he controls. Has he killed . . . ?'

For a brief moment she hid her face in her hands. Then she wiped her nose with the paper towel.

'I never know what's going to trigger him from day to day. Sometimes it's a spot I've missed, another time his shirt is wrinkled . . . On a good day that spot, or the shirt, doesn't matter. Then he can be calm. You just never know. He's unpredictable. But a murderer? No . . .'

Helen closed her eyes. Charlotte could almost see her heart pounding under her sweater.

'No one said anything about being a murderer,' said Alex. 'Have you noticed whether his behaviour has changed in any way the past few weeks?'

'His behaviour changes all the time. What he never does is break his daily routines.'

'Have his routines deviated lately?'

Helen appeared to consider this. 'Now you mention it, Erik has been even more suspicious recently. He found my emergency phone. Or . . . I think he did. Then I was sure he would kill me . . .'

'What happened?' asked Alex.

Helen's shoulders moved up. 'I got an old Nokia phone from the women's shelter because he was constantly looking at my phone. Checking it as if it were his own, and I can't protest. That would be evidence that he's right, that I'm hiding things from him. The emergency phone was gone from the hiding place for several days, but Erik never said anything. Usually he's a person who reacts. He doesn't hold in his emotions, but instead acts on them.'

Charlotte looked at the bruise on Helen's wrist and inhaled sharply. Helen's life was every woman's terror.

'What happened with the phone?' she asked.

Helen tore off a piece of paper towel. 'Suddenly it was back. I'd hidden it in the laundry and one day the phone was there again.' She blew her nose. Her hands were shaking.

'You've never reported him to the police?' asked Charlotte cautiously.

'No, it never occurred to me. Or yes, I did one time, early in the relationship, but then I withdrew my report.'

'Have you documented any of your injuries from abuse? Gathered material that you can use in a possible trial against Erik?'

Helen shook her head. 'It hasn't been possible. Where would I save the pictures without him discovering it?'

Charlotte saw how Helen was wrapping the paper towel hard around her index finger. She wanted to ask the obvious question, why she didn't leave him earlier, but thought that Helen had already asked herself that. Living in constant threat would break anyone down.

Helen put one leg over the other. The whites of her eyes were as red as her nose after all the blowing.

'Erik was so charming when we met, I fell headlong. He also helped me with my father, who wasn't good for me for various reasons. Erik helped me get away from him. And at last Dad went to prison. Erik was my hero, and in the beginning he didn't hit me. He made demands of me and I thought it was connected with Dad's background. My background. It was after I got pregnant that he slowly started to control me. It was so devious that I didn't even think about it at first. I thought it was almost charming, that he was a little jealous and worried. At the time, I didn't sense what it would lead to.'

Both Alex and Charlotte sat silently. Let her talk.

'When Dad was released from prison, Erik forbade me from having contact with him. Even though Dad was like a new person. A better man with sound values. He found God and started to

342

preach. To start with, he also tried to pick up our relationship again, but then he stopped calling out of fear of Erik, because he would take it out on me. My friends tried to help me at first too, but they gave up because I didn't understand the seriousness myself before it was too late.'

Charlotte nodded. 'What kind of contact do you have with your father now?'

Helen gave them a genuine smile for the first time during the whole conversation.

'One day he turned up here in Umeå, outside my workplace. We talked for several hours and since that day he has encouraged me to dare to leave Erik. I wouldn't have got this far without Dad. The last time I saw him was a few days ago in Innertavle. He's found an apartment for me in southern Sweden.'

Charlotte's phone blinked on silent. It was Per calling. She got up and left the kitchen to talk undisturbed.

'I've sent you an email,' said Per as soon as Charlotte answered. 'It contains a video from one of the surveillance cameras on Rådhus Square, right before the explosion. Watch it.'

Charlotte did as she was told.

'Look carefully. We've seen the images several times, but I haven't been able to stop thinking about this video. Now I discovered what we'd missed.'

'What?' said Charlotte, puzzled. 'I don't see anything I haven't seen before.'

'Apparently Erik was at Rådhus Square at the time of the explosion. Do you see him? He's the one who takes cover behind the advertising board. Do you see what he's doing? Just before it explodes?'

Charlotte played the video again on her phone.

'Yes, it's him. Jesus.'

She inspected Erik, but still didn't understand what Per was getting at.

'Look at what he does right after he's placed himself in safety, follow his left hand.'

Charlotte stared at the video. First she saw Erik's jacket being tugged by a person who seemed to want to get him away from there, but then he remained standing still a moment longer before taking cover behind an advertising board. Once there he looked quickly down at his hand, which was half concealed under his jacket sleeve. Then she caught sight of what Per had already discovered. Erik had a phone in his hand and appeared to press on it with his thumb. A moment later came the explosion.

'He detonates the bomb at the scene,' said Charlotte.

'How could we miss that?'

68

Per had gathered the whole team except Charlotte and Alex, who were still with Helen. The briefing room was full this Wednesday.

'We have good reason to suspect Erik Stenlund with probable cause of several murders,' he said. 'Everything points in that direction. Not least after the discovery concerning the bomb on Rådhus Square. But that's not sufficient for arrest, more like a complicating circumstance for him. We need something concrete that can link him to the act.'

He turned toward the TV screen and clicked up a picture of Erik. It looked like it came from a driver's licence.

'Do we know where he is right now?' asked Per.

'According to the school where Erik works he didn't come in today,' said Anna.

'What do we know?' said Per.

'We spoke with the administrator and she said that there's also a student who hasn't shown up, Klara Lundqvist. She babysits for the Stenlund family, and according to several of her friends Erik was driving her to school this morning – her friends seem to have had contact with her on the way there.'

'But she never showed up?'

'No, and another thing they told us: Erik has been unstable lately, and recently had an outburst at one of the staff.'

'Okay, she's the family's babysitter and Erik is supposed to have driven her to school. That doesn't mean anything has happened, but we have to find her. Now,' said Per, and one of the men in the room went out.

'Has the family reported her missing?' asked Kicki.

'No, not yet. But her moped is gone, which is strange because she got a ride with Erik. They're searching for her boyfriend Ibrahim to see if she's with him,' said Anna. She pointed at the board alongside the screen with Erik's picture. There were photographs of Samir, Omar and Ibrahim that had been part of the investigation since the start.

'We've put an APB on Erik and his car. Request everything you can on Erik's and Klara's phones, find out what masts they've been near,' said Per.

Another man on the team got up and was about to leave the room when Per called to him.

'And be sure we get permission to record all communication. I want all the messages that are sent to and from Erik Stenlund's mobile and to hear all his calls. It's a cumbersome process to get that permission, might as well start it already,' he added with a sigh.

Anna waved her hand. 'I've also managed to find out more about Erik, mainly with regard to his upbringing.'

Per nodded gratefully at Anna.

'When he was eight years old he and his mother became homeless, when she was evicted from her apartment in Malmö because of her drug abuse. All their money went on drugs. They lived in doorways, cellars and under bridges for a year. Erik attended school during this period but according to social services he was badly bullied by the other kids.'

'Could that explain why many of his victims have been homeless and found under bridges?' asked Per.

346

'Very possibly. When his mother died he was placed in a foster home in Malmö. After that he hasn't shown up in any police investigations or in the social services database. Apart from one time when the family he lived with was worried about his treatment of animals. They had to find a new home for the family's cat.'

'The first sign of lack of empathy in a child,' said Per. 'Cruelty to animals.'

Anna continued reading from her papers. 'He just barely managed to get through school. That's all I've managed to produce.'

'Keep digging. Talk with the family Erik lived with in Malmö,' said Per, when there was a knock on the door.

A uniformed police officer stood outside. He was the duty chief but wasn't authorized to attend the briefing, which at that moment had locked doors due to the sensitive situation in the investigation.

'Can it wait?' asked Per.

'No, I don't think so. It may concern your case.'

Per left the room and closed the door behind him.

'Ibrahim Hatim's foster parents are here,' said the chief. 'Ibrahim hasn't been home since yesterday evening – they've been searching for him all night. His phone is turned off. He was supposed to take part in a mediation this morning with Adrian Ren and his family, but didn't show up.'

Per ran his hand across his beard stubble. He felt a little irritated at being disturbed in the briefing because of this.

'My God, that's nothing to be concerned about. He probably changed his mind.'

'His girlfriend apparently can't be reached either.'

'That, on the other hand, feels more serious. We've put out a search for Klara. If he's with her then we'll find him. Pray to the gods that they're just somewhere necking,' said Per, wanting to go back to the briefing.

'It's just that his foster parents say that Ibrahim pushed for the mediation to happen – it was important to him. He wouldn't miss it. The family is worried because Samir disappeared without a trace a week before he showed up at Rådhus Square, and now they can't get hold of Ibrahim.'

Per disappeared into his thoughts. This did not bode well.

It may well be that Erik had both Ibrahim and Klara.

Damn it!

69

Charlotte leaned toward Helen at home in her kitchen. The new material from the surveillance cameras was good for the investigation, but Erik pressing on the phone before the explosion on Rådhus Square could be explained away by any defence attorney. They needed to know more.

'Have you been granted a protected residence by social services?' asked Charlotte.

Helen still had a paper towel in her hand and kept twisting it around her index finger. 'Yes, but what happens if I need protection for more than three months?'

Charlotte wanted to say that Erik would be convicted of several serious crimes. That Helen didn't need to fear him any longer, would maybe not even have to move from Umeå. But that wasn't something she could promise.

'We'll deal with that then,' she answered instead.

Helen gave her a weak smile. 'I don't trust the system. No one stays in prison very long in this country. I intend to move to another city and change my name, start a new life.'

Charlotte didn't respond to that. She had nothing to counter with.

'I get to borrow a car that can't be linked to me,' said Helen. 'Then I'll drive myself to an address I've been given where I'll be met by a local women's shelter in that area.' Helen said it as if rehearsing for herself.

Charlotte nodded. She knew that every effort of this sort looked different. The arrangements were adapted to what was possible for the local council.

'How did you get in contact with assistance in Umeå?' she said. 'Was it through someone you met here, someone you trust?'

Helen ran her hands through her curly hair. 'The people at the women's shelter are the only ones I've had contact with here in Umeå. But that's more than I dared before. We've moved a lot, to a different city after one or two years. I don't have any friends. I'm an anonymous mouse wherever I live. It's impossible to make contacts when you can't socialize outside the home.'

Charlotte met Alex's gaze. Neither of them could understand. And no one else could either. Before the school or workplace could discover that something was wrong in the Stenlund family, they had already moved on.

'We suspect that Erik handled explosives,' said Charlotte, changing tack.

'What?'

'Do you know where that expertise came from?'

Helen appeared to think, shook her head.

'Or wait,' she said suddenly. 'One time he left the computer screen on when he went to the bathroom. Then I discovered that he was on some shady site about things like detonations and such. I think it was the dark web, or whatever it's called.'

'Darknet. Did you see what he was doing there?'

'It seemed to be a chat forum for people interested in bombs. But I didn't have time to look carefully.'

Alex leaned forward, fixing his eyes on Helen. 'When was this?' he asked.

'Maybe two months ago.'

Charlotte closed her eyes. This meant that Erik had been interested in bombs long before Samir became his victim. Had he planned to blow up just anyone and Samir happened to become his victim, or did Erik have a different goal with learning to construct homemade bombs? In that case, what?

She looked at Alex, who understood what that look meant. He left the room to make a call. They needed permission to search the house and investigate whether Erik could have contributed to other bombings. She turned to Helen.

'Have you noticed anything here at home? Could he be storing bomb materials here, do you think?'

Helen stared straight ahead with her back bent.

'Oh my God. I don't think so. The children are here.'

'Do you know if he has any other place? It could be a shed, a barn, anything at all.'

She shook her head again. 'I've always been relieved when Erik stayed away from home. Where he went hasn't mattered to me.'

Alex came back. 'Why didn't you call the police when you saw the site he was on?' he asked, a little too irritated. 'You can submit tips about such things anonymously.'

'I thought it had something to do with school or a student, that he was just getting information. I didn't think . . . Well, what happened.'

Charlotte looked at the clock. Where were the folks who were supposed to help Helen get to the protected residence? She and Alex needed to return to the police station and talk with Per.

'Where's Erik's computer?' asked Charlotte.

'He always has it with him, so it's wherever he is.'

Shit, thought Charlotte.

'Has Erik ever been to your job at the dental clinic?'

Helen looked up, seemed to be confused by the question. 'Yes. He really likes to know where I am during the day. He does . . .

spot checks. He thinks I don't understand, but you learn that sort of thing after a few years, and I've been good at meeting people in secret.' She looked out of the kitchen window. 'Why do you ask?'

'Could Erik have taken the tools that disappeared from your work?' said Alex.

Helen looked at them perplexed. 'You can't very well kill someone with dental equipment, can you?' she asked, but then the significance seemed to sink in. 'The woman under the bridge, she didn't have any teeth – is that it?'

'Is Erik careful about his own teeth?' asked Charlotte.

'Manic,' said Helen. 'After every meal he brushes and flosses. Which he also demands of me and the children. They learned to brush their teeth themselves when they were really little.'

Alex pointed toward the bulletin board with the cleaning schedule. 'Can you tell us more about this?'

Helen didn't look up. 'Erik makes a cleaning schedule every week. At first I thought it was charming. That he was so orderly, you know. Not all men are.'

'Does a V mean anything in particular?'

'When you're done with your chore you let him know, and he puts a check mark there, for a completed task.'

'What happens if you don't do your chores?'

'Then he gets irritated and offended. Thinks that we don't respect him. The worst is when . . .' She paused, fixing her gaze on the schedule before she continued. 'He looks for mistakes, wants to find them. Erik gets some kind of sick satisfaction from seeing me scared. After a while I learned that it was half the enjoyment for him.'

Helen fell silent, seeming to have difficulty talking about it. Then she met Charlotte's gaze.

'He often argues. Threatens violence without doing it. Sometimes it's worse than when he actually hits. It wears you down.

Liam has learned to follow the cleaning schedule so that I escape being threatened and beaten.'

The hair on Charlotte's arms stood up from displeasure. *The children must suffer from PTSD*, she thought and wondered where they'd gone. Were they sitting nicely in Liam's room?

'Does he clean the house himself?' asked Alex.

Helen looked at the cleaning schedule. 'No, his name is only there for show. For friends and acquaintances who think that we live in a normal marriage,' she said, then looked at Alex. 'Erik has a similar mark on his forearm by the way.'

'What kind of mark?'

Charlotte had to exert herself not to seem overly eager, she didn't want Helen to clam up.

'Scar tissue that looks like a V, on his left arm.'

'Do you know how he got that?'

'Something from childhood that he refuses to talk about.'

'What do you know about his childhood?'

Helen looked out of the window. 'His father died young, and Erik lived homeless with his mother for a time, before she died from an overdose. I don't know much more than that. We don't talk about it.'

She looked toward the kitchen clock, then at her phone. 'We have to get picked up now. Erik could show up at any time.'

Charlotte knew that the reinforcements would arrest him if he showed up.

'What has he told you about his mother?' she asked.

'Nothing. But one time when he assaulted me, he screamed her name. It was as if he was hitting her, not me.'

'Does he hit the children?'

'No, but they see what happens to me. It's enough that he raises his hand for Liam and Elsa to obey. They always do what he says, without protesting. For my sake. You'll see, I asked them to go to Liam's room and they stayed there. They never object.'

She wiped tears away from her eyes. 'The outbursts usually get worse when he's about to get fired from a job, which as a rule happens after one or two years. Now we're there again. Erik complains about his colleagues, which usually means that they've started to get tired of him. I can't bear another round of it all. I'd rather die.' Helen talked quietly. It was as if the air had gone out of her there at the kitchen table.

'But you've also had problems at work, according to your boss,' said Charlotte.

'Yes, when his need for control increases it affects me in various ways. And I've been forced to meet my support people during work hours. I've found ways to get around it, like a secret agent,' she said, laughing drily.

'You're strong,' said Charlotte. 'You impress me.'

'In the past week I've met my contact person at the women's shelter and Dad in a car in Innertavle,' said Helen, putting her arms around her waist.

'Living in hiding isn't easy, but it must be better than living the way you are now,' said Charlotte.

Helen nodded. 'Many mornings I've woken up and wondered if this is the day I'll be killed. Although in Erik's twisted world we're living in a good marriage. He really believes that I'm happy, despite both physical and mental abuse and control. To survive, I've played along, acted as if the marriage is as it should be because the opposite is too dangerous. Do you understand?'

'I don't think either of us can understand,' said Alex.

'No, probably no one can. For a while I was so desperate that I tried to get my dad to kill Erik. I begged and pleaded on the phone, stood out here on the patio in the middle of the night and said that

I would do it myself otherwise.' She shook her head. 'But he helped me have better thoughts.'

Helen got up to check on the children and Charlotte let her go. For every answer they got, a new question was born. She thought about what they'd heard and fixed her gaze on the cleaning schedule, which looked so innocent. Something you might think was a sweet thing the family did together.

70

Erik closed the heavy door. It echoed from the sheet metal as he turned the key. He had spent several hours in there with Klara. It had been all rigged and ready in case of unforeseen events. The room inside was clean, freshly painted and tidy. There was even a battery-operated heating element to protect from the worst of the cold. He called it the bomb shelter. The space wasn't built for that purpose, but it was like a soundproof bunker. It was impossible to hear that anyone was in there, and he'd put a padlock on the door so that no one could open it.

He needed fresh air, wanted to get away from Klara's frightened look so that he could think. She disturbed him and created anxiety. He needed to distance himself from that for a while. Klara was another Samir. Unplanned. But with Samir it had taken large quantities of drugs to keep him calm, and with Klara almost nothing. Her thin body soaked it up.

What he'd done with Samir was a masterwork. Well-choreographed, like a ballet performance. Every decision he'd made in the bomb shelter the past week had involved enormous risks. But, damn, how alive he'd felt. Simply thinking back to the vest, the explosive device he'd built himself, the terror in Samir's eyes . . . All that made Erik glow with pride. The world had become a better place, thanks to him.

Now he would stage a new performance. She would be placed in a car park in the city with a syringe in her arm. The police would call it an overdose. Nothing suspicious, just a young woman on a downward slide in life. Erik knew that the police had no idea who he was – he'd been careful. Why should they suspect a nice school counsellor who had dropped Klara off at school? He would continue to maintain that lie.

Erik aimed the torch toward the floor. The lights didn't work and the cellar was dark without windows. The beam of light helped him see where to put his feet but also all the rubbish that was in the corridor. Papers, broken glass, car tyres, syringes and bottles. Dried shit was smeared on the walls along with the usual graffiti. There was crunching under his feet; he wasn't sure what he'd trodden on but was careful not to step on anything sharp.

As Erik approached the stairs, the torch was no longer needed. The light from above made its way into the cellar. Shadows from the railing made the walls come alive. Step by step he made his way up, but stopped several times and listened for sounds. Nothing was heard from the bomb shelter. Nothing from up there.

Lena and Samir had spent their final days of life here with no problems. They'd been drugged and easy to handle. Samir had tried to threaten him and he smiled at the memory of how the boy had wandered around the pitch-black corridors after having receiving a syringe of Rohypnol. Tried to find a way out, wobbled, fell. Erik had followed him and felt amused until he was forced to drag him into the bomb shelter and go home. The bomb vest had taken almost a whole week to make. Keeping Samir drugged for so long was difficult and time-consuming. This time it would go faster.

When he came up the stairs, he turned to the right, pulling up the zipper on his jacket. Practically all the windows were broken, so it was just as cold inside as outside. He stepped over a filthy mattress that was thrown in the middle of his path and moved a broken

357

chair that stood in the way. Most of the rooms still had doors, but the cylinder locks and handles were long since gone.

Erik went to a window to get fresh air, took out his phone and turned it on. He had turned off Klara's phone so that no one could trace it. He had missed several calls from the school and from a number he didn't recognize. There was also a text from the administrator who asked if Erik would be coming in today. It had been sent right before lunch.

He looked at the time, which showed 2.53 p.m. Maybe it was not so strange that they were looking for him, but there was no time left to work. He was forced to solve the problems that had arisen. To plan and organize. Other people who lived their lives as brain-dead robots didn't understand that sort of thing.

Erik let the cold caress his cheeks, breathed in and closed his eyes. Collected his thoughts about what he had to do next. Klara's fate was in his hands, and her death would happen without her needing to suffer. She was a person he could feel something for, because the children liked her – not some awful vagrant. Lena on the other hand . . . he despised her. For that reason her teeth were extracted. Like the others. Later he'd found out that she wasn't like that. Not really homeless. He would never forgive her for that.

Erik took in more air, looked around and smiled. He was calm. The first two victims of his life had encountered death in the form of a panic-stricken and intoxicated young Erik who was unable to enjoy the event. Gradually he'd learned to take his time and be completely free from alcohol and drugs. He wanted his head to be crystal clear when he took a life. Experience every movement, see all the details and take in the smell of the victim's fear. Experience again the terror he himself had been subjected to.

Erik turned around to go back to the bomb shelter, to Klara's frightened look, when the phone buzzed in his hand.

It was the neighbour calling. The situation was miserable as usual and several ringtones sounded before he decided to answer.

'Hello, can I call you back?' Erik asked.

'Hi there, are you going on holiday? I see that Helen and the children are putting suitcases in a car with some friends I've never seen before.'

Erik stopped on the top step. 'What do you mean?'

'Yes, I just wanted to ask if you needed help with anything. Should I bring in the post or anything while you're away?'

Erik clenched his teeth. His fingers were holding the railing so hard that the metal cut into his skin.

'Can you do me a favour?' He tried to sound controlled. 'Helen has been a bit confused lately, as perhaps you've noticed. She's doing very poorly mentally. Could you follow them and see where she goes? I have to call her doctor.'

He hoped that the neighbour would think he sounded believable.

'Of course. Call me when you've talked with the doctor. Should I go out and talk with her?'

Erik shook his head, even though the neighbour couldn't see that. 'That would probably only make things worse. Check where she goes, then I'll solve it. Thanks for calling.'

Erik hung up. The neighbour was disgustingly curious and snooped in everyone's lives. He looked up to Erik and was a bit of a chauvinist. Always distrusted the opposite sex. But right now that was a big help.

He took a deep breath and let go of the railing. An endless spiral of shit. Helen was about to leave him. That couldn't happen under any circumstances whatsoever. He turned on the torch just as he heard a scraping sound from the cellar. What was that? Very quietly, he took double steps down the stairs. Rushed ahead through the cellar, past the bomb shelter which he knew no sound could come from. Erik stopped at the end of the corridor, in front of a concrete wall. Slowly he turned around. But all he heard was his own breathing. It was silent and dark all around him.

Erik started moving toward the stairs again, up to the exit. He turned his neck in different directions and noticed that it felt even stiffer than before, as if he'd got a new strain from all the stress.

It was Helen's fault.

71

Per stepped into the room where the family that Ibrahim lived with sat waiting impatiently. The investigation constantly drew him into new conversations and now it was already long past lunchtime without his having had anything to eat. Not good for a diabetic.

Klara's parents had now reported their daughter missing. Alex and Charlotte had been to talk with them. At the same time Helen and the children were on their way to safety. At least temporarily.

Erik was the perpetrator, the serial killer they were seeking. But there was no technical evidence that could link him with certainty to the crimes. Despite that the prosecutor had arraigned Erik in absentia and decided on a house search. Erik was wanted and would be brought in.

Ibrahim's foster parents stood up politely as Per came into the room.

When Per started questioning Apollonia and Martin about what had happened, they basically said the same thing the duty chief had said earlier – that Ibrahim had been gone since the previous day. That they couldn't get hold of either him or Klara. That he wouldn't want to miss the morning mediation with Adrian . . .

As the conversation progressed, Per took off his glasses and set them on the table. 'Can you think of anyone he might have gone to see yesterday?'

'No, he mostly spends time with Klara, but she was babysitting last night.'

Per breathed in. This thing with Klara gave him a bad feeling. She should have shown up by now. 'Could Ibrahim have met up with her anyway?'

'Not according to her friends.'

'And Omar?' asked Per.

Apollonia's eyes flashed. 'I hope not. Last I heard Omar was in Finland, so Ibrahim had been told,' she said with contempt in her voice.

'And Ibrahim hasn't disappeared in this way before?' asked Per.

Apollonia shook her head. 'No. But he told us that Samir was gone a whole week before what happened on Rådhus Square. And Ibrahim has said that he felt pursued by someone. What if he was right? If someone has done something to Ibrahim? You have to start looking for him. We need help.' Panic could be heard in her voice.

'Who is supposed to be pursuing him? Did he know?' asked Per.

'No, Ibrahim wasn't sure if it was even true. It was just a feeling he had.'

Martin looked at his phone and Per saw the hopelessness in his eyes.

'Don't worry, we'll do all we can to find Ibrahim,' said Per. But what the parents said was true. Samir had also disappeared without a trace before he was murdered.

Charlotte opened the door without knocking, standing out of breath in the doorway and handing a slip of paper to Per. He read:

We have located the suspect – he has turned on his phone.

Per stood up quickly. 'I'll send a colleague to take care of your report on Ibrahim,' he said to Martin and Apollonia before he left the room.

362

'Tell me, what do we know?' he said while they moved quickly to join their team.

'Erik's phone suddenly emitted a signal and his mobile is moving along E12 in the direction of Umeå.'

'Have we got the go-ahead to tap his phone?' said Per.

'Yes, approval just arrived from the court,' said Charlotte. 'But we have to send the SWAT team after him. Klara may be in the car.'

'Or else he's left her somewhere. Where exactly did you capture that first signal?'

'By Gubböle.'

Charlotte and Per started to move at a near run toward the briefing room.

'So we know that he's coming from the west, in the direction of town. What has he been doing all day and where has he been? Listen, everyone!' Per called when they reached the rest of the group. 'We have Erik Stenlund's phone in movement on the E12 toward Umeå. Alex and Charlotte, I want you to piggy-back the SWAT team and arrest Erik. Find out where Klara Lundqvist is . . . And Anna, I want to find out about all activity that happens on Erik's phone. We must see all his texts and hear all his calls, now!'

Anna set down her celery juice so hard on the table that it splashed over.

Charlotte and Alex put on their protective vests.

'What's in the direction he's coming from?' said Per excitedly. 'He must have spent the better part of the day there. I'm sure that Klara won't be with him in the car, and if he's done something with her, she's still at that place.'

Charlotte put on her jacket.

'Shit!' Kicki screamed and everyone in the room looked at her. She stared at her computer. 'Erik has turned off the phone again – we just lost his position.'

363

Per pointed at Charlotte. 'Take the manpower you need and drive toward his most recently known location. Find him, damn it.'

'The old Brattby care facility!' Anna shouted. 'He may have been there. I see on the map that it's nearby. It's been abandoned for years.'

'Good, that's worth checking,' said Per. 'You and I will go there.'

72

After Erik left the old care facility, he felt unsure about whether he'd locked the bomb shelter. Distractions were popping up everywhere. *Fucking Wednesday*, he thought and looked at his phone, which was between the seats, charging. The battery had died, but soon he could turn it on again and make contact with the neighbour. Klara's phone was on the passenger seat, the one she'd dropped on the floor of the car and because of that found his black box. When she'd seen the teeth, she had understood immediately. She was a bright young woman. But opening the box had been the same as committing suicide. Too bad, although it was Klara's own fault that she had ended up in this situation. Life had to go on without her. A life without Helen, on the other hand, that was quite a different matter. He needed to talk with her.

Erik put his hand on the gearstick and put it in fifth. The gearbox scraped when he first missed the position and it sounded like the whole car would fall apart. He hated manual gears, but his own car was still outside Brattby House. He'd just acquired the van he was driving – he found it by chance on the internet. Erik felt a little like a cliché. A murderer with a van. But the fact was that it did make it easier to transport the victims. Putting them in the boot of his other car was laborious and involved unnecessary risk. Besides, the explosive materials took up space. The change of ownership hadn't gone through yet and that suited him right now. The course of events during the past week hadn't been optimal. After Lena, things had started to move in an unforeseen direction. His plans had to be put into effect much sooner than he'd expected.

By Kronoparken he slowed down. Further ahead he saw what looked like police cars. Erik turned down the music, drove a little closer to the shoulder. The police drove soundlessly past and he saw them disappear in the rear-view mirror. *Must have been an accident*, he thought.

As he drove on, his thoughts returned to Helen. She was truly ruining this day. What had happened with Klara in the morning was messy enough. Erik was afraid that he would miss details and be incapable of sorting out what was most important. There was too much to be arranged at the same time with the problems that Klara and Helen caused. His routines were upset. The tension in his body produced pressure across his chest and a pounding headache. Where was Helen going? Had she taken off to meet her father or the person in the Volvo? The suitcases the neighbour talked about were worrying. Would she really leave him? Where would she go without him? Erik had to stop her. She couldn't go away or create more problems, it wasn't right. Helen was about to commit the worst mistake of her life. He just needed to get her to realize that for herself.

By the time he reached the Teg Bridge in the middle of the city, the phone was charged again and he turned it on. The neighbour answered after one ring.

'Hey, Erik. You can't just turn off your phone when I'm doing you a favour.'

'Sorry, the battery ran out.'

'I'm driving behind Helen on the E4 going south,' the neighbour said. 'But I can't follow her further than Hörnefors, I have

366

to get back home and take the dog out. Have you talked with her doctor?'

Erik speeded up and aimed for the E4. Conveniently enough he was on the right side of town.

'I understand that and truly appreciate your help. I'm on my way now.'

'So what did her doctor say? Does she need medication or what's happening?'

'I'll take her to the doctor's,' Erik lied. 'First, I just have to pick her up . . . There's a risk that she'll injure herself.'

'What? Is it that bad?' the neighbour said. 'Womenfolk and their weak minds . . . I'm truly sorry.'

'Thanks. Yes, it's really difficult for the whole family.'

'She has the kids with her too,' said the neighbour.

'Yes, that's worrying.'

'There were two women with her at the house, but I no longer see them.'

Erik was about to ask what the women looked like, when the neighbour kept talking.

'Listen, Erik, now I see that her car is turning off here. Where are you?'

'Turning off where?'

'Wait, let me see . . .'

Erik heard the sound of the neighbour's indicator.

'I think that Helen is stopping for petrol. She's driving into a Circle K here in Hörnefors. Do you want me to talk with her?'

'No, you don't need to. I'll sort it, but thanks, anyway. You've done both of us a big favour.'

'I'll head home then,' said the neighbour. 'Hope this works out.'

They ended the call. Erik drove way over the speed limit and would be there in a few minutes. This time it was worth the risk.

When at last he turned into the Circle K, he saw Helen coming out of the store. Her hair was covered by a cap. The children were sitting in the car.

Erik parked a short distance from them. He drummed his fingers on the steering wheel and then reached for the glovebox on the passenger side.

73

Charlotte checked the clock – it was already after five o'clock. Wednesday would most likely turn into Thursday without anyone on the team resting their head on a pillow.

She pushed the earpiece further in, afraid to miss any information from the response team leader who was in the car ahead. She and Alex had left the police station in one of their unmarked cars and were now on their way south on the E4 toward Hörnefors, where they had picked up the latest position from Erik's mobile. The phone tap showed that he was in contact with their next-door neighbour. From what they could hear of the call Erik didn't seem to have any idea that the police were on their way to arrest him. He was focused on his wife.

'How long will it take for Per and Anna to drive to Brattby?' asked Alex, managing to get the car up to 110 kilometres an hour. Traffic was heavy on the E4 and driving too fast was risky.

'It's over twenty kilometres there, so max twenty minutes,' she replied. 'But we don't know if Klara is at the care facility. Per was just going to check the property.'

'If Klara isn't found there, I'll see to it that Erik tells us where she is,' said Alex.

Charlotte nodded. She knew he meant it. Alex charged ahead and used force if required. Although always within the limits of what was allowed – or almost always. She inspected his face from the side. The light beard stubble, the small mouth, pointed chin. And he was ever so physically fit. The energy he radiated said: *I'm going to get you first, before you can get me.* There was something about him that couldn't be resisted.

She turned her eyes to the road again. Alex was driving in the left lane, and the cars moved compliantly into the right lane to make room for the police cortege that couldn't be missed. Charlotte once again tried to call the number they had for Helen but went straight to voicemail. It had been that way with every attempt. She swore silently to herself.

'Have they found anything in the house search at the Stenlunds'?' asked Alex.

'Not yet. The computer is probably the key for us. But Erik guards it like a hawk, according to Helen.'

'It's lucky anyway that Erik doesn't know we're nearby. He would never have turned on his phone and had contact with the neighbour.'

'True,' said Charlotte. 'My analysis is that he's so narcissistic that he believes he's superior to us. Klara has somehow figured out who he is and for that reason he's taken her. Even so, he calmly claimed that he dropped her off at school this morning. He's ice cold. On the other hand, that's not true where Helen is concerned. She's his Achilles heel, the person who can put him off balance so that maybe he makes a mistake.'

They were approaching the place where Erik was headed – the Circle K petrol station in Hörnefors.

'He seems to have stopped there,' said Charlotte.

Alex stayed close behind the van with the SWAT team and Charlotte had to hang on as they turned off the E4. She turned down the thermostat in the car, opened her jacket. Sometimes her body showed signs of menopause. She took out her service pistol and just had time to check it before they were there. As they reached the petrol station, Per called and she put it on speakerphone.

'Have you arrived at the Brattby care facility?' she asked.

'Be there in thirty seconds. Do you have Erik?'

'Soon – we're at the petrol station in Hörnefors where Helen reportedly stopped,' said Charlotte. 'Stay on the phone.'

She scanned the area.

'I don't see either the car Helen was driving or Erik's car,' she said. 'Could they have managed to drive away?'

'Okay, I'm at the care facility,' Per said on the phone. 'Erik is using a different car – his is parked here.'

Then he hung up.

'Then he must be around here somewhere,' said Alex. 'We have to handle this in the right way. Go into the petrol station and ask discreetly to see what their surveillance cameras show. We must know what we're getting into. Then I'll ask the SWAT team to start searching the area.'

74

Anna had guessed right. The abandoned care facility was where Erik had been earlier in the day. Per ran toward Erik's car, parked a short distance away. He tore open one door and looked in. Anna went to the boot and opened it.

'Empty.'

'This is the vehicle Klara was riding in before she disappeared. Get Forensics here and secure evidence.'

The car would be properly examined on site before it was sent on for an even more thorough review.

'Why doesn't anyone take care of this place?' said Anna, pulling a cap over her head.

Everyone in Umeå knew about the Brattby care facility. It had been a reform school to start with and then an institution for adults with learning disabilities. More than two decades ago it closed and now only the dilapidated buildings were left.

Per put on his protective vest and tightened it around his waist. The area would soon be cordoned off and in a few hours darkness would set in. But even now it was just empty, spooky.

Anna took out her phone and reported the find of the car. They knew that Erik wasn't here now, but Per was worried about his need for control. He searched for surveillance cameras around the buildings but didn't see any. Erik also had knowledge of explosives. What if he'd planned to blow up the area if he was caught?

He turned to Anna, who had put on gloves and routinely started going through Erik's car.

'We must start searching the buildings. It's going to take too long to get the national bomb squad to send people here.'

'Isn't that handled through the duty chief at NOA?' said Anna while she stood leaning over the open boot.

'Contact them in that case. I have to start searching for Klara. She must be here somewhere. And call the SWAT team now that we know this is the right place.'

'The SWAT team is already on its way,' said Anna, picking up the phone to contact the National Operations Agency in Stockholm.

Per twirled around to check the area. The row of crumbling yellow brick buildings had once been Brattby House. Windows were broken, rubbish was spread out on the ground along with car tyres and beds. The grounds were extensive. Per counted six buildings in all – a few were two storeys, others had three. Behind them was a large field, and on the other side a forest. They would proceed from Erik's car as they searched through the buildings.

Per took a pair of rubber gloves from his jacket pocket. Anna had ended the call and now came over to hand him a black velvet box.

'This was in the spare tyre compartment.'

Per put on the gloves.

'Look in it,' she said.

Per opened the box.

Teeth.

His stomach reacted immediately and he brought his hand to his mouth.

Damn it, he thought and took a couple of deep breaths before he could look in the box again. White teeth, grey, some with amalgam fillings, others with enamel that looked like plastic. The teeth seemed to be clean – there was no blood on them.

'Here's our evidence. We have him,' said Per.

'But where can Klara be? This is a big area to search through,' said Anna, letting her gaze run across the buildings. Then she turned around as the first vehicle with the SWAT team arrived, almost imperceptibly. That was how they worked. A heavily armed man came running toward them.

'We have permission to search the buildings, one at a time, but at the slightest suspicion we'll back out and await the bomb squad. Don't stray from my side, okay?'

The man fixed his eyes on Per, who nodded. He felt like a schoolboy getting orders from the teacher.

The SWAT team went toward the building closest to Erik's car.

Per turned to Anna. 'You stay here and await information from Charlotte. If Klara is seen with Erik we can break off the immediate search for her here in Brattby.'

He followed the tall man in the black uniform. As a young policeman, Per had wanted to be someone like that, but he didn't pass the tests and then the diabetes diagnosis was the nail in the coffin. Per left his gun in its holster. The people ahead of him had plenty of ammunition. The asphalt under their feet was wet and crunched under their shoes. The SWAT team were wearing head torches that weren't needed yet. He had his torch in his jacket pocket.

'Per, wait!' Anna came running and then stopped abruptly in front of him.

'I'm worried,' she said quietly. 'If Erik has placed explosives here . . . What happens when Charlotte and Alex arrest him and he understands that it's over? And you're all still in there? We know that the bomb on Samir was set off via a phone that Erik had.'

Anna was right in principle. But what if Klara was in danger and they just stood here without doing anything? Per would never forgive himself for that.

'That's a risk we'll have to take,' he said. 'But keep in close contact with Charlotte and Alex. They must take his mobile immediately.'

75

Erik crouched in front of Helen. She was sitting on the toilet seat, seemed too scared out of her wits to really see him. He held her hands, which were shaking. His heart was pounding in his chest. As he brought his hand to her face she recoiled, but he simply wiped away her tears. And his own. Thanks to the neighbour he'd managed to stop her. She needed to be rescued.

'Please, Erik. Let me go.'

He sought eye contact with her, wanted to show that he wasn't angry, just hurt. But Helen looked everywhere except at him.

'But why . . . Why do you want to take the kids and leave me? I don't understand.'

Erik took hold of her hands again and she let him. A good sign. This would work out.

'Helen, I know I can be tough sometimes, but it's because I love you. You know that. Everything I do is for your sake, and the children's.'

'If you love me then let me go,' she said. 'I can't take any more. Erik, let me go. I'll come back. I promise.'

'You want to leave, but come back? And you say that you can't handle any more? I don't understand. What is it you want? You don't seem to know that yourself.'

Erik got up. Her face ended up in front of his crotch. He was standing so close that she couldn't stand up. Her cheeks were shiny with tears. Why was *she* crying? He was the one who was the victim here.

'I see that you're not doing well, Helen, and for just that reason I think you need routines and rules. I know you're in contact with your father again. He isn't good for you. Let me fix this.'

Helen met his gaze and he saw the hatred in her eyes. That made the blood rush in his head.

The blow struck her so hard that the back of her head hit the wall.

Erik crouched down again. Her nose was bleeding and he tore a piece of toilet paper from the holder. Then he carefully took her chin in his hand and wiped away the blood.

'See what you make me do,' he said.

Helen's breathing got faster. She looked at Erik as he cleaned her.

'Shall we go home now? I can forget that this has happened,' he said, getting up again. He opened the toilet door and showed that she was free to leave the cramped space. Carefully he stroked her back as she got up and passed him on her way out to the sink. He wasn't as awful as Helen made him feel.

'I'm not going anywhere with you, Erik. You're sick. You're the one who needs help,' she said.

That was like being hit by a baseball bat right on the head. Who had she been talking with? His beautiful wife was completely brainwashed.

The second blow made her fall to the floor. It wasn't often he used force. Only when it was necessary. Now he had no choice, however much it hurt him.

As he reached out to help her up he heard voices outside the door. Faintly, but clear enough to make out that they were talking about his van.

Erik stood still, listened. Who were they? Police? Maybe he was imagining things. Helen made him paranoid. He reached his hand toward her as he looked at the door that led out from the bathroom. They needed to go home now.

But Helen pushed away his hand and his attention was once again focused solely on her.

76

Per followed the SWAT team into the nearest building at Brattby House. He poked at his earpiece to get it to sit better and stayed close behind the response leader. The man in front of Per was like a wall of muscle and ammunition. He and his team communicated with their hands and fingers; not many words were spoken even though the building was almost certainly deserted. But they couldn't know for sure that Erik was acting alone.

They made their way through corridor after corridor. All that was heard was the crunching sound when their boots hit the floor. With every room they passed, two policemen went in and searched. The further into the building they went, the greater the risk of stepping on something sharp. There were boards with nails pointing straight up everywhere. Per guessed that they'd covered the windows. If Klara was here, it must feel terrifying for her; it was an awful place to be held captive in.

Suddenly the officer in the lead raised a clenched fist.

Everyone stopped except the two policemen who were inspecting one of the rooms. What was happening? Had they discovered something?

But then the two came back out in the corridor and the hand went down. The sign was given to continue.

The group moved ahead. As Per went past the room that the two men had searched, he looked in and shone his torch. There was a garment on the floor – a blue jacket. It looked new. Per recalled what Klara had on when she disappeared. Helen had told the police what she was wearing when she left the house: a pink sweater, a pair of jeans and a blue jacket.

Damn it, he thought, feeling pressure across his chest.

When they came to a stairway that led down to the cellar, the group stopped. Blue blinking lights flashed silently over Brattby House. Now police cars and an ambulance were at the scene. Finally.

The response leader brought his hand over his head and pointed toward the stairs. On his way down Per noticed a stench that increased his worry for Klara. Down here the darkness was solid.

When he heard Anna's voice in his ear, Per jumped.

'Hello, Per, do you hear me?'

He pressed the button to answer. 'Yes, what do you have?' he said quietly, as they moved downward.

'Charlotte called – they've located Erik.'

'Have they secured him?'

'No, there's a situation at the petrol station that must be resolved. But Klara isn't there. Do you have her?'

'Negative,' said Per. 'But she's here, or has been. We've found a jacket that I believe is hers.'

'Okay, I'll pass that on to Charlotte,' said Anna, and then there was silence in his ear.

They were down in the cellar. Per stared into the darkness, using his torch. The group continued to move below ground in what felt like a labyrinth of passageways. He wondered whether they would find their way out again. The acrid odour stung in his nose.

Suddenly the response commander stopped abruptly.

'Bomb located! Evacuate!'

Per turned ice cold.

77

Charlotte was in the petrol station office with Alex and the response team leader, looking at the screen that showed the video recording from a camera inside the bathroom, in the space where the sink was. An illegal surveillance set-up which, according to the employees, was due to problems with graffiti. Charlotte brushed it aside; she had more important things to think about right now.

Erik had just struck Helen so hard that she ended up on the floor. Their reinforcements had secured the area around the room. Erik would not be able to get away.

'We're ready to go in,' the response team leader said.

'We can't storm in with the SWAT team!' said Alex. 'It's still unclear whether Erik has mined Brattby House. If he sees us, everyone there, including Klara, could be blown up.'

'What do you suggest? That we let the woman in there be beaten to death by a psychopath?' asked Charlotte.

Alex tore off his jacket. 'I'll solve this my way. You stay here, Charlotte, and I want two of your men outside the door,' said Alex to the response team leader. 'When I say "fuck it", it's time for you to go in. Then I'll have secured the place. Okay?'

'It will be the same result regardless of whether *one* cop or *several* cops go in,' said Charlotte.

'I've done this before. He won't know that I'm a cop when I step into the toilets,' said Alex, rolling up the sleeves on his shirt. He undid the two top buttons and put his gun in the waistband, before he pulled his shirt over it. Charlotte watched him tousle his well-combed hair. He would pretend to be a regular guy who needed to use the toilet.

'Is there audio? We must be able to hear,' said Charlotte, looking at the woman who had the misfortune of working this particular shift.

'No, unfortunately not.'

Charlotte stamped the floor with her foot. She looked at Alex who was ready to go.

'Leave the phone on in your pocket so that I hear what's being said,' she said.

Alex nodded, called her phone and then walked away quickly, together with two men from the SWAT team. The presence of the police had made the petrol station's regular customers flee the area.

On the screen Charlotte could see Helen sitting on the floor, pressed against a wall. Erik stood leaning over her, gesturing. Then Alex stepped in through the door and Erik turned toward him briefly before he once again directed his attention to Helen.

'You mustn't sit here feeling sad, honey. Come on now, let's go.' Erik's voice was heard in Charlotte's phone. The tone was silky.

Helen got up without Erik's help.

That's good, Helen, thought Charlotte. She saw that Erik glanced at Alex. It seemed like he was considering whether the stranger was a threat or not.

Alex pretended not to care what was happening between Helen and Erik but instead stood by one of the sinks and started washing his hands. But Helen recognized him. Charlotte saw the relief in her face.

'Come now, darling, you'll see that everything will be better when we get home,' said Erik.

Helen crossed her arms across her chest. Blood was still dripping from her nose.

'Excuse me, can you pass me a paper towel?' said Alex to Erik, pointing to the holder that was on the wall behind Helen.

Charlotte saw a shift in Erik's gaze. Something had made him take note of Alex. Then she realized what.

Damn it, she thought. *The gun in Alex's waistband.*

Erik put one hand in his pocket and was just able to get out his phone before Alex shoved him into the wall with such force that he bounced. Alex knocked the phone out of Erik's hands so that it fell down under one of the sinks.

'Fuck it!' Alex yelled and took out his gun, at the same time as the two men from the SWAT team opened the door.

'Police! Down on the floor!' Alex shouted and aimed his gun at Erik, who was standing with his back against the tiled wall. He sank down on his knees and held his hands behind his back without Alex asking him to. Helen held her hands up in the air. Her eyes opened wide when she saw the two heavily armed men.

Charlotte noticed how Erik glanced toward the phone that had ended up under the sink. Alex bent down to pick it up.

'No, no, no,' Charlotte called into the mute surveillance camera. 'Check his hands you lunatic!'

Then Erik took another phone from his back pocket and quickly pressed one of the buttons. *Oh no*, thought Charlotte, seeing Alex notice the same thing. He threw himself over Erik and pressed his body down against the floor.

'Damn it!' Alex screamed as he got hold of Erik's arms.

Charlotte rushed out of the petrol station office so quickly that she knocked over a display of chocolates as she passed. Just then the response team leader's voice was heard in her earpiece.

'There's an explosion at Brattby!'

78

Per didn't know how he got out of the care facility. The others must have shoved him in the right direction. His ears were ringing after the explosion. He felt the heat from the burning building at his back and the fire crackle. In front of him was a blinking blue inferno of light. All he could think about were the boys at home, and Mia. His legs crumpled and he fell to the ground. His palms broke the fall and he felt a sharp pain. His stomach muscles contracted in an attempt to get the contents out, but without result.

He heard Anna's voice while he coughed and looked up, glancing around for the others who had been in the building. They sat spread out on the ground around him, coughing and in pain, just like him. The group had been a few seconds from being blown up completely in there. This insight made Per squint and feel for which parts of his body hurt.

'Per! Talk to me!' he heard Anna say, who crouched down beside him.

He tried to smile to show that he was okay. Then he brought his hand toward a painful spot on his calf and felt something warm and moist. A shard of glass had lodged in his calf.

'The ambulance is here,' she said, grimacing uncomfortably at the sight of his leg.

'Have they caught Erik?' he forced out, lying down on his back. The heat in his body was replaced by cold and dampness.

'Yes, they're taking him to the station. Is Klara in there?'

He thought about the jacket they'd seen in one of the rooms. Klara's jacket.

'I don't know . . . We came to a door . . . The explosives must have been there. Maybe she was inside the building. We didn't have time to look.'

Per looked straight up at the blue sky. He could smell smoke and burned material as an ambulance and fire truck drove into the area.

'Charlotte and Alex must get Erik to talk and tell us if Klara was in there,' he said, pointing toward the burning building.

'Erik detonated the bomb when Alex arrested him. He didn't understand that Erik had two phones and missed one of them.' She placed her jacket under Per's head.

'Yes, I noticed that,' he said, grimacing at the pain in his leg. It increased with every second.

As he sat up to look at the wound, the paramedics came running toward him. He observed the burning building. Police were searching the area.

'Maybe we just blew her up,' said Per, feeling despair.

Anna sat on the ground. She didn't reply, but instead looked at the flames.

79

Erik poked away the dirt under his fingernails. They had driven at blazing speed to the police station, where he had to provide fingerprints, DNA samples and be photographed. His clothes had been stuffed into plastic bags and now he was sitting in a green tracksuit that smelled of chlorine, waiting to be questioned. His assigned attorney was sitting beside him. Erik realized that they must have found Klara by this point. Or in any event, what was left of her. He hadn't pulled out her teeth, so she would be easy to identify. In front of him was a paper cup with water. He sniffed it, didn't trust that the cup was clean – anyone at all could have touched it. The attorney said that this was front page news in the papers. A serial killer was evidently interesting. Erik thought about Helen and the children – what would they think? He needed to get out of here. It was lucky that the bomb exploded. It ought to have destroyed everything. In the bomb shelter was every little detail of the murders that had been plotted by his brilliant brain. Pictures, drawings, recipes, dental equipment, videos. It was his very own deluxe man cave. Erik had forgotten just one thing in the stress with Klara. The box with the teeth.

When the door to the interview room opened, the police from the petrol station strode in. The guy with the tattoos had rolled down his shirt sleeves and cleaned up. He looked rather pleasant, thought Erik. Someone he would gladly have a beer with. The female police officer, on the other hand, was elegant somehow.

They sat down in silence. After that they started setting out picture after picture on the table. Some of his previous victims mixed with his most recent ones. Erik looked at the woman in Umeå whom he'd dumped under the Teg Bridge. There was a lot of carelessness connected with that act. For one thing she hadn't been homeless. For another he hadn't checked whether she actually sank into the river after he pushed her over the edge, so she'd been found much too soon, hanging on a hook. Erik crossed his legs. He inspected his masterwork, Samir – took in every detail in the pictures. These were the ones the police knew about. *Stupid cops*, he thought contentedly. His refined way of helping society get rid of worthless individuals reached further back in time than that. He would never forget the victims in Malmö, especially not the first one because that was where it all started. Stockholm was fuzzy for some reason. Everything in Umeå was as fresh as newly baked rolls.

'What are you trying to say by showing these awful pictures?' he asked the police.

'Wait a moment,' the policeman said.

Erik sighed. He had to tear his eyes from the table so as not to appear too curious. 'How are my wife and children doing?'

'They're fine,' the woman said.

The policeman started a computer that was on the table. Erik sighed again, demonstratively deep.

'Are we boring you?' the policeman said.

'A little. What am I doing here?'

The man laughed scornfully and showed a slightly crooked front tooth. *That's bad*, thought Erik.

The female police officer took over. 'My name is Charlotte von Klint and this is my colleague Alex Alvarez. We are leading

387

this investigation where you are suspected of probable cause of four homicides, aggravated assault, aggravated injury and illegal handling of explosives . . .'

Erik stopped listening, leaned back and let his gaze rest on the pictures. They couldn't put him in prison for any of this. His computer was blown up in Brattby, everything was gone. It was just that little detail with the box, and then Klara and the phone he'd used to kill her. He and the attorney needed a plan for that.

'When can I see my wife?' he asked.

Charlotte looked at him as if he were a little slow in the head. 'Never, I hope.'

'Is she here?'

'I think you should focus on yourself right now, Erik. You're not getting out of this.'

Alex reached across the table to get one of the pictures and Erik reflexively pressed his back against the chair. His head was pounding after the hard shove against the wall.

'I'm going to report you for assault,' he said to Alex.

'Do that.'

'Where is Klara?' Charlotte asked, standing up. She placed herself behind Alex.

Erik smiled. So they hadn't found her yet. 'That's probably up to you to figure out, not me.'

'When did you last see her?'

'When I dropped her off at school this morning, at nine o'clock, perhaps.'

'We can prove you didn't do that. What were you doing at Brattby House?'

'I've heard they have ghost hunts there and I was curious. Just wanted to check, so I went there.'

'And if we say that we found Klara at Brattby House, what do you say to that?'

Erik clenched his jaw. Had they found her or not? They were trying to trick him.

'Really? I didn't see her,' he said.

Alex leaned toward the table again. Erik couldn't tear his eyes away from that crooked front tooth.

'Do you want to remove it or what?' asked Alex, pointing toward his tooth.

Erik didn't reply.

'You do collect teeth, from what we understand,' Charlotte continued, setting out a picture of his black box.

Erik had to summon all his energy not to show what he was experiencing inside. He held his breath.

The box. Which he'd always guarded so carefully, how could he have forgotten that?

'All your victims' teeth gathered in a worn old box,' said Charlotte, stroking her finger across the picture. 'It was found in your car, your DNA is probably on it. Add that to all the other evidence we have on you. But you can still help yourself.'

Erik didn't reply.

'If you tell us what you've done with Klara Lundqvist, we promise to speak with the prosecutor and tell him that you're willing to cooperate.'

Erik looked at his attorney. He was writing on a notepad but did nothing to help him.

Alex set out another picture, taken of Erik a few hours ago by the medical examiner. It exposed Erik's naked body. His secret.

'This scar on your arm depicts a V. How did you get it?'

Erik felt the sweat coming out on the back of his neck. 'An accident as a child.'

'Tell us about it.'

'No.'

'Stig in Malmö. Does that mean anything to you?' said Charlotte.

Erik wiped away the moisture on his back with his hand. His head ached.

There were only two people besides social services who knew about Stig – the foster parents he had lived with in Malmö.

'Tell us about him,' the policeman said.

Stig, he thought. It had been a long time since he thought about Stig in this way. The man that his mother got drugs from and who had raped him under a bridge and then carved the mark on his arm with a bottle cap. The strongest memory Erik had of Stig, apart from the violence, was his teeth. The nausea he felt when Stig's mouth came close. His mother just sat there, high as a kite from the drugs that Stig exchanged for Erik's body. Erik had to fend for himself there under the bridge.

'It was Stig who marked you, wasn't it?'

'That has nothing to do with you,' Erik said quietly, but his voice was tense. He heard it himself. His temples were pulsing in time with his heartbeats. The foster parents in Malmö had betrayed him. They had promised to never tell anyone about Stig, but here sat total strangers who knew exactly what had happened.

'We can stop talking about Stig if you start telling us about Klara,' said Alex.

Erik was stuck in his own thoughts. He had looked up Stig after years of fantasies about revenge and he became Erik's first victim. The most important, and the fastest murder he'd committed. He was young and angry. But it was planned anyway. He found Stig passed out and simply injected a large dose of Rohypnol into him, so that he never woke up again. As far as he knew it had never been investigated by the police. The liberation of payback was like letting air out of a balloon. But the air came back, and back, and back. Erik regretted that Stig had got off easy.

The memories of the man were scattered when there was a knock on the door.

In stepped a young female police officer who handed over a note that Charlotte and Alex read. They appeared to be relieved. Erik became frustrated not knowing what this was about, but soon their eyes turned toward him.

'The room that you exploded at Brattby House has turned out to be empty of human remains,' said Alex. 'No Klara. That's good. But either you tell us where she is, or we're going to see that you're placed in a facility where your other life experiences will seem like a sunny summer day.'

Erik clenched his jaw. He didn't understand. How could the room be empty? Klara couldn't possibly have got out of there. Or was this a mind game that the police were playing?

80

Per let the ambulance personnel take care of his leg. The glass shard hadn't gone in as deep as he suspected and, after a few provisional stitches and a couple of pain relievers, he sat up. He wanted to be there for the questioning of Erik but right now he was needed more at this place. Several units had arrived and the bomb squad was searching the rest of the buildings. Anna was standing a short distance away, talking with another police officer.

'You need to be taken to the hospital to be properly stitched,' the nurse said. 'I can't do more here.'

Per looked out from the ambulance, toward the building that had recently exploded. Half the building was burned up while the other side was intact. The fire had calmed down while the media had done the opposite. They were searching for answers. The place was crawling with journalists now. Over two hours had passed since the explosion, but Per hadn't been able to call Mia yet.

'Do you have any crutches I can borrow? I'm not leaving the area until we know whether our suspected victim is here.'

The nurse sighed. 'Everyone has to be a hero,' he said, getting up.

Per saw Anna turn her back on several colleagues and walk in his direction.

'The room that exploded is completely blown out,' said Anna when she came up to him. 'There's nothing left except for a charred bed.'

'But Klara's jacket was inside the building. She was here.'

Anna nodded. 'Yes, that we know. And we're searching everywhere now. It's still too hot to go into the damaged part of the building. But if she's anywhere near here we'll find her.'

The nurse came back and handed Per a pair of crutches. They were set for someone considerably shorter, but he hopped ahead on them as well as he could to the meeting place. Per looked at the journalists and knew that he needed to make a statement. Although what should he say?

Just then a colleague came running toward them. 'Per, they've found a body on the far side. It's half burned up,' she said, nodding to the building that had exploded.

He pointed at once at the nurse who had taken care of his leg. 'Get there, now!' Per shouted.

Then he turned toward the woman. 'Is it Klara?'

'We don't know yet, but my colleague will meet you over there. I have to keep the media away,' the woman said, walking to the journalists who were shouting questions at her.

Per and Anna set off for the far side of the building. He tried to keep up with her rapid pace, but the crutches only slowed him down and at last he tossed them aside. It was faster without them.

They rounded the building and moved to the burned-out part. The smoke was thicker there and made it hard to breathe. Per felt his eyes tear up. A uniformed police officer met them and showed them the way. They passed a steel door to the left that had been damaged in the explosion.

'This leads to the refuse room which is right above the room where the explosives were,' the policeman said, continuing a couple of steps forward.

The police officer pointed a little further along the outside wall. There was a severely battered body. It had probably been missed in the initial search because it had been well concealed by bushes, which now had been cut back. The face was burned away, as were parts of the motionless body. Per had to turn his eyes away to not feel nauseated and saw that the ambulance personnel were running toward them.

'I suspect that the person was inside the building when it exploded and somehow ended up here in the bushes. Either he jumped or was thrown out by the force of the explosion,' the policeman said, pointing up at one of the windows on the second floor.

'Who is it?' said Per.

'We found an ID on the man. One Ibrahim Hatim.'

Per sighed. 'How the hell did he end up here?' he said to Anna, who shook her head.

He looked around and caught sight of a moped under the debris nearby. It seemed to have been ejected from the building with the explosion. It resembled the description they'd got of Klara's moped, which her parents said was missing. Per pointed at it.

'Could Ibrahim have ridden that here?' he said. 'It looks like Klara's, and we know she didn't come here on her moped.'

Suddenly a shout was heard from another policeman nearby. 'There's a young woman here in the ditch! She . . .'

Silence.

'Rescue them, damn it!' Per screamed, pointing at Ibrahim, as he started moving toward the voice that had called. It seemed to have come from the field in the direction of the forest.

Anna rushed past him and a police car slowly came rolling behind them. The headlights of the car shone into the field. Per had some thirty metres left and swore at his injured leg. It ached from the exertion and he tried to hop on one leg, but gave up and instead ran limping toward the ditch. It must be the place where Klara was.

81

Thursday, 8 September

Klara was wakened by a rhythmic beeping sound. Before she could open her eyes she heard her mother's voice.

'Klara?'

A warm hand on her arm. Klara looked up. Her vision was blurry and she blinked to regain focus.

'She's awake!' her mother called.

Klara turned her head toward the voice. Both of her parents' faces showed up in her field of vision. They were crying. When the memory came back it was with force. Her whole body knotted up.

'Ibrahim?' asked Klara. Her voice barely carried.

Her mother shook her head. 'We don't know yet, he's in very bad shape.'

Klara felt tears running down her cheeks. She raised her arm and remembered what it was like, not being able to move a single body part. That panic she would never forget.

She tried to sit up as two doctors came into the room.

'Lie down, Klara,' one of them said. 'You need to rest. The drugs aren't completely out of your system yet.'

'I have to blow my nose,' she said, taking a tissue from her mother. While the doctors took their samples the tears continued to run. Having muscles that worked was liberating. Something that simple was suddenly so big.

Shortly after that Svea came in and threw herself on the bed. The needles from the drip that was inserted in her arm hurt, but Klara let herself be hugged. She had thought about Svea when she was captive in the room, what would happen with her little sister if she died.

'There are two police officers out here who want to exchange a few words with you,' her father said.

Her little sister let go of her but didn't leave the bed. Klara held her hand and dried her tears.

'Are you up to it?' her father continued. 'It's clearly important.'

Klara nodded. 'Is Erik dead?' she asked.

Her father shook his head. 'But under lock and key.'

Klara closed her eyes and when she opened them again a female and a male police officer were standing in front of her. She had met the woman before at the police station with Ibrahim, but she hadn't seen the man before.

While they introduced themselves Klara's father helped her sit up. He raised one side of the bed and puffed up her pillows. Her little sister was sitting down by her feet and leaned back against the edge of the bed. There was a glass of water on the table that Klara gulped down. After that she listened to the police officers who told her about Erik and what he was accused of. Even though she already knew, Klara felt compelled to bring her hand to her mouth to feel if her teeth were there.

'Klara, we simply need a brief account now. We're going to hold a more extensive interview with you when you're stronger and feeling better. But can you tell us what happened on the way to school, in Erik's car?' said the police officer whose name was Charlotte.

Klara thought about it. It was only a day ago but it felt like an eternity.

'I found a box with teeth in, and he went completely crazy. It was his reaction that frightened me, not the teeth in the box. And then I suddenly understood what it was about. What was in the news, the murder of that woman.'

'How did he drug you?'

Klara brought her hand to her throat. 'He injected something here. I couldn't move.'

'It was probably Rohypnol – it's a muscle relaxant,' said Charlotte.

Klara blew her nose and then picked at the yellow blanket. She didn't want to remember, but the images washed over her like a flood.

'He put me in the back of his car.'

Klara heard her mother start crying again.

'Then he carried me into some room in a cellar . . .'

She leaned her head against the pillow. Looked up at the ceiling.

'I was sure I would die there.'

Her mother took her hand in hers and held it so hard it hurt. Klara closed her eyes. She was back in that room.

'Erik placed me on a bed and took off my jacket. Then he put a blanket over me. The room was completely white, sterile. And big. There was dental equipment on a tray next to me.'

Then she opened her eyes again, didn't want to stay in that room.

'Klara,' said her mother. 'Did he do anything with you? Did he assault you?'

She shook her head. 'No, nothing like that.'

'Okay,' her mother said, and Klara could hear the relief in her voice.

'It smelled like fresh paint in there. I couldn't see the whole room, just what was right in front of me.'

'Tell us what you saw.'

'On the floor, by the door, were what seemed to be paint cans. On the ceiling right above me was a mirror. Like at a dentist. What kind of room was it?'

'We think that Erik created a room for himself at the abandoned care facility, where he also locked up his other victims. You were lucky to be rescued before Erik triggered the bomb there.'

Klara tried to remember other things that she had noticed.

'There was a computer on a bench, it was turned on and the screen showed various rooms that I didn't recognize. I saw cans on a shelf straight ahead, a heating element that sounded mechanical. There was an acrid smell from some substance – the sort of thing you clean paintbrushes with.'

The police officers made notes even though they were recording the conversation.

'I wanted to scream but couldn't. Nothing came out.'

'Did Erik say anything at that point?'

'Yes, he talked away as if everything was normal. It was like he was himself again. He said that he knew what he would do with me.'

'Did he tell you what?'

'No, Erik only said that he knew. And that no one would understand. What was he going to do?'

'That we don't know yet, but you found him with the box full of teeth.'

Klara shook her head again. 'The sick thing is that I wouldn't have made the connection if he hadn't reacted so insanely. Maybe I would have realized it later, but there in the car I didn't understand why he went crazy.'

'What else do you remember? Any small details may be important.'

'That I couldn't move on the bed. And he took my phone – Erik opened it using face recognition already in the car.'

Charlotte sat down on the edge of the bed. 'Did you see him prepare the explosives when you were there?'

'No,' said Klara. 'But Erik entered a code on something that was on the floor by the door. I didn't understand what it was. It beeped a lot and then he put a phone in his pocket.'

Klara closed her eyes again. She didn't want to remember any more, didn't want to feel what she experienced in the room.

'Do you know how Ibrahim ended up in the same building?'

Klara pressed her lips together, before she opened her eyes again and looked up.

'No, or . . .'

She was breathing heavily. The thought that Ibrahim was seriously injured was hard to take in. It was her fault.

'I couldn't get hold of him the morning when Erik drove me. He didn't answer any messages I sent and he wasn't on Snap Map, which was strange. It looked like his phone was turned off.'

'Were you able to alert him somehow?'

She answered with another shake of the head. 'No, but I was just about to send yet another message to him on Snapchat when I dropped the phone in Erik's car. That was when I found the box.'

'We believe that Ibrahim took your moped out to Brattby. Does he have access to the key?' asked the male police officer who had introduced himself as Alex.

'No, but it was always in the ignition. He said that was dumb, that someone could steal it.'

Klara thought about what the police were saying and wondered why Ibrahim had taken her moped. Suddenly it struck her.

'A weird thing happened when Ibrahim and I were at the Stenlunds' a few days ago,' said Klara. 'I was going to pick up my wallet that I'd forgotten and he went with me. But when we were leaving, Ibrahim suddenly seemed really scared.'

'Why?' asked Charlotte.

'I don't know, he didn't want to say what was wrong when I asked him. Could he have recognized Erik somehow? Ibrahim might have seen him when that woman was dumped under the bridge.'

Klara hid her face in her hands. 'He knew that I would be staying over at the Stenlunds'. Somehow he must have seen me get into Erik's car the morning after and then followed us. Otherwise how could he know where I was?' she said, trying to put the puzzle together.

'That's a theory we have,' said Charlotte. 'We'll have to hope Ibrahim can tell us himself someday. What happened at the old care facility?'

Klara took down her hands and looked at the police officers. 'He rescued me. Suddenly Ibrahim was just standing there in the room and said that he was going to call for help. He told me that Erik had left.'

Her shoulders quivered as the tears streamed down her cheeks.

The police officers waited for a moment before they continued with their questions.

'Was he the one who got you out of the room?' asked Alex.

Klara nodded and wiped her face with the sheet. 'Ibrahim found me and carried me out of the building. I was completely limp. He placed me in a ditch away from the building, because he was afraid that Erik would come back and find me. But he had dropped his phone somewhere on the way and couldn't call for help. So he returned to the building to search for it and before he came back it exploded. Then I saw all the blue lights but not him.'

'But the police at the scene didn't encounter Ibrahim. Do you know where he was searching?' asked Charlotte.

'He didn't know where the phone might be, but thought it was in the room where I was held captive. It all happened so fast. He must have still been inside when it exploded. And I was just lying by the ditch, couldn't even call for help.'

Klara drew up her legs and placed her arms around her knees.

'Who is Erik really?' she said. 'I don't understand. He's the counsellor at our school and I was a babysitter at their house.'

'We believe that Erik Stenlund has murdered several people and that he is extremely good at manipulating his surroundings,' said Alex.

'What will happen to him now?' asked Klara. 'He's dangerous. What if he tries to kill me again?'

'He's presumably going to get a long prison sentence. Probably in a psychiatric ward, which will make it hard for him to be released. That's why your testimony is so important. With your help, we should be able to charge him for all the pain he's caused.'

Klara nodded.

'There is someone here who wants to speak with you,' said Charlotte, looking toward the door which was being opened carefully.

Helen looked into the room. 'Hi, Klara. May I come in?'

She nodded and pressed her lips together while she observed the woman she had never really liked. Helen stood by the end of the bed. She had a tissue in her hand that she wrapped around one finger.

'Sorry,' she said curtly.

'For what?' Klara didn't understand.

'I didn't stop you from riding with Erik to school. If I'd known what he'd done I would have . . .' Helen stopped herself. She shook her head and wiped away a tear. Then she placed her hand on Klara's foot, squeezed it.

'I should have seen the signs, sensed something. But I was so consumed by my attempt to escape, to protect myself and the kids. It wasn't the idea to expose you to him. I'm an adult and knew that he was evil.'

Klara still didn't understand a thing. 'You knew that he was evil? Did you know that he murdered people?' Her voice was openly accusatory.

Her mother interrupted her attack.

'Klara, Helen has been abused by Erik for years. Lived in fear.'

Klara breathed in. Helen smiled at her mother.

'Did he hit you?' asked Klara.

Helen nodded. 'He's evil and controlling. Didn't you notice at all?' she asked cautiously.

Klara was working out a puzzle in her mind. Helen's offbeat behaviour, that she was so hard to reach. So that was due to Erik. Klara shook her head.

'No, I thought there was something wrong with you,' she said, laughing in spite of herself.

Helen gave Klara a warm look, for the first time. 'I just wanted to tell you I'm sorry. And tell you that the kids miss you,' she said, and then left the room.

Klara sat quietly. She was still taking in what had just happened when another police officer, this time in uniform, came in through the door and waved her mother to him, who stood up with some hesitation. Klara was glad when she left the room. Her mother's tears made her uncomfortable. Like guilty feelings.

'What did Erik plan to do with me?' she asked Charlotte again and thought about Helen who had been abused.

'Maybe that will come out during the questioning. But we may never find out.'

Her mother was back in the room. She looked sad when she went up to Klara and took her hand.

'Ibrahim is still in a bad way,' her mother said. 'It's not certain that he'll recover. He's been anesthetized to relieve the pain. The next few days will be decisive.'

Klara once again felt the tears welling up. 'He rescued me – he has to survive!'

82

Per took the pizza that Mia had prepped and put it in the oven. The heat that hit his face made his glasses steam up. He was hungry – it was past seven o'clock.

'Do Charlotte and Ola have the energy to come over? You're in the final phase of the investigation,' she said, washing her hands.

'Yes, they want to celebrate with you. And preferably before I start my new position for real. I was also thinking that Charlotte could use a break from the investigation now everything is starting to fall into place.'

'Is it tomorrow you're going to district court with Erik?' asked Mia.

Per poured a glass of red for her. 'Yes, at noon. But we only have a few things to review before that, so it won't be a late one tonight.'

When the doorbell rang, Hannes was quickest. He let in Charlotte and Ola, who greeted him happily before he ran up to his room. Simon was still at hockey practice.

While Ola took off his shoes, Charlotte went into the kitchen and hugged Mia. They hadn't had time to see each other for quite a while, and Mia hadn't had the energy.

'Charlotte, have you heard any more about Anja's plans to become a police officer?' Per asked after he'd welcomed them.

'I haven't managed to talk more with her about that. I'm still in shock,' she said.

'What's that? Anja wants to be a police officer?' said Mia, diving into the conversation with questions for Charlotte.

They talked about Anja while the aroma of pizza spread around the house. Per went out to Ola, who was hanging up his jacket.

'Welcome to Degernäs,' he said, holding out a glass of wine for Ola. His dark hair was combed back neatly and his shirt was impeccably ironed. Per felt a twinge of irritation at the perfection the man in front of him embodied.

Ola held up his hand. 'Thanks, but I'm driving this evening.'

Stick-in-the-mud, thought Per. But he also knew that Ola's father died young of a heart attack during a festive dinner.

'Okay, would you like soda? Water? Alcohol-free beer?'

'Beer would be good,' said Ola, pounding Per on the back as thanks.

He liked Ola anyway, and he was good for Charlotte. He had got her to exercise more and not care as much about superficial things.

When the doorbell rang again Ola looked surprised.

'It's Alex,' said Per. 'I invited him too because he's new in town and mostly hangs out at his hotel.'

Charlotte looked wide-eyed at Per and threw out her arms in an inquisitive gesture.

In response Per made a similar motion back at Charlotte, and offered a smile too, before he opened the front door.

Ola and Alex greeted each other politely.

'Did you hear that a patrol found Lena's red Passat today?' said Alex, hanging up his thin jacket.

'Really, I didn't know that,' said Per as all three went into the kitchen.

'Yes, the duty chief called it in to us about half an hour ago. It was found up by the university area with all her belongings in it.'

'How the hell did it end up there?'

'Well now,' said Alex. 'That will probably come out during the course of the investigation.'

Mia started setting their round dining table, which was in the living room next to the kitchen. Charlotte cut the first pizza into equal-sized pieces.

'Should I get Hannes?' she asked.

'He's eating upstairs, watching NHL and is quite content,' said Per, laughing.

'What shall we say about Klara's testimony then?' said Charlotte, sipping the wine.

Per shook his head. 'You don't dare think about what would have happened if Ibrahim hadn't rescued her.'

'He should get a medal for his effort,' said Charlotte while she continued slicing the pizza. 'He's the one the newspapers should write about, not Erik. Wonder if we'll ever find out how Ibrahim knew that Erik took Klara to Brattby House? Could he really have followed Erik's car with Klara's moped on the E12?'

'It will be interesting to see what the investigation turns up. Maybe he watched the Stenlunds' house if he knew that Klara was babysitting for a murderer. We'll have to hope that he survives and can tell us himself.'

'How great are the chances that Erik will be convicted?' Mia asked. 'You never know, it feels like. Violent criminals suddenly go free despite binding evidence . . . The system seems to have its defects.'

Charlotte looked up from the pizzas. 'There's a lot of technical evidence and his explanations are improbable. Besides, the investigation will be expanded because we're searching for more victims. We still don't know how many he has murdered.'

Alex stood beside Charlotte, who was still struggling with the food on the hot baking sheets.

'My goodness, kebab pizza? You *lunatic*,' he said with a laugh. 'Yes, I heard you when you screamed at me at the petrol station.'

'You missed the extra phone that Erik had – you're the lunatic,' Charlotte said seriously.

'Do you remember the kebab place that was by the police academy in Solna? It was the best in town,' said Alex, ignoring her jab.

Charlotte's eyes flashed. Per thought she seemed happier than in a long time. Ola also seemed content sitting there at the kitchen table. Maybe his suspicions about Charlotte and Alex were exaggerated.

'Yes, and do you remember when I rode past on a bike and the front tyre got stuck in the old train track, and I fell over a man who was coming out of the kebab shack?' said Charlotte.

Both of them laughed loudly.

'How's it going with Kicki, by the way? Did you have that beer?' asked Charlotte.

Alex crossed his arms and maintained eye contact. He waited a long time before he shook his head, without taking his eyes off her.

Per took back his most recent thought while he observed them. It was as if they were alone in the room. Talking about memories and all. He glanced at Ola, who got up from the kitchen table and was now standing beside Charlotte. Alex backed up immediately and leaned against the refrigerator. Ola placed his arm around Charlotte's waist and watched as she set the pizza slices on a big platter. Then he kissed her on the cheek. Per noted the intimacy that Ola previously hadn't shown so openly. But Charlotte seemed comfortable with it, despite Alex's presence.

'Sit down at the table,' said Mia. 'It will be a simple dinner with a little wine.'

Ola nodded and showed his white row of teeth. *Erik wouldn't have been bothered by those*, thought Per.

Alex followed Mia to the table in the living room, where she lit candles and turned off the ceiling light. Charlotte sat down beside Ola, which made Per happy. Alex sat down across from them.

'It will be nice to conclude the investigation,' said Charlotte. 'And how satisfying it feels that a person like Erik is no longer on the loose.'

'But how does someone actually get so sick?' said Per. 'The TV channels are going to make documentaries about him. Serial killers are extremely unusual. It's almost impossible to absorb that we have one here in little Umeå.'

'He seems to have had a frightful childhood,' said Alex.

'How will he manage being locked up?' asked Mia.

'It will probably work out fine,' said Charlotte. 'His personality type does well with routines, and prison is all about that.'

'But he struggles with a lot of demons and the question is whether a correctional facility is sufficient. But I think he'll probably be sentenced to psychiatric care,' said Ola, and everyone nodded in agreement and filled their plates.

Charlotte pointed at Alex. 'Do you remember the guy who went to police academy with us, the red-haired one who used to question everything in class?'

Alex lit up. 'Question-Åke!'

'Yes!' Charlotte was beaming like a sun. 'He's no longer a police officer. Instead he trained to be a psychologist and now works in correctional services, where he handles just this type of difficult case. It would be a dream for him to get to talk with Erik.'

'I'll be darned,' said Alex, and Per saw that he held his gaze on Charlotte a little too long, before he cleared his throat to get everyone's attention. 'Forgive my impudence here, but I wonder if you would mind saying grace with me?'

Per raised his eyebrows. *Grace*, he thought. *What kind of nonsense is that?*

Alex smiled broadly. 'Come on now, a little prayer won't hurt you. It will be super-quick.'

'Now?' said Charlotte.

'Yes, you don't have to if you don't want to,' said Alex, and Per marvelled at his self-confidence.

Charlotte folded her hands. Ola followed but looked just as surprised as Per assumed he himself did.

'Can you pray for a glass of water, since you're at it anyway?' said Charlotte, making everyone laugh.

Alex said a prayer. Per cast a glance in secret toward Mia. He wanted to see her reaction, but discovered that she in turn was sneaking a look at him, with folded hands and her head slightly tilted forward. Their eyes met, followed by a smile. Per didn't understand this guy he had on loan from the Gothenburg police. An odd duck.

The prayer only took a few seconds and when Alex was done Per stood up to go out into the kitchen.

'God heard you. I'll get the water,' he said, pointing at Charlotte.

Mia followed him out of the room. She stood close to Per while he filled the pitcher.

'Charlotte and Alex,' he said. 'It feels like there's been something between them. What do you think?'

Mia nodded. 'My thoughts exactly.'

'It's pretty apparent if you think about how they look at each other and talk. They're like an old married couple,' said Per. 'At the station they're more formal, stiffer with each other. But here . . . Jesus. They're radiant.'

'Could this become a problem, do you think?' asked Mia.

Per looked at her. Her eyes were nicely framed by make-up. The scarf around her head was still there, but wasn't tied as tight.

'At worst, I'll have to send Alex back to Gothenburg, if the atmosphere gets awkward at Major Crimes. It can get damned messy. Charlotte is detective chief inspector now and in a steady relationship with Ola, who also works in the building. Besides, I want to retain Alex. He's a capable detective.'

Mia held up a finger. 'Ah, you swore! What will Alex say about that?' she said, bringing her face closer.

Per shook his head. 'I could tell there was something between them, but I was hoping it was friendship.'

'Should I talk with Charlotte? She's the smartest person I know, so she's going to understand,' said Mia, pointing at the group around the dining table. Then she whispered in Per's ear. 'It's just that Charlotte is head over heels in love with Alex. I've never seen her like she is today.'

Per looked up at the ceiling and sighed. 'Why can't things ever be simple?'

83

Klara was pushed in a wheelchair by her mother. Her eyes followed the yellow stripe on the floor that showed the way to the ICU and Ibrahim. She was still shaky and exhausted from the drugs she'd ingested; it had only been a little over a day since she was rescued from Erik. Besides, she was still in shock over who Erik turned out to be. In her mind she played up all the encounters with him and the family over and over again, in search of explanations or clues that she'd missed. Klara thought about Helen, who had always been buttoned up and stiff. It wasn't so strange considering the fear she must have lived in.

Nice Erik . . . A murderer, a monster. The knowledge that he'd been prepared to kill her . . . Every time she arrived at that thought – *what if* – she had to force herself away from the memories to not be consumed by panic.

Klara fixed her gaze on the floor while she rolled forward. The needle had been removed from the crook of her arm. She managed without the drip now and would be discharged later in the day.

There was beeping in the corridor from various rooms. Nurses went in and out of them; some smiled at her as if they knew who she was.

'You must be prepared for the fact that Ibrahim isn't responsive,' her mother said. 'He has severe burns and fractures.'

Klara bit at a fingernail and answered by nodding. Her mother stroked her head.

She had only received scant information about Ibrahim's condition because he was badly injured. And she had absolutely not been able to see him, not until now. After much nagging it was finally time, and his foster parents hoped that Klara's presence would strengthen him.

The rubber wheels on the wheelchair made a screeching sound when her mother turned toward the intensive care unit. Klara started to feel a little nauseated and took two deep breaths. It smelled of hospital, a particular odour that was hard to put your finger on.

As they rolled into Ibrahim's room, Apollonia was the first person Klara saw, standing at the other end of the room. They passed three beds before they reached Ibrahim's – the furthest in. He was shielded behind a blue curtain. Klara's nausea got stronger and she swallowed repeatedly.

'Hi, Klara,' said Apollonia, smiling between the tears.

'Hi,' she whispered, but didn't dare meet her gaze.

A feeling of shame came over her. Ibrahim had rescued her, offering his own life. Was Klara worth it?

She wiped away her tears and took firm hold of the arm support on the wheelchair, forcing her legs to stand up. They had become more stable. Her feet, covered in hospital stockings, met the cold floor. Her pulse rose from the exertion. Her mother stood nearby, ready to catch her, but Klara felt fairly strong.

Although, when her gaze landed on Ibrahim's body, it was no longer possible to cry quietly. She let out all she was feeling and experiencing, allowed herself to react to what she saw. Ibrahim's mouth was closed. Half of his face was covered by a thin, transparent bandage. Burned skin. Arm in a cast. Dressings and bandages. Ibrahim's long eyelashes rested against his skin. He looked peaceful, and his chest moved in time with the monotonous beeping from the device that gave him oxygen.

Klara's heart burst – as if something literally broke it apart. She sat down on the edge of the bed, careful not to sit on anything. Carefully she took his hand in hers. Bent forward and brought it to her lips, let it rest there while she took in his scent.

'I love you,' she said. Her lips got warm and salty from the tears, and she heard her mother crying behind her.

A doctor stood beside Klara and placed his hand on her shoulder. 'He's going to make it.'

Klara looked up. 'When will he wake up?'

'Ibrahim is being treated with morphine to relieve pain for the time being, although we wake him up sometimes. He has managed rather well anyway. It could have been considerably worse.'

'So he's going to survive?'

'Yes, he will.'

Klara smiled. Her vision was blurry through the tears. Then she brought her free hand to Ibrahim's cheek, stroked it.

'Thanks for rescuing me,' she said in a low voice.

Klara felt how the hand she was still holding squeezed her fingers. Weakly, but enough to replace the heaviness in her heart with hope.

84

Charlotte was sitting in the car with Ola and Alex. The dinner at home with Per the night before had been pleasant but went on a bit too late. They were driving behind the correctional services bus, which was on its way to the district court with Erik Stenlund for arraignment. He would be jailed on remand, Charlotte and the others were one hundred per cent sure of that. The prosecutor would present their evidence against the school counsellor, who had acquired a celebrity attorney. That gave rise to newspaper headlines just as big as for the crimes he'd committed.

The media also speculated about whether there were more victims. There were articles about the mistake that became the start of the end of Erik's crazy murder tour: Lena, who had already been exposed in the press all the way to the bone. Her death was designated the Mermaid Murder and the fascination over her fate seemed greater than over Samir's.

Charlotte looked out of the window. The rain poured down but the air was warmer than it had been for several days. *Hang in there, summer*, she thought.

'I think Per looked pretty good yesterday, after the injury to his leg,' said Ola, driving at a reasonable distance from the correctional services bus in front. He was going to the district court on a different matter and car-pooled with them.

Charlotte sat alone in the back seat. The men in front made her confused. Ola was her security; Alex something else.

'He's okay, it wasn't that bad. I think he's going to feel pretty good over there on the bosses' side,' she said, meeting Ola's gaze in the rear-view mirror. It was serious.

Ever since the evening before, he'd been acting strangely. He was cold. She would talk with him later but didn't know what to say. Ola had clearly been affected by the mood between her and Alex during dinner, even if Charlotte didn't think it was so obvious that he must be jealous. At the same time his suspicions were correct. She did feel something for Alex, but didn't know what. But Ola also made her feel things. Charlotte didn't know in from out any longer, and mostly wanted Alex to go back to Gothenburg. But also somehow not.

As they approached the red-brick building, the journalists showed up like ants around a lump of sugar. Correctional services would take Erik in through the car park, but the photographers were doing everything to get a picture of Sweden's new serial killer.

'I hope they don't publish pictures of Erik before he's sentenced, for the children's sake,' said Alex.

'It's probably about getting an action shot as he's being led into the district court. That creates a little drama,' said Ola as Charlotte's communication radio crackled.

'Okay, we have an incident down in the car park at the district court,' the voice said in Charlotte's radio. 'An arrested gang member from a criminal network is delaying the transport back to the jail. Can you take the usual back way with your suspect, or wait in the car?'

Charlotte leaned toward Ola. 'What do you say? There's no immediate threat against Erik, is there?'

'No, but he will be extremely exposed to the journalists,' said Ola.

'We'll cover him with a blanket,' said Alex as they drove past the crowd of people. Two youths on a moped turned right in front of the car and forced Ola to brake suddenly behind the correctional services bus. Charlotte's upper body was thrown forward but was stopped by the seat belt.

'Damn it! Blasted kids,' said Ola.

Charlotte reported the change in plans to the bus that Erik was riding in and instead it rounded the main entrance and turned toward the courtyard. There was a group from the media there too.

'They've done this before and know where to wait,' said Ola, stopping the car behind the bus.

'Do we have a blanket?' Alex asked.

'In back,' said Charlotte.

She opened the door and stepped right into a pool of water. The rain was pouring down. Charlotte was tired and didn't have the energy to care that she was getting wet all the way into her bra. She opened the boot and grabbed a blanket. The rain caressed her cheeks as she went toward the bus with it. Not until she was standing outside did the guards open the doors.

Erik peeked out, and up. His cheeks were pale and he got up on his own. Then he remained standing with his back bent and his head grazing the top of the bus, while he hesitated to go out. His hands were folded in front of his crotch in handcuffs.

'Oh, look at this weather,' he said, stepping out at last on to the wet ground. He pulled his shoulders back and stretched, before he glanced at the group of journalists, which kept growing. They were flocking from the whole country, as if Erik were a rock star. He remained standing behind the bus, protected from the camera lenses.

'I'm popular,' he said and laughed, but became serious again at once.

No one responded.

'What will happen with Helen and the children now?' Erik asked, turning toward Charlotte.

'They will get peace and quiet,' she said.

His gaze became inquisitive. 'But they're coming here to support me, aren't they?' he asked, and Charlotte realized that he was serious. Erik didn't understand what he had put his family through. She shook her head in response and it was the first time she perceived any form of sadness in his eyes.

Ola and Alex were walking right behind them and made sure the journalists didn't get too intrusive by herding them away from the bus as best they could. Charlotte heard the clicking sound from their cameras, the questions that were asked but which they didn't have permission to answer. A man with an umbrella was standing a short distance away by a large flowerpot talking on a mobile. Charlotte recognized him from Swedish Television.

When Erik started to walk in pace with the guards she unfolded the blanket and brought it toward his head. But he showed clearly that he didn't want to be covered.

'I don't need a blanket. Let them see,' said Erik, as a guard took firm hold of his arm and led him forward.

With the serial killer protected from the photographers they moved toward the door. Charlotte looked at the journalists, but heard the moped again and looked up. It wasn't the same youths who had just driven in front of the car. She was the one who saw the automatic rifle first, but before she had time to react, the two black-clad, masked people had aimed it right at the entrance.

Charlotte acted instinctively by crawling behind the bus.

'Guns! Take cover!' she screamed as the crackling bullets hit everything in sight. The sound of gunfire was followed by metal being hit and people screaming. She heard her own voice and the panic in it. Crouched down, got out her gun and looked out behind the bus.

Charlotte saw the moped disappear. It was all over in a few seconds. She turned around and struggled to catch her breath, which

417

came in spurts. Two journalists had been hit, but were moving. Erik was lying with his face to the ground. Raindrops mixed with his blood on the asphalt. A guard sat beside him and had also been hit.

More shrieks were heard from the journalists. She twirled around and looked in their direction while she scanned for Ola and Alex. Behind the big flowerpot someone was lying motionless. She saw only the legs sticking out.

Charlotte got to her feet. Her heart was about to explode. The gun was still in her hand as she ran toward the motionless man lying on his back.

'Ola! Alex!'

She screamed with the same panic as before.

ABOUT THE AUTHOR

Anki Edvinsson is a familiar face to many Swedes from her former career as a television host, journalist and weather forecaster. Edvinsson more or less grew up at a police station, spending her time with her father and his police colleagues. Her older brother also made a career within the police force.

Edvinsson moved from Stockholm to Umeå in the north of Sweden, where her husband grew up, and joined the local news team. Following her dream to become an author, she signed up for a writing course and began writing the crime novel that later became her debut. After eight years in the town and with valuable insights from her years as a reporter, the setting of the book of course became Umeå.

Curious to get to know her characters and explore the causes of crime – what makes a person choose that path? Who becomes a murderer? – she is studying for a bachelor's degree in criminology at Umeå University.

The Mermaid is the second book in the Detectives von Klint and Berg series.

ABOUT THE TRANSLATOR

Paul Norlen previously translated *A Darker Sky* by Mari Jungstedt and Ruben Eliassen and *Hell Is Open* by Gard Sveen for Amazon Crossing. He lives in Seattle.

Follow the Author on Amazon

If you enjoyed this book, follow Anki Edvinsson on Amazon to be notified when the author releases a new book!
To do this, please follow these instructions:

Desktop:

1) Search for the author's name on Amazon or in the Amazon App.
2) Click on the author's name to arrive on their Amazon page.
3) Click the 'Follow' button.

Mobile and Tablet:

1) Search for the author's name on Amazon or in the Amazon App.
2) Click on one of the author's books.
3) Click on the author's name to arrive on their Amazon page.
4) Click the 'Follow' button.

Kindle eReader and Kindle App:

If you enjoyed this book on a Kindle eReader or in the Kindle App, you will find the author 'Follow' button after the last page.